Out of the night...

"Stength isn't all it's cracked up to be," Kalla said as they walked down the edge of the silent, night-darkened road. Around them the temples of Pagan made dark spires against the stars. "It can be lonely, Mei. Darn lonely. It isn't often you find the person who can fill your life. All my life my dad spent all his money on charlatans—you know that word?—people who say they can reach beyond the grave. He still loved my mother so desperately he wanted to talk to her."

"He loved her very much."

"More than anything." She struggled to hold back the sour taste of failure, because the way things were going with Alex she wasn't going to win her father's approval now, either.

Kalla placed her arm around Mei's shoulder and the younger woman collapsed against her. Somehow it was almost funny that she had to help Mei find control and strength at the very time when Kalla's own seemed on the verge of failing. But it was only fair to help another person learn the hard lesson Kalla had learned early in life.

There was only one way you could live your life. Alone.

"So we'll be strong women together. I'll show you all I know. And maybe you can give me lessons in wearing the longyi?"

Mei looked at her, smiled.

But a hand out of the darkness ripped Kalla away. A wiry arm wrapped around her middle. Two men grabbed Mei and dragged her screaming into the darkness.

"Kalla! Help!" she screamed.

She stomped down on an instep, tried to get free. Oh god she had to, but the rough hand was stronger than the holds in self-defense class.

How could she save Mei, if she could not save herself?

BOOKS BY THE AUTHOR

Written as Karen L. McKee
Ashes and Light
Shades of Moonlight
Judas Kiss
Second Spring
A Different Nightmusic
Shadow Play
Coming Down Christmas

Written as Karen L. Abrahamson

The Unlocking Series
Unlocking Her Heart
Unlocking Her History
Unlocking Her Grace
Unlocking Her Dreams
Unlocking Her Chances
Unlocking Her Doubts

The Sunshine Coast Mythical Beings
Surviving Safe Harbor
Dangerous Haven

SHADES
of
MOONLIGHT

KAREN L. ABRAHAMSON

Dedicated to the people of Burma.

Acknowledgements

Thanks again to the OWN gang and to all my friends who've put up with "the incredible disappearing Karen" while this manuscript was being written.

Special thanks, also, to the puppeteers and puppet-carvers of Burma who took the time to tell a foreign wanderer of their wonderous art form.

Chapter 1 – Spirit Light

Pagan, ancient capital of Burma
Central Myanmar, Modern day

Kalla plunged through tall grass and thorn brush, the ornate wooden puppet clutched to her breast. Spirit light glinted like fool's gold in the stone underfoot. It shimmered pale blue from empty, parched fields and set beacon candles of azure and indigo from the tops of the huge step-pyramid temples that loomed out of the darkness. The rising wind scoured her chilled skin with dust, and the air smelled of ozone and lung-clinging jasmine.

And her fevered fear.

She had to get there. She had to protect.

She stumbled across a dirt road. Through a hedge of cactus, she ripped the red longyi that wrapped her legs and half-fell into a fallow field. Spirit light glinted on her skin.

"No." It came out as a whimper, but too loud in the night as she tried to wipe the shimmering dust away. Already too late. It glowed on her skin—seemed to run *into* her damp flesh. Flickering blue light flashed up her arm, even as she lurched up and kept on. Even as the spirit light seemed to stab into her brain.

And then there was the laughter.

She whirled, her midnight hair sweeping around her shoulders and the puppet. No. Her imagination. They couldn't know where she was. Keep going. Keep going.

The longyi's fabric restricted her panicked stride as she staggered on. The spirit light flashed tingling sparks across her skin, across the puppet, as her palm smoothed the antique figure's fine hair and protected the delicate Votaress' features, from the scour of the wind.

The puppet moved in her grasp.

Insanity, the scientist part of her said. Madness to be out here. Madness to be running like this, into the night and the darkness.

It was darkness that had killed her before.

She squeezed her eyes shut and almost fell across a heap of bricks. Small, collapsed temple. Her breath rang in her ears as she picked her way through, remembering how it had been before, whose temple this had been and the fine teak house that had stood here. A memory of pickled tea and garlic, but the air now smelled of sage and slow-moving river water. From the road came the sound of a jeep.

Military?

Cold sweat in her eyes, but ahead the spirit light shone bright blue flame from Dhammayangyi temple. A mountain with eyes, a yawning mouth. A mountain that would devour her; a mountain that was part of her.

Panting, she stopped, listening to the dying leaves chatter in the rising wind and the bats whoosh through the sky. Towering clouds blocked the moon.

She shivered with need, but the fear held her in place. Her mouth tasted of copper and bile.

To go in that place would mean—*ending? Beginning?* Insanity. She was going mad. The fever raged her thoughts into a whirlwind, impossible to comprehend. But she knew what waited. What had to be done. And that others would try to stop her.

But no one could follow her to the place she would go.

She staggered through the gate, the wind skirling wild Burmese music through the crumbling stone. Darkness, a void waited, but she swallowed her fear.

Do this thing.

And she would save them.

Do this thing.

The night seemed to hold its breath.

Do this thing.

The scent of musk and incense reached her on a fresh gust of wind and she froze, knowing the rough breathing she heard was not her own.

If she moved they would see her, but she had to get past. Get free.

A cautious step.

Then heated hands found her shoulders. Spirit fire swept through her and she knew she was lost.

Chapter 2 - Meet the Darkness

Ten days earlier
Somewhere in central Myanmar:
4 a.m.

Who knew three hundred miles would take over twelve hours and just about every ounce of strength Kalla Jervis had and *still* leave her in the middle of nowhere?

The pitted road lifted under the bucking jeep as she peered ahead through the darkness. The air through her window carried the welcome scents of moisture and life after hours of acrid scrub desert. Cook fires and curry. The strange smells of animal dung and incense. But a whiff of jasmine spurred Kalla's headache to life big time.

She fought the sick feeling as the mutinous jeep slewed around a corner. Damn. She was driving too fast given she had no headlights, but she didn't dare stop for fear this bucket of bolts would never start again.

She tapped the brakes as buildings materialized out of the darkness. A cream-colored bullock too solid to be a ghost lifted its head to stare at her with luminous eyes. Black-stained bougainvillea draped across low wooden buildings, spindly papaya trees, and thick foliage of jack fruit trees and teak. To the northeast, a deeper darkness showed where a lone mountain blocked part of the sky that might, just might, show a hope of fading into dawn.

Kyaukpadaung. Or else she was hopelessly lost. It had to be, by the map she'd studied the last time she'd had light. It meant she was getting close to Pagan and the archaeological project.

She breathed a sigh of relief—the first one since Alex and the others had failed to meet her delayed flight into Yangon.

Soon she could rest and refocus on what she knew—not navigate the problems at home or a desolate country that had far too few street lights and far too many miles of rough roads that had just added insult to her already aching head.

Relaxing, she steered the jeep around a curve that brought her into the centre of town.

Sudden headlights flared into her eyes. Blind, she slammed on the brakes, shielded her sight. The jeep careened to a stop, stalled when she forgot the clutch.

Lights all around—headlights and half-seen figures running and voices yelling—at her.

She fumbled the keys, cranked the protesting engine to get the hell out of there. Her door was yanked open. A hand dragged her out.

"Hey!"

The lights kept her blind. Male voices set off earthquakes in her head. Rice and curry and sweat stung her nose. Hands on her shoulders, her arms.

"Let me go, dammit!" Years of Seattle self-defense classes kicked in and she slammed her heel down on the foot of whoever held her. Jabbed her elbow into his gut. She yanked loose and turned in a fighter's stance as her vision cleared, ready to defend against wild men and bandits.

Not bandits.

Men in tattered green fatigues.

Soldiers, her mind registered. Myanmar soldiers. All with rifles aimed directly at her.

All the heat suddenly left her.

She straightened. Slowly.

Raised her hands. Slowly.

Damnitalltohell, she should have assessed the situation before she reacted. She was always in control, wasn't she?

Unbidden laughter bubbled up to catch in her throat. The whole damn tableau was ridiculous–like a clichéd drawing for a fairy tale or folk story—damsel in distress surrounded by a band of demons. All the picture needed was the handsome prince coming over the rise of the next hill.

Alex would do. Flare of trumpets, please.

At this particular moment she wouldn't mind Alex striding out of the darkness to her rescue. It would be a little proof that she was doing the right thing joining him and the linguist, Simon Renault, on the project.

One of the soldiers barked an order she didn't understand.

"Listen, I'm sorry, okay? You surprised me. I was blinded by your headlights. I didn't realize you were military."

She tried lowering open hands, but the jerk of the soldiers' rifles was pretty international.

So much gun-metal grey, all pointed in her direction. Did they have the safeties on? Heck, did they even *have* safeties?

She could die here and no one would ever know. No one would even come looking for her. No—Dad would look–if he lived long enough. He'd probably get his psychics right on it. Right. Like that'd work.

The strangled feeling too close to hysteria swelled in her throat.

And Alex might look, too, if he knew she'd actually arrived.

The leader of the soldiers nattered at her again. Two men stepped into the circle of weapons and grabbed her arms. They hauled her, resisting, from the safety of the jeep, while another soldier grabbed her keys.

Her stomach plummeted farther. This didn't look like they were going to let her go. What you going to do now, Kalla?

More men went to the jeep's rear and removed her extra-large black roller suitcase and the small trunk that contained her books and precious equipment.

"Hey! That's my stuff!" Because maybe they *were* bandits. The government couldn't be paying soldiers much, by the look of them. She'd heard soldiers on the coast had stolen supplies meant for the typhoon victims. These could be augmenting their wages by robbing unsuspecting travelers.

They unzipped her bag.

"Stop it, damn you!" She jerked in the men's hold. Tried to pull free, and a rifle butt jabbed into her belly.

Her knees gave. There was only pain and indignation. Come on, Kalla, you got to be the careful, methodical, cultural anthropologist you are if you're going to get through this with your skin intact. But….

How are all those fairy tales gonna get you out of this one? She could almost hear her sister's taunting voice.

She opened teary eyes, and the idiotic factoid that these soldiers wore tattered, green-canvas runners on their feet—not boots—struck her as overwhelmingly funny. She was friggin' Alice falling down that rabbit hole, and what nobody had told her was it was really a bottomless pit.

Biting back the hysteria, she struggled to her feet, the grips of the soldiers still too-hot, too-hard on her arms. Others hauled her belongings from her suitcase one by one.

Jeans. T-shirts. Oh god, her diaphragm, brought in anticipation of the reconciliation with Alex that her father had urged. They were holding it up, examining it with their flashlights. The fact they didn't seem to know what it was didn't stop her face from flaming.

"Perhaps, mademoiselle, I may be of some assistance?"

Well thank god, it was English. She twisted in her captors' grasp, but the not-quite French accent didn't prepare her for the man who coalesced out of the darkness.

She froze.

His blue-black hair fell across his forehead in a rough forelock that accentuated black eyes that seemed to drink in everything at once-and find a humor in her situation she just couldn't match. Darkness seemed to cling to him and set all her alarm bells klaxoning. He didn't look French. He was too tall, too athletic, and almost American in the confident way he moved. The fact his high, almost Asian cheekbones and full lips held her gaze just made it worse. This guy was a babe magnet and knew it, and she hated that kind.

The neatly pressed khakis he wore and the khaki shirt rolled up to expose the dark hair of his forearms just reinforced the mess she was: jeans with red earth soiling the knees, sweat-sodden t-shirt from the long drive, her long black hair falling out of its pony tail.

His predatory saunter across the square and sardonic smile set Kalla's teeth on edge. It didn't help that his gaze settled briefly on what the soldiers were examining. One look said this was a man who knew exactly what they held.

His smirk deepened, but he didn't seem to even notice the weapons trained on him. He just waded into the scene with a graceful panther-stride, then stopped and spoke in a long string of fluid Burmese—or was that Myanmarese?-that made the soldiers lower their rifles.

Damn it, if she'd ever been good with languages she'd have dealt with the soldiers just as calmly. Wouldn't she? She shook her hair out of her face.

"I don't need your help." It was a stupid thing to say, but she didn't want to be in debt to this man.

"Pardon?" He said it the French way and motioned around her. "It seems you do, Mademoiselle…" He paused waiting for her to fill in her name, but she'd be damned if she wanted this guy—this Frenchman—helping her. She was dealing with things—or was going to. She tried to shrug loose from her captors, but no dice.

Nearby a car door thunked and she half-turned as a short, barrel-chested man approached. He wore a uniform and one of those over-large military hats that always seemed to go with despotic generals and too many medals on the chest, but….

He barked something and the soldiers released her arms. That was something, even if she didn't want to give the Frenchman credit. She rubbed her biceps, knowing there'd be bruises there later, but all her attention turned back to the too-handsome stranger.

His Burmese flowed like a river; natural. Was it as seductively accented as his English? How had he learned it? Burmese wasn't exactly the kind of thing they'd teach in school, even in France. *All a ridiculous number of questions about a man you're not remotely interested in, Kalla.*

The round-faced officer looked the Frenchman up and down and his frown deepened. He snapped a question, and then held out his hand.

The Frenchman fished in his pocket. Pulled out a packet of documents and handed them to the officer, all the time speaking another of those long strings of Burmese. There was a reason the language was written in its beautiful round script, because that was how it sounded. But this time she caught something. Western words she understood.

The worst kind of news, because they meant this stranger wasn't someone she could just kiss off. The recognition sent her headache jackhammering harder and her vision dimmed, red and black at the edges.

"*You're* Simon Renault?"

Chapter 3 - Un-Nat-ural Forces

The recognition was mutual, and not what Simon wanted. In fact, the small, hostile woman before him made him almost want to turn and walk away, except these days he made a point of trying to retrain the thing in his head to be polite to women.

"And you would be the lost Mademoiselle Jervis, n'est-ce pas?"

Fighting for normalcy, Simon held out his hand. Her startlingly blue gaze flickered to his palm and hesitated as if she thought he wanted to take her hand.

The last thing he wanted, given the moment he'd seen the jeep plow to a stop and the neat curves of Kalla Jervis hauled from the cab, he'd known she was trouble packed into a far too delectable body. More so when he'd seen the rich mouth and exotic Eurasian tilt to her eyes.

Walk away? *Merde*, he should be running.

"Your passport, s'il-vous-plaît."

"My passport."

"I believe I spoke in English, did I not? The kind officer who had you released has asked for identification." He turned to the officer, made a comment about the challenge of working with foreigners and grinned. The smaller man's face remained unamused.

The small points of color on her high cheekbones and the way her hands shook spoke of barely contained resentment as she hauled a sweat-dampened, cotton travel safe out of her shirt.

The scent of her—all apples and roses with an overtone of well-masked fear—set every part of him at alert. Worse when the dark ocean in his head shifted as if she were the moon. *Not now. Merde, pas maintenant!*

"These men-" She motioned to her captors as she plucked her passport loose, "they're taking my things."

At the rear of the jeep, soldiers still rummaged through her bags. She should be used to it if she traveled much, but then Americans were so concerned about the sanctity of their privacy. They should try living in Europe for awhile.

"Not taking. Searching."

Her sharp gaze said she resented his answer along with his help. He should just walk away and let Alex arrange her release from the military, but the way the damnable dark ocean flowed, every cell of his being pulled towards her.

He accepted the passport; her fingers—accidentally?—brushed his.

Pain lanced his skull. The ocean swelled in a blast of damp air, and the Nat's triumphant laughter staggered him back a step. Simon barely stopped his groan.

Jeep lights dimmed and pulsed for a second.

The officer—general by the look of him—narrowed his gaze.

Merde, non!

Taungbyon, the Burmese spirit, the Nat, swirled and tested Simon's controls. He inhaled and built a dike in his head, centered all his concentration into flipping the passport open to scan the name.

Anything for focus. Anything not to drown. It was the only way to not let loose that stormy ocean.

"Suryathai?" He saw the tight clench of her jaw, and took a momentary pleasure that he could cause a reaction in this woman. The thing was, he could see through her taut, resentful mask to the fragile, desirable female—or at least, the Nat could.

"My mother was Thai. She gave me the name of…."

"Of a Thai warrior princess," he finished for her, knowing that said princess had fought to save the kingdom of Ayutthaya and had died in the process. "Interesting. And what great omens led to such a naming? Or perhaps it was a numerological thing? Or a voice from beyond the grave foretelling?"

An angry flare in her gaze.

"The *name* is a family tradition on my mother's side. Not the result of any charlatan's influence." She actually glared at him.

Eyes a man could fantasize about, he supposed. And even in her disheveled state, uncompromising. Still, there was a lushness around the mouth he suspected would show if she smiled.

Or lost herself in desire.

He shoved the Nat's flare back.

"Suryathai. An unusual tradition for an unusual woman?"

Her response was an audible grinding of teeth.

Another weakness—so the control she exuded was more likely a mask. Satisfied, he passed the passport to the general and explained that she was an American researcher coming to join the archaeological research team in Pagan. He pointed out the permits amongst his papers. The general scanned the documents.

"And you are French?" the smaller man scanned the two passports.

"I travel on a French passport. I have dual citizenship. French and American. My father was American, but I was born in France." A flicker of the General's gaze said he wasn't sure he liked this news, but he let it pass and focused on the woman's passport.

"American as well. If she only joins a research team, why does she travel the roads in the dark? It is the act of a spy. Foreigners take over our country. They foment unrest. I will not have such a one in Pagan. It is our heart."

The little man had a posing, cock-fight kind of bravado to his stance, but there was worry also.

"He wishes to know why you drive in the dark. He thinks you are perhaps a spy."

She rolled her eyes heavenward with a truly a 'princess' attitude.

"I rented a jeep in Yangon when no one was there to meet me." The blame was clear.

"And we *were* there as arranged, but there was no American folklorist on the flight." He stared her down, but she just shifted her attention to the officer as if he would understand her.

"The darned jeep had electrical problems. I lost lights about two hours ago in the middle of nowhere. I wasn't about to stop because I didn't know if I could start the darned jeep again. Besides, who knows what's out there in the darkness?"

She scowled up at him as if he was to blame for everything, so he wasn't about to apologize.

"Lions and tigers and bears, perhaps?"

She startled—perhaps surprised he'd read her work on the meaning beneath Frank L. Baum's works on the Wizard of Oz.

"There is no need for impatience, Ms. Jervis. In Myanmar things move slower, take longer, comprenez?"

"It sort of sank in when 240 miles took ten hours." She crossed her arms over her chest in a bitchy look. Then she shook her head and all the self-confidence seemed to run out of her like spilled wine from a glass.

"Listen, I'm sorry I'm being a bitch. I haven't slept in, like, almost thirty-six hours, and what sleep I had before that was on the plane from the States. I'm tired and I have a headache that just won't quit. Alright?" A small pleading smile, fatigue and pain in the those eyes.

And just like that, she was human and vulnerable and lovely, and that made her more dangerous than ever.

He turned back to the general.

"You see? Our papers are in order." He explained about her jeep's problems, promised he would drive the rest of the way in his jeep—he had come to Kyaukpadaung on his way back to Pagan from Mandalay. He had gone there to see if she had perhaps flown there because all the flights to Pagan were full and the phone lines had been down—again.

"If everything is in order, I will take Mademoiselle Jervis to our camp in Pagan and we will trouble you no more."

He half-bowed to show his respect and he could see the general's tension ease. Yes, things were going to blow over. He would get their lost cultural anthropologist back to Pagan and everything would fall into order and he would redeem himself.

A shout brought his attention back to the soldiers searching the Jervis woman's belongings.

They'd finished with her suitcase. Her things lay in a disorganized pile, that interesting little piece of her equipment balanced on top like a cherry on a sundae and he could see her dismay. But now they'd opened the other box of her things and had hauled out books and a carefully bubble-wrapped form

"No!" The woman lost it. She sprang at the soldiers as they tore off the bubble wrap plastic.

Simon grabbed her shoulders as the soldiers held up a small human form—a Votaress puppet, clad in mystical red. All Simon's controls shattered as he tried to understand how this could be.

How her heat blazed through his hands and the warrior Nat, Shwepyingyi Taungbyon, flared blacker than ever before. Darkness roared up through the earth, welled down from his brain as he yanked the woman back, almost into him, too astounded by the puppet to reestablish control.

TAKE HER HERE. TAKE HER NOW. TOO LONG SINCE TASTED WOMAN.

No! *Je regrette!* Simon fought the desire to crush her to him, to capture her mouth. Merde, he was in control. The ancient Burmese Nat had already ruined his life. It would be controlled now!

But the puppet…. His attention wavered.

A jeep engine sputtered and went out. Headlights dimmed to amber.

Damnation! This was his body! His!

He fought back the dark ocean swells even as the woman—*she was Kalla; would always be Kalla and something more*—twisted in his grasp.

Let her go. Let her go. Let her go, and the raging demon will stop.

But he couldn't, could he? Not if he was going to get Kalla Suryathai Jervis—the Princess—to where she was supposed to be.

"Imbécile! Arrête! Stop it, you fool! You think fighting will get you anywhere?"

His words came out in a command—more steady than he would have thought—and she hesitated. He saw her exhausted controls snap back into place even as his nose filled with her scent of apples and roses and—strawberries? Its sweetness left him almost weak with desire.

Praying she'd obey, he released her and the darkness, the roar of the Nat's demands, receded. He fought the tremors tearing through his body. A soldier restarted the jeep, but Simon's nose was filled with the scent of cordite. He might hold on, he might get through this, if he could just stay away from her. It didn't help that they were here, so close to Mount Popa. The Nat was worse here—more powerful so near that nexus of spirit power.

Swallowing, he turned back to speak to the general, but he had stepped away and barked a command to his men to bring what had been found. Simon's mouth went dry; the darkness swirled in his head.

You will not *do this now.*

Low laughter. Simon clenched his jaw.

"Yoke-thei," he breathed as the general took the small form from his men.

I WANT. Was it the woman or the puppet?

Never. At least not now.

Kalla Jervis positively vibrated with fury.

Damn it, he had worked so hard to build controls over this thing that lived in his head. Why now? Why this woman? He clenched his fists to stop the shaking. The Nat prowled his mind, seeking ways to control, to *HAVE.*

    Karen L. Abrahamson

Simon focused on the Votaress—the female shaman figure. The puppet *was* old, very old, by the look of it. The small face of the venerable puppet was painted with a life-like care that one rarely saw in these days of hurriedly-made tourist puppets. From the richness of its red longyi-skirt and the glint of garnet on its red blouse, this one looked like it harkened back almost to the days of the Grand Imperial Stage.

Exactly what his mother had sought to complete the set that had been her life's passion.

"How…?"

"Yes. How?" The fact that the general spoke in quiet, authoritative English almost took Simon's breath away. The man played his cards close to his chest, that was certain.

"You speak English." Her eyes were wide, darting from the puppet to the general.

"Answer his question." Simon sorted the facts that the general had kept his facility with English a secret and that *this* damnable woman possessed the one thing he'd sought as a final tribute to his mother.

"She's mine. I brought her from home." Her chin lifted in a shaky defiance. "She was my mother's, and her mother's before that. She's been in my family for generations, passed down from mother to daughter."

"Like your name?"

She didn't quite cringed, but there was something there—something not quite the truth in her words, and the Nat in his head always knew the truth. He wanted to grab her, shake her, because lying to this general was only going to get her deeper into trouble; but touching Kalla Jervis was about the most dangerous thing he could think of right now.

"Ce n'est pas toute la vérité—that's not the whole truth."

She avoided his gaze. "It *is* the truth that I brought her from home. That's she's been in my family for generations."

"This is—a piece of the patrimony of Myanmar—of the Burmese people," the general said, his face a smooth mask. "You try to smuggle this puppet out of the country."

"No! I brought her with me. I know it's stupid, but I—I had to."

Her utter confusion was almost charming, but Simon had known women who used helplessness as a weapon, even if Kalla Jervis didn't strike him as the type.

"You have the declaration then?"

"Declaration?" Her blank expression, as she looked from the general to Simon, brought the Nat boiling defensively to the fore until Simon shook his head to dislodge it. She shuddered.

"What? Filing paperwork sends ghosts up your back? Not a good quality in a scientist."

Her gaze snapped to his. "I don't believe in ghosts. Or spirits. I'm a scientist, for god's sake."

The Nat flared at her denigration and Simon dug his finger nails into his palms. "Then truly, you have come to the wrong place, for spirits abound in Myanmar."

Were those his words or the Nat's? He steeled himself.

"Merde, woman, did you not read anything I sent? My instructions clearly stated that all valuables and equipment must be declared at the airport, or else face potential confiscation. Did you not see it?"

"I—I saw it. I declared my camera, my computer—but she's just a puppet, a doll." He saw her realization and watched the color drain from her already pale face. Whatever the truth, this yoke-thei was precious to her.

"She's valuable." It came out in a whisper and her absolute vulnerability left him feeling sucker punched.

"She is part of Burma, Miss Jervis. The old Burma I seek to preserve." The general still studied what had been called one of the small dolls, the troupe of 36 puppets that had once played such an important part in the royal court of old Burma.

Kalla's scent of apples-and-roses and the cool green scent of the not-far-off dawn left Simon suddenly feeling weary and old. Far too many things had come at him too fast, like the earthquake-prone landscape, leaving him uncertain.

But there was one thing he was certain of, that the Nat was certain of, and it scared him that the two of them were in accord.

Regardless of everything, Kalla Jervis and her Votaress puppet were two things he was going to possess.

Chapter 4 - Burmeseness

The taillights of the jeep lost themselves in road dust, darkness, and distance as General Ne Setkya turned back to his cadre of men. They could not hide the surprise on their faces—not a good thing in a world where your bamahsan chin—your Burmeseness, or composure— demanded you show no emotion at all.

Of course, the fact he had returned the puppet to the woman and allowed her to leave for Pagan had surprised him as well, though his carefully schooled demeanor didn't show it. There was something about her and the thin rim of blue so startling around the darkness of her eyes. Something old that almost reminded him of… he couldn't quite put his finger on what.

So he had let her go, with the promise that he would make his decision about the disposition of the puppet and would advise her of it later. He knew where to find them, given he knew everything that happened in, and everything about, Pagan.

In dawn's light breeze, the strawberry-scent of jackfruit and the overripe musk of durian were almost overwhelmed by the sweet fruit of the toddy palm. It was harvest time, and fermentation into the heady liquor that quenched many a Burmese throat had already begun. He could almost wish for its heat right now, sliding down his throat as he watched the sun creep up over the Shan Plateau that guarded the eastern passes to Thailand.

Long streamers of light angled through the clouds, shaped like the pyramid-monuments of Pagan, but below the light lay only the oily darkness of the hills, the same darkness that had swallowed his son in the skirmishes with the damnable hill-tribes. The same darkness that seemed to press on Pagan and his beloved Burma—never Myanmar—no matter that his political masters had changed the country's name in 1989.

He pulled his gaze away, because to look too long in the direction of loss was to wear that grief always. Buddha taught that there was only the moment to be lived and so he lived his life as best he could. But he could not forget his son's death by the rebel Karen hill tribes, nor the fact the army had sent him there. Just as Ne Setkya could not forget his duties.

He turned back to the road northwestward, the road to Pagan, just as the sun's rays began heating the air. The distance shimmered with dust—always dust and dying—and the scent of sage as bullocks led their owners into the fields for futile plowing. Nothing grew well in Pagan anymore.

"I will not forget you, Kalla Jervis. Nor the strange man who came for you."

They would bear careful watching. The foreigners brought trouble to Pagan, even when they spoke almost flawless Burmese. The English and German devils disguised as scientists had already stolen too much from Pagan and they kept coming back, always following rumors of treasure. So did the *meihsa* generals who ran this country. Stories said the riots in the late 1990s had been precipitated by the treasure-hungry government's theft of gold from the Mahamuni Buddha in Mandalay.

He straightened, threw his old-man's shoulders back, and inhaled the heating air. It was his sacred task to make sure the treasures of Pagan were never found.

Chapter 5 - Disaster's Sweet Scent

She would do this even if were against all the government's modern ways.

Dawn faded in an apricot sky as Mei hurried across the dusty parking lot to the small dining room of the Beautyland Hotel. The cool air clung to her skin with morning dampness from the Ayeyarawady River, but the dry sighs of the long, parched grass spoke of the heat that filled the ruins of Pagan. As far as she could see, the huge monuments sent long, creeping shadows across the plain.

A shiver ran up her back.

This place didn't look like life-giving rains ever came, unlike Yangon, where the humidity brought the monsoons rolling in from the Andaman Sea and the Bay of Bengal. Here the only sign of life was the over-sweet scent of the single neem tree's yellow clusters of flowers and the dust-grey foliage of the Htaung trees amid the ruins. The place felt of death and age and something waiting. Ghosts.

She shivered again and plucked three of the grape-cluster neem blooms and added them to what she carried, then pushed into the small hotel dining room, determined to keep them all safe.

Swiftly she tied her red head-scarf like a headband around the coconut she'd bought at the Nyaung U market.

"With this, I name you Min Mahagiri, King of Nats, Lord of the Great Mountain and House Nat." Reverently she lifted the coconut towards Mount Popa and placed what was now the effigy of the King of Spirits on a shelf. Below this she spread a saffron cloth on one of the tables against the wall and placed her laquerware bowl on it. She checked over her shoulder.

No sign of Alex or Mr. Hue. Mr. Hue, one of the many Chinese who flooded Myanmar, would not understand her actions; and she could not bear the thought that Alex might look down on her as a superstitious primitive.

She pressed her palms together and bowed to the nat-effigy.

"Min Mahagiri, hear my words. I set out these offerings that you will keep us safe. Three times I ask you. Bring the American woman to us. And Simon. Even Simon. We mean no harm."

She paused, heard a door slam from somewhere in the line of rooms that comprised the hotel, clenched her eyes closed, and rushed on.

"King of Nats, three times I ask you. Hold me safe from my fears, from my past, and let me show myself worthy so I might come to you again. Let us have safe ventures here—and—let me have a place in the world." The last came out as a rushed plea.

A force staggered her back, like great hands on her chest, and her hand flashed to her mouth. What she had said. Great Buddha, what she had said!

Asking a nat—any nat—for aid was courting disaster. She needed to unsay what she had said. Needed to make things right, for the nats were *meihsa*—evil. While it was good to provide gifts to make them stay away, asking for their aid could allow the evil in.

The dining room door banged open behind her and she whirled around. Tall, blonde Alex with the sunshine smile and the golden skin walked in with Mr. Hue, the squat owner of the Hotel.

"Mei? You alright? You're pale." The drawl as the American archaeologist said her name—as if he lingered tasting it—only made her heart race faster.

"Fine. I am well, thank you." She glanced uncertainly back at the small shrine she had made, but not before she saw Hue's disapproval. He marched past into the kitchen and the clatter of pots and pans began.

"Whatcha been doing?"

Alex came up beside her—so close she scented his shampoo of spice and wild grasses. He picked up one of the bananas, but her small gasp stopped him.

"What?" he asked turning to her. "What is it?"

"It is—kadaw-pwe. The offering to the House Nat. You do not touch it."

She couldn't stop the small shiver or the flush of embarrassment. The unseen force still rested across her chest in a warning.

"It is an ancient tradition that still holds in these country places. The nats—the spirits—they are everywhere and must be kept happy."

He must have read the concern on her face.

"Or what?" he asked.

Mei took the banana from him and turned back to the kadaw-pwe. She smoothed the saffron cloth he'd disturbed and resettled the banana so the display was perfect. Then she closed her eyes in obeisance and apology on Alex's behalf, but he stood so close it was like an electric charge in the room that she knew was going to block her prayer. She gave up and met his eyes—a strange pale combination of green and brown, like shadows under leaves.

"Stories say nats bring illness to those who do not make offerings. A child not dedicated to the Nat of his or her village will die. A rice field not dedicated to Boun Magyi, the rice mother, will wither. A warrior Nat not propitiated before battle will lead to disaster."

She waited for the condescending grin all the tourists at Shwedagon Pagoda normally gave her. Alex looked back at the kadaw-pwe and nodded.

"Interesting. So this is to bless our project. Good, I guess. We can use all the help we can get, given how things have gone so far."

He flashed her a smile that left her weak. Could a western man understand? None had, in her life. But then she'd never worked with an archaeologist before.

"So come on and join me. Hue says he can have coffee in a few minutes, and man, I could use a cup. I swear my body clock's all wrong."

She froze looking at the pwe. She would make amends later when Alex was gone. But… body clock? If she was translator, how could she not know what that meant? She was going to bring disgrace on her family when she could not do her job.

"Mei?"

Alex cocked his head down at her, so much taller than she. And too close for propriety. Again, he must have read her confusion. He motioned at a chair.

"You okay? I'm jet-lagged, that's all. So. Any sign of Kalla or Simon?"

Body clock. Jet lag. The phrase meant fatigued—feeling the effect of travel.

"There has been no sign of them." She settled in the chrome chair. From the kitchen came Hue's clattering, but Min Mahagiri's threat loomed behind her. "When I rose this morning there were no jeeps—only the doves in the eaves."

Her father would not approve the fact she was alone with Alex. She studied her hands. "I am sorry you did not sleep better."

"Not your fault. Damn Kalla, anyway. She should have been on that plane." He shook his head and the sunlight through the window caught his shoulder-length hair like the gold wafer encrusting Buddha statues. Still, his worry showed he cared for the missing woman.

"It's not like her. She'd at least send a message."

"Perhaps she tried. Myanmar is not a good country for communication. Things—do not always work."

The way he shook his head said he did not believe it.

"You know Miss Jervis well, then." Do not appear curious. Do not appear concerned.

Alex spread his strong hands on the scarred Formica table top and seemed to study his fingers.

"Yeah. I know her. Knew her. Knew her family. Her Dad's good people. 'Salt of the earth', we say, although he does have a few—odd— interests." He looked up at her and smiled. "We dated awhile."

A pang of jealousy twisted inappropriately and the bright morning light dimmed. But she deserved disaster after what she had done this morning.

She smoothed her face with her *bamahsan chin*, her Burmese calm, and smiled.

"You must look forward to seeing her then."

"Some. Kalla and I." He lifted his gaze at her and shook his head. The wistfulness was quickly shut down, but couldn't hide old feelings.

"Kalla and I have history. But it's all in the past."

It took all her courage to smile. "Perhaps history can be revived? Is that what you hope?"

He looked away, shrugged. "It's just—history. Something we were once, but it's over as far as I'm concerned. I might dwell on the past in my work, but I haven't got time to do it in my life. Get in, get out, move on. That's how I live my life." He grinned.

Perhaps that was how most western men lived their lives. He leaned back in his chair, stretched out his long legs, but his regard felt like heat on her skin. Her body's answering flush said she had to take the conversation back to safer areas.

"You admire her then—Ms. Jervis."

"She's one of the best at what she does. Tenacious. Stubborn. A control freak about her work. Loyal—until you hurt her." He leaned forward, elbows on table, grief on his face. "Then you might as well be dead."

Mei looked to the kitchen, wishing Hue would return with their coffee, wishing she could think of some way to excuse herself because she did not want to be attracted to Alex if he were drawn to another. But the fact Kalla Jervis had hurt Alex already lowered her estimation of the American woman. Alex caught her hand.

"You'll like her, I think."

The depths of Alex's smile surprised her. Since meeting in Yangon, they'd relaxed around each other on the trip north, had enjoyed the evenings talking. But his touch slammed confusion into her like a typhoon ripping into Yangon.

"She's not anything like you, but I think that might be good. Maybe good for you both."

His hand was so warm, so large it enfolded hers completely, tanned skin on her golden. She liked the way it felt. It was not something a Burmese man would do—would never do for her.

"I will check on the coffee."

She extricated her hand, praying he did not see the color in her cheeks. But when she couldn't stop herself from glancing back from the kitchen door, his smile said he had. She had to find time to compose herself.

But Hue was no help. He muttered in Chinese when he saw her, shushed her out of his kitchen, just as the sound of a jeep slowing on the road brought Alex to his feet.

They pushed outside into warming air and sun-glare as a vehicle with two occupants stopped at the pole barring the gate into the hotel yard.

"Finally. I'll get the gate. You get your dad."

Alex strode across the yard as Simon climbed out of the jeep, like a bit of midnight with his tangle of black hair and his sun-darkened skin.

Mei turned and ran, pounded on her father's door, then hurried to her room to recover the welcome gift she had originally brought to the airport to welcome Kalla.

Let this welcome work. Let Kalla be her friend. Let all be well within the team and their research.

From her bathroom sink she lifted the damp cloth she had used to protect the precious jasmine wreath she had bought in Yangon. Unfortunately, time had faded the pale blooms at the edges, but they still filled the air with fragrance. They would have to do.

The jeep had stopped in the shade of the neem tree, and her father was already opening the rear, ignoring Simon as he pulled out a suitcase and a large box. Alex yanked the passenger door open.

The woman who must be Kalla Jervis stepped out shaking her head, and shut the door behind her as if she had something to prove.

"Well, you are a sight for sore eyes, woman."

Alex caught her in a hug so long Mei had to fight back the urge to crush what she held. But Kalla Jervis was not the tall, leggy blonde Mei had expected, and not dressed in the too-revealing sleeveless shirts and shorts too many western women wore. No, Kalla Jervis was small, proper, had a long sweep of almost black hair that hung down her back to her waist, and the face of a—Burmese? Thai?

Alex turned her towards Mei. "Here she is."

There was something unsettlingly proprietary in the way Kalla leaned into him, the way she caught his hand and leaned up to place a kiss too close to his mouth.

Alex grinned down at her. "If your ears were ringing it was because we were just talking about you."

"And here I thought it was just from fourteen hours in a rattling jeep."

"Mei, I'd like you to meet Kalla Jervis. Kalla, this is Mei, our second interpreter. You've already met Simon."

The western woman stilled at Simon's name. He stood back, arms crossed over his chest as if he waited for something. Then Kalla turned shocking blue eyes on Mei.

Eyes the color of spirits. Eyes the color of death. She had to stop herself from stepping back. Kalla Jervis was going to take some getting used to.

"I have looked forward to meeting you." Mei stepped forward and schooled herself to pleasantness and her best English.

She held out her hand, waiting for Kalla to—thankfully—unclasp her hand from Alex's and smile. Those blue eyes mesmerized, like troubled oceans at dawn.

Mei slipped the jasmine wreath around Kalla's wrist. "I welcome you to Myanmar, Kalla."

Her eyes filled with sudden shock as they locked on the flowers.

Then Kalla Jervis slumped to the ground.

Chapter 6 – Darkness and Death

The weight of mountains on Kalla's chest; she cannot breathe. Darkness and desperation and someone beside her. Someone of darkness. Night in the eyes. Night all around as she walks. Dares not run through heated, jasmine-scented air.

Held by the darkness, by the hands reaching, touching. Long sweeps of hair and the faces too like hers, too many eyes and she passes away crying. Knowing it is right. Knowing it is fitting. Knowing it is proper.

But she does not want to die.

Even as the weight and darkness press in to her eyes, her ears are on the wild wings of music tunneling under the earth. Trailing up to the stars.

She wants to scream.

But there is no one to hear her, no one to care under this mountain of darkness, and she has no one to thank for her presence in this place but herself. This is her choice. Her life. Her death. So lonely she could cry for it. Scream for the loneliness of it all, for the weight of the mountain.

The weight of knowledge—if she could only remember.

The weight of years—how many had passed?

The weight of the others holding her in place and she screams, lashes out as their voices fill her head and she can no longer know anything but the overwhelming scent of jasmine and the darkness and the weight of a red mountain and …

"… what have I done! Min Mahagiri, what have I done!"

Kalla fought off the hands that held her, fought up through the red-tinged darkness towards light, and hope. Inhaled a great draught of air, and consciousness slammed home.

Blindness and light. Sun. Day. Scent of dust and man-musk. Shadows, and her gaze locked on a dark face. Dark hair. Gallic nose and those piercing, black eyes that made something dark open inside her like a secret door. Simon knelt beside her.

She almost wished he touched her.

Kalla yanked her gaze away, afraid. And what the hell was going on?

"Kalla? Kalla, are you alright?" Concern in Alex's eyes as he knelt on her other side. Worry. She locked her gaze there. Safety. Normalcy. Control. What she'd come here seeking, apparently.

"Whoa. What was that?"

She squeezed Alex's hand, knowing he was the man her father wanted for her. Maybe she could make her father proud of her just once before he died.

"I was going to ask you the same thing."

She grinned and pushed herself up onto her elbow, and someone brought a sledgehammer down onto her head. At least that was what it felt like. She winced. Almost fell back, but Alex's warm hand caught her arm and she leaned into his shoulder, all the time too aware of Simon's dark regard.

"Maybe you should take it slowly, Mademoiselle."

She ignored Simon and shivered, inhaled the dust, and looked up at Alex. "I'm okay. Just a headache from the trip, I guess. Too much going on."

She brought her legs up and demanded to stand, because she wasn't some swooning woman. She might have had a little difficulty on the trip, but she was Kalla and that was what Alex would expect of her—strength and personal responsibility.

"You're sure you're okay?" He helped her up, held her shoulders, looked down at her with that familiar hazel gaze that wasn't quite any color you found in nature, but that was comfortable Alex, methodical Alex. Alex who also liked to be in control.

"Fine." She nodded and winced at the responding jab of a knife through her brow.

"You had a medical before you came over here, right?"

"What d'you think? Of course I did. It's the drill, isn't it? Or aren't I professional enough for you."

She hated that it came out snarky, but the concern on his face no longer looked quite so concerned—at least not about her. It became the face of Alex Munroe, Team Leader making sure his project was safe.

Just like always.

"I wanted to make sure there were no medical conditions we needed to be aware of. Let's face it, Kalla, when you get it in your mind to go on a project, your health isn't exactly your top priority."

She dropped her gaze, fighting back her frustration. It wouldn't speed up the reconciliation if she recalled that it had been both their decisions that she go the *one* time she got sick.

"I'm sorry, Alex. I'm way tired and I've got a headache that would drop most horses."

But the damage was done, wasn't it. Alex stepped back to the slim Burmese woman—Mei—and touched her shoulder in a way that made every hair on Kalla's neck stand on end.

"It's okay, Mei. She's okay. See? You didn't do anything." He gently turned her towards Kalla.

The wreath of flowers was shredded in Mei's fists. She'd apparently torn it from Kalla's wrist, but the whiff of jasmine still sent a crimson shadow across Kalla's sight.

She stepped back, bumped against Simon who had come up behind her, and jerked away. Darn him for sneaking up behind her. But he was like that, wasn't he? Too tall, too dark, and darn well too good looking. The worst part was he knew it and seemed to laugh at her.

"It's okay, Mei. I'm okay. You didn't do anything."

Simon had been like that since he'd materialized out of the darkness at the roadblock. On the drive to Pagan he had barely spoken one-word answers to her questions, but she'd felt his frequent study of her like a hot wind.

"It is good to hear. You are truly well, Princess?" His dark eyes were locked on her. "You gave us quite the *peur*—the fright—n'est-ce pas? The lovely scientist collapses to the earth like death."

He was mocking her, dammit. Absolutely mocking her, by his use of her hated nickname—he'd somehow known her middle name was her weakness. His gaze watched for her reaction like a hawk watches for prey. Any sign of weakness was going to be fodder for this man, and she'd be damned if she'd give it to him.

"Whatever." She turned back to Mei.

Alex hovered by her. A short, older Burmese man held her hand, and for a moment Kalla resented the woman's use of vulnerability and other feminine wiles to hold men to her. It was as bad as the spiritualists who preyed on the grieving.

But then she saw Mei's eyes—brimming with tears and fear. So maybe the girl really was afraid. It had been her voice Kalla heard as she came to.

"I really am okay, Mei. I don't know what happened, but thank you for your gift." Kalla caught Mei's hand, pried the fingers loose from the flowers and steeled herself to look down at the crushed blossoms. The white flesh seemed to turn brown as she watched, as if they would be dust in seconds. Like the dust sifting across the hotel courtyard.

She inhaled the jasmine scent, and for a moment the flat plain of Pagan was no longer a place of dust and shadows and the huge pyramid temples and stupa that sat like hunkered monsters in the dawn. A flash of torchlight and swaying figures. Scent of curry. Many voices and an overwhelming sense of soul-deep grief.

She managed to not drop the flowers. Managed to smooth the confusion off her face and smile.

"You see? It wasn't you or your gift. It was just my jet lag." She glanced at Alex and grabbed his hand. "Come on. Let's find a place we can all sit down. Any place we can get a cup of coffee around here?"

There. Back in control. She cocked her head toward what looked like a restaurant and he nodded, so she led them from the jeep and into the cool room.

"So tell me, what's the set-up? You were pretty cryptic in your message." But it had hooked her like a salmon on one of her father's trawler lines.

A ceiling fan swung lazily over a central table. The room was really pretty Spartan by western standards, or even Thai expectations. Only a poster by the kitchen door showing Pagan at sunrise with white spires rising over a darkened plain, and at one side of the room a small shrine.

Offering, really. Coconut on the shelf—signifying—she wasn't sure what. The job's timing hadn't left a lot of time for research into the belief systems of Burma, but if it was anything like Thailand, the offering was probably to local spirits or ancestors.

She collapsed in a chair, the headache still thumping like a demon in her head. Alex sat down across from her and Mei settled beside him. The small man - Mei's father, she presumed - stood for a moment.

"I'm sorry," said Kalla leaning across to him. "Kalla Jervis. You must be Khun."

The small man caught her fingers lightly, shook.

"Miss Kalla. I pleased to meet you. Anything you need, you ask and I will get, yes?" He smiled. His round face was topped with a bristle-brush haircut of grey. "My daughter. She will help you."

He touched Mei's shoulder proudly and Kalla felt a momentary pang of jealousy.

"I'm sure she will." She managed a smile at both of them, then looked at Alex, suddenly too aware that Simon Renault had slumped into the seat beside her and stretched his long legs out alongside of hers. He was far too close for comfort, but she wasn't going to give him the satisfaction of shifting her chair.

"Any chance of that coffee?"

And a shower and about 50 hours of sleep.

"Hey, Hue!" Alex called, stopping Mei from going to check with a too familiar gesture that eased her back into her chair. "Can we get that coffee now?"

A grunt and a clatter came from the kitchen and Alex turned back to her, but all Kalla could see was the way Alex hung his arm casually over the back of Mei's chair. Was he courting the woman? That would not do—at all.

"Coffee's on the way." Friendly and matter of fact, but then he looked back at Mei.

"Then maybe you can tell me what this whole darn venture is about? Like I said, your message didn't say a lot. Researching folktales of a forgotten civilization might be enough to get me here, but what makes this so urgent, and what shakes a research permit loose from the Myanmar government when this is virtually a closed country?"

"I'll bet you'd like to know." His face bore that smug little-boy look of excitement she remembered so well.

"Darn it, Alex, you look like when we were undergrads and you'd just come up with the one theory that explained the environmental catastrophe that wiped out a good chunk of the Coast Salish in the Pacific Northwest."

"Can I help it if no one was looking at geology?" He shrugged.

But the puzzled looks on the other's faces made her explain. "We were at a dig at what turned out to be the oldest known Indian settlement in that part of the world. Wonder boy here was the first to come up with the explanation about how the collapse of an ice dam in central Washington released a huge prehistoric lake, resulting in the loss of most of the population. It was a superb piece of work."

"And it led you to connect all the Native folk stories about a flood." At least she thought she saw admiration in his gaze.

She smiled. "When I first saw this tall drink of water sitting next to the campfire with a beer in his hand and this same look of excitement, I decided he was the man I was going to be with." She raised her brows at him, but all he did was glance briefly down at Mei.

"Five years." He said it so matter of factly that it froze Kalla's heart.

"Five years and two PhDs, to be exact." She managed to keep her voice light. Until the fighting was just too much. He didn't appreciate her methodical nature or understand her need to take charge. She couldn't stand his impetuousness and the way he needed to be in control of absolutely everything—even the style of her hair. But she would put up with everything if it would make her father happy with his youngest daughter.

She could do this thing. She could.

An oriental man—Chinese, by the look of the cigarette stains on his fingers—carried a tray into the dining room and clattered steaming cups onto the table. Cups of steaming water, that is. Small orange packets on each saucer.

"What is this?" It came out as uncertain as Kalla was beginning to feel. "Sanka? Sanka's not coffee."

"It is here, Princess. But perhaps it does not meet with your approval?" Simon smoothly tore the packet open, poured the contents in her cup and stirred, then handed it to her.

She swallowed back the desire to knock the steaming water in his face. To tell him what Simon Renault could do with his Princess and the cup of swill he offered.

Instead she dutifully accepted the cup and saucer.

"Thank you." It came out strangled, and that damned smirk of his increased. She sipped.

Swill was right. She should have brought coffee with her. Angry with herself for her pique, she looked back at Alex.

"So? I'll ask again—what's the story? I've come—what?—5,000 miles to find out."

"Guess I really did tweak that curiosity of yours."

"You know the buttons to push. I believe you said something about folktales—ones that haven't been analyzed by every student ethnologist in the world?"

Alex got that full-of-himself look on his face and the puffed up chest she remembered when he held some fact close to his chest. He'd been like that at the Salish dig, too. But everyone had had to put up with it when his brilliance—his ability to look at the dig results from a new angle—had led to the discovery of a second and larger site that had become the first step in Alex's brilliant career.

"I did say that, didn't I?"

He leaned back in his chair, and Kalla couldn't help noticing how Mei seemed to lean towards him. Something in the way they moved framed each other's actions.

Kalla stood up, her headache stabbing into her as she rounded the table. Time to remind Alex of what they'd had. And to stake her territory. She caught Alex's shoulders in her hands and began to massage the deep muscle—just the way she had when they were together.

"So?"

"I think our Mademoiselle Jervis tries to make you putty in her hands, Alex. Something to be wary of, n'est-ce pas?"

Alex pulled away and stood, leaving Kalla feeling entirely foolish for how easily Simon had read her. His sardonic smile only made her hands clench. She rounded on Alex, all the fatigue suddenly resting on her shoulders.

"So are we going to have to play 20 questions, or are you going to tell me why I'm here?"

She was too tired to play adolescent courtship games. She knew Alex. Knew what made him tick and how to work with him. She didn't need to move in like some proprietary, jealous girlfriend. They had history. They'd had chemistry.

That would be enough.

She looked up into Alex's hazel eyes. "Come on. I'm too tired for this."

He must have seen her fatigue because he suddenly smiled that brilliant California smile and draped an arm across her shoulders, pulling her with him as he began to pace.

"It's like this, kid. Weird but true. Seems there were some American doctors helping out with a bird flu outbreak in Yunnan Province of China, just north of the Burmese border. I gather it was a bad outbreak. Very bad. Wiped out a couple of villages and almost wiped out a third, though the Chinese managed to stop it from getting into the international press."

Alex stopped by her chair, eased her down in it with a considerate hand on her arm, then smiled down at the questions that must have been written on her face. Held up his hand.

"Hold on. No interruptions." He started pacing again, rounded the table to pause by Mei's chair, so Kalla's alarm bells rang all over again.

"It's like this. Apparently there was someone on their team who liked to collect folk stories. Amateur. Anyway, he heard a story from an old woman that this was not the first time towns were emptied by disease. She mentioned a great city left barren to the south. That got the doctor thinking, and that got some pharmaceutical company interested. So they came to me."

He resumed pacing, stopping Kalla's questions.

"Pagan is due south of Yunnan province. Between the 11th and 13th centuries it was the greatest city in the region. Then it ended—no one knows why. Some suggest the Kublai Khan's Mongols destroyed the city, but the murals in the temples show few Mongol figures, and those were added after the city was already gone. Others say disease wiped the city out."

He stopped by Kalla's chair again. Knelt down and caught her hand.

"And that's why we're here. To look for evidence to support the disease theory. If we find it, the pharmaceutical company is going to send in a medical team to collect local samples and see if there might be antibodies in the population around here that might help fight the bird flu. I think they're worried about another pandemic, Kalla. And we're here to help them—the first team, as it were."

Kalla pulled her hand free. She shook her head, trying to sort through everything he'd told her and what he hadn't.

"So we're here because of a pharmaceutical company?"

"They send researchers into the Amazon. Why not here?"

She was still shaking her head.

"Kalla, this part of the world is where they figure chickens were domesticated thousands of years ago. If people have been living with the birds that long, why wouldn't some of them have developed some immunity to bird diseases?"

She couldn't answer that. Wasn't a doctor, but…

"So we're here because some woman told a story in another country. They want me to collect local folktales that might substantiate the hypothesis, and you to examine the archaeological remains for further substantiation." There. She'd summarized it and she could tell by Alex's clouded gaze that he'd read her doubts.

"They want our scientific detachment and our passion for knowledge, Kalla. The reason I asked you to be on the team is because I remembered how you always cut through the crap to the underlying facts. You're one of the best at reinterpreting myths and legends. You've retold ghost stories to get at the rational reasons behind the tales. I *thought* you were passionate about your work."

His expression suggested that was the only place he remembered her passion, and she braced for one of their inevitable blowups.

"Alex, I am passionate. I will be. I always have been. I just need more information. Is there a recording of the villager's story? A transcript? Anything? Surely you got one."

She stood up to face him, realized Mei and Khun were standing too; like Thai people, they were afraid of being caught in an unpleasant emotional crossfire. Not Simon. He slouched in his chair, appearing half-asleep.

"Are you questioning me?"

God, she was tired, but she held it together. "No, I'm asking you research questions and you hate it—just like always. I need more than your paraphrase of a paraphrase if I'm to substantiate a link. I need to look at the language used to convey the story. The change in meaning of a word, how a story is told over time—its structure—all can reveal something about the story itself. It could be a legend, based in fact, or a teaching story or something drawn from the Sanskrit *Jataka* tales. I need to see or hear the story to analyze it as a starting point."

"I don't have one."

"So you're expecting me to just run with enthusiasm—not facts."

Alex's handsome jaw was set in the way that said she had asked one question too many. If she was going to make up with Alex, this wasn't the way to go about it.

"Then I guess I'll just have to start from scratch, won't I?" She thought she said it calmly, sweetly even, but the way Alex's face darkened she knew he'd taken it the wrong way.

"Why do you always have to do this?" It came out soft, but oh so familiar—and dangerous.

"I'm just being a scientist, Alex. A scientist is a skeptic, until the evidence proves otherwise. You know that." But he was already gone, slamming out the door, striding across the yard. Mei and Khun looked at her and followed.

She sighed. She hadn't meant for it to happen. She knew his insecurities—that he'd never been able to make his parents happy. It was another thing they had in common.

Outside, Alex disappeared into what had to be his room. It had to be that they were both jet-lagged. Alex didn't normally go off so fast and she didn't normally push so hard. And he was a loving man. One of those unusual men who always thought of bringing home flowers, or helping with household chores. Those were the things she had to hold onto.

Beside her, Simon Renault's feet scraped the worn lino as he stood. He invaded her personal space with his strange, intoxicating scent of incense and man-sweat, and smiled down with the most infuriating mockery. His eyes were pits she could fall into.

"I think, Princess, that did not go well."

Chapter 7 – Cloth, Like a River

The jeep jounced and rattled on the paved road into Nyaung U and Kalla gripped the door handle, inhaling the scent of dust and muddy river water and doubting whether she had done even one thing right since she'd received Alex's invitation to join the research team.

Even her decision to come to Myanmar was questionable. And getting Alex's dander up within fifteen minutes of arriving on site was definitely not the road to reconciliation.

"You are so quiet, Kalla. Is anything wrong?" Mei glanced away as she gracefully steered the jeep around brightly tasseled pony carts.

"Just tired." The woman's glance said she doubted. "And a tad frustrated with myself. Things haven't exactly gone as planned since I got here."

"But did you not sleep, at least a little?"

"Not a bit. Too excited, I guess." Kalla grimaced. Frustrations with herself had stopped her from catching even a moment's restorative rest after the confrontation this morning. "I ended up showering and sorting out my room." But her headache had made even that effort almost too much. She massaged her temples. "You rescued me from the mess."

She locked glances with Mei and smiled. The younger woman had offered to take Kalla to the market in hopes of finding community elders who might share stories. It was as good a place to start as any.

The jeep came around a stand of trees to a shabby collection of permanent wooden stalls, set back from the river; that wasn't what Kalla expected. Grey bullocks lugged huge, wooden-wheeled carts with barrels of slopping river water. Bicycles dodged around the carts, and then there were the jeeps—military green, with soldiers lounging at their sides.

She swallowed as Mei pulled into the curb. Would they arrest her again?

"This is it?" Kalla eyed a woman crouched in the dust, her back to one of the wooden sheds. Before her were two baskets of faded tomatoes and wilted green vegetables. It didn't exactly look prosperous around here—and, with the soldiers, it was questionable whether it was a good idea to even get out of the jeep.

Mei's chocolate eyes showed she didn't quite comprehend the context of the question. "This is Nyaung U market—the largest in Pagan area. Not so good as Yangon markets, but it brings people and it is bigger than the one in the old town of Bagan. It sells the best that Pagan has to offer, but the people here are poor."

She looked away as if she didn't like apologizing for her people, and Kalla realized she had been judging.

"Sorry. I'm used to the Bangkok markets. This is my first Burmese one. It's different."

But the damage was done. Mei's gaze had gone guarded. Perhaps it was the attraction Kalla suspected between Alex and Mei. Perhaps Mei recognized Kalla as a rival.

Well, the girl would just have to stand back, because Kalla's dad had said Alex was the right guy, and Kalla wasn't going to let her dad down. Not this time. Not even if her dad's judgment were based on questionable advice.

As she climbed out of the jeep, the scent of river mud sent pain stabbing her temples. She staggered, but Mei was suddenly there, half supporting Kalla's weight.

"Are you sure you are well? Perhaps we should go back to the hotel?"

Kalla brushed away the help and leaned on the jeep door for a moment. "Just the heat. And the jet-lag, that's all. I can't seem to get rid of this darned headache."

She felt Mei's gaze as light feather touches. The woman was concerned, uncertain. Finally she turned back to the ramshackle buildings.

"This is the market that sells most fabric and laquerware in the area, as well as spices and fruit and vegetables. Many families bring their grandfathers and grandmothers with them. We may be able to obtain stories here—if you are able."

"Lead on—I'm able. I just need to stretch my legs, get some air. That's all."

But it wasn't just the heat and her head. Something about the scent of the water, of the teak sheds baking in the sun, made the scene ripple.

Mei seemed to hesitate, but then her face grew determined. "Kalla, I would like to make amends for what happened this morning. It was my fault. I wish to buy you a gift of welcome, if you will allow it. I thought perhaps a longyi—it would be cooler for you to wear." She smoothed her hands over the slim-fitting sarong that skimmed her hips.

In the face of such generosity, it would be insulting for Kalla to turn her down, even though Kalla knew the woman must not have much money. No one in Burma—Myanmar, she corrected herself—did.

"It's not necessary, Mei. But I accept your gift in the spirit with which it is given. A great kindness." On a whim she caught Mei's hand and squeezed, because she didn't want this sweet woman as an enemy or rival—not over Alex.

"I had hoped we could be friends, Kalla. Might this still be so?" A cautious smile bloomed.

"I'd like nothing better." Kalla clasped fingers with Mei, squeezed. "Friends, then?"

The bright smile that lit Mei's face was almost painful to see.

"I know we shall be." Such proper British English.

Inside the maze of small buildings the sun no longer weighed so heavily on Kalla's head, but the air hung heavy with the river's moisture sticking Kalla's pink t-shirt and jeans to her skin. Already sweat ran between her breasts, even though cloth awnings cut the sun. The scent of curry and garlic and turmeric filled the air.

"You really think I could get by in one of those?" She motioned at a longyi worn by a slim woman working in a stall laden with huge bags of dried—something—shrimp? Fish? Squid?

"A longyi. Yes. They are expected of Burmese people. The government requires it. But the people will like that you dress as them. It is a pleasure to see others take our ways, speak our language."

"Aah. So Simon Renault is well respected here, then."

She saw the slight falter in Mei's light step, felt the way her fingers tightened.

"Simon is—known. He speaks Burmese very well. He spent much of his childhood here."

The caution of the answer was intriguing.

"You knew him?" She stopped to examine a display of black lacquer bowls and boxes, covered with fine paintings of flowers or everyday

Burmese life. Above them hung an array of puppets, but these were poorly crafted things that could never match hers.

"We grew up together when his father's work did not take him to France. His mother was my mother's cousin. Our families were very close."

"He strikes me as a—difficult man."

Again that cautious pause, as Kalla nodded thanks to the proprietor and left the display.

"Difficult. Perhaps. For some. But who would I be to judge a western man?"

Kalla grinned. "As good a judge as any woman. Men are—well—a different species."

"Even Alex?" Mei seemed surprised.

"Definitely Alex. I never could seem to figure him out." She met Mei's steady gaze and realized what she had said. Was that satisfaction she saw at the revelation? "I suppose that's why we were always attracted—the mystery of it all, you know?"

Mei looked away as if thinking on Kalla's words.

"There is darkness in Simon, very unlike Alex. There has been since he was a young man, and it fills me with sadness." Mei's voice was thoughtful even as the change of topic left Kalla a trifle breathless. Breathless again as Mei's face brightened. "Look. Thannaka wood."

Mei broke her handclasp with Kalla and left her leaning on a wooden stall post, trying to regain her mental balance. From sparring about Alex to warnings re Simon to Thannaka wood—whatever that was—was just too fast a transition when she was this tired. The whole market seemed to swing an unpleasant, lazy loop around her, the air shifting against her skin as Mei spoke to the proprietor of the shop and was handed a small stone block and a grey piece of wood. Darkness smothered Kalla's vision for a moment.

Mei ground the wood against the stone in a slow, round rhythm that produced a fine paste she held up to Kalla's nose. It smelled of baby powder.

"See? Thannaka wood. It is good for the skin, protects it from the sun." With light fingers she dabbed the white paste onto Kalla's cheeks, smoothed it on with an intimate and sensual touch. Smoothed it on the backs of Kalla's hands, and Kalla closed her eyes against the overwhelming sense of déjà vu the sensation evoked.

"It keeps our skin smooth and fair, but not as fair as your skin." Mei smiled. "You are very beautiful with your pale skin and straight nose."

"My nose."

"It is not so flat as mine, see?" With a deprecating smile, Mei traced the slight dip of her nose. "No nose. You have one. Perfect."

"Mei, your nose is lovely. Mine is just different than yours, that's all. And I would be better off if I were as kind a person as you. Maybe what I need is a nose like yours."

She was talking nonsense and she knew it, but darn it all, this woman was disarming and charming and lovely and gentle and everything Kalla could never be. She'd spent her life battling for what she wanted and needed—not that she'd ever been particularly successful in getting it—but she'd come to see the battle as part of the getting, and had learned strength from it.

"Let me buy you the Thannaka—as a gift in return, for being my good friend." Against Mei's protests, Kalla purchased the wood and a new small grinding stone and handed them proudly to Mei. "If you're worried, we can share the Thannaka. It feels so cool—almost tingly on the skin."

That brought a true smile to Mei's lips. "You see? We will be like sisters." She held her arm out beside Kalla's, skin to skin. "We are the same, yes? Sisters in skin."

For some reason that sent a chill down Kalla's neck, and she gripped the stall pole against a sweep of vertigo.

"We should get on with this," she said, blinking herself back to normal. What was happening to her? She had lived in hot climates before.

Mei led her deeper into the maze of stalls. Men sold black and red laquerware pickled tea boxes embossed with fine paintings of Burmese scenes. Other stalls sold cheap kitchen utensils, brightly colored spices, but it was the cloth that held Kalla's attention.

Piles of fabric in neat stacks of folded longyi lengths. Sweeps of it, curtains that hung from the sides and backs of the stalls.

All moved, shifting bright colors and swirled paisley patterns in the narrow aisles. Whatever breeze there was seemed to barely reach beneath the cloth awnings hung against stray sun beams, and yet around her the displays of fabric *moved*. Draperies of bright cloth whispered around her, billowed to touch her, lifted like sultry eyelids to give glimpses of stalls, of other narrow ways through the maze. Closed like doors, like tattered funeral shrouds swathing this place.

The passage narrowed and she slowed, swallowed as she tried to catch her breath in the heat. Mei disappeared in the flow of fabric. It moved like Kalla's breath, cloth lifting and falling like the whole market breathed, like the whole country breathed, sucking the air from her. Sipping her breath into the shadows of those long, narrow corridors of cloth.

A glimpse of soldier green.

The dusty earth shifted under her feet and her vision narrowed, narrowed like a corridor that stretched forever before her. Narrowed like the cloth that reached for her, the faces that watched her; and something grasped her ankle and she stumbled. Something reached for her through the curtains of cloth that smothered like water, ran over her like the river, and she was drowning, drowning.

Panicked, she staggered against a wooden pillar that supported one of the stalls. Old woman. Strange face. Strange words that seemed at the edge of almost understanding if she.could.just.push.past.the.cloth.get. it.out.of.her.head.

And then suddenly Mei was beside her, had her hand and was speaking. The world telescoped back, rushing through the cloth like bubbles seeking air, and Kalla popped back into the present, gasped for breath, and brushed at sweat stinging her eyes.

"Oh my god." She would have gone to her knees, if not for Mei's grasp on her arm. Stronger than she looked, a part of Kalla's mind acknowledged.

"Kalla, what is it?" Mei's concerned voice, her smooth palm brushing the sweat from Kalla's brow. "Here. Sit here."

She pushed a stack of folded cloth back into the old woman's stall, spoke to her and sent her scurrying. Kalla half-sat, half-leaned on the edge of the display, smelled the dye of the cloth, the spices, the light lotus scent of Mei.

"I'm sorry. It must be the heat. It has to be the heat and the jetlag." That left her feeling like she was going to her doom? "My head's pounding like there's something inside trying to get out."

A horrid image from the movie Aliens crossed her mind. It would be her kind of luck, but the old woman came running back with a bottle of cold water that beaded in the heat.

"Thank you." Kalla drained the whole thing, felt strength revive her body.

Perhaps that had been all it was—dehydration-induced panic. She hadn't drunk much on the drive north, and the Sanka hadn't been enough. She'd have to watch her water intake. She nodded and pulled herself upright, but still wasn't sure about her legs.

"Maybe something's telling me this is the place I should shop?" She grinned, trying to make light of the situation, and turned to the stacks of fabric in the old woman's stall. She ran her fingers over a length of the smooth cotton that was crimson so dark it was almost black.

The old woman spoke in a Burmese crackling with humor and age as she picked up the folded cloth and flicked it expertly to display the fabric's subtle pattern of peacocks caught with a darker thread.

"She says it is a fine color for you. The color of seers and Votaresses."

"Votaresses?"

Mei smiled. "In the old days, before public ceremonies, a Votaress would make offerings to the spirits. That was our way. That was before King Anawrahta of Pagan turned the people away from the spirits to Buddhism. After that, we made offerings to Buddha. Of course some women still make the nat offerings. Men say it is because women are lesser than men and thus less than the spirits who are men's equals."

Kalla didn't know how to react to that bit of news. The Votaress was interesting. The status of women, well, that wasn't her battle to fight. But Mei's knowledge of things Burmese was going to be a help, she could tell.

Kalla ran her hand down the fabric pattern. "I'd be afraid of getting it dirty."

Mei waggled her head. "Women wear them in the rice paddies and to clean their homes. It is easy to keep clean and easier to wear than those." She eyed the jeans with such distrust it made Kalla smile.

She pushed herself to her feet, swayed a moment. "Okay. Show me how this works, and if I don't look like a fool, I'll get it."

It was a simple matter. Kalla stood with her arms out as women from adjoining stalls came over to help drape her in cloth. Like a river the crimson length encircled her, was folded once in a huge pleat and then tucked into her waist so the cloth draped to her ankles, clung close to her hips, moved with her like water when she took a tentative step. Not binding. Not even close.

"Is there a place where I can pull off my jeans?"

Laughing women fended off the men who wanted to pass by the stall, and Kalla quickly stripped off her jeans, adjusted the longyi around her, and stood—to bright applause and more laughter.

"They say you look wonderful—like you are truly a Burmese sister."

Kalla half bowed as she sleeked her hands down her hips. The cloth was so light, air flowed around her sweating legs and yet still kept her properly covered. She could like this—the longyi didn't impede her movement at all—in fact she felt like she'd worn one all her life. Perhaps there was something genetic about it.

"My mother's side of the family came from Thailand. Apparently there were court dancers from Burma captured in their wars and taken back to Thailand. So maybe I am part Burmese." She grinned. Listened as Mei translated to the other women and caught their excited nods of pleasure.

"The old woman says you remind her of the king's dancers. Her grandmother was one at the Mandalay court for the last king."

"Really?" Kalla turned to the old woman, smiled and bowed her thanks, but then remembered her real purpose in coming to the market today. "Ask her how much for the longyi and if she would share any old stories she might know."

The old woman blushed, shook her head as she answered.

"She says she gives the longyi as a gift to a lost daughter of Burma, but that she has no tales to give that are fit for more than her grandchildren's ears."

Kalla was stunned. The woman could have doubled her price, given Kalla was already wearing the longyi. These had to be the most generous people she had ever met. This gift giving thing was going to be a problem, because it left her indebted and that meant she wasn't in control.

"I can't let her give me the longyi. She makes her living here."

"To not take it will insult her."

Kalla looked at the old woman's expectant face, at the faces of the others, and knew this was a test. She inhaled and sighed. She hadn't exactly brought a lot of money to Myanmar, but this she had to do.

"Alright. Please tell her I will treasure it always. And tell her I would like to buy another length, but Mei…." The Burmese woman stopped in her translation.

"Yes?"

"I can't let you purchase this longyi. I want you to make sure I pay too much for the other length, so that she gets something back for her kindness. Alright?"

That beautiful, blissful smile blossomed on Mei's face. "You are a good woman, Kalla Jervis. Pick another length of cloth and we will do it."

They did—a longyi of yellow-gold, dyed in black and crimson palms and paisley patterns. When Kalla agreed to almost the first price, a wave of laughter ran through the audience of women. They gave Kalla hugs, then wandered off as the grandmother in the stall wrapped the other cloth in brown paper and handed it to Kalla.

"Are you sure she doesn't know any tales? I need old ones. Stories of the people."

Mei translated the request but the old woman only laughed around a gap-toothed smile and caught Kalla's hand. The shopkeeper's skin was like fine parchment, but no, she did not have any stories.

"Are there others in the market who might have tales to tell?"

Mei translated but the old woman only laughed, shook her head and spoke rapidly to Mei.

"She says no one in the market knows tales as well as a woman named Daw Ma Ma Nang. She is a nun, and very old and very wise and has lived in Pagan all her life. She can be found at the Dhammayangyi Pahto—temple—most days. Shall we go?"

On a whim, Kalla leaned up and caught the old woman in a brief embrace. It brought a burst of laughter from the other cloth sellers and a bloom of color to the old woman's cheeks. She caught Mei's hand and joined the laughter.

"I know open displays of emotion aren't usual here, but I just want you to know I don't think I've felt this happy in a very long time."

She followed Mei back through the maze of corridors, holding the joy like something precious—like the Burmese greeting/blessing 'Mingăla ba'. There was nothing to be afraid of here. Nothing to make her feel so strange.

And then they were back at the jeep amid the scent of bullock manure and people heading down to the river. The military jeep was still there, but the green-clad soldiers quit their game of dice as Mei hauled out a map, considered for a moment and then started the jeep.

The soldiers climbed into their jeep and Kalla's happiness disappeared like dust on the breeze. The soldiers' actions weren't by chance.

They were there to watch her.

Chapter 8 – Equanimity

Equanimity. That was what Simon's mother had taught him. It was what he needed now. Peace. Quiet. Balance.

Composure.

In the cool dimness of the hotel room that had been rented for their equipment, Simon could at least pretend he had it and that things were normal. Almost.

The clean, metallic scent of batteries and tape recorders filled his nostrils—low tech, but more likely to be dependable in this country than their radio telephones, portable generators, and laptops. He could lose himself in this mundane work of inventorying equipment with his old friend Khun. It would keep his thoughts and the Nat from where they wanted to go.

Kalla Jervis with the midnight hair and the Votaress puppet he'd been seeking.

The Nat turned, rolled, and Simon opened another box and started to call off items as he lifted them from the box and placed them in stacks along the floor. Khun checked items against their inventory.

For Simon, fighting back Shwepyingyi Taungbyon was a lot like trying to fight back the monsoon rains or the giant naga-dragon who churned the waters of creation at the end of each age.

Just as no one could stop the Creation naga, Simon was beginning to doubt whether he could find that fragile balance and control the Nat.

Again.

He must have stopped calling out the items in the box because suddenly Khun was beside him, looking at him strangely.

"There problem? You stop calling items." The small man's emotionless face demonstrating that famous bamahsan chin that Simon had never been able to master.

"Sorry. I got lost in my thoughts," he said in Burmese. He turned back to the box and pulled out the extension cables and electrical outlet converters. "Cables and converters. I'm tired from the trip last night. The anthropologist. She is not what I expected." Both more and less.

Khun only grunted, and marked the cables off the inventory. That wasn't like the man who had been Simon's surrogate father after Simon's anthropologist father died suddenly in a car accident. Khun was the one who had taught him chinion—the wicker ball game—as a child, and who had helped steady a seventeen-year-old overcome by grief.

"Are you well, uncle-father? It has been a long time since we spent time together."

The smaller man jerked, but only cast a dark glance at Simon. "We have work to do."

The rough Burmese made no sense—as if Khun fought back emotion. Simon considered how best to respond, because he wanted to rekindle the friendship, if not the father-figure.

"How's it going?" Alex leaned against the open doorframe, looking tan and athletic. He'd hardly changed at all since they were undergraduates together. The same good looks that sent the girls swooning.

"We should be finished soon, I think. Khun, do you agree?"

Another grunt, that set Simon's teeth on edge. Merde, what was the matter with the man?

Alex stepped into the hotel room and scanned the neatly stacked equipment.

"Everything looks shipshape. Khun, would you get the jeep ready? I've waited long enough to get out to the temples. I'll give my old friend a hand until we're ready to go."

Alex flashed his familiar grin at Simon and for a moment he almost felt like all the years had melted away, but Khun left so abruptly even Alex noticed.

"Wonder what bug got up his butt this morning?"

"Probably just a little overwhelmed by all this." But there was something that pointed at something wrong between them, and that left Simon feeling a little sick to his stomach. Did Khun know what had happened to Mei?

"He has not worked an archaeological dig before. Things like mining exploration teams, oui. It is the same—requires the same skills—but Khun would be nervous. He prefers to do things correctly."

Alex had the inventory list in his hands and was reviewing the check marks Khun had made. He frowned. "He's made all these little curlicue notations. Like I can read Burmese."

"It's one way to be indispensable, non? Be the only one who can read your notes." Simon grinned. "Desk lamp." Simon set the lamp by the others on the floor. "We're in Myanmar. Burmese script is round, like small moons strung together."

Alex placed a check on the inventory list, his blonde hair swinging around his shoulders. At university he'd cut a swath through the ladies, while Simon had been more intent on his studies. That had been in the days B.N.—Before Nat—as he'd come to think of them.

"Mei and Khun. They'll both do well for this project I think. Both are very reliable—and they both understand the western need for punctuality and performance. Five boxes of batteries."

A check on Alex's list. "They both seem fine. Mei seems a little nervous. I caught her doing some sort of ritual or something in the dining room this morning."

"The nat-kadaw."

"What?"

"The nat-kadaw. An offering to the house nat. I saw it this morning. I hadn't realized Mei still practiced the old ways. Don't worry, though. She's good at her job. Three tape recorders."

"Not worried. I think she'll fit in well."

There was something about how he said it that brought Simon's gaze out of the box. Alex's tone had gone thoughtful, as if he were contemplating Mei.

"She's always been like a sister to *me*." The Nat stirred denial in Simon's head and he sent a dark dart towards it. The Nat subsided into watchfulness, and Simon realized Alex was watching him.

"So how're you liking our latest team member? You had the chance to get to know Kalla a bit on the ride in from Kyaukpadaung?"

A Dictaphone slipped from Simon's fingers and bounced on the bed before he caught it. Before he could compose himself, because the Nat pressed forward at the mere mention of her name.

"We did not talk. She was exhausted, n'est-ce pas? There was un peu de difficulté—a small difficulty—at the village. She was upset."

He saw the concern in Alex's gaze and continued. "The military had a checkpoint. Mademoiselle Jervis drove right into it looking très suspicious with her jeep lights off. It seems there were electrical difficulties with her vehicle. A bit challenging to explain to the local militaire, but she is here."

He shrugged, trying to hide his feelings as he fought back the memory of touching Kalla Jervis. The Nat churned in his head and overhead the light bulb dimmed, flickered, resumed. He steeled himself and paused.

"There is something still between you two?"

Let that be the case. Let Alex want her because that would create a distance between Kalla and Taungbyon, warrior Nat.

"We're—friends. Always will be, because I really like Kalla's family, even if her Dad has some odd ideas." Alex shrugged, but all Simon could think of was the way Kalla and Alex had touched this morning. More intimate than old friends, surely. Was that Alex or Kalla's doing?

"Kalla—she's a powerhouse—brilliant—gifted in her work, though she's sort of stepped back from her career in the last while. I heard her dad was a sick, but never had the chance to get in touch, and Kalla plays her cards close to her chest. She doesn't like people interfering." He shook his head, glanced sideways at Simon. "Why? You interested?"

It took all Simon's strength to stop the nod the Nat would have him do.

"No." It came out more a grunt.

"Better for you, I'd say. Kalla Jervis is like fire and ice in all the wrong places, and the worst damn control freak I've ever met. You saw how she questioned everything I said. For all her charms, a guy would be better off elsewhere."

Not the words of a friend. More the words of a jilted lover—still smarting.

"You describe a woman of strength and conviction, mon ami."

"I describe the most frustrating woman I've ever met. We fought— god—about everything. Sex. Careers. The price I paid for groceries. Not something I'd ever want to repeat."

But along with the vehemence there was a hint of regret that gave Simon pause. For all he spoke of bad memories, there was still something there. But it raised the question of what had happened in the dining room. Kalla's doing? Interesting that the Princess yearned after a man who was not interested in return. Peut-être, this could be amusing.

"Nope, Kalla and I are history only. I've got other things on my mind."

Something in the way he said it brought Simon back to attention. Alex was looking at him—hard.

"What is it?"

"What happened to you, man? I heard about your trouble, but I always figured you for a one-woman man. You were—in school."

His 'trouble', as Alex put it, was the last thing Simon wanted to talk about. He looked down at the pads of paper he was unloading and wished for more than blank pages to distract himself. The Nat was a cloud of whirling black particles—black thoughts that would take control if Simon took his attention away for a moment.

How does one tell an old friend that you are possessed by a Nat? One who has been pissed off for centuries since he was put to death for failing to pay homage to a tyrant's temple. The fact that the man-who-had-become-the-nat and his brother had been Muslim—and would not make offering to a Buddhist idol—had been lost on the king. They were both killed and over the centuries their spirits had become revered as protectors of Burma.

He swallowed, barred the Nat from control, though his head was a maelstrom of wild power, and flickering shadows of mayhem seemed to dance on the wood-panel walls. Mayhem much like the swath Simon had cut at the Sorbonne.

"I had to—how do you say?—'sow my wild oats' sometime." It was his turn to shrug. Let Alex see it as that. Something light to be forgotten.

Instead, Alex grabbed Simon's bicep, swung Simon around to him, even though Simon-Nat could have shrugged him off like a fly.

"There'll be no 'sowing wild oats' on this trip, you understand? I heard about your problems in Paris, Simon. How the hell could I not? Mention ethical misconduct on an academic website and they practically show your picture. You might fuck around with your own career, but you will *not* do it here, with mine. You understand?"

The expression on Alex's face was anything but friendly. In fact, it was so far from the face of Simon's old roommate that the Nat began to uncoil in his head, and his hands clenched into fists.

He fought the cloud of darkness, almost thankful for Alex's presence. He was an ethical man, a trustworthy man who would protect the weaker women. It saddened Simon that he was what needed to be protected against.

"I have cleaned up my act. I look at this as my chance to prove it."
Not now.

The Nat chuckled in his head, whirled like pieces of ocean foam in the wind, and sent a promise of violence lashing through Simon's mind.
No!

"Good. We've got two women on the team and I don't want to see you cause any problems with them. Got that? If you can do that, you'll get a decent evaluation. Understand?"

Simon fought back the Nat, felt the cording of his neck muscles, the tightening of his shoulders, and knew he could take out Alex with just one blow. *NO!* That was Taungbyon's thought, not his own. Overhead the light bulb dimmed to amber and the scent of burning electrical wiring came acrid to his nose.

"Je comprends."

"Good. Let's see you keep it that way. A little self control is good for the soul."

From outside came a short blast of car horn, but Alex and Simon still stood eye to eye as Simon fought for his control. Alex must have seen the darkness, because finally he looked away. Shook his head.

"Sorry, old friend. I don't like this kind of thing anymore than you do, but we've all got to control our demons." He patted Simon's shoulder once, then left him standing in the equipment room.

The light flickered and danced as Simon fought his battle. Demon, indeed. Darkness blinded him as the nat roared its anger. *IT* would not abide by rules. *IT* was a spirit, a warrior, a Nat, not some weakling human.

It took everything Simon had to hold the walls in his head, stop the rage from consuming him. Dark flames all around, a flash of light, and then the Nat was gone—back into the recesses of Simon's mind where it prowled and plotted against him, plotted for Kalla.

The room's light was burned out when he opened his eyes. So the Nat was back to affecting the world around him. Not a good sign.

In fact, a very bad sign, given the proximity of Kalla Jervis.

Chapter 9 – The Influence of Ancients

How do you deal with the fact that the woman who is your friend may also be your enemy? That you have brought disaster on them all?

Mei slowed the jeep as she turned onto the dirt road that led to Dhammayangyi Pahto.

"Wow! Look at that thing!" Kalla said, and Mei did.

"It's—it's like a dark mountain."

The huge step-pyramid-shaped structure crouched alone like a great beast on the dusty Pagan plain, more massive and imposing than any picture she had seen of step-pyramids in Egypt. She touched the brakes and the road dust flooded into the jeep cab, making them both cough.

The dust coated everything—the leaves of the thistle bushes and stunted tamarind trees along the bone-rattling road, the hood of the jeep, her skin. Her mouth. It tasted almost metallic—of death. She shivered and glanced at Kalla, who was leaning forward to stare at the temple.

"Alex is going to have a field day here."

"He will?" Just hearing Kalla mention Alex filled Mei with ill-ease.

"The guy's nuts over his work. When he's working, everything else in his life disappears and everyone better be focused on what *he* needs. Your needs don't matter anymore." A sigh and then a wistful smile. "I suppose we all need that passion in our lives."

A chill ran up Mei's spine, because she liked Kalla, her displays of kindness and understanding seemed almost as if she knew Burmese ways. And yet Kalla wanted Alex. A woman knew these things, could read them in how Kalla acted so proprietary towards him.

"He seems a good man." She tried to keep her voice light.

"Absolutely the best."

The jealousy that knifed through Mei made her hate herself. Who was she to deserve anyone as wonderful as Alex? She had been ruined long ago, and this was what her life was to be. She needed to make her peace with it.

Wanting more was how you created unhappiness for yourself. That was what Buddha taught.

Another glance at Kalla and a need to change the subject.

"You are feeling better?"

Kalla nodded, still intent on the temple.

"I was worried in the market. You seemed almost afraid." And almost not there. If a foreign woman could be so afraid, how could Mei ever find safety?

"I just needed water, that's all." Said distractedly. Kalla hadn't even looked away from the temple as they talked of Alex.

But perhaps things were not as bad as she feared.

When Mei parked outside the temple courtyard, they climbed out, jeep doors thunking with finality. Dust filled the air along with the squawk of magpies and the chirrup of sparrows. Black and white feathers flashed in dusty branches and then darted across the sky. The jeep engine ticked off the moments as they regarded the dark mountain of brick.

The massive temple was so different from mighty Shwedagon in Yangon. The gold-encased Shwedagon covered the peak of a hill and glowed warmly, welcoming the people circumambulating its base. The Shwedagon pagoda lifted its spire up and up and up to tiered umbrellas that glittered at the top.

The Dhammayangyi didn't glow in the sun. Instead it hunkered on the plain and seemed to inhale light. Its seven, dark-red, brick steps lifted into the air, each level with ornate lintels over empty doors and windows that seemed to suck at the sky. And ponder the two women.

Mei shivered, but Kalla seemed fine, just mesmerized by the size of the temple lifting so high against the blazing blue sky.

Then silently, disturbingly, Kalla stepped through the crumbling courtyard gate and stopped. The stiff way she moved made Mei reconsider her assessment.

"Kalla?"

No sign she heard. She seemed too intent on the place. Her face was too pale, and Mei wondered whether she should just grab the foreign woman's hand and get back to the hotel until Kalla was well.

But foreigners came to Burma and took—did—what they wanted.

The temple's huge main door yawned onto the courtyard where scrub grass and twisted trees grew amongst fallen mortar from the courtyard wall. Kalla's blank stare at the temple sent a shiver up Mei's spine.

"They say the king who built this temple demanded the bricks fit so tight together even a pin could not be pressed between them. Only the courtyard walls crumble."

Kalla nodded, but her gaze only rose to the corn-cob shaped finial at the top of the temple.

The little hairs at the back of Mei's neck stood on end.

"Kalla? Is everything alright?"

Kalla glanced at her then, and at last her gaze seemed alive, present. She smiled, but it was a puzzled smile.

"It's strange. There's something about this place. I have this weird sense I've been here before." She shook her head and her grin broadened in a way that eased Mei's concerns. "Probably just the fact I've visited other lost cities. After a while they all seem similar."

Kalla crossed her arms over her chest and cocked her hip, all foreigner now, all scientist in the considered gaze she gave the temple. Then she shivered.

"The darn breeze is cooler than I'd expected."

But Mei felt no breeze in the courtyard. There was only late morning sunlight reflected off grey soil.

Shadows shifted in the towering main door, and a skeletal old woman clad in pink nun's robes stepped out into sunlight. Her head—shaved bald—gleamed in the sun and her lips were stained red from betel.

She motioned for them to approach as she settled herself on a piece of white cloth she had spread at the edge of the doorway. Before her, on the cloth, lay a small display of incense sticks and chained marigolds for those who had forgotten to bring offerings.

"Mingăla ba."

The old woman grinned, revealing the red-stained teeth of the frequent betel user. Her eyes were the darkest Mei'd ever seen. She looked beyond the nun, into the darkness, and saw that the opening was a Buddha sanctum. Two standing Buddha figures waited. Perhaps, if she made offering, Buddha would protect them from the error she had made this morning.

"Are you, Daw Ma Ma Nang?" she asked in Burmese.

The old woman smoothed the white cloth under her marigolds. "I am her."

"We were told you know many stories that you might share."

The old woman grinned her red grin again. "Is it not a good day to make offerings and meditate on the teachings of Buddha?"

Mei glanced over her shoulder. Kalla stood in the sunshine as if transfixed by the huge door, and her total stillness left Mei nervous.

"This is Daw Ma Ma Nang, Kalla." Mei used the honorific of Daw. "Shall I make your request?"

Kalla didn't even look at her. "Please."

"Kalla?"

"Just ask her." It was as if the darkness of the entrance held Kalla in place.

Mei turned back to the old woman and purchased a stick of incense. "My friend is a scientist from America. She is seeking old tales of the end of Pagan."

The old one's lined face cracked in a thousand wrinkles as she cackled. The sound echoed too loudly in the courtyard, but it seemed to break Kalla's concentration. She knelt in front of the nun.

"Please? I would like the stories. It's to help people all over the world."

Her face was so earnest Daw Ma Ma Nang must have seen as Mei translated. She nodded, patted the cloth beside her to indicate Kalla should sit beside her in the shade of the temple, but Kalla would not. Fear seemed to flood her features and suddenly Mei was uncertain of this nun.

Kalla glanced at Mei and then at the incense she held. "I'll wait here if you want to make an offering."

"Are you certain?"

Kalla glanced at the sanctum and visibly shivered.

"I'm fine Mei. I've told you that." She tossed her head impatiently. "Now go make your offering and quit treating me like I'm an invalid. When you're finished we'll arrange a time to meet with her."

Reluctantly, Mei left them. She did not fully trust the nun, and checked over her shoulder as she entered the dim cave of the Pahto. Her concerns had to be unfounded. A nun took vows—in the ancient days, more vows than even the monks did. But there was something about Daw Ma Ma Nang and this place.

In the sanctum the two white Buddha figures—Gautama, the current Buddha, and Maitreya, the Buddha of the future —gazed impassively at her. Gold flake offerings decorated their hands and faces. The ground in front of them had been swept clean except for fresh marigolds and a single stick of incense trailing looping smoke up toward the high, shadowed ceiling.

Mei knelt and lit her incense stick, standing it in the small bowl provided for such things. Behind her, Daw Ma Ma Nang was talking excitedly to Kalla.

She focused on the Gautama Buddha, prayed he would listen to her, hear her words and help her.

But before she could begin, Kalla gave a small cry. It knocked the prayer right out of Mei's head.

She sprang up, turned, and found Daw Ma Ma Nang had hold of Kalla's hand. She sat frozen, blue eyes wide and black with fear.

Mei made the door as Kalla yanked to her feet and staggered back from the temple.

"What are you doing?" Mei demanded. "Can't you see you're frightening her."

So strange. So strange, when Kalla was the strong one. The foreign one. But Mei had failed Kalla—failed to protect.

Daw Ma Ma Nang's gaze had locked on Kalla, and the air in the courtyard had gone cold as if clouds covered the sun, but there were no clouds in the sky.

"Tell her—I am her friend," the old woman ordered, and automatically Mei slipped into translation. "Tell her I will tell her stories at my home tomorrow."

The old woman paused, chewed her lips for a moment, and the world seemed to pause as if awaiting her next words.

"Tell her I have waited for her for a very long time."

Chapter 10 - Watchers

The only thing General Ne Setkya hated more than the Burmese military government were the foreigners overrunning his country. He leaned back in his chair, aware of the clock on his office wall ticking the night away, but kept his gaze locked on the stout Chinese man standing in front of his desk. The man didn't even sweat under Ne Setkya's gaze, and that was troubling—because all foreigners sweated in the heat of Pagan, even at night.

Except the damned Chinese.

Not that Ne Setkya had any issue with Chinese people per se. China had brought aid to Myanmar when the west turned its back in economic sanctions against the Burmese junta. The Chinese were fine.

As long as they were in China.

But the 'Old Man' of Myanmar had decided—probably under pressure from those same Chinese—to allow immigration and so the Chinese flooded in until, in parts of his beloved Burma, it seemed that everything of value was owned or operated by Chinese. The Chinese would take over—breed the Burmese out of existence—just as the Kublai Khan had tried to overthrow the country. Of course, the Burmese were still here and the Chinese were not, but how were his impoverished people ever to become prosperous with the voracious foreigners taking over everything?

Ne Setkya smoothed the expression on his face, ensuring his bamahsan chin. This Chinese however, this Hue, was a tool, and Ne Setkya would use whatever tools were at hand. Even if the Chinese might be a spy. He tapped his fingers on his desk.

"So. Tell me of these people who have come to the Beautyland. What have they done since they have arrived?"

Hue shook his head, his gaze less than friendly. Superior, almost. As if he questioned whether he needed to answer at all.

Ne Setkya set his hands palm down on his desk.

"You will tell me—if you value your license to house foreigners." His glare seemed to do its job and Hue looked away. Ne Setkya might be old and feeling older every day, but he was still a general to be obeyed.

"They have all arrived now. There is an American archaeologist who leads them. He seems very determined, not the usual lazy American. There is another—French or American—I'm not sure. He is full of dark scowls and speaks Burmese, and there is the foreign woman who arrived late. She collapsed once, and still does not seem right. The other woman and her father, the Burmese...." the disdain in his voice said much about what he thought of the people he lived among. "She hovers around the foreigners like a beggar seeking alms."

Ne Setkya looked up at Hue when he stopped. "And the foreigners? How do they react?" Not that he truly cared, but the father would certainly stop anything untoward, and that might be a point of conflict to be cultivated.

Hue shuffled his feet, but continued. "The archaeologist shifts around her like a moth drawn to flame. This does not sit well with the foreign woman. She acts as if the archaeologist is hers. The father sees this dance and is not happy. He is not full Burmese, I think. He reminds me of the people you see in the hills near my old home in Yunnan. Kayin."

That name stopped Ne Setkya from pondering the other information Hue had given. That there were potential frictions amongst the party boded well—but Kayin or Karen blood?

Ne Setkya stood, paced past Hue to the window where the moonlight placed a long finger across the water as if pointing westward. One day the foreign researchers had been here, and already a sense of doom filled his gut. The river water smelled like death.

So many had died at the hands of the Kayin and Karen hill tribes, his son among them. It left him with no one to pass his responsibilities to.

"Kayin." He turned back to Hue, fighting back the too-rich stew of emotions.

Many Kayin had died at the hands of the genocidal government. Even after the death of his son, when thoughts of revenge had filled his head, he could not stand what the generals did. Time in meditation had made him sure of it. The government medical aid to the Kayin people had been advertised as an attempt to win the people's hearts. Instead, Ne Setkya knew, it was a means to genocide.

"They are a filthy people," Hue said as if he sensed some of Ne Setkya's distaste.

"They are a people beset—just as Burmese are beset—by foreigners." The inoculations given to the Kayin were infected with the HIV virus. It would wipe out the Kayin, just as surely as colonial Americans had wiped out the Indians by giving them smallpox-infected blankets. It would just be a little slower.

Hue remained silent as he realized Ne Setkya was no friend to the Chinese immigrants.

Perhaps the government would turn on their own people next. But then, they already had. Greed and loss of bamahsan chin had resulted in too many people dying—lost to typhoons and starvation. The Pagan plain had withered. In the course of his lifetime, huge sandbars now blocked the mighty river. He did not like the change and what it foretold. The end times came unless....

He looked out to the broad river seeking calm in its darkened waves, for what hope was there of reprieve?

Along the water's edge, small cook fires spoke of the river people pulled up onto shore. They drove the teak down river to the mills of Yangon. Such a simple life and simple cares. Food for the evening meal, the strength of the wind. The strength of the knots that held their large wooden rafts together. They did not know their world was dying—would die, unless changes were made.

He yearned for such simplicity, but turned back to Hue.

"What are their plans? What do they seek?"

Hue shook his head. It was shaped like an anvil, broader on the top, not round and neat like most Burmese.

"They look for something. That is all I know. English is not my language, but the archaeologist goes to the temples to explore, and the foreign woman went to the market seeking storytellers."

"Storytellers? A strange thing to seek in a dead city, don't you think?" Hue met his gaze, did not look away. Finally he shrugged.

"What do I know?" At least in that he spoke the truth. Actually, his words were more or less confirmed because Ne Setkya had had the blonde man followed as he toured the temples and had had the old cloth-seller from the market brought in for questioning. The woman was seeking stories for some reason, and had been sent to Daw Ma Ma Nang. That difficult old woman would need to be questioned. She had had strange insights in the past.

A knock came at the door and Ne Setkya frowned at the interruption, and frowned deeper when Colonel Aung Aung stepped inside and saluted. The man was newly arrived from Yangon and so suspect for his allegiances.

Ne Setkya eyed the Colonel's thin face—like a naga, a serpent, really—with those hard, reflective eyes. A man with too many personal ambitions. A man to be watched.

"What is it?"

"General, Sir." He snapped to attention. "I bring news that the foreigners are all at the hotel for the night. Our men watch from just down the road and will advise if there is any change."

"You interrupted for this?"

The way the man's eyes kept flitting to Hue, it was more likely the good Colonel wished to know the General's sources. He had felt the Colonel's gaze on him too often. The man watched and waited, like a predator. Well, Ne Setkya knew how to pluck the fangs from such predators, and Hue was not much good with his lack of English.

"Thank you for the update, Colonel. Now take this out of here." He nodded at Hue, but the Colonel did not move for a moment and Ne Setkya went cold.

Then Aung Aung grabbed Hue by the arm and dragged him from the room, the door slamming just a little too loudly behind them. Ne Setkya's chill didn't leave, and for a moment he yearned for the simplicity of the monastic life he had tasted as a boy.

But that was not to be. He looked at the door that had closed behind Aung Aung.

After years in this position, Ne Setkya could read men well, and what he had read in the moment of the Colonel's hesitation was his own fate. The Colonel had been sent, and that meant Ne Setkya's task as observer and guardian was in jeopardy.

Because someone was watching the watcher.

Chapter 11 - Votaress

Darkness, and the iridescent woman danced. Red longyi flowed, jewels glittered on bodice, pennant of dark hair in the wind of her movement, red scarf tied across brow, the silken scarf around her breasts shifted like water with her sinuous dance.

Around her rang dragon thunder and wailing darkness.

She trembled, half fell at the boom and crash as she raised the offering bowl, then went to her knees. The offerings disappeared and she rose, danced, danced in the air. Light poured from her pale skin as her expression reached ecstasy, reached enlightenment, and she whirled, stopped. Thunder crashed, darkness wild and wailing.

She stared into the night, and right into Kalla's eyes.

Shocked awake, Kalla found herself staring at the puppet on her dresser. Thunder still rumbled. Light sent fingers into her room, a single long yellow streamer from beyond the window curtain illuminated the face of the Votaress. Kalla pushed herself up, struggling to understand.

Dream?

Waking dream?

Now that was a stupid thought. As if she had had some kind of vision. As stupid a thought as her father's belief in the afterlife.

But she didn't remember closing her eyes—or opening them again. Hallucination? It sure as heck wasn't what it appeared to be—a wooden puppet dancing.

She swung her legs off the bed and a wave of dizziness struck. Her head throbbed like someone banged a huge brass gong right between her ears, leaving her tender inside. Shakily, she went to her dresser, picked up the Votaress. Had she placed the puppet there? In that position? She couldn't remember.

She had barely managed to take off her clothes before she collapsed into sleep after returning from the temple yesterday.

Well, almost sleep. There had been dreams that included Simon Renault far too prominently. The man was trouble; just the way he looked at her told her that. And the way she could actually feel his heat whenever he was near her. She shouldn't be so aware of him. She definitely shouldn't be dreaming about him.

The little puppet stared at her with its dreaming black eyes, its lips slightly bowed in an expression that would have been rapt if she were alive.

"You look like her, don't you?" Kalla smoothed the long tresses. "Mama would have looked just like you."

She was nuts talking to the puppet, but she had all her life. She hugged the little figure.

There was no way she was leaving the Votaress behind when she left Burma—no matter what that General threatened. The Votaress was family, and had been a solitary comfort to a very lonely little girl.

"And I'm having dreams she's dancing for me. Good one, Kalla."

She caught sight of the time on her alarm clock and swore. She'd overslept, and Mei was probably waiting for her and Alex would be soooo unimpressed. Not to mention how Simon would mock her.

The shower shocked her fully awake and she hauled on a t-shirt and almost pulled on her jeans, then remembered the longyi. She looped and awkwardly folded the fabric around her waist and checked herself in the mirror as she brushed her hair. Have to do.

Grabbing a notebook and the tape recorder she'd taken from stores, she rushed outside into too-bright sunlight and humid air, and almost crashed into Simon, who stood on her porch as if he'd been about to knock.

"Princess." His name for her made her clench her teeth.

"Stop it. Just stop it," she spat, the headache flaring in her head. His dark gaze and good looks made her pulse jump, but he stepped back from her. Overhead the sky was a brilliant, heated blue, hard on the eyes.

"Stop what, Princess? Vous êtes belle—you are lovely—in your golden longyi. Would you have me not acknowledge it?" His smile taunted her as he glanced past her to her room. He was dressed in neat khaki trousers and a shirt just a shade too similar to the crimson the Votaress wore. She had to yank her gaze away from his strong forearms, exposed by the rolled-up sleeves.

Beyond him, the early heat shimmered across the Pagan plain. No dark clouds. No clouds at all. So… how had she heard thunder? It left her shaky. He left her shaky.

"Stop calling me Princess. I'm not one. I'm Kalla. Just Kalla. Got it?" She checked her watch and scanned the courtyard. One jeep, still in the shade under the neem tree. No sign of Mei, and would this man just get out of her way?

"Kalla, I wish to speak to you of something."

The earnestness in his voice turned her back to him. She raised her brows in question, but he must have seen her need to be gone. His expression changed as he thought about what he was going to say.

"Never mind. If you seek Mei, she waits in the dining room. She is worried about you. She said you had difficulty with the woman you are interviewing today."

Was that a hint of real concern? Well surprise, surprise. Maybe the guy was more than some arrogant Frenchman. Or maybe he was trying to find a weakness he could use.

Or he was trying to get her into his bed.

She shook herself. She was letting her imagination run wild.

"I'm fine. She just surprised me yesterday." She couldn't meet his gaze, stepped around him because she didn't want him to see the truth. Daw Ma Ma Nang had terrified her. When the Nun had tried to embrace her, it had felt like she was trapped and couldn't breathe. The nun had tried to drag her into the temple, and there was no way on God's green earth she was going in there. The strange thing was, she had no idea why.

"Mei said you had difficulty—almost fainted in the market. That you seemed afraid."

She ignored his comment for what it was—a way to find her vulnerabilities—and started across the yard.

"Kalla?"

His use of her name half turned her back to him.

"You will be careful? We do not wish anything to happen to you."

His dark gaze was too intense to meet and she wondered whether he was speaking in the royal we, speaking of the research team, or something else—which was a stupid thing to wonder, given he was certainly talking about the research team.

"I'm always careful." But she saw him stiffen at the coolness of her response and knew she shouldn't be such a bitch. "Thanks for the concern."

The tightness of his face softened slightly and she headed for the dining room.

Mei met her with relief on her face and waited while Kalla made a quick breakfast of Sanka and something that was a reasonable facsimile of toast.

"Alex and Khun?" she asked around a mouthful.

"They are at the temples in old Bagan town. You are pale again today, Kalla. Did you not sleep well?"

"Just dreams. Too many dreams. Jet lag, I'm sure."

Mei looked at her with concern, but Kalla waved it away. And then they were on the road, Mei following the Nun's directions, but turning small glances at Kalla that twisted her gut with frustration. She was well, dammit.

Daw Ma Ma Nang lived in the village of Old Bagan, in a small, walled courtyard house along a side street toward the river. Unlike the rest of Pagan and the area around Dhammayangyi Pahto, here Pagan showed signs of life and water. People. Broad-leaved tamarind and eucalyptus trees. A neem tree spread boughs covered with lacy yellow flowers over the pink-bougainvillea-covered wall, and over it all came the sound of the Ayeyarawady River—a low hush as if something large and powerful shifted unseen through the land. Through the spreading trees, ancient pink spires and huge red pyramids stood like manmade mountains. Lovely, venerable, peaceful, but everything inside her vibrated with—fear?

Come on Kalla. You eat fear for lunch—remember. But things had felt so— off—since she'd arrived in Burma. Well, she was in her element now. Stories.

She knocked on the faded wooden gate overhung with the pink flowers. A small gate window opened and someone peered out. Then the door was unlatched and Kalla and Mei faced a tiny, bald woman draped in pink robes.

Mei spoke and the woman ushered them inside to a yard that had been swept clean of the falling neem blossoms.

"It is a traditional Burmese house," Mei offered. "They are usually steep-roofed and stilted like this. Then the people can gather in the shade underneath during the day."

Kalla peered up the stairs to the wide door into a single open room with a railed, second story platform. It would be cool in that house, lifted up into the breeze.

"It reminds me of Jim Thompson's House. It's a tourist attraction in Bangkok, with traditional Thai architecture. The concept's the same, though—open flow of air." She cocked her head, studying the building. "You know, this place might only have rolled up bamboo mats, but I like it more than all the expensive stuff in the Thompson house."

It was true. There was something soothing about the way two young nuns swept the floor and another hung newly washed pink robes on a line at the rear of the house. Kalla inhaled neem and incense and tea, and felt calm come over her.

"It's lovely."

"It is how our houses used to be. Made of Teak."

"But I thought religious people lived in monasteries."

"The men, yes. The nuns are different. They do not beg, but are able to work for their food. I think, if they begged, they would not get so much as the monks do."

Kalla nodded, knew she had known what Mei told her, but not how she had known it.

"Mei, thank you for being my guide—interpreting and teaching me about your country."

Mei's tentative smile made Kalla realize just how easily bruised Mei was—like a pale frangipani flower.

Then Daw Ma Ma Nang came around the house to the neem tree and gestured Kalla and Mei to join her.

For stories. Kalla fought the tight, unreasoning knot of fear in her belly.

Firmly, she followed to where a young nun spread a white cloth on the ground beneath the tree for Daw Ma Ma Nang and set up two low, wooden stools. Daw Ma Ma Nang folded herself cross-legged on the white cloth and spoke.

"She offers us tea."

"That would be lovely," Kalla said, but one look at the nun had brought back the strength-wasting fear.

The nun had waited for her for a long time. It must be a mistake in the translation. The woman couldn't have said anything more than that she would wait for them today. Which meant Kalla would have to take extra care because Mei's translations were suspect.

But that wasn't what she'd thought last night. Last night she'd been shaken enough that she'd thought about listening to the signs and just going home.

Signs. Right. Like she was going to go all weak and woo-woo and run away now. Her father probably would have told her to, but Dad was always watching for signs, while she purposely confronted them.

Kalla doggedly explained the interview process and the simple equipment to the nun, and how she would like to hear stories of Pagan's last days.

Daw Ma Ma Nang slipped a green wad of betel into her mouth and began to chew. The thick red juice from the leaf and the nut stained her lips and teeth. Kalla could only hope it would not affect the stories. Betel was a slight narcotic, even if it were used all over Southeast Asia.

When the tea came, they drank in uncomfortable silence.

"How long has she been a nun?"

Mei asked and translated. "All her life. When she was only six her parents sent her to learn. Her brother followed her to the monastery, but he returned to normal life. She did not. Her calling was here. She asks how long you have collected true stories."

True stories? It left Kalla impatient at her own uncertainty about how to answer.

"I've loved myths and folktales since I was a child. I read everything I could get my hands on. I used to pedal my bike to an Indian reserve so I could hear the Elders tell their stories of how the earth was made. I guess I've always wanted to understand what was important enough for people to remember and teach each other. In the old days that was important. Not like to today."

Where the heck had that come from? She'd never really thought about it before, but it was true. Fairy stories and folk tales had provided a miracle-filled hiding place for a motherless girl. But sitting in the presence of Daw Ma Ma Nang, who actually still told the stories, who looked old enough to maybe even have *lived* them, made all Kalla's adult efforts to collect, dissect, and analyze somehow cheap and tawdry. It had never been like that before.

"Tell her I want to learn."

The old nun chewed her wad of betel in a slow, mesmerizing motion. Then she smiled her crimson smile and hawked toward the garden wall. The splatter-pattern of red stain on grey stone said she had done this many times.

She began to speak in a voice as mesmerizing as the river, her liquid words almost dragging Kalla under. Mei translated as Kalla pushed the tape recorder 'on' button and took notes of points that might be of interest to Alex's research hypothesis.

"In ancient times there was a young woman who loved her husband very much. She was a beauty and had a bright butterfly that all could see. So lovely was she that when a great taw-saun—forest nat—saw her, he fell in love.

"He came to her in the night and spoke his love for her, but the beauty was faithful to her husband. She turned the taw-saun away and slept in her husband's arms.

"The next day the taw-saun came to her again, professing his love. But the beauty said she would love only her husband for as long as she lived. Then the beauty became very sick. She lay ill in her house and could not cook meals or carry water. Her children became hungry and her husband could not work his fields because he cared for her.

"In the night the taw-saun came to the beauty again. She was caught in dark fever and barely knew her husband, but the taw-saun made himself known. 'My love, he said. I offer you your life and the love of your husband and children if you will also love me'.

"The woman dearly wished to remain with her husband and family. Her children were too young to be without a mother, and, truly, the woman loved the forest as well. So she agreed to the taw-saun's proposal. She sacrificed herself to the taw-saun, and the nat took her for his wife. She became well. The beauty became a great Votaress and made many predictions for her people. Because of her great offering to the forest nat, all Burma flourished."

The old woman stopped and hawked, again, at the wall. Sunlight through the leaves dappled her bald pate, and the rush of the river was like an echo of the woman's voice. The old woman's silence left Kalla with a sense of loss.

Daw Ma Ma Nang's story carried within it the rhythm of Asian tales, and the not-so-happy-ending. So this was a true tale. Kalla looked down at her pencil and paper. Not much. Not much at all.

"Ask her: The butterfly she refers to—it refers to the woman's soul, doesn't it? The woman had a lovely soul that she gave to the nat, and Burma flourished because of her predictions. She had illness, but cured herself by giving up herself." Not much there. Nothing about endings. Nothing about great illness and devastation.

Mei questioned Daw Ma Ma Nang and the old woman nodded.

Kalla frowned, quickly classifying what she had before her. This was not a legend of the past; this was a folk tale—a teaching story of moral or religious significance, but it did not come from the ancient Sanskrit or Pali sources. That meant it might be strictly Burmese in nature. Interesting in its obliqueness, but not what she needed. Not what she liked, either, with its emphasis on 'spirits'.

She glanced at Mei, who sat as still as a statue, her hands folded in her lap with a patience Kalla couldn't fathom. It was as if the people of South Asia—the rural people of Thailand, the people of Burma—

were simply part of their world, while the people of North America might cover the earth but were never part of it.

"Tell her—tell her it is a good story, but…. Does she have a story about Pagan?"

Mei translated. "She says she has many stories, but they are not for yet. There are other stories you must hear first."

"Must hear?"

Mei shook her head, clearly sharing Kalla's frustration. "I tried to get more information, but that is all she will say. She says she has finished her story for today, but we are to return tomorrow and she will tell another. That is fine with you?"

"'Is that okay with me' is the correct phrasing." Kalla caught the Mei's flinch, but let it go. What was it about the story that the nun felt the need to tell it first? These stories always needed to be taken in context.

"Ask if this is a story she always begins with. Is it a story to set the stage with blessings?"

Mei asked and the Daw Ma Ma Nang threw back her head and laughed a deep-throated belly laugh.

"She says you have a mind like a little bee, always buzzing, buzzing and so it cannot hear. She says it is time to listen in quiet, Kalla."

The nun's soft reprimand left Kalla feeling like an upstart puppy batted down by an older dog, and she didn't like it. She was just doing her job by trying to control variables. *If* that was what the nun said, and not Mei's misinterpretation.

"Fine." She snapped her notebook closed.

"All stories are lessons, Kalla. They come from unexpected places. Perhaps Daw Ma Ma Nang has one for you."

Kalla turned a cool eye on Mei. Was she suggesting that Kalla wasn't doing her job properly? Or was this soft rebuke just a way to jab at Kalla's confidence because of their mutual interest in Alex? Well it wasn't going to work.

"Thank you, Mei. But I know my job, and I know about stories."

Mei looked uncertain, and Kalla could have kicked herself again. She wasn't here to undermine Mei's confidence. She looked down at her notes and hated to admit what she saw.

"Damn. I was so busy pushing for stories *I* wanted I forgot to consider the story's presentation." She'd stopped listening once she'd realized it wasn't specifically about Pagan. Hell, she had even stopped taking detailed notes. Thank goodness she had the tape.

The wind gusted, startling her when it rattled the branches, and Daw Ma Ma Nag threw her head back and cackled so hard Kalla thought the old woman might break into a million pieces that would fly off on the breeze.

Suddenly cicadas sang again in the trees. Magpies chortled and Kalla realized she'd been lost in a pool of silence. How long had they sat here? Kalla's butt hurt from the stool. Hours?

She pulled the tape machine to her lap, punched it open, and hauled out the cassette. She would review it later, see what she'd missed.

Then she frowned. The tape hadn't turned.

Alex would not be pleased.

Chapter 12 - The Heat

In the late afternoon sunshine, the door to the equipment room yawned suspiciously open. The sight stopped Simon as he strode across the dusty Beautyland parking lot, the compound, as he had come to think of it.

An unsecured door was not proper procedure, even though it was Alex's preference. He preferred ease of access to his equipment, just as he had preferred ease of access to his girlfriends back in his glorious university days. Back then the two of them partied and cut a swath through the ladies and then crammed like mad for their respective courses. Of course, back then, cutting a swath had had an entirely different meaning.

But the open door was an invitation to theft that Simon didn't like.

Rustling inside suggested that whoever it was wasn't being particularly careful about their actions. If they had made a mess of his and Khun's organization, there'd be hell to pay.

When his eyes adjusted he almost turned away. Then his pride took over. Damn the Nat and damn Kalla Jervis, who had drawers pulled open and equipment strewn across the room's bed.

"What the hell do you do, Princess? Redesign my storage to your taste, perhaps? Find a better way to inventory?"

She whirled to him, her eyes guilty and then stubborn. All in a flash. All in a flash that made him cross the room to her, almost grab her and shake her as the blackness in his head swirled into a mad whirlpool to suck him down. She was too close.

NOT CLOSE ENOUGH.

He wanted that soft body in his arms, that mouth under his, and the trouble was that he knew it was not just the Nat's yearning. There was something powerful in this woman, something that drew him at far too many levels.

"I was trying to find a set of batteries that work."

The annoyance in her voice was like a bucket of ice water, but the Nat still churned. Still demanded Simon take her.

She flicked her fingers at the equipment on the bed. Batteries. Every package opened, the batteries mixed together.

"Merde!"

"None of them work. Not a damn one." She placed her hands on her hips and lifted her chin at him in annoying defiance. "I suppose *you* were responsible for them."

It took all his strength not to grab her.

"Actually, I was, Princess." Good. It came out cool, controlled. "I say again, your majesty, what petit problem do you have? How may I be of service to make things better for the Princess?"

Bright spots of color formed on her cheeks that would have been lovely if not for the fury forming in her gaze. Actually, even angry she was lovely.

"You really work at that, don't you? Busting my chops? What, you have a problem with women who know what they want and take it? You prefer the helpless kind? Someone you can subdue and control? Mei's type, maybe?"

It was too close to the truth. That, and the way she stepped up to him as she spoke, set him back a pace, because he didn't dare let her closer or he *would* take her.

Her lush lower lip just demanded to be kissed, her mouth and neck devoured. The blackness whirled in him and the single light bulb overhead dimmed almost to amber. Then all the tension in her suddenly went slack. She rubbed a hand over her eyes and stepped back, turning her back on him.

Simon fought down the Nat and the light bulb flickered, then returned to almost normal.

"Listen, I'm sorry, okay? I didn't mean to be a bitch. I've just had one hell of a day." Kalla looked sideways at him, contrition in her gaze. "My tape recorder didn't work and I had been depending on it, so I hadn't taken complete notes. I spent most of the afternoon trying to fill in my notes from memory. I can't have the same thing happen tomorrow." She motioned to the mess on the bed.

"I've tried them all. Every last battery, and none of them work. I even tried them in the other tape recorders. None of them work either."

She shook her head, her long hair flowing over her shoulders, a strand catching at the corner of her mouth that he had to stop himself from smoothing away.

"That makes no sense. I bought those batteries myself. They were new."

"Maybe Burmese batteries are no good?"

"That is the truth. I brought these from Bangkok."

He swiftly tried different batteries in the recorder. In each of three recorders. None worked.

"You see?"

The hint of triumph in her voice grated.

"I was going to try my reading lamp. I know *it* works."

"Do you purposely try to annoy me, or is it just something you do naturally?"

The surprise on her face and her silence were what he was going for.

"So tell me, s'il-vous-plait, what was so important in this tale today that you made such a désastre of my storage room?"

He felt her gaze as he checked batteries.

"That was part of the problem. It wasn't a story that seemed important in any way. It was about a woman who was seduced by a nat. I'm assuming the nat was a nature spirit. She became his spirit-wife."

She had lost him at the mention of the story, at the mention of the nat seducing a woman, because it was far too familiar a story.

The grief of a great love lost was one of the few things he'd felt from the Nat when he was under the spirit's control. That and the overwhelming sense of anger that it had happened. The need to mask that grief in debauchery and drink.

A dark wind raised the ocean inside him, and he felt the Nat's vibration of need.

It is not her. It is not Min. She speaks only of a story.

A sudden gust of wind rattled the room's windows. Kalla glanced at them, thankfully oblivious to what went on in his head.

"Nats are not just nature spirits, though there are nature spirits as well. This whole country is filled with them. There are forest nats and the rice mother and nats of the hills. There are also the 37 great Nats—the spirits of those who die tragically."

Kalla's whole body went suddenly rigid.

He stayed silent, not wanting to go into the matter further and wondering why he raised that point at all. She did something to him—made him do—say—stupid things and that made him angry. And her as well, it seemed.

"I would have thought you would know these things, Princess. You study culture, do you not? Not even great kings or Buddha could rid Burma of its Nats. So both learned to accept them."

Her face closed tight as a lotus blossom, any camaraderie she'd displayed erased.

"What? You do not like the beliefs of the people? I thought scientists guarded their objectivity."

"Folk beliefs," she hissed and shook her head. "I should get the lamp." She headed for the door as if something chased her.

"Un moment, s'il-vous-plait, Kalla. Je m'excuse—I apologize. Somehow you bring out the worst in me, n'est-ce-pas? The story you were told—it is the story of the making of a votaress—like your petite yoke-thei. They also are said to have a nat—a spirit. The nat of the Yamani tree they are made from."

Uncertainty flooded her gaze and told him what he wanted. She also did not know how to react around him. There was something between them that drew and repelled at the same time—like a thirsting man drawn to too much water so the water made him ill. Still, she hesitated, her gaze watchful.

"Perhaps we may discuss your puppet? A safer subject?"

She gave a sharp nod and then escaped out the door. Simon inhaled as if he had been holding his breath since he saw her. He grabbed one of the tape recorders and changed batteries yet again, then chided himself on the futility. Then Kalla was back at his side, surprising him by returning.

"Last night I dreamed of the Votaress. She was dancing. When I woke, I realized I was half awake and looking at my puppet." She handed him the lamp, clicked it on. "You see, it works."

Simon replaced the lamp's batteries with four from the mess on the bed. The reading lamp flashed on again.

"Aah. It is not the batteries who offend, n'est-ce pas?" He flipped the tape recorder over, fished a screw driver from a tool box. "Your puppet—the yoke-thei. She is very old and very precious, but I think you know this. She was once part of a troupe that would have carried news across the land. In those days the puppeteers believed their puppets lived. They fed the puppets when they ate, washed their hair when they bathed, and kept them with great care."

"You've made a study of them, then."

"A little. My mother was a collector. It began with a gift from my father of an ancient puppet he found during his work in this country. But she became enamored of the small dolls and began to collect the antique figures, determined to complete a set and then gift them to the Museum of Culture in trust for the Burmese people when they are free." He glanced at her, hoping she would understand how important this was.

"So you learned from your mother, then."

She hadn't understood. He was going to have to be more direct.

One screw, and then the second came loose in his hands; and she stood so close to him he inhaled the apples-and-roses fragrance of her hair. The Nat swelled against the bonds Simon put in place, but he forced himself to continue.

"As I grew older she almost treated them as her children. Perhaps you do as well, non?"

Kalla smiled, her face made golden in the late afternoon light through the door. "Not quite to that level; your mother must have loved them very much. But she is precious to me. All I have of my mother."

Not what he wanted to hear. Simon glanced at her, saw the barely hidden anguish of old grief. Definitely not what he wanted to hear. He knew something of that kind of pain. The third small silver screw came loose in his palm.

"Perhaps your puppet really danced. Perhaps in Burma the puppet's spirit takes control again." He felt Kalla stiffen again.

"There's no such thing as spirits."

Her voice was so adamant he looked at her. Strain whitened her lips, but he could not help himself. He plunged on.

"Kalla, I must ask you an important question. Would you consider selling your puppet? To me?" He saw her face and rushed on. "I swore to my mother on her death bed that I would finish her collection. I have searched through museums and antique shops seeking a puppet that would match the antiquity of hers. Yours is the first I have seen. Please, Kalla, consider it. For the Burmese people." And for me.

But she was already shaking her head, pulling back, and he knew he'd erred in even broaching the subject.

"No way. Never. She's a family heirloom. Not in a million years. Besides—my father and sister would have to agree, and they never would."

He should have waited until there was more friendship between them. To distract them both he twisted back the tape recorder's plastic motor panel.

A mess of wiring was all that remained of the neat coils and small solders that connected power to the motor. His skin went cold. Unless you were a small motor specialist, he doubted it was possible to repair.

"What's going on here?"

Kalla and Simon spun back to the door and Simon realized they had stood with their heads almost touching as they looked at the tape machine.

Alex stepped into the room, looking from one to the other of them with suspicion in his eyes. Simon stepped away from Kalla, holding up the machine like a shield, because the last thing he needed was Alex thinking that something had happened between them—even if something had. He glanced at her, saw a hint of darkness and confusion in her blue eyes and looked away before the Nat uncoiled.

"It seems we have un petit problème, mon ami." He pointed out the torn wires, hoping for a distraction. "Sabotage."

§

Kalla fell back a step, feeling confused and guilty and just a tad resentful that Simon had tried to use their momentary camaraderie to buy her puppet. Here she was, wanting to follow through on her long-ago engagement to Alex, and he'd found her sidled up to Simon. It didn't make sense that she stood so close to him when he raised such ire with his request.

She was supposed to be with Alex. Had made up her mind about Alex after her father had pronounced Kalla fated to marry him. Against her better judgment, she'd decided then to get over herself and finally make her father happy.

Even if Alex Munroe wasn't necessarily her choice.

Alex eyed the exposed tape recorder innards, but she could see by the way his gaze flicked back and forth between her and Simon that he knew something was going on—even when there hadn't been.

But something had happened. Even the room's air smelled different. Ozone and incense and Simon's musky soap and water. Tension seemed to hang like a fog. At least she'd made it clear that the puppet was not for sale.

"Sabotage?" Alex scanned the mess on the bed.

"It seems our lovely ethnologist found the tape machine did not work. Now it seems none of them do. Someone has ripped their wires loose. I was about to check the other things here." He motioned to the other equipment and Alex's face paled. His precious equipment.

"You can't be sure. The tape recorders could be faulty. It could be only that."

"Peut-être." Simon glanced at Kalla and she felt the hunger of the look, knew it would be clear for anyone to see. "What do you say, Kalla?"

He called her Kalla, not Princess. Perhaps it meant a temporary truce? Or he was trying to butter up to her for the puppet.

"I…," she couldn't take Simon's side. Alex wouldn't appreciate it, even if Simon's response was the logical one. "I couldn't say."

She was ashamed even as she said it. Since when had Kalla Jervis ever allowed a man's favor to color her perspectives? She knew she'd let Simon down, but this was Alex. The man she was supposed to marry. She just had to make this work.

"Kalla, you look exhausted. Still jet lagged, I'll bet. Why don't you head back to your room and I'll check in when I'm done here."

Alex's attempt at solicitousness came out more as an order and everything inside her twisted, even though she *was* tired. She managed a nod, turned to the door. There she turned back.

"Well?" Alex's question to Simon came out harsh.

The two men were opposite sides of a coin. Alex, copper-bright with his California surfer-dude good looks and his casual approach to everything in life except his work. Simon, with his shaggy profile and smoldering gaze.

Smart, both of them, but even Alex even in bed had never evoked the nervous excitement that Simon could arouse with a simple turn of the eye in her direction. Or a touch of his hand.

Simon had already moved across the room, checked through drawers and boxes, and hauled out the satellite telephone, clicked it on.

He frowned when nothing happened.

He clicked it again. Still nothing.

His gaze caught on Kalla, seemed to hesitate, and she knew it was time to leave. She did, hustling back to her room as the sun finally disappeared and blue light filled the heavens.

Let Alex come to her. Maybe he wanted to talk about them. Maybe he would confess he had never gotten over her. They would kiss and she would seduce him right then and there and seal the deal.

A part of her felt sick at the prospect. It wasn't her modus operandi to be calculating. But this time she needed to be in control to do what Dad wanted. She could—would—do that, at least.

     Karen L. Abrahamson

In her room she pulled off the longyi, pulled on her shorts and shorty sleeping shirt, knowing the sight of her legs, of her midriff, would tempt Alex. It always had.

When the knock came at the door she was ready. Seated cross-legged on her bed, papers and books around her, just as she had been the first time Alex had come to her, had made love to her.

"Come in."

The door opened and Alex paused, clearly understanding the scene.

He hesitated, then seemed to sigh and step inside. Kalla smiled up at him and saw the way his gaze settled on her legs.

"Hope you don't mind." She motioned to herself. "I thought I'd take your suggestion. This damn jet lag is making it hard to work." She rubbed the spot between her eyes associated with the third eye.

"Headache?"

"You got it. A hum-dinger that just won't seem to go away." She smiled ruefully and cocked her head. Then patted the bed next to her. "We haven't really had a chance to catch up. What've you been doing the past three years?" But she knew. She'd checked. "You haven't changed at all, you know."

"And neither have you." He stood over her, clearly hesitant to sit beside her on the bed, and that made the whole thing a challenge. She smiled up at him sweetly.

"You've been well?"

"Never better."

An awkward pause.

"My god, we sound like strangers, not friends. Not lovers." It had never been really great between them, but they'd been friends, lovers, fiancées even, monogamous together because of their mutual interest in their work. They'd introduced each other to their respective families. Everyone had thought they'd made a great couple—until the bottom fell out and they both realized that they were about the worst-suited couple ever. He'd complained she never just cut loose in bed, and wanted to control everything else. She'd thought he never paid enough attention to her in bed—and only paid attention to his own needs in his work.

They'd ended with a crash and burn that had resounded in the Anthropology/Archaeology worlds.

"We're still friends, Kalla."

He said it too gently and she felt a chill up her back, but forced her smile brighter.

"So we're both well then." It came out lame. Then she leered sexily and patted the bed. "Two healthy animals. We could see where it leads...."

Alex shifted, clearly uncomfortable with her play. He looked toward the door as if he wished he'd left it open, and that just pissed her off.

"Listen, sorry. Grab a chair, if you prefer." She stood, went to her dresser and pulled out an industrial sized bag of M&Ms. "I haven't anything to offer you except chocolate." And myself, dammit. You could take me.

But he only allowed her to pour a few candies in his palm. Even made sure their hands didn't touch. She tried to make light of it.

"The taste of home. I always bring some when I travel. Gives me my chocolate fix. But then you knew that."

She settled back on the bed, grabbed a brush and started brushing her hair in a motion she knew had always struck him as intimate. Alex stiffened in his chair and she knew he remembered when they had been together. She had sat like this then. Had shared chocolate that she had always called the lovers food. There was something between them. Always would be. Once he'd brushed her hair for her.

Now he only looked down at the candy in his palm and cleared his throat.

"So. I thought we might discuss how today's session went. What you learned."

She couldn't meet his gaze. The brush tangled in her hair and hurt when she pulled. She used the pain to distract herself. She never was a good liar. When she looked back at him, it was with resolve.

"Not great. This Daw Ma Ma Nang has her own mind about how things should go. I asked for stories of the end of Pagan and she told me a story about a woman getting sick because a spirit wanted her as his seer. I don't see the relevance, but the nun insisted."

She shook her head, at a loss. "I tell you, the fact that the first person I talked to started on about spirits took me a little aback. Then I tried to check whether this was a story that must be told first, because it's not only what is told, but also how, but Mei just told me that each story has a time and today was that story's time. I wondered if she missed my meaning or the nun's. It's the problem of translation—like I mentioned to you yesterday about that story from Yunnan."

Alex stiffened in his chair and she wasn't sure whether it was because of how she'd doubted the Yunnan story, or because she'd critiqued Mei. Either way, she needed to tread carefully if this were to work.

"You still doubt my story?" Not Mei then. That was something.

"Not your story. Simply the version of the story you received through translation. As I said, the specific words in a sentence can change the nuance of meaning. Think of it as like the positioning of an artifact at an archaeological dig. It changes the meaning of everything else around it. Your translation loses that context."

"So if the Yunnan story isn't the problem, you're telling me you're not happy with Mei's translation. Is that it?" He stood, his movement jerky, and she knew she was losing him. Knew she had to act now, quickly, if she was to win this man.

"No." She stood, papers scattering around her. "Mei's fine. Really." She went to him, pressed her palms on his chest, and stood so close he could not mistake her meaning.

But Alex only caught her arms and set her away.

"What's going on, Kalla? You couldn't get out of my life fast enough a few years ago." The look on his face was hard and questioning. She wanted a different look.

"Funny. The way I remember it, you left me in the dust." She couldn't keep her sarcasm out of her voice.

"Let's not go there. Recriminations and blame won't get us anywhere. We have to work together. Now I repeat—what's this all about?"

She swallowed, approached him again. This was do or die time. She had to make this work. "It's about us. I made a mistake. I realized it when Dad said you were the best person he'd ever seen me with. When he said he thought we were good together - and he hoped we'd reconcile."

"Is that what he really said, Kalla?" The probing look he gave her made her look away.

"You know Dad. He's still trying to get messages from beyond the grave. His latest psychic told him we were fated to be together."

"Is that what you think?" He held her gaze until she finally had to look away in acknowledgement of what he didn't say: that their relationship was mortally flawed. She'd never known him to be so certain of himself.

"So how is your dad? You didn't say much on the phone. Only that he'd been sick." His voice was gentle as if he understood something she didn't want to acknowledge herself.

Oh god, this really wasn't going well at all. She hadn't intended to use sympathy to get Alex. But if that was all she had....

"It's cancer—or was. Pancreatic, and his own brush with death has him more certain than ever that he can reach out to Mom. He's in remission or I wouldn't have taken this job. He wanted me to go and I thought maybe it was time to undo an old mistake. Ours."

The silence in the room stretched far too long. Then Alex's hands were on her shoulders, turning her to look at him, lifting her face so he could see the traitorous tears in her eyes. She swiped at them, impatient with herself, but he caught her hands, wiped the tears away with his thumbs.

"I'm sorry to hear that, Kalla. Your dad's a good man. Very good, and I pray the cancer stays in remission. But you shouldn't have come. For the work, yes, but not for us. We were never good enough for either of us."

"But...."

"No buts. We'll always be friends, but it's over. Has been over since way back when, and you know it as well as I do. Doing this for your father, and wishing it's so, can't make it into something it never was."

The trouble was, he was right, too right, but it didn't make accepting defeat any better. There still had to be some way to make this work.

"Alex—really. It could be good between us if we worked at it."

"The topic, that chapter in our lives, is closed. I didn't come here to talk about us. There is no us. I came to talk about the work." He sighed, put the chair between them, and a part of her knew it was over. Too over, and she had failed her father again.

The headache that had been a dull thumping in her head increased to a Scottish tattoo. She rubbed her head, closed her eyes for a moment.

Alex nodded and went to the door, stepped out into the last, tangerine light of evening. She let him go, rather than appear pathetic. She couldn't stand pathetic. There was always tomorrow to deal with this.

To make things right. To fix things for her father.

Chapter 13 – Darkness and Moonlight

Darkness like fog veils and wild music. Kalla runs, frightened, fights to get free. Chill air, sweat scented. And he follows, sends her crashing through thorn brush, through rice paddy, then up into jungle. Breathless and bloody.

Because he comes.

Loping tiger stride, silent and deadly. Tall. Ebon-haired. Night-eyed when he catches her, turns her to him because he has wanted her always.

Has haunted her dreams.

Will not accept her refusal.

His lips find hers. Prove him right. Prove she wants him, and she does. She wants the forest. The fluid power that flows through her in his arms, and she looks in his eyes and….

Falls into darkness. Falls where women line the chasm. Faces and hands reaching. Touching. Smothering, and then THE woman is there, and Kalla knows it was from this she was running. Not the man. Never the man.

Votaress—dancing. Swaying body. Prophetic rapture. Offering herself as crimson cloth swaths her body, scarf streams around her bodice, and her hair is dark as space between the stars. Dark as the man's eyes. She turns and Kalla startles back, screams.

The woman looks at Kalla with Kalla's own eyes.

She bolted upright, blinking, her breath harsh in her ears.

What was that? Where was she? Who was she?

The air smelled of sour sweat. She looked around and found only darkness and moonlight. Bedclothes tangled her legs. A stream of moonlight found the Votaress puppet, casting the little face with almost living rapture. As if she could move to the wild music that still rang in Kalla's ears. And smile.

Kalla shivered at the memory of the dark man's powerful hands on her flesh. His desire left her trembling. She crossed her arms over her chest. The trouble was, she had desired him back.

"You are one sexually frustrated puppy." And she was wide awake, her body pulsing with the need to move. Lose herself in the plunging oblivion of sex—and she just knew where *that* had come from, and it wasn't Alex.

"Like you're going to let that happen."

She stood, stripped off her sleeping shorts, and wrapped a longyi around her waist; high marks for ease of application.

Her damp sleeping shirt she tucked into the waist. Maybe—maybe she could slip into Alex's room. Rekindle things in a more intimate way than talking ever did. Because she sure as heck wasn't going to follow through on anything with Simon.

Slipping her feet into her Keds, she went outside and stood in the night air. Cooler, but not cool. The breeze still parched and the sky clear of clouds. Since she'd arrived here, she'd come to have a different appreciation of clouds. In Seattle she'd never appreciated how they shielded from the baking sun. How they gave life-giving water. Both something that didn't seem to occur much on the Pagan plain. It was a parched, dying place except for the narrow strip of land along the river.

She looked at the hotel doors. The store room door was probably locked after the sabotage that none of them could understand. Should she really seduce Alex? It was a logical next step, but it would cost her pride and self respect. What if he turned her down?

She shivered at the possibility.

That would make her the lowest of the low, and she didn't know if she could stand that right now. She'd been rejected too many times in her life already and the grief counselor at the hospital had said that was why she tried to control what she could now.

She needed to think this through. Decide on the best course of action. Acting impetuously would only get her into trouble.

She stepped down from her doorway and started across the parking lot. A long walk would help. Something to tire her out and help her sleep. Maybe get rid of this sexual energy that had raised its head at the most inappropriate time.

Midnight insects buzzed in the neem tree. Batwings blotted the stars. She smelled dust and distant river water. The Ayeyarawady River truly was the vein of this country, flowing north to south, and echoing into her head like her own pulse.

"Kalla?"

The soft voice made her heart leap and spun her around. Mei stood in the doorway of her room. She came to Kalla.

"The moon is full of the old man and his rabbit, but knowing he is there does not help me sleep." Her slim finger motioned to the waxing moon, traced a silhouette on the white disc. "I thought some air would help."

"I don't know if it has anything to do with the moon, but I couldn't sleep either. I thought I'd go for a walk." Mei stepped back, head bowed as if she did not wish to intrude. "Would you come with me, Mei? It would be nice to have company. You could tell me about the old man and his rabbit. I haven't heard that story before."

Where that came from, Kalla wasn't sure, because she had wanted to be alone. But tonight her dream, her attraction to Simon, had disturbed her.

The smile that bloomed on Mei's shadowed face said Kalla had done the right thing.

"I would like that very much."

"Then come on, girlfriend. Let's blow this pop stand and put some miles on us."

Momentary confusion filled Mei's face.

"That's good old American vernacular, Mei." Kalla caught the Burmese woman's hand and led her to the single bar across the courtyard gate. She looked down the road.

Silent. Straight. No traffic. And suddenly the plan to wander the plain between the dark temples of Pagan seemed like the most wonderfully brazen thing to do because *she was not afraid, dammit.* Not even after the dream. She hiked up her longyi and scooted over.

Turning back, she found Mei watching her.

"You coming?"

"Are you sure this is a good idea?"

Kalla motioned at the flat plain with its night-blackened monuments. "You see anything that's out to hurt us?"

Mei looked back at the hotel, but then, far more gracefully than Kalla, sat on the bar and lifted her covered legs over the barrier.

"So that's how you do it." She looked down at herself. "I think I need lessons in being graceful. I'm used to wearing jeans, and I never was very good at being a girl." She caught Mei's hand again, and started south along the road toward Old Bagan. "So about that rabbit?"

"It is a children's fable about an old man who only had a rabbit and was terribly lonely. One night the moon goddess heard his prayer for an old woman to keep him company, so each day she would come down to him and help him winnow his rice, and each night she would return to tend the moon. Finally the old man found out who she was and begged to go live in the moon with her. Children are told that if they are not crybabies they might see the man in the moon even today."

Kalla had to slow her pace to match Mei's and that let her mind click into researcher mode, analyzing the little story. A romance. The close relationship between spirit/goddess and man. Perhaps a teaching tale for small children about not crying because the Burmese, like the Thai, did not believe in great shows of emotion.

The two of them walked silently, listening to the rush of the wind rattling the dry grass and brush. The air whistled through the spires of small, abandoned pagodas.

"Archaeologists say they think all these little brick spires were built in the courtyards of noble's houses, but because the city was all of teak, the monuments are all that remain."

Mei looked at Kalla with dark, luminous eyes, and Kalla could see why so many western men fell in love with Asian women. Such a woman would make any man feel strong, the protector. Which was sort of counter to everything Kalla was and believed in.

"You know so much about my country and yet you've never been here. You must be very wise."

Kalla chuckled. "Now there's a thought. I know my field—folk tales—and a bit about related fields, but I've missed out on a lot of the other stuff. Like social skills." She inhaled and went for it. "Mei, I'm sorry if I was hard on you today. I can't explain it except to give excuses that aren't very good. I thought it would be different here. I thought I was doing the right thing coming. Now I'm not so sure, and all that talk about spirits, and then having the tape recorder broken. It was too much. But I still shouldn't have acted like I did." It came out in a rush and was a relief because she'd felt bad all afternoon, but hadn't known how to broach the subject. "Please forgive me?"

Mei studied her face, her dark gaze so serious Kalla thought for a moment Mei wouldn't forgive.

"Kalla, when I learned a woman would be coming on this team, hope filled me. I wished to learn from her what it means to be a woman in the west, to understand about men—and women."

It came out in a rush that made Kalla look sideways at Mei. A flippant remark died on Kalla's lips when she saw Mei's earnestness. If this was about Alex….

"Mei, I haven't exactly been lucky in the man department."

"But you are so certain, so strong."

At that Kalla did laugh. "And that can be a problem. It seems men don't always want certain women, and they sure as heck don't want strong ones. Even those who tell you otherwise."

"You mean—they lie to you?"

The stricken look on Mei's face stopped Kalla cold. Her own problems suddenly disappeared and a horrible suspicion filled her gut.

"Mei, why is this so important?"

Even in the moonlight Kalla saw the flush of color up the younger woman's neck. She hung her head, would have hidden her face if her long hair had not been twisted back in a bun.

"Because I need to know. I want to understand. I want—I want to stop the hurt." The last came out in a pained little gasp, as if she choked on the words. Scrubbing at tears, she looked up as Kalla pulled her into a hug.

Dread filled her. Did Mei love Alex? Was that what this was about? How would she deal with that news?

She looked over the darkened plain and wished she could rid herself of the guilt and jealousy that surged in her gut.

"Love is painful, Mei. I know. I'll tell you everything I know, but it's not much. To be good at love, you have to know what you want and be clear about it. If you aren't clear, how can the other person know?"

Not that that was working particularly well for her at the moment.

"But you understand western men."

She laughed again. "Now there's a novel concept: Kalla Jervis understanding men." Just how did she think she was going to be helpful? "I only—maybe—understand the few men I've known, and then not well. We never really know anybody, do we?" She held Mei away, saw she had regained her composure. "Come on, let's walk and talk."

Mei fell into stride with Kalla and they walked in silence, then: "You are so confident. Even the way you walk says it. Burmese women walk with a much smaller pace."

"It's the longyi."

"Is it? Perhaps, but it has trapped us walking behind our men. In the west women stride out like equals."

"That doesn't mean things are any better between the sexes. I think it might make men afraid of us. It makes us competitors, not lovers." At least that was what she had come to think with Alex. "The last guy I was serious about—he was the chair of the Anthropology department. When our relationship ended, so did my hopes of tenure."

"He fired you?"

"No. Simply made it clear that my career at Western Washington University was over."

Mei was silent a moment. "But because of your strength you know men. You know when they speak the truth. They do not lie to you."

Mei's face held a desperate need to have this confirmed that evoked protectiveness in Kalla. And confirmed her suspicions.

"You met someone, didn't you? Was it Alex?" Because she'd kill him if he'd hurt this sweet woman.

Mei's fingers tightened on Kalla's hand with a strength she would not have thought possible. "Myanmar—Burma—is not so good these days. Even people with education cannot find work. To help my father I work sometimes at Shwedagon Pagoda as a guide and translator. It is not so bad. I meet people from across the world and I practice my English and my Spanish and my French, which is good for me. Sometimes it gives me hope."

"And you met a man."

Silence, and then, "There are many businessmen who come to Yangon. For negotiations and to oversee their businesses. They wish to see the golden pagoda—the Shwedagon—and seek a guide to take them."

Silence again, except for the rattle of grass like old fragile bones, so Kalla waited as a shiver ran up her back.

"His name was Richard." She said it with the sweetest lilt, one that set Kalla's heart on edge. "He worked for the English and he came many times to Shwedagon. He said it was to see me."

Mei's fingers squeezed Kalla's as Mei looked out into the shifting grasses towards a small grouping of decrepit brick spires. Once they would have shown the grandeur of a people. Now their decay was a fitting backdrop for Mei's tale.

"He said he cared for me. Said he wished me to come away to England with him, to marry him. He said he loved me. Then he asked me to come away with him on a journey to Mandalay—it was what a western woman would do to seal our love, he said. I thought—I thought I wished to be western—it would be good for my family."

The silence and the whoosh of batwings and the cold stare of the stars sent a greater chill down Kalla's back, because she knew what came next.

"You went, and he left you, didn't he?"

The darkness hid Mei's imperceptible nod. "He said he would send for me, but he never did. I don't understand. He said he loved me."

Kalla squeezed her eyes shut trying to find some way to help Mei understand when the story made Kalla so angry she could spit.

"Men—don't always tell the truth. No one does. But in relationships, western men are not like Burmese men. Burmese men—I think they still have courtship rules they must live by in your culture. Am I right?"

"To be a good Burmese, you treat women with honor; you do not tell her one thing and do another if you are an honorable man. If you fail to be honorable, you may bring the wrath of the Nat, Lady Three Times Beautiful."

"It isn't like that in the west. We don't have those rules anymore and we don't have Nats. Some men—and women—take pride in how many partners they can have outside of marriage. So each person must take responsibility for themselves. Control their own actions and do only what is right for them. That's why women are so strong, I think. Because we each must fend for ourselves."

And that was the truth as she saw it, wasn't it? It was why she took control of so many parts of her life—because there was no one else to depend upon. No fairy tale knight in shining armor. No one to help. Especially not in her father or her sister.

"Mei, perhaps it would be better if you sought a Burmese man in your life."

There, that would deal with the Alex issue as well, though she felt bad saying it. But she didn't know if Alex could be trusted with this delicate woman.

Mei was silent for so long Kalla finally looked at her. In the moonlight, silver tears streaked her face. When she realized Kalla saw, she swiped them away.

"I am sorry. I lose my bamahsan chin—my composure? —I think that is the word. It is my sad tale, but no Burmese man will want me now. None have wanted me for long and long. I think perhaps I will be alone always, and so I must learn strength from you, friend Kalla."

"That I can teach." But bitterness sat heavily on her tongue. "But it isn't all it's cracked up to be. It can be lonely, Mei. Darn lonely. It isn't often you find the person who can fill your life. All my life my dad spent all his money on charlatans—you know that word?—people who say they can reach beyond the grave. He still loved my mother so desperately he wanted to talk to her."

"He loved her very much."

"More than anything." She struggled to hold back the bitterness, because the way things were going with Alex she wasn't going to win her father's approval now, either.

Kalla placed her arm around Mei's shoulder and the younger woman collapsed against her. Somehow it was almost funny that she had to help Mei find control at the very time when Kalla's own seemed on the edge of failing. But it was only fair to help another person learn the hard lesson Kalla had learned early in life.

There was only one way you could live your life. Alone.

"So we'll be strong women together. I'll show you all I know. And maybe you can give me lessons in wearing the longyi?"

Mei looked at her, smiled.

But a hand out of the darkness ripped Kalla away. A wiry arm wrapped around her middle. Two men grabbed Mei and dragged her screaming into the darkness.

"Kalla! Help!"

She stomped down on an instep, tried to get free. Oh god she had to, but the rough hand was stronger than the holds in self-defense class.

How could she save Mei, if she could not save herself?

Chapter 14 - Apples and Roses

Simon rolled off the bed into darkness, stood and dragged his fingers through his hair.

Merde! How was he to sleep?

The damn Nat roiled in his brain like a naga coiling, uncoiling, pulsing with anger and a need he could not set away. Even his mother's meditation teachings did not seem to do it.

Damn Alex for his confrontation. As if Simon had anything to do with the damage to their equipment. And damn Kalla for arousing the Nat as she did and for denying him the puppet. But he was kidding himself, wasn't he?

He couldn't blame her—it was his task to control. In the past he'd done things without remembering them. In the bad days. In the days when the Nat had gained control. But wasn't Shwepyingyi Taungbyon taking control more and more in Kalla's presence?

Merde!

Breathe in, out. Calm himself. Center himself. The woman's blue gaze stared back at him and the Nat roared - wanted the weight of her breasts in his hands, the feel of her thighs around him and he would plunge into her, take her, *make her his. Own her.*

"Merde! Non! Vous ne pouvez pas l'avoir—you cannot have her!" He paced the room—small, too small—like a tiger's cage. He would not be trapped as a spirit wife, obedient to his Nat.

"Sortez de ma tête. Get. Out. Of. My. Head." To be a citizen of the world, an American abroad, and have this anachronism as part of him was not what he had planned for his life.

But the need, his arousal, stormed through his veins like a searing madness that he combated with cold, clinical thought.

It had been like this in Paris. Then, when the Nat had won time and time again, he had hunted the streets—at least that was what he had called it. Prowling the Place de la Sorbonne for female students. Leading them into debauchery. The nat replayed the scenes of his prowess over and over and over, until Simon had considered suicide to stop the madness. Only his will to live had stopped him.

It was his mother's meditations that had saved him. They had helped him—until now.

Until Kalla.

He had to get out and away from this claustrophobic room.

Simon hauled on jeans and, bare-chested, slammed out his door. Barefoot, he padded across the courtyard.

"Hey, man. What's up?"

Simon whirled, fist ready. He had beaten men half to death when they disturbed his pleasures in Paris.

Not his pleasures. He wanted release from this thing in his head. Had wanted it for years—and now he was here—too close to where it had all begun.

Alex faced him, his golden hair gone grey in the single light over the dining room door. He took a drag on a cigarette while he looked up at the sky and then eyed Simon like he was some strange beast.

"You know, I never saw so many stars before. Not even at some of the digs I've been on in Cambodia and Indonesia. There's something about this place. A sacredness."

Simon was tempted to just walk away, but Alex seemed to wish to mend fences. It was a struggle to control the Nat's whirling darkness. Simon pressed it down into an uneasy pool of endless anger and grief and desire. He glanced at the sky where the moon set, the stars cascaded across the heavens.

"The night air is clear tonight. Usually there is much dust on the plains of Pagan."

The light over the dining room door flickered and pulsed.

"That so?" Another drag of cigarette and another glance at Simon. "That usual attire around here?"

Simon glanced down at his bare chest. His skin gleamed darkly, showing the definition of hard muscle. It was against Burmese modesty, but when had a Spirit Wife ever been modest?

"I was hot. I needed to walk."

"Seems like there's a lot of that going on. Caught sight of the women heading out for a walk about twenty minutes ago. You're not aiming to mess with them, are you?"

There was warning in Alex's voice and the Nat rose at the challenge. Simon fought the internal battle, knowing the Nat hoped for a confrontation—*and* a meeting with the women. The light dimmed almost to nothing.

"I just need to walk."

"Well then, maybe I'll walk with you. Make sure there's no trouble."

A curt nod was all Simon could manage. His brain seethed with the Nat's frustration and anger—and with his own anger that, like an addict, no one believed he'd gone clean.

He strode across the courtyard, vaulted the pole and kept going. The pavement was warm under his feet, the air cooled his chest, but could not cool him. He was hot for a woman. But not just any woman. It was like he could scent her in the air. Apples and roses, strawberries, and a hint of ancient jasmine that sent the Nat quivering.

He could grow addicted to that scent.

"So I gather you've known Mei and her dad a long time."

Simon glanced at Alex, keeping pace. The man might be shorter than Simon's six foot three, but he was slim, rangy, and athletic as an American thoroughbred.

"They are family. Mei and I almost grew up together."

It came out in a rough growl. Predatory, and he knew Alex heard it, had his own protections in place.

"That so. She's a nice girl, that Mei."

"Elle est belle. She is a lovely woman. Like a sister, though we have grown distant over time."

"That so."

If the man said 'that so' one more time, Simon just might turn the Nat loose, let him use his fists.

"She is a woman to be treasured, not mishandled." He looked at Alex, studying him because he knew about Alex's old conquests in University. Was he the same man? Casual sex pervaded these types of academic expeditions.

"She should be treated with honor and respect—not casually."

"That the pot calling the kettle black?"

Simon fought down the nat and his guilt.

"I try to turn over a new leaf." His voice sounded brittle, even to his own ears, and he could see Alex's disbelief. "I want no trouble. I want to see Mei safe and happy."

Alex gazed down the road as if he could see through the darkness to the secrets that had led to the death of Pagan. Or maybe he was only looking for Mei.

"Well don't look at me for trouble either. I like Mei. She's smart and classy and about the most lovely, delicate thing I've seen in a long time. She makes me want to be very careful I don't scare her."

It was an unusual sentiment coming from Alex, so maybe the man had changed. Simon sought words to caution that this could not be a brief *liaison amoureuse*, because Mei would not understand such a concept. It was not the Burmese way.

A scream preempted his words. Mei's scream.

He ran.

Gravel bit his bare feet. Didn't matter. Ahead, on the road, people struggled. Someone fell. Mei—screamed again, pled for release—and he knew that plea. Had heard it before, and it froze his blood.

That meant the other figure—fighting—could only be Kalla. He remembered her at the road block, how she had initially fought the soldiers.

The Nat whirled up in his head, demanding release, demanding violence.

And a part of him *answered.*

Non! Control. Mei's screams echoed against the brick monuments that dotted this part of the plain.

Against the Nat's wishes he leapt off the road. Left Kalla, when all he wanted was to go to her. A male figure had a woman pressed against a monument.

With a roar, Simon was on him. Tore him away, slammed his fist into his face as Alex grabbed Mei.

Simon threw the attacker's body aside, whirled, sought violence. Mayhem. Blood.

Mei sagged in Alex's arms. The Nat roared in Simon's head. Consuming the logic, the reason.

In danger. Kalla in danger.

Two bounds through deep grass took him back to the road. Two men attacked her. He grabbed one man by the arm, twisted, heard bone crack. The man screamed as Simon tossed him aside.

The second man took one look and ran. Shwepyingyi Taungbyon wanted to pursue, to hurt, but the scent of the woman caught in his nose.

Her. He swung back to Kalla.

She stood, chest heaving, hands fisted, and anger seething in her huge blue eyes gone black. She nodded at him, then left to go to Mei.

The Nat growled in Simon's throat. He clenched fists made raw by impact. *She should come to him. She should melt into his arms.*

He would show her, make her.

"No. *Sortez de ma tête.*"

As if the nat would listen. It had never listened. His head turned, following Kalla's scent, and he stepped back into the brittle grass. Broken brick cut his feet, but he hardly felt it. Kalla was on her knees beside Mei. Mei huddled against the blackened brick, her arms wrapped around her knees as she rocked.

Merde, he remembered that look far too well. Fought back the Nat. Felt bile in his throat.

"How is she?" His words came out thick and almost slurred. Alex glanced up at him.

"In shock, I think."

"Mei? Mei can you hear me? It's Kalla."

Mei simply rocked harder.

Simon looked into the night; the sound of a jeep rattled over the plain, covering the moan of the wind that seemed to run like blood in his ears. "Someone comes. We should get her back to the hotel."

"Mei? Can you walk?" Simon knelt down beside her, went to gather her in his arms but she yanked away, huddled against Kalla. It left him bereft and full of shameful memories. He met Kalla's gaze and stood. Would she understand what Mei's reaction meant?

"Mei? It's me, Alex. I'm going to pick you up and get you home? Okay? Understand?"

He slid an arm behind her and she seemed to fold into him. He lifted her and settled her against his chest, his chin resting against her head, in a display that caught Simon's breath for its honest caring. Alex kissed her hair.

"Let's get you home."

Then he was striding through the grass, leaving Kalla rigid beside Simon. She couldn't seem to take her gaze off Alex.

"I couldn't get to her."

"You should not have been out here." So close to her, the Nat rose like a vortex in his head, sucking away all his controls.

He had come out here to find peace, and now this? Alone with the object of the Nat's desire. Where was there safety? Where could he go to get this thing out of his head? Get back to the hotel where others were around and could stop him.

The Nat's laughter deafened him. And suddenly he had Kalla's wrist in his hand.

"Let go of me!"

He couldn't let the Nat control what happened next. Fear had him dragging her through the grass. He heard her longyi catch in it. Then they were on the pavement and he was almost running, knew she had hiked her longyi up to keep pace even as she twisted in his hold. Knew he wanted to see those ankles, those calves, to run his hands along their toned length.

The bite of teeth on his hand shocked him into releasing her.

The Nat reeled at her attack and Simon managed to press it back, back into the seething darkness of his brain. Taungbyon could not believe a woman dared assault him.

So Simon, alone, faced Kalla Jervis's fury.

"How dare you! No one touches me like that. I'm not some cavewomen to be dragged off by my hair."

She stood, said hair wild about her face, her breasts heaving very nicely, merci beaucoup, against the thin cotton of her pink, shorty t-shirt. Her body positively vibrated anger, and the glare, the way her lips were parted, made Simon—not the Nat—want to take her in his arms.

If he wanted to live dangerously.

Frankly, living with the Nat was danger enough.

"And you, Princess? How dare you place yourself in such danger?"

"*I* wasn't in danger. *I* know self defense. *I* was doing just fine, thank you." Her glare said she was close to striking him and he wondered how the Nat would react—hell, how he would react—because right now he was feeling damn unappreciated and aroused.

He fought his emotions under control as tight as the bonds he had placed on the Nat. Just facing her, the spirit rattled the bars of its prison, threatened to break free.

"So perhaps I should not worry about you, Princess Kalla." He let the sarcasm drip, saw anger tighten her face. "But Mei is not so capable, n'est-ce pas? You said yourself you could not help her."

That stopped her. She looked away.

"It's still no reason to manhandle me. Alex had Mei safe. We should be with him to help."

"Oui. But instead we fight because the Princess got her feelings hurt. Because someone else assumed control." He thought of Alex's words. "Is that what it is with you, Princess? You must run the show? Is that why Alex rolls his eyes at you? Why he cares for Mei, not you?"

Her flinch said he'd hit her tender spot directly. So his reading of it had been correct. She'd hoped to rekindle things with Alex, but Mei's sweetness had put an end to that.

Good. She deserved to be brought down from her high horse. *Good, because it opened the way for him.* He forced the Nat's eagerness back.

"I've no time for this shit."

She wheeled, started down the road, then hiked up her longyi and began running so Simon had to sprint to catch up to her. His gaze was drawn by the flash of her slim calves. The scent of apples and roses almost dissolved his control. How did she do that—make him feel weak with need of her?

When they reached the Beautyland, the place was lit up. Mei's room stood wide open. Loud voices came from inside. Mr. Hue wrung his hands at the doorway.

Simon and Kalla pushed past the hotel owner and found Mei on the bed, Alex holding her hand while fending off Khun, who tried to push Alex away.

"Leave. Leave now. I her father. I care for her."

At least Mei seemed aware now. She sat up, still clinging to Alex's hand.

"I am fine. Stop worrying over me." Her gaze locked on Kalla. "If I had been as strong as Kalla, I would not have been in such a situation." She turned back to Alex and her smile was soft, one Simon remembered and had not seen for far too long.

"Thank you, Alex." Her gaze dropped in propriety, but she could not hide the flush that flooded her face, nor the way she shivered. She was attracted to the Californian.

"They didn't hurt you?" Simon asked, but Khun blocked his attempt to go to her.

"You leave."

"She's my little sister. My cousin."

And it was true. Mei was dear to him, had been since they were children. Close enough he'd smuggled her books and magazines when the Myanmar government had shut down the Universities and the borders. He'd corresponded so that she could practice her translation.

Khun shoved him back, then leaned in, his breath scented with pickled tea and garlic.

"You think I don't know what you did?" he said in Burmese. "Mei cried for days at your betrayal. But still she begged to come on this job so that she could practice her translation. I did not want her to come with you here, but I love my Mei. I want her happy. And so we come and your kind take her into danger." His unfriendly gaze flickered to Kalla, and he switched to broken English. "She lead my daughter to where men like you hurt her. She no friend. You leave. Take her."

Simon froze. He could not deny the truth of Khun's words, just as he could not deny the way Mei looked at him with fear. His concern for her now could not undo his past actions.

Grief made it hard to breathe. These were his last family, but they did not want him anymore. It left him finally, irrevocably alone.

Except for the Nat that had caused the rift.

He nodded, went to grab Kalla's hand, but stopped for fear of the Nat and Kalla's ire.

"No. Kalla, stays. She is my friend."

Khun turned back to his daughter and started to argue—until Mei broke into tears. She buried her face against Alex's shoulder as the archaeologist stroked her hair, and Khun relented. Kalla went to the bed, while from outside came the sound of jeep engines and voices.

Simon was not wanted in the room. He was the enemy, when he had never meant to be. Outside Mr. Hue's voice rose in excited Mandarin. The tone clearly spelled trouble.

Simon stepped out onto the porch to see what next disaster required his intervention. Across the yard, Mr. Hue raised the pole from the parking lot entrance, and two military jeeps barged in. Their headlights swept the darkness and came to rest directly on Simon. He shielded his eyes, heard the slam of doors and one voice in Burmese.

"By order of the Myanmar government I confiscate the unauthorized equipment of this place."

The Nat swept darkness across Simon's gaze. A million stars collided in his head. But even the heavy scent of neem could not replace the perfume of apples and roses.

Chapter 15 – A Precious Thing

The loud voices turned Mei and the others toward the door and sent another shudder through her. It made her wish she could be confident like Kalla.

Alex must have felt her tremor, because his arms tightened, comforting, warm, while the sound of barked orders and yelling brought back memories of soldiers in the night—the way they took people away after the riots of the late 1990s. Soldiers had burst into her father's Yangon home because the family was well known to have links to the West. Her father had even been detained for a short while.

"What's going on?" Alex's voice was sharp.

"Soldiers." And Mei knew this was more of the disaster she'd caused by her selfishness.

Khun went to the door. Simon's raised voice came, clearly, angry. Always a strange rage dwelt too close to his surface. "We must stop Simon. If he goes too far, the soldiers will not accept it. He will end up injured, or worse."

Her father stepped out into the dark muttering something about young fools, and Kalla rushed to the door just in time to be pushed back by two green-clad soldiers. They shoved into the room and barked an order in Burmese.

"They say we are to relinquish all foreign equipment by order of the Tatmadaw—the armed forces. We are to leave now."

Alex shook his head, held Mei to him. "You're too shaken already. You need rest—not this."

One of the soldiers jerked his gun at the door, ordered them to leave. Kalla still stood where they had shoved her into a corner.

"We must go. Kalla, go. To stay will cause trouble."

Mei went to get up as Kalla ducked around the armed men to the door. Alex shook his head.

"No. They're not forcing you out of your room. There's nothing for them here. You have no equipment." He set her from him, on the bed and stood.

"She's not leaving. She's sick, you understand?"

"Alex, no. I'm fine. I will be fine." But he ignored her, focused on the soldiers. His larger size kept the men at bay, but that would only work for so long. "You'll only make things worse. They'll hurt you if you don't do as ordered. I know."

The warning must have finally sunk in, because he glanced in her direction and that gave the soldiers their chance.

A rifle butt slammed into Alex's gut. He doubled over. Tried to fight as the soldiers propelled him backwards into the wall. Alex was stunned by the impact and then caution flooded his face. And pain. He must have seen the cold determination in the soldier's eyes because he suddenly turned to Mei.

"Come on. We better listen." He helped her up, draped his arm protectively around her, and eased them around the army men. As they stepped outside, there came a crash behind them.

Overturning the bed, probably. She felt Alex stiffen, caught his hand, and felt his strong fingers close over hers and squeeze.

"They shouldn't be allowed to do this." His words came out as a low growl. "In my country there'd be hell to pay."

"But this is not your country." How could she make him understand? "This is Myanmar. All one can do is live quietly and obey. To do otherwise can mean death or disappearance. There are still dissidents held since I was a child."

"Aung San Suu Kyi. I know."

She shook her head. "More. Many more."

Two military jeeps stood in the centre of the parking lot, their headlights illuminating the front of the hotel. Mr. Hue stood by the dining room, wringing his hands. The others had been herded together and were held under guard as a thin, precisely-dressed officer barked orders.

Mei had seen his kind before. They usually worked in the Tatmadaw offices and were being groomed for upper positions. As a result they strutted like roosters who thought they owned all of Burma. This one strutted too, even though he was in the dusty outpost of Pagan.

The hotel doors were all open. Soldiers carried armloads of equipment from the supply room, electronics from Alex's room.

"My notebooks!" Kalla cried and lunged forward, but Simon caught her arm.

"Leave it be. Arguing with them will only make it worse," said Simon.

"Says the pot calling the kettle black." Kalla stood toe to toe with him. "If you hadn't tried to bully them into leaving when they first got here...."

Darkness seemed to flow across Simon's face, and Mei cowered back against Alex. She knew that face. Years later it still haunted her and hunted her in her dreams.

"Kalla, it is done. Simon did the best he could."

The grateful look Simon turned in Mei's direction almost made her regret her fear of him. But Simon was darkness incarnate—now. He was not the fun-loving youth she had so loved as a teenager. She had always thought she would marry him—but not this beast that walked as a man.

But Kalla seemed to listen. She stepped back beside Alex. "So what do we do now, fearless leader? You wanted to be in control."

Alex scanned the parking lot, and if anything, his embrace seemed to tighten. "There's not a lot we can do. Watch what they take. Make sure we all live through it. Complain to the government afterward."

Kalla rolled her eyes. "So no one's going to do anything to stop this?"

She swiveled, hands on hips, to face the soldiers. "We'll see about that."

"Kalla, no!" But Mei's shout didn't stop Kalla from marching toward the military officer. She got two strides. Three.

Perhaps she was going to prove that sometimes you could take control of a situation.

Then the officer turned, saw the woman approaching in her longyi and he shouted at his men before Kalla spoke.

To arrest them all. To take them away.

To be disappeared.

§

When the rough hands seized her and the rifle barrel jabbed her side, Kalla knew she'd erred.

She raised her hands.

God, what had she been thinking? She'd been a damn fool to try this. Again. But it was a matter of pride wasn't it? A chance to show Alex just what he was losing?

The trouble was, as she quick-marched it back to the others under guard, all she saw on his face was disgust and—well—pity. That was the worst thing of all. That and Simon's dark, predatory regard.

She steeled herself, expecting his 'Princess' comments and Alex's recriminations.

"Not too wise a move, Kalla. Look what you've done."

Armed soldiers herded them towards one of the vehicles and Simon slid in beside her.

"You are well? The weapon did not injure?"

"I'm fine," she snapped, waiting for the other shoe to drop.

"It was well tried, but foolish. These soldiers do not know how to listen."

That surprised her. She looked up and caught a glimpse of concern in his gaze, quickly masked by anger as a soldier stabbed his rifle between them, shoved Simon and Khun away from the vehicle. She stopped dead in her tracks.

"Simon? Where are they taking you?" Kalla asked.

Mei called to her father, her eyes full of tears and suddenly the seriousness of their situation hit home. This wasn't just some annoyance Kalla could take over and control. This was the military power of Burma come to take them away. And she had caused this.

"Where are they taking Khun?"

Simon spoke to his guard, but the man only jabbed his weapon at Simon, forced him and Khun to keep walking.

"Do not worry, Kalla. Khun and I—we know how to take care of ourselves."

And then they were driven under guard out beyond the courtyard gate, the night closing around them.

Kalla stood frozen, hating her uncertainty. Anything she might do would just cause more trouble. Finally she obeyed the weapon thrust in her direction and followed Alex and Mei to one of the military jeeps. At gunpoint they climbed inside, and all she could think of was how lonely the Pagan plains were. How, if you died out there, no one would know.

"Where are you taking us?" she demanded, but the soldiers slammed the door shut on the three of them, Mei squeezed between Alex and herself.

"Good work, Kalla. Really did a lot to improve things."

She looked out the window at the hotel. A huge pile of their belongings stood in the centre of the courtyard. Soldiers began loading them into the other jeep while others kept bringing things from their rooms.

"I was just *trying* to help."

"Just like you always 'help'. Take control because no one can do anything as well as you."

His sarcasm hit home and she knew he was right, but when no one else is ever around to run things, you have to step in. Take control because no one else will. She'd learned that growing up, and she would not feel guilty about it.

"It's who I am, Alex. I'm never going to be the woman who sits back and waits for someone else to make her decision for her."

And that was why it was never going to work between them. She had to accept that fact and that Mei was probably the best match for Alex. The young Burmese woman made him happy. She'd seen the way he cared for her—not that Mei was likely to allow Alex to make *all* the decisions.

He'd never even looked at Kalla in the fight by the monuments. It had been Simon who had come to her rescue—not that she needed his help.

A cold wind seemed to blow through her as three soldiers climbed into the jeep. The driver started the engine and drove them out into the night. Dry fields flashed in the headlights, she caught the smell of the river, and then they reached a concrete building on the road that ran between Nyaung-U and the old town of Bagan.

Alex was silent as they were ordered out of the jeep. He held Mei close, leaving Kalla feeling loose in the dry wind and dust. From the south came the ominous flash and rumble of heat lightning. She looked up at the building. Grey. A single bare light bulb on the exterior. The kind of place you could go into and never come out of.

"We'll stay together. Stay safe," she said to reassure herself as much as anything.

But the soldiers had other ideas. They grabbed Alex, tried to push him away, but he wouldn't relinquish his hold on Mei's hand. Not even when they cracked a rifle butt against his head.

He staggered, but shook it off.

"I'm not leaving you. Tell them, Mei. Tell them I'm not leaving you."

Mei shook her head. "There is nothing that can be done."

She eased her fingers from his and the desperation in his face almost broke Kalla's heart. He'd never turned such fear and need on her. Never such love. Had she ever known it?

Sighing, she caught Mei's hand and held fast. "I'll protect her, Alex. Depend on it. I'll keep her safe—for you."

And then he was gone, half-dragged by the soldiers. And there was only the concrete bunker and what waited inside.

Chapter 16 – A Dawning Darkness

"Thank you for saying you would protect me." Mei's disembodied voice cut through the darkness and for a moment, just a moment, Kalla managed to push away her mounting panic.

Darkness so thick it seemed to press in like the too-close walls of the room where she and Mei waited. Not much larger than a closet, their bodies pressed together, hot and smelling of coppery fear as they crouched on the floor. No sign of the door. No sign of light.

Kalla's breath came in little ragged gasps that betrayed her control. It was like—*like being caught in the dreams where something pursued, only this time she'd been caught. Only this time the weight of the concrete building was around her, waiting to collapse, to crush her. Wasn't Pagan frequented by huge earthquakes? Hadn't there been massive damage in the past?*

A little moan escaped her lips and Mei's hand tightened on hers.

"Kalla? Is something wrong?"

"No!" It burst out, more a denial to herself than to Mei, but she felt Mei's body stiffen. Kalla managed to find the words. "Sorry. For some reason this is hard."

It took everything she had to keep the shudders at bay. To not appear foolish and weak. And the worst part was that there was a part of her that wanted to embrace the darkness and the crushing weight.

"This kind of thing would not happen in your America."

Kalla managed to focus on the comment, push away the panicked need to just give into the fear, pound her fists raw on the walls and scream.

"No. No, it wouldn't happen like this in America. Or at least I like to think so. But things aren't the way they used to be since 9/11. The government has more power to hold people now."

"Do you miss it—your home? Your family? They must worry about you."

"Not so much." The old bitterness rose and Kalla closed her eyes from the outer darkness to peer into the inner. "There's only my Dad and my sister. They have their own—lives. They don't think about me much." She didn't need the painful memories of them. Dad so caught in his own need. Sharon only able to look at Kalla with blame in her eyes—when she was clean enough to have any look at all. The fact that Sharon had come home claiming to be drug free and planned to stay with Dad while Kalla was away had done nothing to erase all Kalla's doubts about her sister.

"Would you like me to tell you a story?"

Kalla squeezed Mei's hand. "You think you aren't brave, but you are, Mei. Very brave and kind. Please tell a story. It will help to keep our minds off the darkness."

"Then I will tell you about the Galon-bird and how he became a salt-maker. The Galon is a creature of the old days—from when the earth was young. He has a bird's head with fierce beak and teeth, a human body and wings. The Galon is mortal enemies with the Naga—the dragons that live in the world, that will one day churn the waters into a new creation."

Kalla held onto the words, focused on the story and how it was told. Be controlled. Be a scientist, not some scared, claustrophobic weakling. Two mythical creatures. Perhaps a teaching tale—like the little story of the old man in the moon.

"This Galon-bird was one day flying through the air when he saw a naga-dragon strolling through the forest. The Galon swooped down to catch the naga, but the naga saw him and, to escape, turned himself into a human and joined a King's party that was hunting nearby.

"The Galon bird was puzzled by the disappearance, but soon guessed what had happened and also turned himself into human form to look for the naga."

Transformation. This tale is about transformation. Things that are not as they seem. It seemed like the theme for Kalla's entire time in Pagan. Mei was stronger than she looked. Alex did not love Kalla—and frankly, that news was almost a relief.

"The naga knew he had to escape, so, when the King's party met a group of merchants traveling to the sea, he transformed into a merchant and went with that party on their journey. The Galon-bird checked all the people in the King's party but could not find the naga, and then realized what must have happened; so the Galon caught up with the merchants and joined them, searching for the naga.

"The golden naga was now becoming desperate, for this was a most stubborn Galon-bird. At the shore of the sea, he made a mad dash to the water and dove into the waves to return to his home before the Galon-bird could catch him. The Galon-bird wept in disappointment, for he wished to eat that particular naga.

"The Galon-bird decided he would wait for the naga to come out of the water and capture him then. The Galon-bird turned himself into a human and joined a village of salt-makers who lived on the sea-shore. For years he watched and waited, ready to take action to catch the naga. He died there, an old, sad salt-maker, for he never saw the naga again. Perhaps his spirit still waits."

When Mei quit speaking, Kalla blinked. A part of her felt such intense sadness at the tale she had to fight back tears.

"To die sad and alone after spending your life in a futile venture. I thought you'd tell a happy tale, Mei."

"It is an old tale intended to point out the foolishness of the Galon-bird. To hold onto that naga-dream for so long."

For a moment Kalla wondered if Mei was trying to tell her she was a fool to want Alex. Well she had been, hadn't she. A lot like her father and his dream of reaching her mother.

"Well thankfully neither of us are Galon-birds. We live our lives. We move on."

"We do." But there was sadness in Mei's agreement. A hint of regret that echoed Kalla's. "But the past haunts us both, I think."

A noise interrupted Kalla's reply. A thin strip of light came from under the door and Kalla reached for it, bathed her fingers in it, then stood revived. She was no longer floating in darkness. The cell coalesced around her.

Yes, Mei had been stronger than Kalla, had shown her just how weak Kalla was, and she didn't like that fact. She would redeem herself now.

"Stay behind me Mei. It's my turn to be strong now."

§

The pale features that faced General Ne Setkya worked hard to hold defiance. It was the American way, he supposed. Bravado. Effort even when the situation was insurmountable. In a way it was much like his role in life.

"Miss Jervis. We meet again. I apologize for this unfortunate mistake."

Confusion in her eyes, and he knew he had disarmed her. She had expected a fight and suddenly she did not know how to approach him, was uncertain whether he was enemy or friend. That was as it should be. He allowed his lips to curve slightly in a smile.

"My Colonel is an eager man. He leaps in sometimes—without considering the harm to others. You are both well? You have not been mishandled?"

He ushered them smoothly out of room, but the Jervis woman suddenly regained her voice.

"How dare you lock us up like this? Where're the others? Where're Simon, Alex and Khun? We did nothing wrong. Your colonel pulled us from our beds and confiscated our belongings with no reason, and now you expect us to be happy?"

He considered her belligerence. If she was a citizen, if she was anything but what she was, he would be tempted to wipe away her snarl. She needed to learn respect and responsibility. But his bamahsan chin demanded otherwise.

"Come with me, Miss Jervis. Your friend will be taken to another room."

"No! We stay together."

"I am afraid that is not possible. I must gather your evidence individually or it means nothing."

"Evidence?"

"I am told you were attacked this evening. I would like your statement, and given I am the only English speaker...."

A slight flush on her cheeks said he had surprised her again. Unbalanced, she would cooperate, which was what he had intended. Perhaps now he could obtain straight answers about these researchers' intentions. Perhaps now he could put his disquiet to rest.

"But... I promised I would protect Mei."

"And I give my word she will be well. As will the others." As well as anyone in his country. But he needed answers and in that, Colonel Aung had done well to separate the prisoners. If the Burmese woman held the truth, she would tell.

He led them through the halls of the concrete bunker, knowing she would notice the rank odor of Chinese cigarettes and sweat and—perhaps—fear. It would maintain her uncertainty, though he had always attempted to keep fear to a minimum.

Finally, he handed the Burmese woman off to one of his soldiers, admonished him not to harm her, and hauled the American into his office and to a chair he had had brought into the office for this purpose.

She was worried—he could see it in her eyes. Let her stew in it.

He went to his window, stared out at the night sky and the river carrying stars toward the sea. Tonight, though, the view did little to calm him, but let her think so. Let her consider him a slow-thinking Burman.

"It is the first time I have had a foreigner in my office. You are American, I believe."

"Of course I'm American. You saw my passport at the roadblock."

"Aah. Of course. I forget myself. As Mr. Renault is American and Mr. Munroe." He smiled in her direction, not liking to expose his teeth so much, but it was the American way, was it not? All those photos of fulsome-toothed politicians.

"And your reason for traveling in Myanmar?"

The woman rolled her eyes, went to stand, but the look on his face must have stopped her. She settled back into her chair.

"As you know, we're here for research. Strictly research. I'm a folklorist. An Anthropologist. I collect old stories and look for the underlying truth that led to the story being told."

Ne Setkya looked away from her, back out to the water, again seeking solace in the quiet movement of the waves and wind and the rippling stars.

Not to be. There was too much death in Myanmar, too much old death in Pagan—and more that would come if he could not protect things.

"And what stories do you seek in Pagan?" He held his breath, dreading the answer.

"It's no secret. We're researching the end of Pagan—what happened that ended this great civilization. That's all. There are theories about the Mongols. Theories about disease. I'm looking for stories that might tell of the ending. It's all in our permits—if you'd look."

He heard the sarcasm in her voice—but none of the tension of maintaining an untruth.

"Documents may lie, Ms. Jervis." Of course it was just as likely people did.

"Well I don't."

He turned to her, saw the firm set of her jaw. Truly this was a woman of will. He could admire the way she hid the fear he smelled on her. Almost Burmese of her.

"Then perhaps you can enlighten me about why you were out amongst the monuments in the middle of the night? What stories of the end were you hoping to uncover in the dark?"

A slow dawn of comprehension crossed her face. It showed intelligence and a firming of resolve. If not for the fact it was so obvious, he could have admired her. But in Myanmar one did not survive by allowing others to read what you truly thought.

"Is that what this is all about? Because we went for a walk after dark? I thought you wanted statements because Mei was attacked?"

There was interest there, keen observation in her gaze that momentarily left him uncertain. Could she read his concerns? His hopelessness?

There was something unsettling about this woman—more unsettling because he could not place his finger on it. She seemed almost as if she could understand his hopelessness, had perhaps experienced something similar.

"Tell me about this walk. What was its purpose?"

"Its purpose?" She looked at him, the considering gaze going quiet, watchful. "It had no purpose. I couldn't sleep. Mei was awake, too. Something about the night—or this place, I guess. I needed to clear my head, so we walked."

"Among the monuments."

"Yes. Down the road among the monuments. Where can you go in Pagan that isn't among the monuments? The darn things are everywhere. Great hulking things."

It was good that she grew impatient. Things could be revealed in a word poorly considered.

"You do not like our great treasure?"

"No I don't." She hesitated, perhaps as surprised as he at her vehemence. "They are huge, dark, and unfriendly spaces. I find it hard to believe people would want to go in such places." She shivered. "And they still make offerings."

Interesting. Most tourists expressed awe at the size and number of the temples, fascination with the frescoes, and frustration they could no longer climb to the top of the huge pahto.

"You do not like the dark and yet you choose to go walking in it. An odd choice, Miss Jervis. Perhaps a choice motivated by other desires. Perhaps you and your friends seek something other than stories?"

A knock at the door interrupted her answer, but already Ne Setkya could see the realization of her error as he barked an impatient order to enter. A soldier poked his head in, said that Colonel Aung Aung wished to speak with him, but did not wish to disturb the interrogation.

It took everything he had to maintain his bamahsan chin. The damnable Colonel acted as if he ran the Pagan military station, dared to call Ne Setkya to report to him, and yet he did it in a manner that Ne Setkya could not ignore.

He swung back to the woman and wondered at her dislike of the dark. In Pagan, darkness brought relief from the heat and from the view of the death that was all that remained of Pagan. Darkness brought ghosts and remembrances of the glorious past.

Her fear was something to consider.

"You will remain here." Then he left the room, with orders for the soldier to guard the door, and went to find Aung Aung.

Chapter 17 - A Typhoon Wind

Let this day be cancelled. To Simon the night had been far too short, too much of it walking to the military building and then being held in a too-small cell until, suddenly, they had all been released. It made no sense—no sense at all.

They had been set outside the station to find their own way back to the Beautyland, Kalla bristling with anger, Khun sullenly silent and Alex and Khun concerned for Mei, who was nearing exhaustion.

It had made for a difficult walk back through the darkness. When they'd reached the hotel a predawn rain that was not enough to end the drought, but enough to destroy precious equipment, had made it a mad rush to get their belongings moved back into the rooms from the heap where the soldiers had unloaded them.

The only thing positive was that Mr. Hue had stood guard over their things so that nothing was stolen—as far as Simon knew.

But in the jumble of belongings in the storeroom, how could anyone tell? The heaps of equipment set the Nat swirling in the back of Simon's brain, and that made it hard to concentrate and harder to sleep. It was like the damned creature knew—just knew—what was to come today.

As a result, after he'd sent the others to bed, he had fussed with the mess for the remains of the night. That and paced to control the fury in his head. Someone had attacked Mei and Kalla.

He inhaled the room scent—dry cardboard, metal and dust and the fresh scent of rain from the open door. Unusual to get rain. The Pagan plain was almost desert, and it was only going to get worse because the monsoons were shifting, changing as the world's climate changed. The light shifted from the pale pink of dawn to the golden of early morning.

An entire day with Kalla Jervis to look forward to.

That had been Alex's last words to them. There would be no research teams of only women. Simon would translate for Kalla, Mei for Alex. It would mitigate the risk. It also played nicely into the hands of the budding romance he saw between Alex and Mei. It would keep Khun preoccupied as well.

It had sparked Kalla's ire, and caused a small explosion that had ended when Kalla had stomped into her room. And it left the damned Nat strutting like a ram in rutting season and a metallic taste in Simon's mouth. He would need to work with great care today.

The sound of voices brought him to the door before he could stop himself. *Merde.* The Nat had too much control. But it was not Kalla in the courtyard.

Alex and Mei stood expectantly in front of their respective rooms, peering out over the plain.

The rain had softened the golden light. A pale mist rose, making the hard, red brick of the monuments seem to melt and run with pink. The trees glowed, their dust washed away so that the world looked young again. As young as the couple that stepped down off the doorstep and towards the neem tree, their bodies parentheses for whatever was growing between them.

The Nat shifted in agreement and a stab of grief and remembrance went through Simon—both the Nat's and his own—as Alex plucked a blossom from a low-hanging branch and tucked it behind Mei's ear. Her soft laughter caught at Simon's chest. He wanted her to have happiness and knew he had caused her only grief. He should—he would—apologize.

But not now. Now she deserved time for whatever developed between Alex and her. The look on Alex's face said this infatuation was more than casual, more than a *liaison sexuelle.*

They stood so close together, the tension of not-touching almost perceptible. Almost more than Simon could bear.

The Nat flexed like a cat in a box, testing his bonds.

No. Focus on the doves cooing in the branches, the fall of purple bougainvillea along the fence. Think about what you will need for today's work.

A quiet spot. Time alone. Kalla.

He yanked back from the door, saw Alex jerk at his movement. He knew Simon had been watching.

"Maudit. Je ne suis pas un voyeur." He crossed to the dresser where he'd stacked pads of paper, pens. Glanced longingly at the tape recorders.

Khun had tried to find a local mechanic who could fix them—in a country where everything seemed to crumble away as soon as you put your hands on it, the Burmese were good at making things work.

But still things crumbled like paper bags in the rain.

Like your will turns to dust around Kalla.

Like the years return each of us to dust. There is only spirit. Only now.

Simon stopped. His thought, or the Nat's? Usually Shwepyingyi Taungbyon did not convey his thoughts so clearly. Usually they were only an assault of emotion. But this was coherent thought and longing—and longing was something Simon understood.

A swirl of agreement and the sensation of something running through his brain like the fur of a cat. Or scales. Tricky, this Nat. Hard to know if he was enemy or friend; or was it only that Simon had gone mad sometime in his youth and there was no Nat at all? Only delusion.

But the sensation had been so familiar it staggered Simon back, because this was as if the Nat filled him, was part of him, had depths like an iceberg deep in Simon's soul, and he had not realized it.

If Shwepyingyi Taungbyon was that large, how could he ever control him? What hope did he have of dislodging him?

He would. He had to, with his mother's meditations.

When he stepped out of the room at eight a.m., the light mist had turned the day humid. His khaki shirt stuck to his skin, only emphasizing the heat burning from the Nat. Kalla had said the nun expected them early this morning. She should be up and ready.

He strode three doors down to her room, hesitated, then knocked.

"Come in."

He pushed open the door, but didn't enter. There was no need to press his luck. Already the Nat uncoiled with attention, setting Simon's teeth on edge.

"So, Princess. You have finished your beauty sleep?" She stood, slim as a reed, fair as Minthamee—a Burmese princess—her golden longyi skimming her hips. His gaze caught at the way her t-shirt outlined the outer curve of her breast. Even to his ears his taunt sounded petty.

She didn't rise to his bait.

Her face was distracted as she turned to him, but when she looked at him he saw her anger. And frustration. So. He'd gotten under her skin.

That was good because it would make her stay away.

"If you're going to make this more difficult, maybe you should just explain to Alex why his high-priced researchers aren't doing their job." It came out in a snarl he could almost admire. In France the women were not so powerful, would not show their frustrations so naturally. This he could almost enjoy like a cat with a furious mouse.

"So you wish me to tell him the Princess does not play well with others?" He stepped into the room, enjoying the way she stiffened, and all her attention locked on him.

Then her shoulders slumped.

"I play fine. But I'm tired and I can't find anything in this mess." She swept her hand at the heap of belongings in the room. "I couldn't sleep. I tried to sort through this stuff, but it just seemed to overwhelm me."

She scrubbed a hand over her face in a way that was charming in its strange combination of strength and vulnerability. It left him guilty that he'd teased her.

"If this keeps up I'll be as hopeless as my sister."

"Sister." Interesting. He hadn't thought of Kalla as having family. More as if she'd sprung from the brow of a god fully formed.

"Sharon. She's a bit of a write-off. Smart woman, bad choices. Drugs. That scene." She shook her head as if dismissing the matter, but the fact she'd said it so emotionlessly spoke volumes of a long-standing control.

"That cannot be easy."

"You get used to it." She was still sifting through the pile of belongings, then stopped and shook her head so her hair swung in a mesmerizing sweep around her shoulders. "Dammit. I don't understand. It should be here."

"What? You are missing your notes? You can start another notebook."

She turned to him, but it was like there was a film over her gaze, as if she did not truly see him.

"Not a notebook. It's my puppet. I've been looking for her all morning and I can't seem to find her. I didn't see her last night, and all I can think is that the soldiers took her."

Simon scanned the room, a sinking feeling in his gut. "Not too likely, given the General gave orders for everything to be returned. At least that was what Hue said."

"You don't know that. And you said she's valuable. Someone could have stolen her." She was sifting through the main pile of clothing again. Lifting a stack of papers she'd already shifted. High points of color stained her cheeks and Simon tried to make sense of it all. Yes, the puppet was valuable. Could she have been stolen by the General?

She pulled dresser drawers open and left them. Wiped her hair back. Crossed back to her clothing and began tossing pieces onto her unmade bed.

She shook her head. Shook her head. Shook her head and muttered and Simon suddenly realized what she was doing. The Nat was poised. Ready. Watching like a snake.

"Kalla?" Simon spoke softly, because in the short time he'd known her, he'd seen Kalla was a driven woman, but this was not like her. This was something *wrong*—unnaturally obsessed.

She kept searching through the garments, then moved to a jumble of shoes on the floor.

"She should be here. I left her on my dresser. She has to be here."

Simon crossed the room. He heard her quick intake and exhalation of breath, smelled heated apples and roses as he caught her wrist.

"Kalla!"

He had to stop this, whatever it was. Get her out of this loop, even while the Nat roared with need and desire that rip-tided over Simon.

She stared up at him, blue eyes wide, the pupils swallowing the color. He could lose himself in those eyes. Wanted to fall. Felt the unnatural heat of her flesh in his hand and saw a deep sense of recognition float up through the darkness of her fear.

"What are you doing?" Her voice was soft, breathless and scented with mint.

"You are acting *folle*—crazy. You look places and then look again and again. If the puppet was not there the first time, how could she be the next?"

"I—I don't know. I—I swear she moves at night. I feel like she's hiding. Playing tricks. She has to be here and I just have to find her."

The blue-black of her gaze was so earnest it was clear she didn't hear the craziness of what she said. Her body strained in his grasp, wanting to return to its hopeless task.

What had happened to the Votaress was a serious concern, but right now his concern was for Kalla.

Kalla gone strange. Kalla in his grasp, so close he felt the heat of her, her scent overwhelming his senses. And Shwepyingyi Taungbyon's roar was a typhoon that sent his flesh shuddering.

No. Not now. She is unwell.

WELL ENOUGH.

The wave of possession crashed down on him, left him fighting for control. Any control. And suddenly Kalla was against his chest, his arms around her and he took her lips with his own.

Sweet. *Like he remembered.*

Warm. *As only she could be.*

He buried his face in her hair, ravaged her lips, her neck. *By the Kings of Heaven, he would have her here.*

The slam of her palm against his cheek rocked the Nat back. Sent Simon back a pace, still caught in the sensations of her.

Soft under his hands. The taste like mint and—yes—rosewater. The yielding pressure of her breasts, the tight muscle of her back, her ass.

Mon Dieu, what had he done?

She faced him in fighting stance, but the huge black of her gaze had diminished. This was Kalla, furious and blue-gazed as a Burmese devil. At least she was not the half-crazed woman he had found in the room.

"How dare you! I told you last night, no one touches me like that." He could almost smile at the way she was la petite fury ready to take him on. She stomped her foot and backhanded his kiss off her lips.

That did make him smile, but she was already casting about for the puppet again.

"Aah, but Princess, you told me not to drag you. You did not mention kissing was also forbidden. A tragic thing, n'est-ce pas? No kissing." He straightened to his full height and looked down at her. Her frustration was so clear he couldn't help laying on the French accent a little thick. "Now the French - they believe that kissing is a good thing. And I who have one foot in both America and France so in this I must agree with the French. See how it has relieved you of your worry for the Votaress? And given you are relieved of that care, perhaps you would like to care about the fact we are going to be late to meet with your nun if we do not leave immédiatement."

Her gaze flashed away from sorting through tangled bed sheets, picking up clothes, to his wrist.

"What time is it?"

"Almost nine o'clock. I believe that was the time you had set for the meeting?"

"Nine? But it was just seven…." She crossed to her bed, studied a small travel alarm on the bedside table, shook the clock. "But how?"

"*Le temps n'attend pas*—time marches on, Princess. Are you ready to go? Perhaps you can ask the others if your puppet appeared in another room." Her puzzlement was clear. "Did you not say you thought the puppet hid from you? Perhaps she prefers another mistress."

"Now who's talking crazy?" She said, disgusted.

She gathered up a stack of notebooks and pens, then turned back to him with resolve on her face.

"We'll go see Daw Ma Ma Nang, but then we're going to see that general to demand my puppet back."

So she would make the best of this, just as he would, but the taste of her filled his head and the Nat reveled in her flavor of mint and apple. The creature grew like a cyclone in Simon's brain, even as he tried to figure out what could have happened to the Votaress.

Not a good start to his day. Not good at all.

Chapter 18 - Hands Madly Clapping

To hold off the Nat, Simon focused on the long-faded paint of the small gate he faced. Weathered russet. Peeled in strips. For some reason the old paint was not a good thing.

It suggested this was a well-established group of nuns, older—and that they would be more caught in the old ways. Would probably be less approving of a man entering their home.

Well there was no choice, n'est-ce pas? Kalla needed stories and this nun had them. He glanced at Kalla. She stood beside him, her lips in a tight, disapproving line at his presence and her continued preoccupation with the disappearance of the puppet. She had sat that way through the short jeep ride to the nun's home.

"Would you just knock? Or is that beyond you?" The snap in her voice could almost make him smile but his battle with the Nat left him without even the ability to consider the puppet's loss.

"I think it may be improper for me to be here."

"Well what choice have we got, given Alex's edict? We have to make the best of this."

Simon ran his hands through his hair.

"The best. I thought perhaps that was the kiss this morning." He put all his charm, all the force of his accent that had always worked quite well on women, into his smile and knew her hackles rose by the way she almost snarled. It was becoming increasingly easy to rile her— good, because it kept her at a distance. "But perhaps you would prefer to challenge him? I believe you know him well—very well?"

She reacted with a nice bit of color and tossed her black hair back so it shimmered in the morning light. He wished she hadn't worn it loose on this of all days. He wanted to catch that mass of hair in his hands, bare her throat to his lips. Instead he rapped on the door.

"I don't know Alex at all anymore. Things were over between us long ago." But her voice held a tinge of sadness that made him regret his dig and sent a twinge of jealousy through a part of him. Actually, both parts.

"So we shall try this thing, then. And then we shall speak to the general, though I do not like to go there again."

From beyond the gate came the murmur of voices. On the road, the usual russet-robed monks made their morning rounds with their black begging bowls, and a pony cart clip-clopped past, bells and harness jingling gaily in the dusty air. Overhead, doves crooned to the new day.

The small gate's window opened and a young, bald-pated nun peered out. Simon explained his role as translator and the window closed with a force that made him suspect it wasn't going to open again.

"Not an auspicious start, Princess."

"Can't be any worse than the way the morning has gone already." She wouldn't meet his gaze.

Perhaps she felt it just as he did—the drawing—and was repelled by it. Perhaps she knew what he was and loathed him for it. She was, after all, an anthropologist. She should understand about nat possession.

"You worry about the Votaress."

She did look up at him then, with swiftly masked vulnerability. "Damn straight. My dad'll have a fit if she's gone." But it was more than her dad's reaction she was worried about. Her gaze said the puppet meant a great deal to her—perhaps even more than his mother's dying wishes?

Abruptly the gate opened and an old woman stood there. Kalla half bowed.

"Mingăla ba," she gave the traditional greeting. "Simon, this is Daw Ma Ma Nang." She pointed at Simon's chest. "Simon Renault. Tell her you will translate for me today."

Simon swore silently at the way Kalla always had to assume control, but he bowed his head at the nun and explained that Mei could not attend, but he was an experienced translator and would be pleased to assist in the conversations if Daw Ma Ma Nang would allow such a foreign man to enter.

She stepped up to him, looked up at him with black eyes caught in a net of wrinkles so deep he thought of fisheries bringing strange creatures from the deeps.

Perhaps she saw a similar strangeness in Simon because she reached up and with a dry palm, traced the line of his cheek as calmly as an old gypsy fortuneteller at a French country market. Then she stepped back and ushered them through the gate.

When it shut behind them, it was like they had stepped back in time. No sound came from the street. The breeze rustled the purple bougainvillea, water sloshed as a young nun washed clothing. The scent of garlic and shrimp and pickled tea came from the house. The earth around and under the teak structure was swept of blossoms, the building scrubbed clean and glistening.

The nuns were an industrious lot. They had to be.

Daw Ma Ma Nang seated herself under the lone tree in the yard, barely waited for Kalla and Simon to seat themselves before launching into a tale that used the age-old characters of the rabbit and the tiger.

Simon relaxed into the task of translating the traditional story of the scheming city rabbit and the kindly country tiger. Beyond the wall, the monuments of Pagan lifted lotus-shaped peaks a hundred feet into the air. A few were restored—white as the spires of Paris's Montmartre, but most were dark with age. *Once they had been few, young, vivid against the blue sky.*

Simon yanked away from the Nat's thoughts and realized Kalla was looking at him.

His translation faltered. He looked down at his papers. His pencil had traced the shape of her face, the angle of her jaw, and he froze.

The Nat held too much control. Even now Simon's nostrils expanded, seeking the heady scent of Kalla's skin.

Daw Ma Ma Nang's story droned on. He jerked his attention back, and found he had leaned toward Kalla, his pencil had shaded her skin, shaped the slant of her eyes. He could scent her apples and roses fragrance, feel her softness against him, even over the heat of the sun, the smell of dust and wash water and thanaka wood being slowly ground to a paste by the young nun who sat at Daw Ma Ma Nang's side. He yanked himself upright and realized he had lost the thread of the translation.

Merde! He had control. He was a man, not a rutting animal. Or spirit!

He grabbed the edge of his notepad and held on for dear life. Focus on the words. The words.

He had lost them.

"Pardon, Daw Ma Ma Nang," he said in Burmese. "Please repeat what you last said?"

How long had he wandered lost in his thoughts. How long had she told the story? How long had Kalla waited with her blue gaze was on him.

To have that gaze locked on his as he moved in her. To have her shout his name.

Stop!

The old woman sat like Buddha under a bodhi tree, the shadows of the breeze-blown leaves dancing across her face. Simon wondered if he had made that order out loud. Except for the glitter of her eyes, she could have left her body.

A cold chill ran through him and the Nat stirred. Overhead, something more than the breeze stirred the leaves and fluttered the purple bougainvillea. Simon stiffened in fear.

You will not do this.

The low laughter of the Nat filled his head.

"We are finished with that story of cruelty," Ma Ma Nang said startling him back to attention. "I will take tea and then I will tell a new story and you will listen."

It was more than he dared, to look at Kalla. The Nat was too close to taking shape.

"She's going to change stories, but wishes to take tea now. She says she's done with the story of the rabbit and the tiger—that she has told what must be told of the rabbit's cruelty."

Kalla shook her head. "I can't quite get this. Your translation seemed spotty at the end—incomplete." Her look challenged him to deny it.

"I'm sorry. There is something here, something strange. I feel like we step outside of time."

Was that laughter on her lips? *Because he would kiss it off of them, taste her laughter.*

But she did not give him reason; she shook her head still considering her notes.

"I swear it's this whole damned place. Pagan. Even the name spells trouble. Change the pronunciation and you have something beyond accepted religions."

"So you think this place causes your dreams?" He tried for humor, something to get rid of the Nat's pressure. Instead she surprised him with a small half-nod.

"Maybe. I know it has got to be the atmospherics, but I've had a headache here like I never get at home. Makes it hard to focus."

He stretched his neck, eased his shoulders, and craned back to look at the sky. If she knew the real level of strangeness in this country she might run screaming. To be possessed was an evil thing.

"Burma—Myanmar—holds many overlays of belief, and many ghosts." Again that flinch in her. "Pagan was one of the places of horrible killing on religion's behalf. Once this was a place where people believed in spirits and alchemy and other things. King Anawrahta tried to purge these beliefs at the start of the golden age of Pagan. He wanted a pure form of Buddhism, so many people who held to the old ways were killed. He eventually relented—with new rules that set the nats almost lower in stature than the people—even though he allowed nat statues at the edges of the great temples. If you go to the phatos around Pagan you will see them."

She shook her head, then grimaced. "Then perhaps it's all those ghosts making people question things—their beliefs. Their way of living."

Her blue gaze made him weak. It made him want what he had seen between Mei and Alex this morning. The way their bodies had curved together.

The Nat's power stirred and Simon fought it. Beads of sweat ran down his back as he met the nun's gaze.

She chewed her betel like a limousine cow chews cud, but her eyes were knowing black holes.

"Did you know in Burma there are still people wedded to spirits? They call them Spirit Wives and Nat-dancers. They wander the country with false visions and prophecy."

Kalla jerked towards him and he knew he could never have what Mei and Alex had—because there was a third being involved in any relationship he might have with Kalla. He was one of those charlatan-transvestite-dancers and it sickened him.

"Simon? Are you all right? Your face has gone strange."

It was hard just to inhale, to accept the small glass of tea provided by the young nun who set out a tray with a laquerware container that held the traditional Burmese snack-mixture of pickled tea leaves, dried shrimp, and garlic. Simon helped himself to a spoonful, fighting to settle himself.

"This animal tale—it's a teaching tale, I think. What role do the rabbit and tiger usually play in these stories?" She brushed back a loose strand of hair.

Her touch would be light on his chest.

Simon twisted his thoughts away. Ça va mal finir - it would end badly unless he focused on her question.

"My mother used to tell me these old stories when I was very young. The rabbit—he is usually like a human hero with all good qualities—so this is an unusual tale."

Kalla glanced at the old woman, and he could see Kalla's thoughts turning over in the way her gaze narrowed and her finger tapped the pad of notes she took. She had a quick mind—one that brooked no fools—or demon-possessed men.

From the street came the sound of children passing by, their laughter filtering through the bougainvillea. Overhead a sparrow chirruped in the branches. Finally Kalla stopped her ruminations and smiled at him.

"You're fortunate you have your mother's stories and her understanding. I lost my mother early."

She looked so fragile in that moment. Like a single reed that could be blown down by a high wind.

"Is that what drew you to this work?"

Her gaze fell back to her notes. "No—maybe. I don't know. The work seemed natural. I've spent my whole life trying to find meaning—a look, a phrase, a folk tale. Small things." She looked up at him and her eyes were bright with emotion.

"My father—let's just say we weren't close until lately… and now I'm here." Her voice faded away.

So being here was not an easy thing for her. Perhaps he could play on it—get her to leave and thus relieve himself of temptation. Set the Nat to rest.

But a part of him suspected the Nat would never rest now that it knew Kalla Jervis existed in the world.

Did he truly wish her to leave?

A magpie squawked above the yard, sending the little sparrows fluttering as the larger bird settled on the steeply pitched roof of the house. Kalla followed its flight, and the graceful arc of her neck almost stole Simon's breath.

"Darn birds. They're a plague in Seattle. They used to steal food from my dog's bowl."

Her oblique glance left Simon fighting the Nat back. This was the first decent conversation he had had with Kalla; he did not want to destroy this fragile peace.

"There are always plagues like those birds. Petits problèmes. This country was a large part of my life growing up. I grew up in a household that was American and French and many kinds of Burmese. It made for an—shall we say—interesting, life."

"And I thought Thai-American was bad. But my mother's family might have originally come from Burma. It was why I joined the team."

Kalla's admission brought the Nat raging forward. Simon's vision paled. The breeze picked up. Leaves fluttered above him like hands madly clapping.

Fight back. Find something mundane to talk of. Something that will hold you together.

Kalla leaned forward, unaware of how the soft swell of her breasts fell against the fabric of her t-shirt. The apple and rose scent of her hair reached him and he realized he had shifted towards her again.

The nat roiled inside him. Demanded freedom. Demanded Simon take this woman—now.

Here.

No matter the others around. The blackness rose, raging.

His fingers dug into the old wood of his seat, tore the edge of his notebook. But the breeze had increased. The bougainvillea blossoms rustled.

The old nun spoke.

Simon jerked his way free of the spirit. Her words were a music he needed, an interruption from Kalla. He couldn't look at her, couldn't scent her, couldn't feel the heat of her, though he swore he could hear the quick beat of her pulse.

"She tells another story," Simon growled. His head—too full of Kalla, too full of memories of his mother's puppets, of Kalla's missing Votaress. The images kept sliding together, distracting, urgent, almost more than he could bear.

"There was, in old Pagan, an alchemist," Daw Ma Ma Nang said. *"He was very great. He worked and worked and, with the aid of his apprentice, found the secret key to making gold…"*

The nat-form whirled within him, seeking to coalesce. Seeking control. Simon tightened his grip on the stool, held to the sour-bitter taste of the pickled tea. *It will not happen now! It will not happen here!*

You. Cannot. Have. Her!

Daw Ma Ma Nang's words floated in and out of his awareness. *"… Alchemist's stone… filled pots with gold… great wealth, but he was not a greedy man…"*

He translated, but it was by the skin of his teeth. Stop! He wanted to yell. He wanted—no, needed—to get up, move. When he moved, sometimes he could work the Nat through. It brought the battle into the physical—something that was easier than these internal battles.

But he could not spring to his feet now.

"Simon? What has she said?"

Her voice. Kalla would *whisper his name to him in the throes of their passion.*

Non! He gripped the tops of his knees, digging in so hard he knew he bruised flesh. "She says the alchemist received the king's permission and he and his apprentice placed the alchemist's stone in every pot in the city. This wealth allowed the people to build many temples. That is why Pagan is so rich with monuments."

To find the words took all his strength. Yet the old woman continued. He had to pay attention, could not afford to blow another of his translations—they were too key to the work, but the Nat roiled forward, ready for battle.

The old woman's words. Focus. Focus.

"The alchemist watched this great building and was happy to see the holy Buddha's teaching spread among his people. Great were the gold and silver spires of the city so that people came from the four directions to see it. Nothing could equal it."

Simon scribbled madly, translating for Kalla. The nat loomed in his mind; the darkness was a great pacing beast.

"When the great temples were built, the alchemist was ancient. He had done many good works and was friend of the spirits because he had also made sure that the mighty temples recognized the spirits of land and tree and pond and river.

"He took with him his apprentice, and the two traveled to Mount Popa."

Simon jerked at the name. He glanced up at the nun and found her gaze locked on him. The Nat seemed to stare back at him from the woman's dark eyes. Simon clamped his closed. Swallowed. Translated.

"They walked high on the mountain with the spirits beside them—such spirits who loved them. The trees of heaven sent down vines and creepers and blooming plants. They came around the old alchemist and his apprentice, wrapping them gently, and began to lift them up and up toward the sky.

"But alas, the apprentice was a young man. He still had a mother in Pagan. The heights caused him great fear and, being a wise man, though not so wise as his Master, he spoke. 'Master,' he said, 'I am not so worthy nor so wise as you. I am not ready for this journey. I would return to my mother, and there I will remember your work and celebrate it. And await your return.'

"The old alchemist saw the wisdom of his young friend. The vines gently lowered the apprentice, as the other vines lifted the great alchemist beyond the world.

"And so the young apprentice returned to his mother with gifts from the alchemist. And there, until he died, he waited for the alchemist to return. He waits still."

The words rang in Simon's ears like music through deep water. The rush of waves, of wind, inundated his hearing, could not be denied.

The hot wind rattled the leaves overhead, raised a dust devil in the yard, tore blooms off the bougainvillea. It carried the scent of dust and old earth. And death, like that which haunted the Pagan plain. And ghosts.

Weak. He was too weak.

The Nat fell on him like a tiger on prey—just as it had done before. All the women of Paris for the taking. Debauchery, and fighting and—mon Dieu—where would he wake in the morning? What would he have done?

He leapt to his feet; the stool fell over. Get out before he hurt someone.

Kalla.

The old woman yelled, raised her robes to cover her face. Kalla spoke to him, but he couldn't hear her words. Couldn't see.

There was only the laughter, the roaring. The dark oncoming wave.

He would grab the woman and have her!

The gate. Get to the gate and away. From here. From her. From her softness and ripe mouth. From the danger. Then maybe he could put himself back together.

Kalla was on her feet, calling his name.

He shoved her aside and ran.

Chapter 19 – Rationale for Nerves

"Simon!"

He was gone like an infuriating gust of wind by the time Kalla got to the gate. The street was still. Doves crooned overhead and the jaunty jingle of pony cart bells came from down the road. The wind blew through the dry grass that edged the road and carried with it the scent of—was that incense?

The scent caused a shiver up her back and broke the spell of concern that held her.

"Darn it, Simon. What the heck's gotten into you?"

Another of his jokes, probably. Another way to attack her certainty, and as she swung back to the gate she caught sight of the jeep and her full predicament sank in. Simon had the keys.

"Damn that man." She growled it because the speed with which he'd left and the fact he'd disappeared with an almost supernatural skill suggested he wasn't coming back anytime soon.

She went back into the courtyard and bowed to the nun, who now gazed serenely at small birds pecking seed near the house. Daw Ma Ma Nang shook her head, spoke in rapid Burmese that was far beyond Kalla's grasp of 'Mingăla ba'.

"I'm truly sorry he behaved like that. He shouldn't have left. He was—is—just rude sometimes and doesn't seem to realize how he offends people. I don't think he really means it—most of the time. Not with you, anyway. Maybe with me?"

She realized she was prattling on as if the nun made her nervous, and maybe Daw Ma Ma Nang did—had, since Kalla first met the woman at that Dhammayangyi Pahto.

"I should go. Not disturb you anymore. I figure I can catch up to Mei and Alex at the temple where they're working." She bowed again, gathered her things, but the nun climbed laboriously to her feet and caught Kalla's hand.

The old woman's palm was dry as dust, hard from labor and hot as if a furnace burned inside her. The firm grasp was discomfitingly strong as Daw Ma Ma Nang stepped in close.

Black gaze that showed no color in the eye, only pupil and white. Kalla felt herself studied, weighed and—when she tried to pull loose—as if she'd missed something dearly important as the old woman spoke. Her tone was urgent, so urgent and it sparked a small fire of fear.

What if the nun wasn't going to let her go? What if Daw Ma Ma Nang was part of those kidnap rings Kalla had heard about years ago where women were taken and sold to the Middle East?

She knew she was being stupid, but the way Daw Ma Ma Nang looked at her, the way the nun's fingers were claws around her wrist—on top of everything else that had happened in Pagan, Kalla had to get away.

She yanked loose, sending the old woman stumbling. Then she grabbed her notebooks and ran.

Out the gate, swore again at the useless jeep and headed—what?—south? Was it south she needed to go to find Alex? Behind came the old woman's voice calling Kalla's name.

She just ran, feeling mightily foolish as she did so. Daw Ma Ma Nang was just an old woman. But that didn't slow Kalla's swift retreat.

Past a cluster of young monks laughing together, past a young woman carrying a basket of fish to market, past walls of old stone that seemed to press in at her, bougainvillea that seemed to trail long runners to catch her. Then she was on the main road heading south against a steady stream of Burmese walking, cycling toward the larger town of Nyaung U.

She slowed to a walk and tried to calm her breathing. Checked over her shoulder. No sign of the nun, or any nun for that matter. So her concerns had been foolish and she'd lost control. Again.

The whole of Pagan and everyone she met seemed to be pushing her to do so. At home she wouldn't react this way. First, there'd been her competitive attitude towards Mei when the young woman had done nothing. Then throwing herself at Alex. Animosity with Simon. And then there had been the general.

She looked suspiciously at the faces around her.

All smiling.

She was being ridiculous. Again. It was like this entire place eroded everything she'd always thought of herself.

Shaking her head, she firmed her stride down the road, forced herself to smile and greet the people along the road. Was so tired of faking it and mouthing 'Mingăla ba'—to the apparent delight of the locals—that she almost shouted in relief when she saw the research team's other jeep pulled up in front of another huge pahto.

But this one was different. Where Dhammayangyi stood dark and brooding above the barren plain, this stood flushed-white—almost filled with a pink pearl's nacreous glow. It stood at a curve in the river, in a courtyard filled with trees that had been hung with antique temple bells. The air rang with the gentle, many-toned ting, ting, ting, amid the shadows of the leaves. The breeze off the river was welcome after her long walk.

She passed through the small row of tourist gift shops and then into the pahto. Gawdawpalin, the sign said. Meaning 'Platform to which homage is made'.

Long cool halls of white turned golden in the oblique sunlight that came through the many doors and windows. The wind seemed to whisper here—but the whispers were interrupted by a low boom, a tremor, and loud voices.

One voice in English. Alex.

Kalla skidded around a corner in time to find a thin, longyi-clad, Burmese man standing toe-to-toe with Alex. The Burmese came up to Alex's chin, and stood so close he had to crane his head back to make eye contact. He was motioning at equipment spread on the floor, and chopping with his hands in a motion that left no question but that he was upset at whatever Alex had done.

With Alex leaning his blonde height over the Burman, the scene would have been funny if both parties had not so obviously been angry.

And if there was one thing Kalla knew from living in Southeast Asia, it was that a show of emotion was seriously out of character.

Whatever Alex had done was serious.

Chapter 20 – Time's hands

"What's going on?" Kalla came up to Alex and Mei, just as the little man shook his head and stormed off down the sun-gilded corridor, clearly still fuming about what had happened.

"Dammit," Alex swore under his breath. "I mean, come on? I didn't hurt anything." He motioned around at the pale walls, the white-faced Buddha-figure seated in a niche across from one of the doors.

"The man—he says you dishonor this place that is the greatest achievement of Pagan." Mei's gentle admonition did nothing to wipe the annoyance off Alex's face. "It was almost destroyed in 1975, by an earthquake. The caretaker worries your machine is like an earthquake and may bring Gawdawpalin down."

Alex snorted. "Not going to happen. There isn't enough power to do that."

"What'd you do?" Kalla asked, eying the equipment spread on the ground. It looked something like one of the machines used in cardio resuscitation with paddles and wires, and was connected to a laptop and battery pack that Kalla hadn't even known Alex had brought.

Alex knelt and began carefully dismantling the equipment and placing it in a foam-filled pelican box that would protect it from water or concussion.

"You missed the show. It's something I rigged up to look at the interior of these buildings. Thankfully I've had it in my room so our saboteur didn't get it. Everyone says these temples are solid except for small relic chambers buried in the centre, and yet there have always been rumors of something more in Pagan. Treasure, perhaps. I took the technology used by archaeologists looking at what's under the earth, and modified it to work above ground in buildings."

He motioned to the computer screen, still turned on.

"See here. Spaces should show up as a ghost on the computer screen. This would be the relic chamber," he said tapping the screen that showed a foggy mandala shape. The muzzy picture showed what looked like an ultrasound with a darker shadow in the middle.

"And you nearly got us kicked out for that?"

Alex's gaze turreted up to Kalla and she knew she had seriously erred.

"I'm a scientist, Kalla. I'm doing *my* job. And while we're talking about jobs, what are you doing here? I thought Simon was translating that nun's stories for you?"

She fought back her anger at the way he immediately tried to make her the guilty party.

"I'm just concerned, is all. After last night. I mean, that general was so suspicious of my walk—it's like he's afraid we're looking for something. I was considering escape out the office window before they released us, and they sure as heck didn't give us any reason for any of it.

"As for me and Simon, it seems my illustrious translator had other ideas. In the middle of things he took off. I've no idea where he is."

She stood with her hands on her hips, ready for Alex's next jab, and ready to enter the fight if necessary, but Alex glanced at Mei. She had knelt beside him, was silently coiling the wires and passing them to Alex. Alex closed his eyes and his sigh was audible.

"Sorry. The caretaker just got me upset. I didn't mean to take it out on you. I just wanted to try out the equipment and I thought Gawdawpalin would be as good a place as any. I didn't think of the earthquake damage. I should have tried it out elsewhere—will, as a matter of fact. I'd just decided to head over to Dhammayangyi when the caretaker and I got into it. You might as well come."

It took a moment to believe that Alex had held himself in check. Always in the past, his first reaction to Kalla's questions had been to fight.

Mei's influence. It had to be. Or it was just Kalla who brought the fight out in him. Kalla smiled down at Mei, even though the thought of Dhammayangyi filled her with disquiet. Still, it was time she got back in control of herself.

"Sounds good. I'm not going to get anymore stories today. And maybe after Dhammayangyi we can go past the General's office. I think one of his men stole my Votaress puppet." She shook her head. "Simon was going to take me, but…. I tell you, he shot out of there like he had a demon on his tail."

Mei shifted uncomfortably, as if she had something she wanted to say. What was it she had said before? Simon had darkness inside him? Madness, more like. He'd acted like a mad man today, had had that sort of look in his eyes.

"Your puppet from home?" Alex asked, distracted by settling the equipment into the padded case.

She nodded at Alex. "What other puppet is there?"

He rolled his eyes at her sharp tongue. "I still can't believe you brought the damn thing here." He must have seen the twist his words caused because he sighed again. "Fine. After Dhammayangyi we'll go to the general's office—that is, if Mei feels up to translating."

Kalla saw Mei's hesitation.

"Don't worry. The general speaks perfectly good English. All you have to do is get me into his office."

Mei's relief was evident as Alex snapped his equipment case closed and stood.

"So let's blow the pop-stand before the cops come." Alex hefted his case of equipment over his shoulder. "They'll have to find us in Dhammayangyi."

He led them out of the pahto, past three novice monks who were no more than ten, clustered in the first Buddha sanctum. Their laughter said they were hell-bent on causing trouble. Certainly their impish faces told of plots hatched and monastic rules broken.

Kalla grinned at them, gave them each a pen, and followed after Mei.

"You should not encourage them, you know. They have taken vows that are far too easy for a boy to break."

Kalla rolled her tongue into her cheek. "Then consider my gift tests of their obedience."

Mei only shook her head. "Oh how the west corrupts our children." Then she grinned. "They will be glad of the pens when they return to school. Burmese pens and paper are of poor quality. They will thank you for your gift." She turned back and spoke to the boys who each in turn thanked Kalla with a grin and a bow.

"Our youth must have manners, even in these times."

"Well, you're doing your part. I missed you with Daw Ma Ma Nang, today. I think she was uncertain about Simon. No doubt she won't let him back in after today."

 Karen L. Abrahamson

"Then perhaps we will work together again," Mei said noncommittally.

Kalla stopped her in the middle of the courtyard, the bells dinging around them like the music of clouds, so light and full of spaces.

"Mei, if Alex said I didn't want you as my translator, he was in error. I just didn't understand the story Daw Ma Ma Nang told or why she told it. I got impatient. I'm sorry."

Mei's gaze was clear, thoughtful, and full of a peace that Kalla wished she could experience.

"It is nothing, Kalla. In the past. Is that not what Buddha teaches? To let go of grievances before they eat you whole? We all carry our own dooms."

She grasped Kalla's hand, and the warmth and friendship of her smile brought relief to Kalla. "Besides, we have been through too much since then, have we not? We are the sisters we spoke of that first day."

"We'll be sisters of the best kind."

"Is there any other kind?"

Kalla thought of Sharon, back home with Dad. "I've never had an easy relationship with my sister. I'm younger, but I've spent most of my life rescuing Sharon from something or other." Not that it ever did any good. The woman seemed hell-bent on self-destruction.

"Are you two coming?"

Alex was loading his equipment and Kalla felt the first stirring of ill-ease at the prospect of visiting Dhammayangyi. Mei had been with her that day. Mei had seen.

And she must have seen Kalla's hesitation as well.

"Are you sure about Dhammayangyi, Kalla? You gave me a true fright the last time."

Mentioning it brought it back too clearly, the darkness and the sense of waiting and the pulse of pain in her head. She realized it had been there all along since the day at the pahto, but she had simply become used to the dull thud behind her eyes as if some monster pounded at its prison.

"I'm not sure. I don't know. Just thinking about that place gives me a chill, but I'm an adult. There's no reason for me to be afraid of that place." She sighed. "I think this whole plain has left me a little unhinged. And now my puppet has disappeared. It must be the soldiers never gave it back—or that general. Simon offered to buy it from me to complete a collection his mother had, so it must be more precious than just a family heirloom."

And there'd been his kiss.

Her fingers went to her lips. His lips had been hard, demanding, and yet…. There was an underlying gentleness she had responded to. The smell of him was like musk and incense and dry leaves, and she somehow knew the scent was just him. Not soap. Not aftershave. As if he was a temple creature.

"Kalla? What is it?"

She jerked back to the present, too aware that just thinking of his strong arms brought more than a little shimmer of heat to her body. More heat than Alex had ever evoked on his best day. She glanced in Alex's direction. He was busy loading his equipment in the jeep.

"He kissed me," she said. "I think it surprised us both." The heat flared in her and it was just plain stupid. Probably just a matter of not having been with any man for far too long. Simon was available and so her body was interested. Biological clock and all that.

But the alarm on Mei's face made it necessary to reassure her.

"Don't worry. I'm not interested. He's too confident. Too assertive. Too infuriating." And too damn sexy for his own good, with that dark tousled hair, that accent and those mysterious eyes that just showed a little too much hunger.

"Be careful, Kalla. Simon is—unpredictable. There is something—hungry—in him."

Kalla caught Mei's hand. "Would you quit worrying about me? I'm fine, alright? I know how to handle guys like Mr. Simon Renault." Or she hoped she did. "Now let's get going to that darn Pahto. I'll be fine. Besides, I could use a little chill right now."

She fanned herself against the heat, but Mei seemed to ponder her answer, her gaze shifting over Kalla's face until she felt a little foolish even acknowledging her hesitation. She was a scientist. She shouldn't even be having these conversations.

"In my culture, Kalla, these things might be attributed—that is the right word is it not?—to ghosts too close by. There are hungry spirits in the world. They are the ones held in the dark parts of the Wheel of Dharma. People who have not deserved hell, but neither do they deserve rebirth as human or animal. They live among us, thirsty for our lives. Perhaps what you feel is such a one. Perhaps it is a warning."

And that was seriously not what she wanted to hear. She grabbed Mei's arm and steered her towards the jeep. "You know what you could do for me? Tell me all that stuff's bogus. I don't believe in spirits or ghosts—hungry or otherwise." But there was a little ticking of nerves in her gut.

Buddhist beliefs. Sure. So if she followed Mei's logic, there was a spirit out there who saw her as designer clothing come to town. Perfect.

In the jeep, they roared away from Gawdawpalin, leaving behind the caretaker who had come out to wave a fist at them one last time. Very angry indeed.

They curved away from the river, heading past the matted htanaung trees and eucalyptus that grew within the red walls of the ancient city of old Pagan. Then they were past the crumbling structure and out into the dry wastes of the plain. Dust rose in long streamers from a plow dragged by two dun-colored oxen, and Kalla wondered how anyone could grow anything in the barren fields.

The sight of Dhammayangyi brought a bright stab of pain behind her eyes and an involuntary groan. For a moment she was blind, but she felt the jeep slow, stop, heard voices from somewhere far away beyond the palm she used to press her brain back into her forehead.

When her sight returned, the sunlight hurt her. Alex and Mei were dim shadows turned to her, and inside her something red and black stirred, whirled like blood in her vision.

"Kalla?"

It took what seemed like hours to recognize her name, to find a response in her brain.

"I... I...." She what? Was going to die of the pain? Wished she could? She wanted to lie down. She wanted to turn off the sun, the sounds of the day. The rumble of the jeep was enough to set her screaming if she hadn't bit down on her tongue until she tasted copper blood.

Then Mei was beside her, had pressed her back on the seat, cool hands on her face, and the jeep was moving again, bumping over the pavement.

It was—strange, wonderful, a miracle. Suddenly the weight lifted from her head, her vision cleared until there was only a rippling quality as if she saw the world through water.

"What—what happened? Where are we?"

"Heading back to the hotel."

"No!" Kalla struggled upright. "No. I'm not sick. We can still do research."

Alex glanced back from the wheel. "Good. I'm heading to Thatbyinnyu, then."

He twisted the jeep wheel for a U-turn across the road and headed back past the dark bulk of Dhammayangyi. Kalla averted her eyes. Mei held her hand.

"So what is it about you and Dhammayangyi?"

Kalla straightened at Alex's question and felt Mei's worried glance. This collapse was stupid and the fact Alex had seen it left Kalla chagrined. That made it twice she'd collapsed on this trip and that really wasn't acceptable. She'd always worked to be strong, to make him proud like she'd always tried to make her father.

"Let's call it a past life experience and leave it at that. Needless to say, a doctor's appointment is one of the first things on my list when I get home."

"Wise decision."

She shook her head and realized that type of movement was still unwise. The jeep bumped along a gravel road, sending her clutching for the door handle, but then Alex guided the vehicle to a stop before a huge pahto.

"Welcome to Thatbyinnyu—the Omniscient Pahto."

"Thanks for stopping." She rubbed her head, then looked at the structure. "It looks like a wedding cake. One that got 'McArthur Park'ed - left in the rain so all the white icing is washing away."

The huge, square, stepped structure lifted so high above when she stepped out of the jeep she had to crane backwards to take it all in view. Dark doors and windows dotted the structure and yet didn't evoke the sense of menace she got from Dhammayangyi. Pinnacles and corncobs and ornate lintels decorated the step edges and doors and windows.

"It's the tallest pahto in Pagan, but we don't know if it was ever consecrated and used as a temple. Used to be you got the best views ever over the plain, but the government doesn't allow people above the ground floor anymore. There's a huge Buddha on the second level, and legend has it that the King used to light bonfires higher up that could be seen across the plain."

"You really have made a study of this place, haven't you?"

Alex grinned like a kid let loose in a candy store. "Do you know how many archaeologists would kill for the chance to be here—to do this research? Hell, UNESCO and the Myanmar government haven't allowed any research beyond documentation of the site." He patted his equipment case as if it were a favored pet dog.

A favored dog that could rear back and bite them, if the caretaker's reaction at Gawdawpalin were any indication.

"You sure you should be using that thing?" She was surprised at her caution, and that surprise was mirrored in Alex's expression.

"This little baby is harmless, I promise. It does no damage at all and just gives us a peek to whet our appetites. Frankly, I'm surprised that there haven't been researchers in here before with something like this. But then, it hadn't been invented yet." Another grin—the proud, boyish grin of a kid who has fixed his bike and nailed his first bird house. She'd always liked that in him.

"If you're sure."

"Always. Now you feeling alright? Mei, maybe you better stay with her in case she has another one of those spells."

The solicitousness of his tone raised hackles on the back of Kalla's neck.

"I'll be fine. I'm not a child to be cared for. Or an invalid. I'm just—allergic to a certain pahto. Or I've got hungry ghosts after me, like Mei suggested."

She strode past Alex towards the huge building. "What's that?" She pointed to a smaller, but still large structure to the northeast.

"Tally zedi. They used one brick for it, to every thousand bricks in the main pahto. That platform over there is where the temple bell once stood." He pointed with his chin to large stone supports to the southwest. Beyond it rose the white, frosted peaks of Ananda Pahto, the main temple still in use among the ruins.

"Too many bricks if you ask me."

"It takes what it takes."

That was true, but it didn't stop the little tremor of nervousness that coursed through her as she neared the entrance with its two guardians that, according to the stories, could only be nats. The door stood as tall as three men, dusty floor illuminated by the sunlight that seemed to have to push against the darkness of the interior. In the dimness beyond, a white, serene face almost set her back a pace until Alex came up beside her.

"Buddha."

Kalla nodded, but the scent of fresh incense and lotus reached Kalla's nostrils and her stomach slowly somersaulted as if the memory of Dhammayangyi still rode her cells.

"How do you know it was never consecrated?"

"We're not sure, really. But none of the jataka plaques were ever hung, as far as we know. There should have been over 500 of them. It has some fine murals from the later period of Pagan, though. I'll give you a tour before I run the test."

He led them inside, to where the Buddha sat above puddled wax and the ash of incense sticks and faded marigolds. So this place was used as well. Buddha remembered, even though the history of this place had faded into sad memory. Kalla stood in the sanctum and let the feel of the place sink in.

"It feels sort of sad. All this effort, and it was left to crumble in the sun. All the crumbling brick—sort of like a metaphor for the saying ashes to ashes, dust to dust. Even great mountains like this can crumble and fall."

"Did you know they figure the first of these structures were built to represent mountain caves?"

The fact Alex's words so clearly echoed Kalla's brought another shiver up her back. What was it about these temples? She looked up, too aware of the weight of all those bricks above her and the way they crumbled in time's hands. To either side, corridors stretched from the Buddha sanctum to encircle the huge base of the temple. Distant pools of light showed where other doors and windows might provide escape.

She marked them.

"See here, Kalla." Her eyes had barely adjusted and he was dragging her into the cloister near the seated Buddha. Mei stood close by his side as he played his flashlight across the dim reaches of the ceiling vault.

Kalla looked longingly back at the outside where the sunlight caught in the low-walled courtyard would have been a relief from the darkness. Sparse trees spread sparser shadows across the ground. She forced herself to follow the beam of Alex's flashlight.

Color leapt into existence, coaxed by the light on the arch of the ceiling. Gold-clad Buddha and crimson-clad kings strode across the arch. A white elephant stood with trunk raised to Buddha seated beneath his bodhi tree. Kings knelt before him.

"That's Buddha as a teacher," Alex said nodding. "And here…" he flashed the light further down the ceiling… "here is the scene of Buddha realizing things aren't great in the world.

The light shone on another scene—this one of an emaciated man fallen on the ground, Buddha as a young prince riding past and truly seeing.

"All life is dukkha," Kalla whispered.

"What?" Alex asked.

"She said all life is suffering and illusion." Mei nodded. "It is Buddhist knowledge. This life is illusion that we paint for ourselves out of our desires. By desiring we cause ourselves suffering."

Alex lowered his flashlight for a moment, the light skittering across the lower reaches of the ceiling and down to the floor in a motion that almost turned Kalla's stomach.

"Are you telling me that I'm just imagining this place, and that you'll cause me pain?" He stepped closer to Mei, looked down at her in a way that spoke volumes of the relationship that was developing between the American and the young Burmese woman.

Color flushed Mei's cheeks prettily and Kalla had to look away, regret gnawing at her gut. She would never have someone look at her that way—so determined to make it work. Her own drive and determination always pushed away whoever she was interested in. After all, few men could match her intensity.

A pair of dark eyes under mussed hair came to mind, but that was just plain madness.

Without the light playing across the ceilings, the murals were lost in veiled darkness. The colors had been so vivid, so vibrant as they celebrated the historic events that had been this Buddha's life. Someday, according to Buddhist belief, another Buddha would arise—Maitreya—the future Buddha, just as there had been many Buddhas in the past.

Teachers, they were individuals who had reached enlightenment—an understanding of the true nature of the world. Buddhist belief said through this understanding they were able to escape the cycle of reincarnation and the suffering.

Not something she was going to do anytime soon, apparently.

Shivering, she crossed her arms against a cool breeze whispering through the corridors. Dust motes shone in streamers of light. Min and Alex murmured together, their voices magnified, echoing until it sounded like a host's whispers filled the corridors. A host lost and waiting like the women in her dreams.

That stopped her. This place was having way too weird an effect on her.

The way the light fell, the way the sound echoed—it reminded her of something, of some place, and yet she couldn't think of any place like this she had ever been. It was almost like she knew something but was afraid to admit it.

Her gaze slid down the wall, but caught on something just at the edge of the gloom.

"Alex, what's that?" She pointed up at the shadow.

Alex was setting up his equipment at the side of the Buddha. Not paying too much attention to whether he offended the locals, but then that was Alex's way. Focus on the science and forget the niceties. He glanced up.

"What are you talking about?"

"There. It looks like another painting."

He shrugged and bent over the equipment. "It is. There are a series of small murals along the walls below the main paintings. The surveys say they were added later, after the main murals were completed. Folk art, mostly. Little pictures of village and farm life. Probably added after Pagan had faded from its glory days—maybe even after the Mongols were here. There are little figures that look Chinese. Not really important."

He was in full Alex mode now, completely distracted with his boys-and-toys equipment. Kalla grabbed the flashlight from him and played it over the wall.

A small figure sprang into view. A blue longyi gleamed in the darkness. The figure knelt, holding out a small bowl containing something yellow that glittered in the light. Around the figure, tall palm trees waved and a foolish country tiger peeked out from amid the brush.

Kalla studied the image. An offering probably, but to what? She couldn't see the Burmese making an offering to the tiger recalled as such a foolish symbol of country life.

She slid the light along the wall, finding another of the small paintings. This was of a man in a rice field. At the side of the field stood a woman with babe in arms.

"Interesting bits of family life," she commented. "The man works, the mother stands watching with their child."

Mei looked up from where she helped Alex and shook her head.

"That is not the man's wife. That is Boun Magyi—the rice mother. See the rice around her neck?" Mei came to her, pointed at the standing figure. "The farmer has to propitiate the rice mother or else his crops will fail—all of them—including his crop of children. This man has made offering—see the little twist of rice stalks by his heel?"

The image was as Min described. Another offering and not to Buddha. But in Southeast Asia Buddhism still contained remainders of older religions.

She left Alex and Mei to walk down the corridor, shining her light on any images set at the same level of the wall. Strange these paintings should be here, given they were added after the time Simon said the King had ended nat worship.

Now that her eyes were educated, she could spot the images in the recesses of the corridor. There was another tiger image, this time the animal strode the forest. There an image of a King on a forest-covered mountain.

A little frisson of excitement ran through her. There was something in these pictures that was important, if she could just figure out what.

She needed to document all of them. She needed Alex's camera and then she needed to spread the photos out in front of her to see the story they told her. For there was a story here, she knew. From the Neolithic times, men had used their hands—the pictures they drew—to tell stories, until the development of cuneiform writing had set man on a path away from hieroglyphics.

"Kalla, come here. I want to show you something."

Alex's voice interrupted her excitement. His words echoed down the corridor to her, somehow sounding like they came from years away. Whatever he wanted to show her could not be more important than this.

"Kalla?"

She turned back to him, her hands clenched, and realized her body ached as if she had been walking through deep water.

"Coming."

She reached them and found Alex crouched among loops of wire, a framework of wire rods holding two paddles against the brick wall behind the Buddha image. His grin held all the excitement of a kid at Christmas.

"Thought you'd want to see this." He sat cross-legged in the dust, his computer, with a plain blue screen, in his lap. A happy grin filled his face as he typed commands into the machine.

A little beep, and the conglomeration of wires around the metal scaffolding began to hum.

"After this we'll know whether there's any truth to rumors of secret rooms and buried treasure in Thatbyinnyu. The sonar runs through the mass of brick and reflects off the opposite walls and comes back to get read by sensors in the brick here." He pointed to small probes he'd pressed into the bricks. "Ready?"

He didn't wait for a reply. He touched a button on the computer and a low boom sounded that Kalla felt in her bones. Dust shimmered down from the ceiling.

Another boom ran through the ancient structure and Kalla went cold. Bright flecks of paint shimmered as they fell. The darkness that cloaked the ceilings seemed to flood down over her. It was falling. The ceiling was truly falling.

She had to get out.

She would die in the dark, smothered in brick.

Alex reached to touch the button again.

"No! Stop! You could… you could… damage things."

It took everything she had to gasp out the words. She couldn't breathe. Her lungs ached for air. She turned. Ran blindly towards light.

Slammed into strong hands.

Simon of the dark eyes. "Kalla. There you are."

Beyond him, armed men.

Chapter 21 – Lies and Deflections

Kalla was warm under Simon's hands, but confusion and—fear?—radiated from her. Her blue-black gaze, the way she'd burst from the temple, it was like a demon was on her tail.

And so she ran right into another. The Nat surged forward and Simon shoved Kalla away. He'd barely managed to put himself together, and now this. Taungbyon grew more powerful every moment Simon was in her presence.

It didn't make sense. He'd been around desirable women in the past. But being around Kalla Jervis was the worst.

The confusion drained from her features. Well—at least partially. She was no longer le petite animal trying to escape the predator.

"Simon?" He watched comprehension metamorphize into serious pique. "Damn you, Simon! You left me."

Aah. That was more like his Kalla.

"Princess! You missed me. Perhaps you worried about your servant?"

"Shoot you, more like." Her face tightened at his use of Princess. Her hands went to her hips, her chin raised in that charming way that tempted him to smother her protests with a kiss.

DO IT! He yanked his attention away, denied the Nat.

"You ran off and left me trying to explain to Daw Ma Ma Nang. Like that was real successful. And I *was* worried—more fool me. You took the keys, too, you bastard. You left me to walk down to Gawdawpalin to find Mei and Alex. Thank god they were still there."

Then her gaze flickered to the soldiers at the gate behind him and her belligerence drained some. "Why are they here?"

"They had arrived when I got here. I just have longer legs and beat them to the temple. I thought perhaps you called the general to you?" He grinned, ran his hands through his hair in a way he knew usually charmed women. On this one, though, it didn't seem to work. Kalla stepped past Simon as the soldiers arrived.

"Do they speak English?"

"I think perhaps not. It is not so common for Burmese to speak English well. The general is an unusual man."

Unusual indeed, as the General followed his men through the gate. Simon had last seen the man last night. He had stepped into the doorway of the cell where Simon waited, had looked Simon up and down.

"I believe you are a dangerous man, Monsieur Renault," the general had said in English. "It sits in the air around you. It seethes in your eyes. But I will not have such things in Pagan. Do you understand?"

Simon had nodded. Had wondered just how much the man's dark eyes really saw. The general was no fool, that was certain.

"Good. Then see that it remains so. And see that my ruins remain as they are. I will not stand grave robbers or treasure seekers. The West has robbed my country enough—the English. The Germans. The French."

"No worse than your own leaders."

The only sign that the comment had hit home was a slight flaring of Ne Setkya's nostrils and a scent of heat from the older man's body. Fear? That was what Taungbyon said. Fear of Simon or the statement?

"My leaders are not here to guard Pagan. I am. I will not add the Americans to my list of thieves and brigands."

"Why tell me this?"

"Because you are a man of influence, a man whose blood may assist him to understand Burmese ways. Your records say you have been here many times. Let me warn you that such visas will not continue should there be further issues. Do you understand?"

"You threaten me?"

At that, Ne Setkya smiled. "I am not a man of threats. I am a man of facts. You understand? There will be no more problems. No more wandering the ruins in the night."

"I'll do what I can, but I don't lead this party. I can only influence."

"And I only deal in facts. It will be as I said."

And then Ne Setkya had left him to the soldiers who had hustled him out of the cell at the rear of the building and around to where Alex and Mei had huddled together. Khun had joined them a short while later, looking pale and shaken, and then Kalla, more subdued than he'd seen her before.

"Mingăla ba," Simon stepped past Kalla to face the small uniformed man. "We pose no problem here. We simply conduct our research."

Ne Setkya simply nodded at his soldiers. Two turned their rifles on Kalla and Simon and urged them towards the temple.

"What's going on, Simon? What's happening?"

The strain in Kalla's voice made him look at her. She was dragging her feet, the fear back in her eyes as she looked at the door to Thatbyinnyu.

"I don't want to go back in there," she whispered.

Where was the controlling Ms. Kalla Jervis, now? This was—this was more like the woman he had met in her room this morning. Emotions laid bare.

It wasn't like her.

A low boom came from inside the temple as the Nat swirled in Simon's brain. He wanted to hold Kalla, comfort her.

Take her and make her his.

Simon jerked towards the temple entrance. "What is going on?"

"Alex. It's Alex. He has some kind of machine."

"An illegal machine," Ne Setkya spat. He ordered his men into the pahto. The clatter of their footsteps echoed from the darkness. Alex's voice rose. He yelled and then suddenly appeared holding Mei's hand, herded by the armed men. Behind him came two soldiers clutching a mass of wires and metal and a humming computer.

"What the hell's going on, Renault? What's this all about?"

"How should I know? I just arrived, n'est-ce pas?"

Ne Setkya forced himself between Simon and Alex. He glared up at the blonde man.

"You endanger the temples. You force me to defile a temple with armed men to stop you."

"I haven't done anything! I've got permits! Perfectly legal permits to be here and conduct research." Alex's fists were clenched. He'd pushed Mei behind him. "Your men had better treat that equipment carefully! It's fragile, damn it." He tried to push past his guards to reclaim his equipment but the weapons stopped him. Then he turned back to Ne Setkya clearly prepared to go toe-to-toe with the general. Not a good idea.

"Alex, perhaps there is a misunderstanding. Perhaps if you explain to the good general what you do."

Alex's glare rested momentarily on Simon's face. "I don't need your help. I can defend myself, given your translation services don't seem to be particularly important to you these days." He turned back to the general.

"I'm simply doing what the permits allow. Surveying the site."

"Your permits say nothing of machines. They speak of visual inspection, that is all."

"I think you better look again. I can do what I want as long as I'm not digging."

Ne Setkya stepped up to him, a slight flush on his neck, the only sign of anger. The man was a master of bamahsan chin to control his physical reactions so well.

"You are wrong. I wrote the permits. I know what is in them, and I know that your machine digs in a new way, an electronic way that stabs through the heart of a temple." He peered up into Alex's face and must have seen the look of surprise that flickered across Alex's features. "I am not a primitive, Mr. Munroe. I understand such things and that such things are not allowed in Pagan. You will not use such tools again."

He barked an order to his men to take the equipment to their jeep, then turned back to Simon. "Monsieur Renault. Again we meet under unfortunate circumstances. I think, perhaps, you do not try hard enough to keep things in order."

His hard gaze caught on Simon's, and the Nat flared inside him. *He could—would—defeat this little man in battle.* But he dared not.

But Kalla pushed past Simon before he could respond.

"General, a word if you please?" She faced him with her hands on her hips and a look of such belligerence the General's color streamed a little further up his neck.

"Ms. Jervis." A small bow.

"My Votaress puppet has disappeared. She was in my room before your soldiers swept in last night. Now she's gone. I can only assume one of your men has stolen her. I would appreciate it if *you* would return *her.*"

The accusation in her voice was clear. Given the general's perspectives at the road block, Kalla had come to the conclusion he was behind the puppet's disappearance.

"Ms. Jervis, my men are honorable. No such thing would happen."

"Well then what else could have happened to her? No one else has been in my room."

"General," Simon leapt to intervene. "It is a little mystery we must solve. It would be most appreciated if you could speak with your men.

Perhaps the puppet was loaded in a jeep and was not noticed at unloading. Perhaps she still rests there."

"Simon…."

He silenced her with a glare and forced all defiance out of his gaze as he looked back at Ne Setkya. "I will explain to the others."

The general met his gaze, all expression masked. Finally he nodded. "I will speak to my men." He turned to go, but then stopped. Turned back to Simon with a quick, dismissive glance at the others. "See that you keep order in other things as well."

Then Ne Setkya strode across the courtyard, his soldiers at his heels. In the sunlight the dust of their passage filled the air like fool's gold.

And then they were gone and there was the sound of the doves, of Kalla's ragged breathing, and the hiss of debris falling from the temple.

She turned on him. "How dare you treat me like a child in front of the General. I could have dealt with him myself."

"And leave the man with no means to save face? I thought you were an anthropologist, Princess?"

Her furious expression only increased, but then Alex grabbed his arm.

"Renault, I need that equipment. You better damn well fix this."

Chapter 22 – Cold to Freeze Ayeyarawady

General Ne Setkya knew his hands shook.

For fear his driver would see, he kept them clenched into fists in his lap as his men drove back to headquarters.

It would never do for word of weakness to get back to Colonel Aung Aung.

Nor for the Colonel or the government to get their hands on the American's equipment.

He knew he'd erred by bringing everything back with him, but in the face of the woman's confrontation about her damnable puppet, he'd had to demonstrate his authority. Now his men muttered over the archaeologist's equipment in the back seat, smoothing their hands over the slick computer case and curiously tugging at the wiring and paddles. The fact they had confiscated the computer was serious. Anyone with reasonable computer skills could determine the program and possibly copy it.

It would provide the Myanmar government with the ability to assess the presence of treasure troves in any of the great monuments in the country. The Old Man would be greedy in its use. The generals would fight over it. They would sweep the country of its heritage, sell it, and Burma would simply cease to exist.

The people would be outraged and there would be riots and more killing. Just as there was always too much killing. And nothing would change.

His son.

Ne Setkya used a cough to cover his wince of pain, as the jeep pulled up before the military building. Colonel Aung Aung stepped out onto the front steps, imposing as he loomed above Ne Setkya.

The man tried to take control. Had been cultivating Ne Setkya's soldiers with small gifts and favors since his arrival, and there was nothing Ne Setkya could do about it. To confront would show he knew the other man's mind, and that they were not in accord.

It was time for Ne Setkya to call in old favors and perhaps have Aung removed from Pagan, before the man could gain more influence and possibly get his hands on what had been confiscated today.

"What have you done, General? You look upset."

Ne Setkya looked up the Colonel, knew the thin man tried to undermine him again, and that his men all paused to see how their General would react.

"Upset? Hardly. I stop the foreigners from mischief is all. Potential damage to Thatbyinnyu."

"Thatbyinnyu pahto? I had heard of a strange machine used in Gawdawpalin, but no damage was done, I thought."

Ne Setkya swept up the stairs, motioned the men with the equipment to follow him, but saw the gleam in Aung's gaze as he eyed the computer, the strange structure of wires and metal.

"You confiscated their equipment." There was almost admiration in Aung's tone.

"What else? They defile the temples and go beyond their permits."

"Aah."

"Bring it."

Ne Setkya swept past the front office with its pall of Chinese cigarette smoke and stench of old curry, and down the hall to his office. He had the equipment set on his desk, then ordered everyone out. Saw Aung's resentment as he was left in the hall.

"Colonel." Aung swung to attention. "The foreign woman claims her Votaress puppet was taken in your raid last night. She says it was not returned. Please investigate with the men."

Aung looked momentarily surprised, but then nodded, even as his gaze slipped past to the equipment on Ne Setkya's desk. Ne Setkya closed the door in his face.

There was no question but that Aung was dangerous to Ne Setkya and everything he held dear. Keeping him busy dealing with the woman's puppet would be a boon. Ne Setkya flipped open the computer and the screen sprang to life, showing a foggy image of what must be the interior of Thatbyinnyu. The general recognized shadows and blank spaces on the screen that could be corridors and stairways at each outer corner.

If this machine could show these things, what would stop it from showing where some other open space existed? A place where something precious hid.

He went to the window, peered out at the hard glittering waves and the blue-checked sails of the fishermen. On the far shore, a normal scattering of bright cloth showed where women set their laundry to dry. Burmese culture, and at risk because of this device.

His people were peaceful. His people tried to live in rhythm with the world around them. But that would end if his government used such a machine.

Something must be done.

Aung had to be gotten rid of. The man had sharp eyes and a sharper mind. A naga mind that was intent on making Ne Setkya no better than the Galon bird. The search for the puppet would not keep him distracted long enough.

Sinking into his desk chair, he dialed the number of his patron in Yangon, General Bo Htin.

Long ago, when Ne Setkya was a new officer in the Myanmar army, then Colonel Bo Htin had taken a liking to the intelligent young soldier. He had taken Ne Setkya as his adjutant, and his career had risen as Bo Htin's had until finally Ne Setkya was given commands of his own.

Still, having that connection to one of the country's top generals was a safety net Ne Setkya did not often draw upon.

The phone buzzed in his ear. Buzzed again. Again. The phone lines in Myanmar were unreliable at best and the army had resisted the use of cell phones for sensitive military conversations. For all he knew, the lines could be down between Pagan and Yangon again.

Which would mean he would have to find another way to deal with Aung Aung. Perhaps one more permanent.

A click, and Ne Setkya's concerns were allayed when a young male voice filled the buzzing line.

"Offices of General Bo Htin."

No 'how may I help you'? No 'good afternoon'. No traditional 'Mingăla ba'. Simply stating a fact that the person at the other end could decide how to deal with.

"General Ne Setka calling for General Bo Htin." Keep it official. Keep it simple.

"Good afternoon, General. The General is busy right now. Would you like to call back later?"

"Tell the General I am calling. I will wait."

The line clicked and Ne Setkya stared at the foggy computer screen, then down at the keyboard. How to erase the whole thing, that was the question. He began jabbing keys, listening to the small beeps the computer made when he did something in error.

Finally, in frustration, he pressed his whole palm down on the keypad. Pressed. Used the side of his fist and banged down until suddenly the screen went dark. No lights flickered on the keyboard.

Maybe he had done it. Erased it. He flipped the screen down and yanked the wires loose, not caring if things broke. This would not be used again. Would not.

And where was General Bo Htin? The wait had stretched too long, as if Ne Setkya was not an almost-son to the grand old general.

Ne Setkya inhaled, exhaled and fought to steady himself. This was not like him, but there were too many pressures and he was no longer a young man. Truly it was time for his return to the temple and the peace he had had as a novice monk so many years before. He sent his tension forth on his breath. Heard the phone click and that smooth young voice again.

"General Bo Htin will speak with you General."

Was that a slight disapproval in the young man's tone. He could be imagining. He had to be.

Then the phone clicked once more.

"Ne Setkya, old friend, how are you? How does Pagan treat you?" General Bo Htin's gravelly, old man's voice boomed across the wires and Ne Setkya relaxed. Things were the same between them. His sense of strain in the adjutant's voice was all an illusion.

"I am well, Sir. I still find purpose in the plains of Pagan."

"Always were a homebody, weren't you, Ne Setkya? Frankly, I'm surprised you haven't gone back to the temple by now. I always thought that was where your heart was."

The comment gave him pause. Bo Htin had known of Ne Setkya's deep beliefs, but never had there been a doubt that he was a career officer. He had worked hard for that image and to maintain it.

"A strange thought, old friend. This uniform is like my skin."

"Aah. Good. That is what I wanted to believe, but after your son's death—well, I had heard the fire seemed to fade from your belly. I thought perhaps you needed time and assistance to regain yourself."

A cold wind blew through the window and right up Ne Setkya's back. This was a slight against his bamahsan chin. Yes, he had grieved for his son, but he had kept his men working.

"I thank you for your concerns. I believe I have kept operations running smoothly in Pagan. The loss of my son—a fine officer—was—difficult, but all life brings suffering, does it not?"

"I suppose it does—to those who cannot care for themselves."

Ne Setkya stared at the receiver. It did not sound like Bo Htin spoke of Buddhist practice as the means to deal with one's desires. "I am sorry to interrupt your busy day, but I wished to speak with you about another matter. The archaeological team here at Pagan."

Silence a moment on the phone, almost as if Bo Htin listened to another, and then: "Aah yes. The research team. American. A French-American interpreter and a Burmese father and daughter assisting. What of them?"

Perhaps it was just the adjutant providing information in the background, but Ne Setkya no longer had the sense that this was a private conversation between old friends. There was a strange hollowness to Bo Htin's voice, an echo on the line. Speaker phone?

Ne Setkya was no longer so sure he'd done the right thing by phoning.

"Did I pull you from a meeting, Sir? If so I am sorry to interrupt."

"It is fine that you called. There is a common interest in your fine work. That is why we sent our trusted Colonel Aung to assist you."

That rocked Ne Setkya back. He had known the man was sent, but that Bo Htin had been part of that decision....

The Old Man and the Generals no longer trusted the General of Pagan. They felt a spy was needed. The plastic phone receiver groaned in Ne Setkya's fist.

"He is a fine man and officer, it seems." His voice sounded calm, didn't it? No change in inflection. To say he did not want the Colonel here, to say the man was a problem would be a slight to Bo Htin. One did not make such comments and retain one's place in the military structure.

"There have been problems with the archaeological team. They have been exploring the ruins, and collecting old stories, yes, but there has been an incident today. One has brought a device to use in the temples." He would not tell them it allowed views through the bricks to the secret spaces within the pahtos. "It has upset the caretakers immensely. They say it offends the sanctity of the temples."

Again that humming silence. Then Bo Htin came on, his voice as jovial as ever. Too jovial, perhaps.

"For as long as I remember, you have played guardian to Pagan, old friend, and have kept the place safe. But perhaps the times are changing and deserve new methods.

"We thought so when we received the request to research the fall of Pagan. It would be good for the modern Myanmar government to aid the international search for a cure to the avian influenza. For that reason we modified the permit you prepared. Did you not notice?"

They had modified the permits?

The office was so cold he expected the Ayeyarawady might be frozen beyond his window. They had never modified his permits. His permits were his to write—to protect Pagan from the treasure seekers who would damage the ancient monuments.

But to admit he had not seen the changes would be to admit he had failed. He hauled a copy of the documents from the file in his desk. Scanned down, and found the deleted clause amongst the most standard wording.

"I know you have allowed all forms of research except for digging. I wished to check, because the foreign process threatens the delicate murals in some of the greatest sites. I thought perhaps to modify the permits; return them to their old form."

The chuckle on the phone was edged with steel. No friendly camaraderie here, and Ne Setkya suddenly felt his age, the settling of his muscles around his waist, the way his brain had slowed with the years. He would not have failed like this in the past. Perhaps it truly was time to retire.

But he could not allow men like Aung Aung to control Pagan.

"But I hear that is not an option. No matter then. It is the concern of an old soldier for the old ways. We will deal with these archaeologists in the spirit of modern Myanmar. Thank you for your time, General. Again, I apologize for interrupting so important an old friend."

"Aah, Ne Setkya. You are never a bother. But see that Colonel Aung is able to examine this equipment. It may be of use to glorious Myanmar, yes?"

"Again, my apologies, old friend. I do not have the equipment to give." It was a little lie. He would return the equipment immediately to make it true.

Silence and then: "I understood you confiscated the equipment."

The cold froze Ne Setkya's bones. He sought for an answer. Another lie because it was clear that his job, his life, everything that was important in the world, were at risk.

"I had sent it back with one of my men. Perhaps he has not delivered it. I will check, of course."

With that he eased the receiver back to the cradle. His hands shook when he released the plastic and his legs were too weak to stand, because he knew.

After a lifetime of deflecting his thieving military master's attention from Pagan, he could do so no longer.

Chapter 23 – Hell on Earth

It was all too much for Kalla. In the rumbling hulk of the jeep her head still throbbed from the argument that had raged between Alex and Simon from the moment the soldiers had left with Alex's machine. Her body was still tense from the way Simon had simply shut her down. The only reprieve had been when she and Simon drove back together, leaving Mei and Alex to their own jeep.

Not that that had been much better.

The drive had been strained; Simon's face dark with anger and something else, barely controlled. Rage. Despair. It was like he fought some great force the way he gripped the steering wheel so hard his fingers actually blued. Sweat beaded the edge of his hair.

"Are you alright?" she asked, not really wanting to break the silence.

"Je vais bien, et toi?"

Kalla parsed out the meaning using vaguely recalled high school French. "I'm fine. I could have dealt with the general, you know. I would have given him an out, if you'd given me a moment."

He glanced at her, and the dark consideration of his eyes brought a flush to her skin and a heat to her body she did not want. Regardless of the memory of his kiss.

"Perhaps," he said. "I could not be sure."

That set her back, because it hinted that he had not been trying to annoy her, but perhaps protect her. She realized perhaps she was just allowing her imagination to run wild when she attributed some nefarious motivation to him.

"Why'd you take off?"

No response. She sighed.

"I was worried, you know."

Another glance, this time with an intensity that made her think of finding a quiet spot hidden amongst the monuments. Of Simon's strong hands on her skin.

"Chérie, I think you fool yourself. You do not care for me. It is your work that concerns you. Your stories."

"No. I was worried about you." She felt silly trying to convince him she cared. She wasn't sure whether she did. "Heck, I'd worry about anyone, but I need you." Another flick of that dark, dangerous glance and she swallowed. Maybe she did care. Who else had she met that left her feeling hot and bothered like this?

"I mean, sure. I want my stories. Who else is going to translate?"

She looked front and centre out the windscreen, considering how Simon had still avoided telling where he had gone, why he had gone. He'd come back looking disheveled, with fresh, dark scabs on his knuckles. Was that blood on his collar?

But they'd said nothing more until they pulled into the parking lot of the Beautyland, and then Simon had climbed out and rejoined the fight with Alex.

And their words seemed to only make her headache worse, as if she still stood in the darkness of Thatbyinnyu, the pulse of Alex's machine booming through her feet, and the entire brick temple about to come down.

Like the entire world was about to cave in.

Maybe it had. Her Votaress was missing.

§

"Damn it, Renault, I need that machine. I have the permissions and that damned general friend of yours had no right to confiscate it."

Simon leaned his weary frame against the wall next to Mei's little kadaw pwe, his arms crossed over his chest. Let the man rant. It was no use trying to explain. Alex would not listen when he was like this.

At least here, closer to the offering bowl Mei had replenished this morning, Taungbyon's pressure seemed to ease a little.

"Well, what do you say?" Alex had stopped his pacing, faced Simon standing so close the Nat whirled at the invasion of Simon's personal space. Not good. Not good at all, given how he had spent his late morning.

He cracked his knuckles, and the scabs over his fists broke open and oozed. Mei and Kalla drank tea at the formica table, trying to ignore what went on between the two men. Khun was in Naung U trying to get a second set of ignition keys made to ensure what had happened today did not happen again.

"Answer me, damn it!" Alex's face was belligerent enough Simon could just wipe the expression off.

"I have tried to explain to you, but you repeat yourself five—ten—twenty times and it makes no difference. The ruins of Pagan have a special place in Burmese history. The Burmese do not like anything that damages that place."

"The damn permits don't forbid equipment like mine. Only excavations were excluded. I was fucking surprised when I saw the papers. I know past teams have been limited to documentation."

"It is odd. Perhaps the general does not agree with the permits. He seems to be—how do you say?—old school?"

"Old school or not, that's my equipment. It's delicate and I want it back. Now. So what are you going to do about it?"

"At this moment?" It took everything he had not to curl his fist, use it on this cocky upstart American.

Respect! Does he not realize he faces the greatest warrior Burma had ever known?

Simon wrestled the Nat back.

"At this moment I think I will drink a cup of tea with our female friends and try to forget how you harp at me. That way I will not do something foolish."

He eased himself past Alex, smelled the other man's rage like a heated cloud around him, and then settled into a chair beside Mei. At least with Mei he was safe. Safer than sitting next to Kalla.

She looked at him with wide blue eyes, but something simmered beneath the surface. Concern? Something more. Yes, there was enquiry there, a part of her wanting to know more of him. The Nat almost purred with pleasure except that Simon was reminded of the sound of a naga-tail rattling. Even across the table she was dangerous.

"You have recovered, Princess?"

When she stiffened, a part of him hated himself for goading her. Kalla was strong willed, yes. She was annoying and smart and lovely and full of life, and every one of those qualities had become more and more seductive to him as he had come to know her. No wonder he was having trouble with the Nat.

He was buying into the lust.

Mei poured him a cup of tea and he wrapped his palms around it, turned his attention on his friend. Considering all they had been through, she looked well. The shock that had so scared him the night of her attack was gone. But there was reservation about her when she looked at him. She even scooted her chair slightly sideways—to give him room or to put more space between herself and him? Her face told him it was probably the latter.

It hurt, because he knew what caused it and could never undo it. She would not meet his gaze.

"Mei," he began, and felt her freeze. "Thank you," he finished, feeling just a tad helpless. "I'm glad you are better after last night. You've been through so much."

At that her gaze did flicker to him and away.

"Kalla and I were just speaking of the challenge our work faces now. After this morning Kalla is concerned that Daw Ma Ma Nang may not welcome you back." Her uneasiness came through.

Kalla nodded, cradled her tea cup in her hands, her gaze narrowed on Simon. "You've done a good job avoiding the question so far, but what happened this morning? What was so important you had to run out of there like a demon was on your tail?"

From the frying pan to the fire. His father's old saying leapt to mind. He'd avoided Alex's rant only to face Kalla's inquisition, and with the full force of Kalla's, Mei's, and Alex's gazes upon him he would be hard pressed to avoid answering.

He followed Kalla's gaze to the broken skin, the scabs that had formed on his knuckles. Teeth could do that to skin. So could broken noses. Her blue gaze found his.

"Your hands were fine before."

The Nat's low, satisfied chuckle filled Simon's head as if Taungbyon dared him to reveal what had happened, how he had sought revenge for the attack on the women. He'd run from Kalla, and Taungbyon had swelled with rage at her loss.

Thorn brush and cacti and Htanaung trees and the ubiquitous red brick underfoot as he'd plunged away from the nun's home. Away from the perfumed neem, the brilliant bougainvillea and the life along the river and into the dry lands. Running. Past an old man and his oxen rising like dust from the dry fields, apparitions the wind would tear away. Running, past Thatbyinnyu and Ananda Pahtos and out along the road to the maze of smaller monuments.

Just get away. Get far from Kalla and her scent. But even here she filled his nostrils, his head. He stopped. Panting, sweat running down his face, the sun too blinding and the plain simmering like damned Hades, and he was trapped here.

As he should be. As he had been for most of his adult life.

But Kalla's sweet scent was on the air. And something more. Mei's fainter scent of frangipani and—male pheromones of sweat and power and the stench of toddy wine. Still here from last night, the logical part of him knew.

Mei's injured face. Kalla fighting alone in the dark, against two assailants. She would not have been able to hold them off for much longer. Even drunk there were two of them and only one of her.

Fury at the chance she had taken, at the men's actions.

So what if Taungbyon/Simon had almost done the same to Mei when Simon was first possessed. Taungbyon had been maddened by his years without a woman—not that that was any excuse. But there were other predators out there. In the years since his almost-assault on Mei he had learned control. These men—they had not. Were no more than animals.

The Nat's rage fueled his own as he turned like a turret, letting the wind carry the men's scent to him. There.

Taungbyon rose as a black cloud swirling. Simon held him back, held him back, and yet he was already running, loping across the dry fields of grass, towards Nyaung U. Towards the river. Predator seeking prey.

There. A dusty road that followed a dry canal bed towards the river. Five old monuments, no more than twenty feet tall, jabbed crumbling fingers against the sky like he would jab fists into attackers.

Was he not Taungbyon? Was he not the protector of Burma?

Simon slowed, inhaled the scent of the river and the teak logs running toward Yangon. The scent of men and toddy wine was stronger, and came from the monument closest to the point of land. He trod through the fallen debris, not caring if the sound of his footsteps carried. Not caring if his hair fell into his eyes.

There was only the scent of the men. The scent of their blood. The feel of *his* blood coursing through his veins.

He was alive. Here. More powerful than ever. With the choice of this strong one, Shwepyingyi Taungbyon had wed well.

And then he had been among the men. Three of them, surprised out of a drunken stupor by a demon's attack. Dark-visaged Taungbyon had come for revenge.

Simon barely controlled his shudder, and looked back at Kalla's waiting gaze.

The truth was, he had lost it. Had joined the spirit's rage and—mon Dieu—he had enjoyed it. Too much.

"I was overcome. Ill." That at least was right. He had to be careful lest Kalla see through a lie. He had no doubt she would. Somehow she knew how to read him too well. "I did not want to offend Daw Ma Ma Nang. So I ran to find a place to be sick."

Her gaze was back on his hands again. He put down the cup, flexed his fists.

"I fell. In the rubble. The bricks." He shrugged. Fell upon three men and left them bloodied and begging for forgiveness. "So what do we do now?"

Alex slid into a chair beside Kalla, his arms crossed belligerently. "You tell me? My work is stymied without that equipment. Kalla needs more stories. How're we going to fix that?"

It took everything Simon had to quell the Nat. Even though the assault had satiated the spirit's rage, Alex seemed to be able to bring it out again. Simon could not chance losing it. God knew what damage he might do.

"It seemed the General believes our papers do not allow such equipment. Perhaps we simply must approach him to point out his error." He glanced at the faces around him. Alex, at least, had relaxed some of his belligerence. That made it easier to control the uncoiling of the Nat.

"Well, why didn't you suggest something like that before? We can head over there now." Alex stood, clearly intending that Simon come with him to the military building immediately.

"Mei, feel free to correct me, but I am going to suggest that we delay the visit to the General at least for this day. Ne Setkya seems an honorable man. After that Colonel arrested us last night, it was Ne Setkya who released us. It was Ne Setkya who allowed Kalla to keep her puppet."

"But she's missing now. The General might have taken her himself."

"And now he knows you suspect something like that. He cannot afford an incident."

"That really is your Dad's old puppet?" Alex looked at Kalla. "I can hardly believe he'd let it out of his sight."

Her gaze darted at Simon and she colored slightly. So she hadn't quite told the truth of the puppet's ownership to the General.

"My family's puppet. It actually came from Mom's side of the family, but Dad…." She looked away as if it was hard to speak of it. "After she died, he thought it could provide a channel to help him communicate with her."

There was so much anger and hurt in her voice Simon knew she didn't want to talk about it further. "If Ne Setkya has erred—or taken the puppet—he will fix things, I believe. But to go immediately leaves him no space to be triumphant with his men. It will put him in a defensive position, and a man in Ne Setkya's position cannot afford that. He will hold the equipment—and the puppet—to save face, I think."

He caught Kalla's almost thankful glance. Mei nodded in agreement.

Alex swung to her, clearly not liking what he heard, and for Simon it was a double triumph. Mei, who had hardly spoken to him since he arrived in Burma, was actually agreeing with him.

"We would be better to allow him to decide to release the machine, Alex. At the earliest, we might approach him tomorrow, but I think perhaps we should allow him to bring the machine back to us. In the meantime I believe I have an answer to Kalla's problem." She looked at Kalla.

"My puppet?"

"No, your need for more stories. You have said that Daw Ma Ma Nang does not fully meet your needs."

Something about her words, and the way Mei glanced at him, caused a shimmer of concern up Simon's back, but he was more than happy to have the conversation change direction.

"That's true…. Her stories are so indirect." Kalla's reservations came through clearly.

"You do not like the smiling old nun?" he asked, and she colored the shade of new roses.

"But you do not wish to depend solely on one person's stories, correct?" Mei continued.

"It's better if you have numerous sources," Kalla agreed, ignoring him. "The commonalities of the stories tell you a great deal. I'd hoped to go out to some of the other villages in the area. Pagan is a big place. Daw Ma Ma Nang can't be the only elder with stories."

She brushed her hair back out of her eyes in a typical feminine gesture. "Frankly, I'd like to get back into Thatbyinnyu again, too. All those folk murals. Alex, I have a feeling there's something there. Photographing those could keep us busy until you get your equipment back."

"I thought you gave up ruins for folk tales."

"And I thought you remembered that people used pictures to tell stories far longer than they've used the written word."

Alex glanced at Kalla, but Mei's presence distracted him. He shrugged in the absent-minded way of the man-in-love so that Simon almost smiled. Alex Munroe may have met his match this time.

"But there is a better way." The intensity of Mei's voice turned everyone to her. There was excitement in her eyes, the pleasure that comes of knowing you can truly please another person. For Simon, it reminded him of a much younger Mei: one who had tagged behind Simon, copying what he did, so eager to please, so trusting—until he destroyed that trust.

"When I was in the market to purchase food for the kadaw pwe, an old woman told me that she and her son are going to a festival that will draw people together from all over this area. It is very large and very popular."

Simon stiffened, felt the Nat stir, the ghost of a chuckle. She could only be talking about one thing but, powers that be, please make him wrong.

"If we go there, you could talk to many people from all over Pagan and Burma. Gather your stories easily."

"No!" Simon sprang to his feet, barely controlling his shaking. "She speaks of Popa. The kadaw-pwe—the festival of the full moon. It is a wild place: no place for women."

The Nat burst its chains; cycloned in his head, tore his thoughts loose, Simon loose, and lost him in the cloud of the Nat's glittering presence. He was aware the others looked up at him expectantly. He was aware of Kalla's blue eyes. Wanted them. Recognized them.

Would have them!

"What's the problem, Renault? If it gets Kalla what she needs, it's what we should do. Besides, we've been hard at this. Maybe we should do as you suggest, take a day and let things cool down so the General can do the right thing."

No! The faces turned to him were already resolved. He could smell it on them, just as he could smell the lotus-scent of attraction between Alex and Mei. Smell Kalla's waiting apples-and-roses heat.

He had to get out of here. Could not go to Popa. Dared not go to the place where his dissolution began. He pushed his hands through his hair, trying to push back the Nat.

Useless. The others were nodding. Alex glanced his way.

"Too bad, buddy. Looks like you're outvoted. We'll head up to Popa tomorrow."

Chapter 24 - Popa

The feeling they had made the wrong decision rode Mei like an oxen's yoke. Many times through the night she'd regretted her suggestion. There'd been something wildly afraid in Simon's eyes. And the feeling of ill winds blowing had followed her this morning on the long bumpy jeep ride from Pagan towards Popa.

Though she had never been to a pwe, she knew they were wild. Still, there would be monks there, and elders who would remember the stories and share.

"We should have asked my father to drive us," she whispered to Kalla, who sat beside her in the back of the shuddering jeep.

Instead they'd left him to sort the storeroom and await the return of Alex's equipment. Simon could have done that.

"He looks like an angry monument." There was almost satisfaction in Kalla's whispered reply.

Simon sat hunched behind the jeep's wheel as they bounced across the potholes on the road to Mount Popa. Outside lay only the barren fields, the stands of toddy palm, and the farmers harvesting the last of the nectar that made the potent liquor. Much of their stock would already be at the festival, if Simon were to be believed.

He'd stormed out of the kitchen, his face almost black with rage. He hadn't even stopped for Kalla, though she'd tried to follow him, calm him.

And that was a new thing, that Kalla would try to help Simon. One that deserved watching.

But Simon had left anyway. The only surprise was that he had come back.

"Look." Mei pointed out the misty, blue bulk of Mount Popa. as the land began to rise, the air clearing of Pagan's dust. The hills beyond the fields were covered with forest.

"I can't believe how different it is here." Kalla said.

"There's not so much dust, and you can feel the moisture." Mei rubbed her arms as she stared out at the forest that covered the flanks of the mountain.

Kalla's pleasure was clear. "Pagan—it seems like an old museum, filled with dead things, but here the world seems alive again."

Simon snorted from the front seat. "You will think 'too alive' after you see Popa."

"Simon, would you just stop? I've been to Mardi Gras in New Orleans and to festivals in Thailand. People drink and get rowdy. So what? The old folks won't, and they're the ones I want to talk with."

Mei saw Simon glance at Kalla in the rearview mirror. He held there just a moment too long and the glance sent a shiver up Mei's back. The eyes were the same as those that haunted her nightmares—black and greedy. She looked away, but knew Simon was aware. Or whatever it was that looked out of Simon's eyes.

Something was wrong. Horribly wrong, and had been since the decision was made. The Simon that had come from his room before dawn this morning had brooded over his breakfast, his gaze rarely leaving Kalla. She had seemed at first unaware of the regard, but then a slow flush of color had risen up her neck and face. She'd avoided Simon. Had stayed close to Mei.

Alex turned back in his seat and smiled.

"You okay?"

"I am well." His attention was a relief but she still had to force a smile.

Things were wrong enough that this morning she had gone to the dining room and pleaded with great Min Mahagiri to intercede, to heal things, but the House nat had seen fit to do nothing.

Mei's fault. She had wasted the nat's power by asking for and receiving a great gift—Alex's love.

But the disaster was coming. She knew it every time she looked at Simon's face.

Coming soon.

§

Kalla tried to ignore the affectionate exchange between Mei and Alex and stared out the window.

Popa rose like a blue god out of the haze of forested countryside. It was like the forests flowed in waves out from the mountain, and perhaps it was so.

"If I recall my geography correctly, the mountain creates a cooler microclimate than the rest of Burma's central plain."

Mei broke her eye contact with Alex. "Is that why you do not wear your longyi today?" She motioned at Kalla's jeans.

"Exactly. Though at the moment I'm sort of regretting it." She fanned herself in the muggy closeness of the jeep. Opening the windows wasn't much of a help because of the dust. "It looks like it's an extinct volcano." She motioned at the cloud-covered mountain-top, then caught a glimpse of Simon's face in the rearview mirror.

Simon was the volcano now. Not so extinct, either, judging by his face. The danger she'd sensed in him before was barely covered with a veneer of civility.

She chose to ignore him, leaned forward to peer between Simon and Alex. "With all this life, it's hard to imagine I thought of ghosts when I drove through this area the first time. The ghosts are all in Pagan." She said it with a haunted laugh and caught Simon's glare. Ghosts hung in Simon's eyes, too.

She yanked her gaze away.

"At least we'll get the stories I need. We can finish our job and I can head home." She paused, looked at Alex. "Sorry, but I'm worried about my Dad. I was awake all last night with this feeling something's gone wrong."

"You're sounding like your Dad. Next you'll be telling me you're dialing the psychic hot-line or something," Alex teased.

"Shoot me if I do. Those darned charlatans have bilked enough money out of the Jervis family." She heard the acid in her words. So, apparently did Alex.

"He loved your Mom, Kalla. You can understand that."

Kalla closed her eyes, bit her lip.

"Sure. He loved *her*." And she was going to disappoint him one more time because she couldn't even reconcile with Alex. "The sooner I get home the better."

"He'll be okay, Kalla." There was a gentleness in Alex's voice she hadn't had turned on her before.

"Thanks."

She was so hot she took a chance and rolled down the window to stare out at the increasing number of farms as they neared Popa. The wind carried the heady scent of ox manure, sweet toddy, and flowers. Bright lines of freshly washed clothing flapped in the breeze. Children played around the houses. There were gardens of lilies here, and bright banks of bougainvillea. More as they drove into Kyaukpadaung. Purple flowers weighed down the fronts of buildings. Scarlet flame trees bloomed overhead.

Life. She hadn't realized she was so thirsty for it. So why was she so uneasy?

At the crossroads she almost expected to see the general's roadblock, but there was only one jeep, two soldiers lounging in the cab drinking tea from a small tea stall. Handsome people in longyi carried babies and bundles with the air of festival-goers as they walked the long straight road that led to the mountain.

Almost there. Anticipation had her leaning forward, gripping the back of Alex's seat. The trouble was she wasn't sure if it was eagerness or dread that thrummed in her belly.

"So tell us about the festival, Simon. You obviously know something about it."

If anything, his scabbed knuckles turned whiter on the steering wheel. He stayed silent as he eased the jeep into the stream of people and crowded vehicles heading for the mountain. The small pickups that doubled as local buses overflowed with men seated cross-legged on the jury-rigged roofs, while the women were crammed inside.

"It is an old festival, one that dates back to before Pagan. At that time thousands of animals were sacrificed to the Nats, but King Anawrahta stopped that. UnBuddhist, n'est-ce pas?"

"Un- a lot of things, if you ask me," Alex muttered.

"It is not like western festivals. Or perhaps it is like festivals were in the west very long ago. The spring rites, and so on. It is a celebration of the thirty-seven great nats. They were numbered by the King generations ago. There are, of course, hundreds of nats, and over time some of the nats transform and change, but there have only been 37 recognized as the great nats. Of course there are others that are important as well. Great warriors, mostly."

His tone was surprisingly bitter. The fact he knew so much about the nat belief was surprising as well. Her interest in knowing more about the place warred with her total rejection of all things involving the spirit world. "How do you know all this?"

He was silent again. "I came here as a young man."

Kalla felt his glance through the rearview mirror and wondered what had brought him here, but he held that story to himself.

"Popa means flower. In ancient times this mountain was covered in blooming trees. It has changed over the years, though it is still very beautiful."

The wistfulness of Simon's voice sent a shiver up Kalla's back. He was the strangest, most troubling man she'd ever met. And he drew her like crazy.

She jerked back in her seat.

You are not following through on this, woman. Not. The last thing you need is another failed relationship, and what else can happen when you hook up with a bad boy? Things fall apart.

"You sound like you were there, Simon—in ancient times. And regret them?"

Her little dig hit home and he actually winced, which was something for Mr. always-on-the-offensive Simon Renault. But he continued on.

"Much history has taken place here. It was believed that beautiful ogresses lived on the blossoms of the mountain. King Anawrahta formed an army here when he was seeking to regain his throne from a usurper. It is also the birthplace of Burma's greatest warriors—the children of a great warrior and a mountain ogress—who will defend Burma until the ends of time."

Silence again, as if he had to decide what to share. Then.

"The festival is three days, one day before the full moon, the day of the full moon, and the day après—after—the full moon. It is a time of pranks and small thieving and rowdiness. That is the word, yes?"

His French accent had suddenly gone thick, as if he no longer paid attention to his English, and her little feeling of concern increased. She caught him looking at her again and she looked away from the hunger, glanced out the window and across a sloping valley to the mountain. Gasped.

"My God! Look at that! Look!" She almost leaned out the window at the sight.

Half way up the mountain's flank rose a single rock spire like a spike driven into the earth. Clouds wreathed its peak, but sunlight glinted golden where the cloud thinned. Something was built on the pinnacle peak and white roofs spiraled up the sides towards it.

"What is that?"

"Popa." Simon said it without a glance, his hands gripping the wheel as if he were afraid the jeep would try to take control. "Min Mahagiri, the King of the nats, lives atop that spire with Sister Golden Face and the others of the nats."

"Spirits, you mean. Nats are small, bothersome insects." If she kept up this banter then her own nerves wouldn't show, because the sight of the pillar and the discussion of 'spirits' just sent her stomach through a whole series of dips and rolls.

"They are nats in Burma, Kalla. And each year the nats of Burma return here for the festival. Correct, Simon?" Mei carried on the story, seemed to want to pull Kalla back from where she leaned on the door.

She sat back again and inhaled Simon's scent of musk and incense as the road rose up the mountain and curved in amongst the trees. Traffic slowed and vendors sold yellow-fleshed jack fruit and strawberries along the road. The air was thick with the sweet scent of fruit and the flash of bright bird wings.

"It's beautiful. Lovely." So why did the anxious thrumming increase in her belly? Energy. That was all. Being cooped in this car for a few hours and all this unpleasant discussion of spirits that were just too 'present' to these people.

Simon pulled over to the side of the road.

"We walk the rest of the way. It'll be gridlock beyond here, so if we want to be able to head home today, I'm parking here."

With that he climbed out of the jeep and joined the flow of people up the mountain, leaving the others to catch up.

"Darn it, Simon, slow down." Kalla pushed through the people and almost caught his arm, but stopped herself. She met his moody gaze, recognized the hunger there, and looked away.

"Listen, I know you didn't want to come today. I just wanted to say thanks." She felt lame as she said it.

More so when he simply walked away. Damn the man.

The crowd congealed into a long snake that coiled up the road and then turned to flow down amongst buildings that surrounded the base of the pinnacle. Kalla stopped beside Simon, the people flooding around them.

Tents and awnings were scattered down the mountain slopes among red-roofed buildings. Restaurants blared Burmese music. Other, more discordant, music echoed off the pinnacle and seemed to reach into Kalla's gut and pull. Her knees went weak with the stink of rotten fruit, alcohol, and marijuana. Amid the eddying flow of people, individuals spun and danced.

"It looks pretty wild, but I don't see any spirits." She said it to goad him and to convince herself, because this place left such a weird feeling in her gut she could almost believe some of the folk-nonsense Simon was telling her.

"It will get wilder." Simon's voice carried a low growl of promise that set Kalla's hackles on end.

Alex and Mei joined them, as a group of people pressed past.

"What the hell?" Alex nodded in the group's direction.

Men, Kalla thought. At least, the five o'clock shadow on the heavily rouged and mascara'd faces suggested it. But they wore sheer, silken shirts over longyi folded and tucked women's style - not knotted at the front as men wore.

"Nat Ka Daw - Spirit Wives," Simon muttered.

And then Kalla's academic training kicked in. Transvestitism and transsexuality were far more openly displayed in Southeast Asia. In Thailand, male corporate managers went to work as women. Articles in Bangkok newspapers celebrated the transsexual.

"In Southeast Asia, the cultural belief is that these people walk between the normal and the spirits—the nats." She let it sink in. "Oh my god. We're talking a festival that celebrates spirit possession, aren't we?"

Fear flared in her belly.

Simon's dark gaze turreted towards her and held. "Not just celebrates. I said the nats return to Popa. If they are to communicate, they must join with someone."

He was just too bloody serious, and all her years of having to look the other way while her father wasted his life finally got the better of her.

"You're telling me there really is spirit possession? That you believe in it?"

Again just that dark glare, and for a moment she thought she saw something move there in the depths and could almost believe. She suddenly didn't want his answer.

"Spirit worship is one of the oldest belief systems. We can still see vestiges of it in our Catholic beliefs in the holy spirit." She fell back on the platitudes she'd tried to hold onto when dealing with her father.

Downhill, the group of Spirit Wives disappeared into the crowd. She should have expected this kind of festival, if she'd only been thinking instead of reacting. In a tightly controlled culture like Myanmar's, there needed to be safety valves. Places for people to let off steam so that the rest of the time they could adhere to the strict moral standards of the culture.

 Karen L. Abrahamson

This type of festival provided a license to untie all the cords of civility. Simon was right. Things would get wilder. Drunker. More stoned.

And she thought she could get stories here.

Think again.

Chapter 25 – Old Stories and Hope

"They have gone to Popa."

Ne Setkya's office fan stuttered over his head, as if the news gave it pause. He stiffened in his chair, but maintained his smooth face. From beyond the office window came a wind off the river. The sails would be bright today and filled with light, but here in the office the reflections off the water were like spirits on the walls.

The news disquieted him. It was like a hungry ghost passed too near.

He gazed up at Khun; the little man also kept his face clear as he faced Ne Setkya's desk, but there was a decided belligerence in the little man's stance. They were of an age, Ne Setkya thought. Both remembered a time before the military wrenched control of Burma from a civilian government. Both had raised families during the hard times.

The difference was that Khun still had his child, while Khun's people had killed Ne Setkya's son. He hardened his heart to the Kayin man, even though there was little likelihood Khun had had a part in the young soldier's death. He would think of Khun as a tool—no more. Not a father who worried for his child.

"What purpose?" It came out as an order, and the stout Kayin-Burmese frowned as if he did not understand the question. As if he would make Ne Setkya work for every word he spoke.

Ne Setkya flexed his jaw and inhaled deeply. Matters were becoming out of control. General Bo Htin's duplicity. Colonel Aung's increasing disregard for Ne Setkya's command. Researchers who conducted research he had always forbidden in the past. If they had used that damnable machine beyond Gawdawpalin and Thatbyinnyu, what would they have found?

The room was cold as he turned his gaze on Khun. "There are all manner of things that may happen to a young woman at Popa, U Khun. Even a young woman amongst friends. We must work together if she is to be safe, correct?"

The man's stubborn features folded, all Burmese composure lost. The girl was the child of his heart, just as Maung had been to Ne Setkya. For a moment Ne Setkya regretted the not-so-veiled threat.

"They go for stories. The foreign woman needs stories, she says. I wished my daughter to stay with me, but Alex would not have it, nor would he have her travel only with Renault after his disappearance yesterday."

Ne Setkya pondered the unwelcome news. How was he to keep these foreigners safe if they continued to do foolish things? He looked back at Khun.

"Your Ms. Jervis has accused my men of theft of her puppet. My men have checked their vehicles and the doll is not to be found. I suggest it is most likely that one of your number has stolen it. Do you wish me to enter a full investigation?"

Khun's hurried nod was what Ne Setkya wished to see. "Good. I suggest your group investigate. Perhaps speak to Mr. Hue or his staff."

A knock at the office door interrupted.

He had asked not to be bothered, but the door pushed open to reveal Colonel Aung. The man stepped smartly into the room, snapped off a salute that just barely escaped insolent.

"Sir. A patrol has brought in three men, badly beaten. They were found in the ruins near the river. They are drunk, but they claim that they were attacked by a—nat." The last came out with a smirk.

What did Aung think Ne Setkya was? A fool?

"You interrupt me for this? I expressly told my guard I was not to be interrupted."

"I felt you might wish to know, Sir. The men admit to the attack on the two research team women. They claim that mighty Taungbyon walks the world again. That he fell upon them for their wicked ways and warned them of destruction if they attacked women again."

"An interesting means of obtaining an admission of guilt." Ne Setkya looked back at Khun.

His face was a mask, but there had been a small intake of breath at Colonel Aung's news. Had Aung caught it? Possibly not, because the Colonel bowed slightly, turned to the door.

"Colonel."

Aung stopped.

"Send in the guard. I am finished with this man."

When he was alone, Ne Setkya went to his window, breathed in the moist air. The sky carried a pall of dust lifted from the dry plain that settled on the back of his tongue. Dry leaves rattled in the wind.

Tales said that once Pagan had been a garden, a paradise that had allowed a great civilization. But the great King Anawrahta had sown the seeds of Pagan's destruction even as he led the country into one of the greatness civilizations Burma had ever known. Destruction that Ne Setkya's alchemist ancestors had warned of and had tried to guard against.

But too late and now, with the death of his son, Ne Setkya's line was ending.

He considered the Kayin's news. The research team gone to Popa.

Home of the nats. Last bastion of their power. He thought of the woman, thought of the man, and of the news Aung had brought.

Disturbing news. Perhaps hopeful? Could Taungbyon walk this world again?

A gust of heated wind set him shivering.

During the Festival of Lights there would be more than stories afoot in Popa.

Of that he was sure.

§

Apples and roses. Even over the scent of marijuana, of alcohol and heated bodies, Simon scented Kalla.

She and the others followed him through the crowds, flesh brushed against him as if sensing the Nat that walked as a man. Wild music wailed, up, up through octaves unnatural to the western ear.

But to Taungbyon it was a call to come forth. To dance. To live.

The Nat struggled in the strangle-hold Simon kept on his brain. Burning black smoke. Black sparks of power.

It was almost too much, and Simon *had to* keep control. There was no choice. What would he do in this place if the Nat took control? What he had done in Pagan was disastrous enough.

Simon flexed his fingers, the satisfying impact of his fists against flesh still clear in his head. The cries. The begging. If Simon hadn't managed to wrestle back control while the Nat was busy gloating, he might have killed those men.

But I did not.

Taungbyon's booming thought staggered Simon. The Nat's power had grown. How could Simon possibly control the thing like this?

You will not.

It's this damnable place. It was how you took me in the first place. He'd come for the festival, flushed with the successful defense of his doctoral dissertation and an offer of a post-doctoral fellowship at the Sorbonne. He'd thought it would be fun, had partaken of the pot and the toddy wine and reveled with the villagers.

But the drugs and wine had opened him, just as they did for the villagers. At the time he'd thought it was just a chance to cut loose. To go wild after all the focused hard work.

I came to you and set you dancing. Why would I leave one so suited to my needs?

And Taungbyon hadn't. Not even when Simon sobered up.

"Et maintenant nous retournons où tout a commence," he muttered. And now we return to the place it began. The Nat coiled around him, echoing his words. "Damn you."

"Pardon me?" Kalla had come up next to him. He had stopped at the side of the large open area where most of the crowd was focused. A pair of huge, white, elephant statues guarded the entrance to the stairs that snaked to the peak of Popa. Most of the crowd streamed that way to pay their respects to the King of Nats before the party truly began. Taungbyon urged such action, but that was about the last thing on Simon's mind.

Apples and roses. Crisp and soft.

"I said nothing. The crowd—it will only get worse."

Kalla glanced around her, her blue eyes unnaturally vivid in her Asian features. What was it about her eyes that seemed to haunt him even when she wasn't around? Strength and vulnerability.

"Is there any quieter place we could go? There's no way I'll get stories here."

"There are the monasteries. They are scattered down the mountainside. Many of the pilgrims to the festival take rooms at them. We might find a person taking refuge from the noise."

"Then that'd be a place to start." She looked up at him and little lines around her eyes said she was fighting a headache again. "Are you alright?"

Her concern surprised him.

"Why do you ask?"

"Because you didn't want to come here. Because you've been quiet since we arrived."

Her awareness surprised him and set the Nat struggling against its bonds. Apples and roses. *He would bury his face in her hair, taste her breasts.*

He groaned inwardly.

"I am fine." He pivoted away. Perhaps among the monasteries it would not be so bad. There would be quiet. The music would not incite the nat.

Perhaps all would be well.

Perhaps by returning to Popa he could rid himself of the Nat. He held to that thought, ignoring Taungbyon's wild laughter. If he could force the Nat to chose another to dance, perhaps his possession would be over.

Almost forgotten hope swelled in Simon's chest. Perhaps such a thing was possible. He shook his head as he led them down among the monasteries with their round windows and egg-shaped images of the nats.

He'd had hope before.

Chapter 26 – In Their Flesh

There was something seriously wrong with Simon. His flesh was hot enough Kalla had felt him even when she stood apart. The scent of heated copper and incense had seemed to ooze from his flesh.

And his scent, his presence, set a part of her humming. Something deep in the secret places of her body could have rubbed herself against him like a cat.

It was why she had asked Mei to translate for her.

In the red-sided monastery with the strange Humpty-Dumpty-shaped statues that guarded the stairs and entryways, she faced the old monk Simon had found. The air smelled of frangipani and incense and the sunlight shimmered on the branches of the trees and on the swept earth of the monastery compound. Young, ochre-clad, novice monks looked at Kalla and friends strangely, and then laughed and ran away.

"Kalla, are you alright?"

Mei looked at her, concerned, and she found a feeble smile. "Sure, just watching the kids."

She nodded at the shaven-headed novices, playing just beyond the monastery gate. Their looks had suggested she was kidding herself thinking she could find what she needed here—or had overlooked something so obvious even the children knew.

She rubbed her hands together. "Just give me stories."

They sat in one of the open cells that lined the rear of the courtyard. Mei had told her it was a resting place for pilgrims, but to Kalla it just looked like a barren room. No bed, no blankets. Not even water unless that was what was in the clay pot by the open door. Across from her the old monk sat, cross-legged, his russet robes smoothed over boney knees, his betel-stained lips and teeth looking vaguely vampiric as he sipped the tea he had brought for them.

If this cell was where the visiting monk stayed, then he simply lay down on the hard ground and pulled his robes around him. These people lived far more simply than she could imagine.

She adjusted her cross-legged position as strains of the festival music ran fingers down her spine. In the courtyard sparrows fluttered among the leaves. Alex and Simon had gone to get food as both a gift to the monk and for themselves. They shouldn't be long.

Which meant that she should get on with this interview. She turned back to the monk who sipped his tea, his gaze turned inwards as if he drew the old stories from some great depths.

"Mei, perhaps you can ask if we can begin."

Mei spoke to the monk and he smiled, nattered back, his voice like raspy sandpaper. Grinning, Mei turned to Kalla.

"He reminds us of the custom we have in Burma when a person sneezes. We say 'May you live more than a hundred years, and may you be free of all diseases.' He believes it speaks to times long ago when sneezes and diseases were thought to be caused by evil spirits."

The old man nodded, smiled. Nodded more as Kalla noted the comment and smiled encouragingly. This was more like it. A bit of information that actually had to do with disease, even if the mention of spirits was not what she needed right now.

The old man began to speak, his voice counterpoint to the strains of wild music that seemed to build in strength beyond the courtyard walls. The scent of marijuana teased her nostrils. The crowds must be overflowing down the mountainside now.

Mei's voice became a light, insistent after-beat to the old man's. *"Once there was an old woman who lived with her son and daughter-in-law. The old woman was very happy to be with her son. She was proud of him, but after the marriage it did not take long for her to realize her daughter-in-law hated her.*

The daughter-in-law claimed the old woman was a burden. She ate too much of their food and took too much space in their home. She was too old to be much aid in the fields or in the house. So the daughter-in-law told her husband to take the mother into the forest and tie her to a tree so she could be eaten by tigers. They would tell everyone that the old woman died of disease.

The son was so in love with his wife, that he did as he was bid. He tied his mother to a Yamani tree, deep in the woods. His mother was old. She would die soon anyway. So the old woman waited to die.

In the night the tigers came and they were large and hungry and had sharp teeth and claws. The old woman shook with fear, but she also apologized to the tree, saying she was very sorry that there would be blood and marks on the smooth, white bark.

The taw-saun—the tree spirit—heard the old woman and took pity on her. He tickled the old woman's nose so she sneezed, Achoo, Achoo, and frightened the tigers away.

The taw-saun was so delighted with her care of his tree that he set the old woman free and left her a great pot of gold for her goodness.

Kalla scribbled furiously, trying to keep up with the words, trying to stay focused when the story seemed to get into her blood so that she could almost see the old woman, smell the tiger-musk, feel the fear, and hear the tinkling of bells around the taw-saun's ankles. There were questions she needed to ask, but they were lost in the need to hear, to record, and to consider the presence of a spirit in the story.

When the old woman returned to the town, the daughter-in-law was jealous of the old woman's wealth. The daughter-in-law had her husband take her into the woods and tie her to the same tree.

In the night the tigers came for her, but the daughter-in-law had concerns only for her own safety. Still, she sneezed as the old woman had, and frightened the tigers away. The tree spirit, though, saw through the woman's greed and made sure she became very sick with the disease she had pretended to have. When she went back to her husband's house, he too was taken ill in the flesh, as were all who lived as they did.

The ending of the monk's story left a silence that was filled by dove-call and the swelling music that had seemed to weasel its way into the story until the taw-saun, the dying people's wails were swallowed in the wild tones. As if the music helped tell the tale.

Kalla considered what she had. The shadows had shifted so that sunlight now fell over her shoulder to light her notes.

"This is the most graphic story I've heard so far and the only one that truly speaks of disease. Clearly it's a teaching tale, but is it a folk tale—something made up long ago? Or is it a folk-legend—something based on facts?"

Mei translated the question and the old monk only laughed and shrugged.

"He says it is a teaching tale. Beyond that, he cannot say—except it is a very old story."

Kalla tapped her lips as she considered. "A forest spirit gives gold in thanks for caring for his tree. Not too likely. A king might have gold to give. Inferior gold, of course, because pure gold was kept for royalty, but gold. So not a legend."

Mei remained silent.

"So what is the story telling us? Why was it necessary as a teaching story? Don't mess with spirits?"

Mei translated Kalla's rhetorical question, but the old monk answered.

"Perhaps it is the importance of kindness, even to spirits?"

Kalla hid her first response, which was to roll her eyes. A sound behind her turned them all towards the gate.

Alex stood at the courtyard gate, his fair hair tousled, his clothes sweat-stained and in disarray. He scanned the courtyard and swore softly, the look on his face sending a chill up Kalla's back.

"Alex, to swear here could offend the nats, and you do not want them against you!" The real fear in Mei's voice surprised Kalla. Could this city woman still believe in such things? Were these old stories still in some way real?

"Fine. I'll just think it, then. Have you seen Simon? I lost him in this madhouse forty-five minutes ago."

Chapter 27 – Music and Blood

The heat. The florid scents of marijuana and incense and lotus. Music wild as Simon's pulse, wailed in his head and pounded in his veins. Bodies boiling with the copper of their blood, with their need to break free, to be.

Human.

MORE THAN HUMAN!

Taungbyon's voice crashed through Simon's defenses. Brought a groan to his lips as he staggered against an old man in the crowd.

"Kàunbadhǎlà?" Are you well, the old man asked.

"Nei Kàunbade." I am well. So growled Taungbyon, who controlled his tongue.

Simon shook his head. Shook his head again. And tried to turn away. Get back to the monastery and he might be safe. Alex and Mei and Kalla would help. He'd been a fool to think anything good could come from this place. That he could rid himself of Taungbyon unless the Nat wanted to leave.

Ahead, the crowd had formed a circle around a band of Nat Ka Daw and their musicians. The main Spirit Wife stood in the centre of the circle, a microphone in his hands, his diaphanous clothing and his long hair lifting in the mountain breeze. His face was painted like a Parisian whore and the Nat stirred, stretched, and growled its disgust.

Not Nat Ka Daw of Taungbyon. Farce. Charlatan. Shwepyingyi, of the Taungbyon brothers, knows who he possesses. That one is here!

Darkness cycloned in Simon's head. Fury and despair. Lust and devotion. Rage and compassion. And yearning. The pain of long yearning.

Him? Taungbyon? He could no longer tell the difference. The swell of emotion tore Simon's controls, threatened to overwhelm as he reached the edge of the Nat Ka Daw's circle.

Not him!

Not what Simon desired. He had fought for so long to regain himself.

Not enough. The music demanded him. The heat and the incense insisted. The moon pressed him forward, even in daylight. God help him if he was here after dark when the real dancing, the real possessions began.

The Nat Ka Daw fluttered his hands over his face, harangued the audience for offerings and money, and lifted his scarves even as the music rose. Wailing from the hne flutes, pounding from the metal pattala and the circle of brass kyaynaung gongs.

Not this. Not this.

The beat of it pained him. The scent of copper blood, the heat, the pillar of Popa—a giant phallus in the sky—all conspired against him. Hard won barriers collapsed. Blackness flooded through.

Too late.

Never soon enough.

The Nat swept over him like a monsoon wind. It raised his hair off his neck, arched his neck back.

Pain. Loss.

A low moan escaped. This could not happen. He would not let it happen!

The moan changed to words, changed to triumph.

Simon leapt into the centre of the open circle. Crouched, he growled at the charlatan Nat Ka Daw.

No! Simon tore at the Nat, fought for control. His body was his!

The Nat Ka Daw fell back as the great Shwepyingyi Taungbyon rose up, staggered once, and then paced the edge of the audience in a prize fighter's stance.

"LET NO ONE QUESTION WHO I AM!"

Wind rose around Simon, tore at his clothing as he clung to his body, clung to the force that filled him, that seduced him to give up— become one with the Nat. The blackness enveloped him and was not the cold dark he feared.

Instead, it was a swarm of colors. Red and blue. Yellow and green that ran against his face, into his eyes, his ears, his mouth. Color like a fire in the belly. Heat like a forge—the furnace of the King of the Nats—Min Mahagiri who resided on Popa.

Simon jerked once. *Choose!* the Nat demanded.

Twice. *Me and be strong. A god. You and only man. Weak. Those are the choices.*

Three times. Swept away on the force of it as Taungbyon asserted control.

Simon/Taungbyon drew himself up. Taller than the mountain. The puny Nat Ka Daw passed him a bottle and Simon/Taungbyon threw back his head. Drank deep of the bitter toddy wine.

It burned down his throat and he leapt at the crowd. They leapt back, screaming in delight.

Another long pull and the music filled him. The rhythm caught him, pulsed in his blood, and he lifted his feet in the slow, ancient dance.

The music. Stomp.

The wine. Stomp.

Burning blood, and there was no option but the power.

He was no coward. He was Simon.

Stomp.

And whatever Simon had become.

Chapter 28 – Red Vision

"What do you mean he's disappeared?" Kalla leapt up, thanked the old monk and rushed to Alex. "What happened?"

"Like I said. We went out to the restaurants, but the lineups were gawdawful. I went to check out another place, but when I came back Simon wasn't there. I thought maybe he'd gone to check on one of the stalls along the road—we'd talked about it—but he never came back. I've been searching since then."

Alex shook his head like he always had when he was disgusted by something someone had done. He'd never had any better tolerance than she had for other people's foolishness. It was one of the few things they had had in common.

"I should have known better. He wasn't right from the start. I should never have asked him to help with this project, but who else knows Burma and could translate as well? The damn country's been almost closed for years."

Kalla looked at Mei, knew they shared the same look of concern for Simon, but Mei was actually shaking, her eyes filled with tears.

"No!" she whispered. "Min Mahagiri, no."

"Mei? What is it?" Kalla caught her shoulders and felt the younger woman's shudders.

"It is my fault. I brought on this disaster."

"Just because you thought to come here, doesn't make this your fault. This place isn't that big. We'll find him." Then the episode at Daw Ma Ma Nang's came to mind and she whirled to Alex. "Oh god, is the jeep still there? Did you check?"

"No I didn't check. I came back here to make sure that you were okay. Simon Renault can take care of himself." That head-shake again, but he caught Mei's hand. "Everything's fine, Mei. I was worried something might have happened to you."

Alex's solicitousness of Mei was starting to grate on Kalla's nerves.

"We're perfectly fine. Our friendly monk told us stories. Finally one about sickness. I think we did the right thing coming here, but I need more time."

"Then I'll leave you two and keep looking. The damned man has got to be somewhere."

Kalla looked longingly back at the monk, but knew continuing the stories was not an option.

"You're right that Simon hasn't been right. He's been difficult other times, but today something was wrong. It was like he wasn't well—a fever of something. He didn't want to come here. It was like he knew something was going to happen." The wail of the festival music cut through their conversation.

"It is my fault. I asked the nats for a gift. Now they ask for their payment."

Mei's words sent cold shafting through Kalla. All the little hairs on the back of her neck stood on end. Mei's face was deadly serious—ridiculously serious, given what she had said.

"Come on Mei. You don't believe in ghosts." Kalla closed her eyes. If everyone had been dreading this trip, then why the heck were they here?

Because of you, Princess. Simon's words, his taunting name for her caused a frisson of shame to run through her. Because she needed stories, people had set aside their feelings.

Somehow she'd taken control to get what she wanted. She'd come here to Burma, left an ill father behind without his most precious possession so she could reclaim a past love.

"It's my fault we're here, Mei. Mine. I'm the one who wanted to get the stories as quickly as possible."

Like that had worked.

Maybe what Simon had said was true. All his taunts. Maybe she was just fooling herself about being in control. "We better go find him. We're a team. We don't let anyone get lost. I can get the stories later."

Hitching her notebook bag onto her shoulder, she started out the gate, Alex and Mei coming behind.

"Kalla, I'm not sure this is the best course. It's wild out there—you saw. And it's only gotten wilder in the couple of hours you've been here. It's not a good place for a woman."

She looked up at him, saw his concern, and knew that once he might have looked at her that way. Not now.

"Keep Mei with you. You know I'm pretty good at taking care of myself. We'll meet back here in an hour."

Then she ducked out of the gate, past the grinning Humpty-Dumpty figures, hoping like heck Simon was okay and they could put things back together again.

Alex hadn't lied. The press of people had spread down the mountainside and in among the eucalyptus and teak and tamarind that shaded the monasteries. Groups of men drank their Toddy wine. A man and woman kissed passionately in the shadows.

They'd probably be doing more than that before the festival was over. All the propriety of Burmese culture was coming unraveled. The crowds tried to push her away from the main area at the base of the pinnacle.

At the main open square Kalla stopped, caught a glimpse of Alex's copper hair, Mei close to his side as they went to check on the jeep. Good plan. She'd do a circuit of the grounds and then meet them there. In the meantime, Alex would keep Mei safe with his life. The guy was hooked, there was no question. Mei, with her quiet, considerate ways, was his choice, his match. Kalla had never stood a chance.

Well she couldn't control everything in life, but she could take control of the search for Simon Renault. She tugged her t-shirt down over her jeans. In this crowd she was beginning to regret her decision to wear the heavier trousers. Sweat ran down the backs of her knees and had formed a channel between her breasts.

The air reeked of pot and liquor and too many bodies, even though a breeze fanned the mountain slope. It was warm, brought up from the plains, so it wasn't as cool in Popa as she'd expected.

Another thing she'd been wrong about.

The discordant music wailed up octaves humans weren't supposed to hear. The festival musicians had taken the tonality of Asian music and turned it inside out, so it seemed to raw the skin—at least hers. It made the jostling crowd hard to bear.

She staggered in the current of humanity, and a man caught her arm, steadied her. He spoke to her in Burmese but all she could do was shake her head.

"I don't speak Burmese. Sorry."

She pushed on through the crowd, the marijuana so strong she was lightheaded. A part of her responded to the crowd's excitement, the music. No longer so raucous.

As if a part of her remembered.

Just remember what you're doing here. This isn't an exercise in studying a culture. This is a search for a missing man.

But it was easier to remain the observer, in control. Observe the effects of the place, the people, the noise, the drugs, on herself and those around her. Watch how they moved through the festival, circulating from musical group to musical group.

A flash of color caught her attention, an eddy in the crowd's flow. One of the Spirit Wives. What had Simon called them? Nat Ka Daw? The centers of the wildness that was unfolding. They would be possessed, would enjoin others to be claimed as well and that would lead to a wild debauchery such as these people rarely saw. She shivered.

The tide of people took her closer to one of those whirling spectacles. People were caught like waves against a shoal. Music blared, seemed to echo through a chamber in her head. A rough, raucous voice berated the crowd. Music reached higher, higher, until it was painful to hear. Around her dark bottles of sweet-scented toddy wine quenched thirsty throats.

It was hard to breathe in the press. Hard to think with the pot smoke cloying her nostrils, with the heat.

A single voice roared and someone leapt into the air in the half-glimpsed open area claimed by the Nat Ka Daw. A woman not far from Kalla staggered, pushed forward, and was yanked into the void. She moved woodenly, whirled as if someone turned her by the shoulders. A glimpse of shin as her longyi rode up, then the crowd closed around Kalla.

That voice. Her head throbbed.

Burmese spoken in a taunting tone.

Simon?

She craned up on her toes, but the sea of bodies blocked her. If it was Simon, what the heck was he doing?

She stopped, suddenly uncertain, but the press of bodies seemed to push her forward.

Did she really want to know? Did she really want to subject herself to his ridicule—because he *would* make her concern a joke?

She had to at least know he was alright. Then she could go back to her stories.

A new swell of music, and pain stabbed between her eyes. For a moment she went blind, but then darkness edged her vision like the start of the worst kind of migraine.

Her pulse pained her ears. Pained her worse as it seemed to join with the music, and set her innards trembling. Maybe she should go find Alex. Send him here to get Simon.

But that would show that she wasn't capable.

Another roar, and the crowd pushed back against Kalla. Voices, bodies, pressed around her but she couldn't move. She was held in place as the boundaries of the Nat Ka Daw's domain opened towards her like a spreading disease.

She should move back to safety. But the scientist in her wanted to see. And something else. Something that felt the pull of the music, that *liked* the pulse deep and low down in her body. That *yearned* for it.

A veil of red tinged her vision.

She shook her head against the strangeness that was more than being half-stoned on second-hand weed. More than the heat.

The crowd's shift suddenly left her at the edge of the open area, the open air cool against her face. The woman she had seen, four others, and the Nat Ka Daw all whirled in what was supposed to be spirit possession.

A shout and a seventh figure leapt at her from the edge of the crowd. She almost screamed, fell back against the man behind her as the huge, dark figure approached through the veil of red.

Simon.

And something dangerously not-Simon looking out from his eyes.

Chapter 29 – Screams and Whispers

Her.

Apples and roses and he had known she would come. Had smelled her through the crowd, had sent out his call and she had *answered.*

Simon/Taungbyon saw it in her eyes as he reached for her hand, dragged her into the open area. She would dance for him as he would dance for her.

But she resisted. Fought against his hold until her hair came loose from its pins at the back of her neck and cascaded around them both.

Curtain of night. It would shelter them together.

He released her and she rubbed her wrist, took a step away, but the crowd had closed behind her, and urged him on. Simon Taungbyon grabbed a bottle from the Nat Ka Daw, tasted. Rot gut. Not fit for this woman of apples and roses.

He roared at the crowd and was handed a bottle over the heads of the others. Tasted. Smooth and hot down his throat. Pulsing in his gut.

He pushed the bottle at her and she held her hands up to ward him off, still seeking a way to escape through the crowd.

Not this one. She would never escape, did not truly want to escape.

He saw it in her eyes, felt it in the heat pulse through her body.

"He gives you the good stuff! Drink!" Someone called in awkward English that sounded strange and out of place.

Her eyes finally came to rest on his face and he saw her strength and resolve as she held out her hand.

"Just one sip."

He handed her the bottle, but still kept it in his clasp, moved with her as she tipped the bottle for a sip. He tipped it further, so she gasped, choked, came up sputtering, and a part of him that was deeply Simon knew it was wrong. Knew he should not force liquor on her, knew what it would bring.

But another part, the powerful part that was Simon/Taungbyon rejoiced, felt the liquor course through and heat her. Cheeks like roses, lips damp and parted, and fury in her gaze.

"Drink." He ordered.

"Not on your life."

"Drink."

He dropped down into a dancer's stance, raised one foot and stomped.

The mountain trembled under foot and she started, aware of his power. Aware of him just as he was aware of her. *Apples and roses. The fall of long silken hair and memory of lips full and soft, like her skin would be soft, yielding under his hands.*

Music ululated upwards through octaves, through the air carrying Simon/Taungbyon's triumph to Min Mahagiri alive in his shrine. This time it would not be debauchery. This time it was her.

Her lips parted.

Kiss her.

Instead he pushed the bottle at her. She shook her head, but something wild filled her eyes. Something daring. She grabbed the bottle, raised it in salute, then drank long and deep before handing it back as she wiped her lips.

Full lips.

"You don't scare me, Simon Renault."

"Scaring is not what I had in mind, chérie." He barely managed to find the words. Caught her wrist and pulled her to him. "*It is time for this, non?*"

Apples and roses and fear and lust. A part of her knew what came and wanted it. A part of her buried so deep it was only glimpses, but Taungbyon had known since he saw her. Had waited and wanted an eternity of years.

He looked away from her eyes, black rimmed with blue. Roared at the crowd and drained the last of the liquor from the bottle, then dragged Kalla—that was her name now—into the crowd.

She still fought, twisting in his grasp as the people parted around him, called out encouragement, ribald suggestions. He needed none of them; he knew what he would do.

The forest.

Sunlight streamers through stands of tall teak, tamarind, and wild papaya. The scent of old leaves and new growth, the feel of earth underfoot, pulsing with life. With renewal. Long and long since he felt that renewal. Since he felt whole.

He dragged her into a glade on the mountainside and released her. She stood furious before him. "How dare you! You had no right!"

Simon/Taungbyon could almost laugh. "I brought you where you wished to go. There is no need for feigned anger. Not here. Not between us."

Words were difficult to form when it was sensation you desired. The feel of her in his arms. Her lips answering to his.

"I didn't ask you to bring me wherever this is."

"But your eyes put lie to your words."

"My eyes."

§

And it was truth. Even though Kalla narrowed her gaze at him, she knew it. Felt it like her heartbeat, like the beat of the music and the liquor in her veins.

She was meant to be here. Had wanted to be here since—when?—since the first time she had seen this dangerous man coalesce out of darkness? At least since his first kiss.

Dark and dangerous and openly desiring her, he stood above her, shaggy hair in his too-black eyes.

She should walk away because this was too dangerous and Simon Renault threatened everything she knew about herself. Control. That was what she was good at and this man—he brought a heat into her that said he was about anything *but* control.

"I should go."

He threw back his head and laughed so it echoed under the leaves, seemed to echo in her head as well.

"You cannot even lie to yourself."

She didn't appreciate being laughed at. Had never liked it.

Her fists curled and she swung at him, but he caught her wrist easily. One tug brought her next to him. Scent of musk and incense and dried leaves filled her head. Drunker than she thought.

Heady scent and the heat of him. Before she thought she was on her toes, kissing him, arms clasping his neck, his strong hands pulling her into him.

Hard muscled belly. Rough-cut silken hair. Hard lips that drank from her as demanding as she was of him.

His lips slid from her mouth, found her neck, her ear, and she arched herself for him. Felt him hum against her skin. Wild music that answered inside her.

A rhythm she would answer. Knew how to answer as the red stained her vision. Wanted to answer as his hands came up under her shirt to cup her breasts. Thumbs found her nipples through her bra. Taut with desire, she groaned, pressed into him.

"Simon."

"I am here." His voice thick.

She stepped back, her breath quick, her pulse ragged.

"You would stop now, Princess?" But this time it was not a taunt; it was a cherishing. Confusing.

She shook her head and stepped back another pace. Voices in her head made it hard to think. Hard to do anything but respond to this man, this creature, this desire.

She stripped her t-shirt up and over her head, stood, daring him, as she unclasped her bra, as she stepped out of her jeans.

It was inevitable, wasn't it? They would be together. The heat had been there since the beginning. Get it over with and she could get on with her research.

But the heat in his black eyes said it was more. Much more, as she stepped up to him, as she pulled his shirt-tails loose, ran her hands up over smooth skin and felt him shudder.

He pulled his shirt over his head, pulled her into him. Breasts against washboard stomach and he groaned as his palms cupped her buttocks, his fingers found the edge of her silken panties, sought inside.

Lips on hers again as his hands explored, his tongue tasted down her shoulder, down her breast to her nipple. She clung to his head as he bit, his fingers easing the silken fabric over her hips and down, down. She stepped free as he went to his knees, clever fingers at her cleft, seeking until she gasped, until they dipped inside her from behind even as his lips trailed over her navel and lower.

Found her.

She held on for dear life as he moved, couldn't stop the moan, the shudders that rode her, that brought a single cry from her throat. As he had her, readied her, lifted his head to peer at her from his mane of hair, from the darkness of his eyes.

He stood, stripped his jeans off and pulled her to him, against his length, and the red veil increased. Increased, and the pounding in her head was a demand for more. So much more as he half lifted her, and she parted her legs for him. Ran her moisture over him, wanting.

The head of him against her, parting. The swell of him inside her, pressing.

Deeper, and she didn't know if she could do this.

Deeper. He rammed her against a tree, wild eyed and wanting, needing something that had been too long coming, and she opened. Opened to him as he moved.

As he eased deeper, as he slammed into her, as he found her core. Beyond. Cried out. The world shimmered as they moved together, as she accepted him in. The red grew, shining over his skin, the trees, the sky.

She wanted. Oh god, she wanted. *Had hungered for so long for this. This man.*

Moving inside her as she plunged to meet him. Not enough, never enough. *Time. Years. Lifetimes.*

Suddenly he released her, pulled loose and set her on the ground, turned her so she braced against the tree, arched her back as he took her from behind.

Warm bark under hand. His hands on her hips, her breasts, his breath on her neck as he bit her, plunged into her, and she was wanting. More.

Of him.

More.

Of life.

More of the feel of the earth underfoot, of the tree under her palms, of his movement.

Movement. The crimson growing, filling her as the spasms started, as the thundering shudder shook her controls away. As he throbbed inside her as she went blind. *As she was falling.*

Falling through the chasm, women on either side, eyes flashing past, hands reaching, and the crimson grew in the chasm, was everything, and the votaress was dancing as Kalla slammed into her.

She screamed as he thrust one final time, his hands holding her hips to him, buried so deep she felt his release, released herself and her knees collapsed pulled them both down in a heap.

"Min Gyi!" she cried, naming him for who he was—long loved and lost.

"Min," he whispered, cradling her in his arms. And she knew he named her for herself.

Chapter 30 – Hard-edged Blue

"Damn it to hell, I should never have let her go off alone."

Alex held Mei's hand as he dragged her through the crowd. They'd waited for Kalla for two hours and then had gone looking. There'd been nothing to find.

No sign of Kalla amid the crowd, and that worried Mei, for Kalla Jervis was a woman who would do as she said. She always had as far as Mei knew. It was the woman's primary quality. Absolute control.

Which meant that something must have happened—and with the soldiers that had appeared on the mountain a few hours ago, Mei was even less certain.

"Perhaps she has gone back to the monastery by now."

"We checked there an hour ago. No, she's somewhere in this crowd. Probably got lost in documenting her observations if I know Kalla."

Mei looked up at Alex. His shirt was stained with sweat. Worry-shadows filled the corners of his eyes even in the half-light of dusk. But he was lying to himself, or perhaps to her to deal with the fear they both felt.

"Kalla is very focused on her research," she allowed. But the pwe—the festival—was a wild place. If a group of men had decided to take her…. She shivered at the thought. Most of these festivals were wild, but no one got hurt. Society might allow a little wildness, but not rape. Never rape.

"Perhaps the soldiers caught her. Perhaps she did something."

"That'd be like Kalla."

"You speak as if she's always causing trouble."

Alex shrugged as he scanned the crowd that milled between wires of multicolored lights and torches. Pilgrim's firelight dotted the hillsides and down into the fields below.

"Kalla has a knack for it. At least in our relationship. She wanted one thing and I wanted another. Always getting in each other's faces. She can take care of herself."

And she didn't need you, Mei realized. That was what had really ended their relationship. Alex wanted to be needed, just as Mei did. What he hadn't realized about Kalla was the loneliness Mei had seen in her. Kalla needed as well. She just hid it by taking control. Hid it from herself, as well.

"So what do we do?"

Alex shook his head and Mei followed his gaze to the sky. The full moon already sat like a fat man. The festival would continue as long as its light lit the sky. When it set people would drop where they were, to sleep, only to party even harder tomorrow when the moon was truly full.

Already in the shadows there were figures locked in embrace. Among the trees along the road, she saw movement that suggested more than that, and the air. The air itself seemed to reek of lust and letting go.

It was not a good place for her and Alex. It was not a good place for Kalla.

And it was most certainly not a good place for Simon Renault.

§

Fading sunlight sent fingers through the trees when Simon woke in a crushed bed of ferns and small, sweet flowers.

How long had they been here?

His hand rested on Kalla's hip.

Min's hip, the Nat corrected.

Her bare buttocks pressed against him in a most intimate way.

Seductive. Things to enjoy with a woman who rests thus.

He hardened as he ran his hand up over her lean side to the warm swell of her breast, her nipple still taut from their lovemaking. The scent of apples and roses and a faint hint of jasmine filled his nostrils and he knew he would carry that scent always. On his hands, in his head, no matter how much he bathed or time passed.

"Mine," he whispered and pulled her to him, kissed her neck and felt her respond. A small sigh escaped her lips.

He would turn her over and take her slow and easy as the night rose into the sky. He would see her skin turn silver in the moonlight, her eyes dark as the sea.

How many times had they'd made love this afternoon? The forest had filled with their cries of passion as they came together again and again.

They had walked together, found fruit to slake their thirst, then come together again.

"Merde." Where were their clothes?

Clothes are no consequence. We are gods among men. Can walk naked for all to see.

"In your dreams, maybe." Simon muttered the American saying.

He thought he remembered how to find the first clearing, but it was some distance away. They would never find it in the dark, and they had obviously been here for some time.

Some time. Taungbyon's satisfaction was like a contented cat. *This woman. Mine.*

Simon could agree with that. Kalla brought a peace to him. A satiation of the desire that usually beat in him even after a day such as today.

He sat up and stared down at her. Smooth skin. Wisps of dark hair he gently pushed back from her full mouth. He leaned down to kiss her, tasted himself on her lips, as her eyes flickered open.

Blue gaze through black lashes. Kalla, not the other. *Not Min.*

Simon smiled as the Nat roared his disapproval.

"Bonjour, Chérie. As-tu bien dormi?" He caught himself. "Have you slept well? It has been a most enjoyable day, n'est-ce pas?"

The gaze widened as she registered his bare chest. Suddenly filled with shock and she was on her feet, across the clearing, crouched down looking wildly at herself, and then at his nakedness.

"What the hell have you done, Renault?"

"Pardon?" She was playing games, surely. Had to remember the wild passion, the tenderness and desire. But her eyes said otherwise. Hard-edged blue of fear.

"Where the hell are my clothes?"

"Not here." He shrugged and saw her anger take hold over her fear. "I was going to wake you so we could reclaim them, Chérie. It would not do to walk into the festival au naturel."

She swiped at loose hair that fell around her face and stood, ignoring her nakedness. "You damn well better get me there, Renault. I don't know what you put in that liquor, but it's about the last thing I remember."

He stood, scanned her body in a fashion that let her know there was far more he remembered, and then enjoyed the color that flooded up her shoulders to her face.

"Aah, but I think you do recall, ma petite. We did many things this afternoon."

She shook her head. "Not me. Not by choice."

"You are about to tell me you would not do such a thing, be so wild."

He stepped up to her, caught her head in his palms, and planted a slow, passionate kiss on her lips. Her body yielded to him, trembled and almost sagged as he stepped away. Taungbyon raged to take her again, but Simon would not.

We gentle this one, my friend. Not by force.

The great nat acquiesced for once.

Those blue eyes were on his face.

"You see, ma chérie, there are things your body remembers and wants more of."

But she shook her head, her hair flowing over her shoulders to give only sexy glimpses of a shoulder, a breast, the roundness of a buttock. "Try anything and I'll—I'll...."

"What? Scream? Beat me up?" He knew he should quit taunting her, but somehow it was so easy, so wonderful to see the emotions course across her face. She was so alive. Made him feel so alive.

"I am sorry. I should not toy with you so. Come. We find our clothes."

He went to hold her hand, as he had when they had wandered in the woods, but this time she resisted. He let her, even though it was her touch he wanted. Best not to force too much. She had enough to get used to.

The feel of a well-used body, for one.

And the fact that another being dwelled inside.

Chapter 31 – Pain and Moonlight Wanting

So strange. The air against her skin like cat's fur as she followed him through the trees. The feel of the mountain hummed under her bare feet and she couldn't recall a time she'd felt this. The scent of growing things and moist soil and—Simon. Bare back and strong buttocks as he strode through the last of the dappled light like a god. Or something more feral.

Simon/Min Gyi.

No! He was Simon, just as she was Kalla. She knew no Min Gyi. Or Min, for that matter.

But the names—the other names that sprang unbidden in her head—seemed to ache in her, just as her body throbbed in a delicious, bone-weary, curl-up-together-and-sleep, kind of way.

She crossed her arms over her breasts, determined not to let him see how he aroused her. How she wanted him still.

But *she* didn't want him. It was her body—pure lust. And something else deep inside her that she didn't—couldn't—trust. Something that had made her throw caution to the wind and do something she darn-well regretted now. How was she going to work with this man when every time he looked at her, she'd know what they'd done? What hadn't they done? She might feign forgetfulness, but in truth, even through the red tinge of the memory, it was painted indelibly in her head. The sensations. The want. The desire and how they met it, each ministering to the other until their wanton cries filled the forest.

And she still had wanted more.

So little time in this life for the pleasure they'd found together.

The way they'd given up themselves to be part of something more. The two headed monster. Hermaphrodite in ancient Alchemical texts. Man and woman joined.

Hold onto those clinical thoughts. Be the scientist you are. Simon Renault was nothing more than one of those typical research team trysts.

She shook her head. "Here I was worried about Mei and Alex, and look at us—naked as jaybirds wandering the woods."

Simon glanced knowingly over his shoulder. "A very pretty jaybird."

Good one, Kalla.

"Well I've got you out of my system now. It's done."

"Oui?"

Another too-knowing glance. Well, she could put up with his knowing glances. She could. It was only for another week or so.

The light was amber, lost in the tree-tops, as the sun fell too low to reach the forest floor. It would be dark soon, here. Dark soon enough at the festival as well. That would be when the real madness began.

"How much farther?"

Simon shrugged, the movement rippling up his back and sending a surge of heat through Kalla. She remembered that back. The feel of him under her hands as he moved.

Stop it. Stop it. Anything with Simon would never work. He was too unpredictable and wild. Dangerous.

And she liked it.

"Simon do you really know where you're leading me? Because if I don't have clothes in my hands in five minutes, I am going to be plenty pissed off. You don't want to see me pissed off, Simon. I've been told it isn't pretty."

It came off sounding lame, but Simon stopped, leered back at her in a way that made her clutch her arms around her chest harder.

"Are you cold, Princess? Because otherwise there is no need to cover yourself. I know your charms."

She ground her teeth at his pointed once-over that lingered far too long. Then he started walking again.

Furious, she watched him go. Birds sang their evening songs and flashed bright feathers in the tree tops. Something moved in the underbrush and she thought she saw eyes. She scuttled after Simon.

But the mountain felt strange. The hum she'd noticed as soon as she woke resonated inside her as if she were connected by a vibrating cord that ran from her navel.

And there was something else, as well. Whenever she closed her eyes she immediately was back in that chasm, immediately falling towards the red-clothed Votaress with the blackest of eyes. And that woman was waiting.

Another movement in the brush and Kalla hurried up, was right on Simon's heels, so close she could touch him and she knew he was aware. Knew, as if she could read his mind, he wanted that touch. Would turn to her, hold her, lower his lips and taste her.

The red stirred inside her and Kalla jerked back, stumbled in the clearing they crossed. Simon caught her arm so fast she didn't even see him move. He set her upright, looked down at her as she jerked free.

"I'm fine. Just fine."

He cocked his head, that dark hair shadowing his gaze. "You do not look it. You look pale. Beautiful, but pale."

He tried to stroke a strand of hair from her face, but she jerked away, knowing his touch was dangerous.

"I'm tired. I want my clothes. And that darn headache is back with a vengeance." She looked up at him and hated herself for being pathetic. "Please Simon. Just get me my clothes. I want to go home."

"Then here you are, Princess. I am to serve."

Again that gentleness in his voice so she wasn't sure how to take him. Taunting or cherishing? Simon Renault was no man to cherish women. He'd obviously had a lot in his life, if Alex's comments were true. But the look he gave her as he half-turned to show her clothing discarded nearby brought an ache to her heart she hadn't felt before. It left her breathless and wanting to touch him, and saddened that she dared not.

It was hard to dress. Hard not to recall how he'd slipped her panties off, how she'd disrobed. She knew she flushed as she pulled her clothes on, that she could not meet Simon's steady gaze.

But from the shadows of her hair she watched him. Proud like some wild animal. Broad V of chest. Slim-hipped and powerful and oh-so-much a man. A shame when he was clothed. It was like a wild beast imprisoned. He should be naked always.

When he caught her eye, he grinned rakishly as if he knew what she'd been thinking.

"Better, Princess?" This was a taunt. "Shall I lead you to your chariot?"

"We need to find the others. Alex and Mei must be worried sick."

A shake of his shaggy head. "Peut-être they have done as we have. There are many glades on the hillside."

"Mei would not. She's a proper woman."

"Aah. And that would make you very improper given how we spent our afternoon?" She hated his grin. Hated the fact he was right.

"But then, when is loving ever improper?" He faced her. Towered over her and forced her to look at him. "This was not just sex, Kalla. There is something between us. Something ancient and pure. You know it."

He nearly caught her shoulders, but she ducked away, past him. There was noise down the hill. Music. That had to be the way to go.

"Ancient and pure in a pig's eye. I don't know anything of the kind."

She plunged through the trees, escaping the intensity of his gaze and his words.

They didn't mean anything.

He followed her down the slope, never trying to aid her as she slipped and slid through moist soil, as if in her shoes she was less sure footed. Certainly the hum of the mountain was less. Clothed, she felt less aware of Simon as well. Well, maybe not less aware.

Less vulnerable.

The wail of music grew and suddenly the trees ended and she stumbled out onto the road that was filled with stragglers coming up to the festival. The sweet stench of marijuana hung in an actual cloud over the throng. It immediately went to her head, so she fought back a stupid grin. No way was she going to let Simon think she was smiling about what they had done. She was about to plunge into the crowd when his strong hand fell on her shoulder.

"Do not." His voice was soft—a fist in a velvet glove. "It can be dangerous here after dark. I will lead. Stay close."

He released her then, leaving her to her anger at his preemptive actions, at the way he wanted control and challenged hers. Damn him. But he was already disappearing in the crowd and it was wild and—

She plunged in after him, elbowing her way until she caught up to him.

The closer to the pinnacle they got, the more people there were. Tightly packed, dancing and singing together. Drunken together. Groping together. Nat Ka Daw's berated the crowd with voices that were almost hoarse. The music ran up and up and up, until her flesh crawled and her body hair stood on end.

Someone caught her waist, swung her away from Simon in a dance. She punched at the person, but she was being passed from hand to hand. Simon? Where was Simon?

And suddenly he was beside her. A roar in Burmese, and the hands were gone from her. She stood stunned in a small open space as Simon turned to her.

"I told you to stay close." He grabbed her wrist before she could stop him, pulled her through the crowd, down into the treed paths that led to the monastery. Now the party had spilled well down the mountain. Sighs and moans came from the shadows. A small fire flickered over drunken faces.

And then the round doorway of the monastery was in front of them, he dragged her inside and Kalla pulled loose, rubbed her wrist.

"Kalla?" Mei's voice as she materialized out of the dark.

"And Simon." Kalla glanced up at him. Darkness on his face as if rage walked close to the surface. "You bruised my wrist."

"And worse things would have happened if I had not claimed you."

"Claimed me? You claimed me?" She rounded on him now. He'd had things far too much his way and that was darn well going to change. "I'll have you know I'm a grown woman. No one claims me, except me. You got that? Let me say it again—I'm my own woman and I don't belong to you or anyone. Can you get that through your thick skull or do I have to have it translated for you?"

The mountain hummed under her, around her, became her pulse and joined the pounding in her head so she knew she was going over the top, a little crazy, but for some reason she couldn't stop.

"Get that smirk off your face."

His face smoothed a little, but it did nothing to lessen the knowing blackness of his eyes. Maybe it was because he knew everything that set her screaming and she hated that he knew. Or maybe it was that pain he caused in her heart, and the headache between her eyes, and the fact she couldn't blink without that red-draped woman looking back at her.

"Pardonnez-moi, Princess, for making you blush so prettily. I will remember my place from now on."

That damned smirk was back.

"Kalla, where were you?" Alex came up behind Mei, his hands on her shoulders possessively. His face was far from friendly. "And you, Simon?" Much less than friendly.

"I—I found him at one of the Nat Ka Daw performances. He—he took me on a tour of the place." She couldn't meet Alex's gaze, was sure he would see her bruised lips, the mess of her hair. "I'm sorry. We lost track of time."

A look from her to Simon.

Alex was angry. "Do you know what's going on out there? There's no way we should be here. A man tried to grab Mei. We should have left hours ago."

"I said I'm sorry," Simon replied stiffly.

"You would have been a hell of a lot sorrier if I'd had the jeep keys. I'd have left the two of you here. Totally irresponsible—both of you. And I would have thought better of you, at least, Kalla." Alex's disgust flushed his face, even in the silver light of the moon. He swung to Simon. "You irresponsible son of a…." He bit off what he was going to say. "Just get us back to the jeep."

Simon stayed silent, as if he knew he'd erred. He glanced at Kalla, held out his hand, but she refused to take it. No way was she allying herself with him.

His gaze clouded, his lips tightened and she knew she'd hurt him, but it was too darn bad. Simon Renault assumed too much. She was going to teach him that. He led them back out the gate, Alex at the rear, keeping Mei and Kalla between himself and Simon.

"I'm not a cow to be herded, Alex," she said after the third time he urged her to keep up to Simon.

When they reached the jeep, the moon had risen to glaze the pinnacle roofs with silver, filling the festival with a swirling, ghostly mist. Spirits. She could see why people believed in them here. Tendrils of the mist came from under the trees, placed cool fingers across her cheeks, and again she felt the mountain's hum, the pressure behind her eyes.

She shivered but Simon's gaze was like heat against her skin as he held the door for her.

"You are—alright?" Again that—tenderness?

"I'm okay." But she wasn't really. She wanted to touch him. Wanted his arms around her because maybe that would dissipate the headache that was building to pile-driving intensity behind her eyes. But doing that would only make things worse.

She climbed into the jeep, the mountain's hum in her bones, and avoided his eyes. There were too many reasons things couldn't work with Simon and that made her inexplicably sad.

"I'm sorry," she murmured as the door thunked shut. He probably never heard and she wasn't about to repeat herself.

The drive took forever through the moonlight that flooded the landscape. Gradually the hum of the mountain was replaced by the rattle and roll of the jeep and the stench of diesel, but the headache didn't go. Every time Kalla closed her eyes it came on stronger. And the red-clad woman—whoever the she was—glared back from Kalla's brain. It left her aching, uneasy, and unable to sleep as the forests of Popa disappeared into the ghostly Pagan plain. Worse, it left her with the sense she'd made more of a mistake by her rejection of Simon than by her tryst on the mountainside.

She made up her mind to talk things out with him.

When the jeep came to a stop in the Beautyland courtyard she could have cried with relief. She just wanted a bed and sleep and to forget all the stupid things she'd done today. At least she had one good story. That was the upside.

The downside was she had seriously damaged her professional relationships. Tomorrow she would fix things with Simon, because regardless of how she denied it, there was something between them. He'd been right when he said it.

The Hotel was in darkness, except for a single finger of light that came from the dining room. Khun and Mr. Hue pushed out the door to greet them, the light through the window illuminating Khun's unfriendly face and what he carried.

"My puppet!" Kalla sprinted to meet him, clutched the Votaress to her chest. "Thank god. Thank god." She whirled to Khun, not caring if he was shocked by the tears in her eyes. "Thank *you*! So the general did have her. He had his men bring her back."

Khun didn't meet her gaze. Instead he shook his head and turned that unfriendly glare on Simon.

"Miss Kalla, the general did not bring today." He half-bowed to Alex. "He send Mr. Alex's equipment. That was all. I decide to look around here." Another glance at Simon, that seemed to burn through the night. Khun looked back at Kalla. "I find Votaress in Mr. Simon's room."

It felt like a block of ice filled her lungs, her gut, her bones.

Kalla, still holding tight to the precious puppet turned to face the man. "How—how could you?" All the emotional upheavals of the day shredded her composure and the tears of happiness she'd felt at the puppet's return soured on her cheeks. "What do you have…? What have I ever…?" Everything she wanted to say just caught in her throat and he didn't even have the good grace to say anything—simply stood there, with smoldering darkness on his face.

"Is that all today was, too? A way to finish the job of tearing me down? You just can't stand to see a woman capable of standing on her own two feet, can you?"

She was openly crying and hating herself as she did.

"Kalla, no." Finally he spoke, but there was no way his weak protest could undo the fact—the *fact*—that her puppet had been found in his room.

"Don't even try, Simon. I should have checked your rooms as soon as she disappeared. You're the one who wanted her enough to try to buy her."

"You really think I'd steal your puppet? After today?" His standard smirk had become a scowl.

"You took her before today, remember?"

"Kalla." He caught her shoulders. "Listen to me. I wouldn't do that to you. I know what she means to you. I have no idea how she got into my room."

But she didn't care if there was a glint of earnestness in his gaze as if he could will her to believe him.

"The facts speak louder than any of your lies, Simon. And to think I almost thought I liked you." She spun on her heel, intent on getting away from all these people and getting her puppet under lock and key.

"Miss Kalla?" Khun again, and she didn't want to stop. "Miss Kalla, please."

"Yes?" Sighing, she turned back to him, but again he wouldn't meet her gaze.

"Ms. Kalla. While you were away, a message came." He held out an envelope, neatly sealed. "I did not open it."

For her. The headache beat in her head as she clung to the puppet and tried to comprehend what a message could mean. Not good news. Never good news.

She felt the others watching her as she walked away from them and used the light from the dining room to see as she pulled a single piece of paper from the envelope. Read.

```
    Kalla. Hope you are alright. Regret to
inform you. Dad took turn for worse day you
left. Died two days later. Funeral on Sunday.
Sorry. Love, Sharon.
```

Chapter 32 – The Forever Corridor

The earth shifted as if an earthquake had struck and Kalla staggered. Shock took out her legs. She went down hard, to her knees in the courtyard dust, unable to breathe the heavy scent of the neem. Nothing in the night-bound courtyard moved.

Not true. Not true. The message had to be another of Sharon's lies. Sharon was always lying to cover her addictions. It had to be a lie.

"Kalla? Kalla what is it?"

Voices around her, but it was Mei's voice she heard. Mei on her knees, gentle fingers taking the note from her, passing it to Simon.

"No!" She lurched to her feet. "Don't you dare touch it, you evil bastard. Don't you think you've used me enough already?"

She grabbed back the letter and stumbled towards her room. She needed time to think, to get home. If this headache would just stop she could think more clearly, plan.

She wiped at her crimson-stained vision and realized her cheeks were wet. Dammit, she was stronger than tears.

"Kalla."

An unwelcome hand on her shoulder that sent tremors down her spine and spun her around. Simon looked down at her, concern on his face, and she didn't want his concern, dammit. Didn't want anything to do with a liar and a thief.

"What has happened?" Again that gentle voice.

"None of your business." It came out blunt and thick with tears that had flooded through the breaches in her control. It had to be a lie. Dad had said he was okay, that it would be good for her to go on this trip, get out there after she'd put her career on hold while she helped care for him.

"We are too small a group for secrets, Kalla. You will need our help to deal with whatever is wrong."

She squeezed her eyes shut, but the crimson woman glared out at her so fiercely that Kalla was suddenly afraid. Unfortunately, what he said was true. But she couldn't look at him. Wouldn't, because he was the most hateful, manipulative, and abusive man she'd ever met.

She turned to Alex and Mei and inhaled to steady herself.

"It's my father. He's dead." Be matter of fact. Cool. Formal. "He was sick—very sick, but he told me the cancer was in remission. That he was well so I could accept this research team."

The betrayal stabbed her to the core. That she had to share it only made it worse.

"I have to get home."

"Of course you do." Alex's conciliatory voice, his pat on her shoulder helped, but she wanted a hug. Needed arms around her, someone to tell her everything was okay and yet she knew if she allowed herself to be that weak she'd cry like the world had ended. Her Dad gone. It couldn't be.

"Oh, Kalla." Mei caught her in a hug. "Oh my sister, hold tight to me."

Kalla did, the puppet caught tight between them. "My Dad—he was the one who hugged me—and now he's gone." Little sobs jerked at her core, at her words, and she hated the weakness. She pushed Mei away and scrubbed at her eyes. "Who am I kidding? That was a lie. Dad was never there for me. Never. Always out on his salmon boat or with his damned psychics. Now I have to get home. What do I have to do?"

She saw the shock on all their faces at her bitter words.

Finally Alex nodded. "Hue says the phone lines are down, but tomorrow we'll get you on a flight to Yangon and home. We'll take care of everything. Okay?" Alex met her gaze carefully. "Okay?"

"Fine. But don't talk to me like I'm broken, dammit. I can do things myself—tomorrow." She stepped up to her door, clinging to her puppet for the strength to maintain her front. Her room. Quiet. She didn't look back at them as she went inside and shut the door. She heard their voices as she barely made it to the bed. Sank down.

Her headache surged forward, shattering her vision, as she looked down at the beautifully crafted doll on her lap. The room a sickening kaleidoscope of too many shapes and colors. But closing her eyes brought the shape of the woman, her black void of eyes that looked far too similar to the Votaress's painted face.

Kalla gripped the doll until she swore she heard the wood moan. She released it and rubbed her temples. What was the matter with her? She'd dealt with problems before. Had dealt with Dad's illness through the worst of it.

Sharon was probably falling apart just like Sharon always did. She'd be back into the drugs and the booze in a heartbeat. It was a wonder the message came at all. There'd be a hell of a lot of stuff Kalla'd need to take care of when she got back to Seattle.

If the pain wasn't going to let her sleep, she might as well start making a list.

She stood, intending to start with locking the Votaress in the travel case, but the world did a slow roll around her and her knees sagged. She sank back onto the bed.

Not good. Not good at all.

Just as she'd made a mess of just about everything. Actually, absolutely everything. She might have control, but every one of her decisions was faulty.

She set the puppet aside and bent to retrieve the bag of paper and pens she'd taken to Popa.

The movement brought a stab of pain between her eyes, a noise like glass shattering, and the scent of incense and jasmine so intense she tasted bile.

Falling.

Vision pinpricked.

Falling through darkness.

She slid off the bed, grabbed blindly for the covers, pulled them on top of her as she slumped-slammed onto the slatted wood floor.

And everything went black.

§

Simon turned from the closed door, when every part of him wanted to follow Kalla inside, wanted to be there for her even if she didn't want it. Wanted to make sure she believed him that he'd had nothing to do with the puppet's theft—no matter what the facts suggested.

He understood her shock. Had felt the loss of a parent—both parents. Knew the pain. Instead he looked at Alex.

"She will need a flight. I will get Hue to direct me to one of the local agents. See what can be done about a ticket for first thing tomorrow."

"It's late, and maybe Kalla's right. Maybe you've about done enough on this little venture, Simon. Maybe you've done enough altogether and should be moving on."

Karen L. Abrahamson

"Just what the hell are you suggesting?"

"I'm suggesting that maybe we've all had quite enough of Simon Renault. Maybe we'd be better off without you here."

Simon looked from Alex's unfriendly face to Mei's open fear and to Khun' scowl.

"You actually believe I'd take her puppet?"

Alex shook his head. "Truth to be told, I don't know what to believe anymore. But it's pretty clear something happened today between you and Kalla. She hasn't been the same since you came dragging your butt back at that damned festival looking like the proverbial cat that ate the canary. She, on the other hand, looked like a shell-shocked soldier. You care to enlighten us, or shall I just let my imagination run wild?"

Alex's innuendo almost broke the Nat loose, for Kalla/Min was no woman to be used and left. Simon's control slipped and the Nat flooded in, raised him up until he could almost destroy Alex with a glance.

"What happens between Kalla and me is personal. Private—no matter what you may think."

"Well Kalla doesn't seem to think so, big guy. As a matter of fact, I'd say she wants exactly nothing to do with you."

Simon thrust his hands in his pockets to stop from throttling the team leader, and met Alex head on. "And there you are wrong." Good. His voice was steady—not at all as he felt. "Who better among us to help Kalla? You, with your fine language skills who has abandoned Kalla for another? Mei, who cannot protect her? Khun?"

They looked at each other, suddenly uncertain. "You see? Morning will come soon and this is an emergency, n'est-ce pas? I will contact the travel authorities and see what can be done."

And then he would lose her. It could not be helped.

Taungbyon's roared protest made the world disappear.

§

Falling, and Simon's touch is on Kalla, his hands trying to catch her. She reaches for them, wants them on her, wants comfort.

Misses and falls. Falls alone, and then….

Dark corridors stretched—forever?

But Kalla walked somewhere, pacing the darkness. She had purpose, even if she had no idea what it was.

From somewhere she produced a candle. The single white flame hissed and guttered in a chill breeze that whispered past the bricks, blew along the floor, disturbed the hem of the red longyi she wore.

Votaress crimson.

The air reeked of dust and incense, and her stomach rolled sickeningly. Bright ceiling murals sprang into existence in her candlelight—complex mandala of blue and red and yellow representing the cosmos. Golden Buddha figures bloomed along the walls.

And her purpose was ending. Grief. Grief so powerful the candle shook in her hands. Pain cut the full feeling of her heart. But this was as it should be.

The candle guttered, faded.

Movement in the air as someone came. She must do this before they stopped her. A gust of wind, and the candle guttered out. In darkness she ran the forever-corridor, trying to remember.

To know what she would do.

Veils lifted. Thinned. Faded. Almost a memory. Almost knowledge. Small footsteps.

But she was on the floor tearing at the veils. The veils…. A sheet?— that had fallen over her face. She yanked it aside and found herself staring into wide black eyes.

She almost screamed. Scrambled backwards away from the little figure under her bed, and came up against her dresser.

Votaress. Only the puppet. Kalla fought to steady her erratic breathing.

She'd spilled the puppet onto the floor when she fell. That was all it was. Staring out at her with those black eyes and wicked smile like the face of the woman in her dreams.

Almost as if it had been doing something forbidden and had barely managed to get back in place before she opened her eyes.

"It's a puppet. Only a puppet. So what the heck are you so afraid of?"

She dragged the little figure to her, smoothed the human hair over the cat-sized skull. Tugged the vermillion robes into place.

"So where have you been, Madam? Out visiting the countryside? Looking for your brethren? Or conversing with my father in the astral plane?"

Another silly, bitter thought, but the lifelike figure looked like it could almost answer, and her pulse still raced.

From outside came the sound of the restaurant's screen door bumping loose on its hinges like a metronome to her pulse. No voices. Her room was dark except for the light shining over the dining room door. Who had turned off her light?

She hauled herself up onto the bed, brushed her hair back from her face. Weird dream. Probably the product of what she'd been through today—she glanced at her bedside clock—make that yesterday.

Corridors and darkness and the woman and something closing in. She'd had that feeling before. Mandalas on the ceiling. She'd seen similar drawings and statues at Thatbyinnyu, but knew that wasn't where she was in her dream. *Vision.*

Dhammayangyi.

And that was something she certainly wasn't going to believe. She ignored the shiver that went up her spine and considered. The dream was most likely her subconscious trying to educate her conscious mind. The subconscious was always better at processing seemingly disconnected pieces of information.

So something was at Dhammayangyi. She just needed to find out what, and to do that before she left tomorrow meant she had to overcome her ridiculous fear of the place.

Now.

She had her shoes on, was on her feet and at the door with flashlight in hand before she caught herself.

"Just what do you intend to do in the middle of the night?" she murmured to the darkness. "It got you in trouble before."

But then she'd had Mei with her. And not going out had her standing here talking to herself, which could *not* be a good sign. Go to Dhammayangyi, have a look around, and that would be the end of it.

She stepped out into moonlight and cool air before she could second guess herself. The pounding pressure behind her eyes seemed to lessen.

"You see? You just needed fresh air."

The scent of the neem tree was heavy in the night, its yellow flowers whitened by the setting moon. Dying petals fluttered in a steady rain that brought a pang of grief. Her father.

She hadn't been at his side. Hadn't even grieved when he died. No, she'd been here—rutting on Mount Popa like some animal. Not even doing her job. And not winning Alex back, either. She felt sick at the thought.

Well, she would do her job, because it was all she had now. She might have been brought here for stories, but there was something in the temples, too. Something in all those little murals and something about Dhammayangyi. The more she thought about it, the more certain she was.

The quiet in the courtyard said the others were probably asleep, but one of the jeeps was gone. Odd.

Cicadas buzzed in the neem and bats winged overhead, their high-pitched cries oddly fitting on this ghostly plain. Wind raised a thin pall of dust across the moon, but a damp river scent lingered in the air giving a sense of life in the darkness.

She vaulted the bar that gated the courtyard, then checked behind her. Nothing moved. The insect song paused. In the distance a goat-bell tinkled. Yes, life, like a faint promise, even in this stark barrenness. She waited and finally the chorus began again, so she started down the road in a swinging walk.

Dhammayangyi Pahto sat to the southwest of the hotel in a field of moon-grayed grass and dust that undulated in the wind. After half an hour and a brief time huddled amid the ruins when she heard the roar of a jeep engine, the temple's huge bulk rose like a small mountain waiting to crush her. Swallow her. She entered the courtyard cautiously.

Darkness oozed from Dhammayangyi's doors and she knew something waited there. Déjà vu of herself walking, of holding a candle, of cool air around her legs.

Kalla shivered, but she'd come all this way.

To Burma. To Pagan. To Dhammayangyi. As if this had been predestined, Dad would say. But what did Dad know?

Stubbornly, she flashed her light over the entrance. A golden face leapt out of the darkness and she leapt back. Almost turned.

Stopped.

Stupid. Stupid. You saw the Buddha figure last time, and the two nats by the door. Squaring her shoulders she turned back to the temple, paused at the step.

Go. Just do it.

She did, and the darkness took her breath away, left her heart pounding so hard she thought it might escape her chest. A vibration like the mountain-hum at Popa seemed to run through the structure. Her headache answered and it was hard to see. The scent of incense flooded into her. A sound…. Footsteps? They faded like echoes, made her uncertain if she'd heard anything at all.

"Get a grip, Jervis." She shook herself.

Her words ran down the corridor. Came back to her in whispers. Were those footsteps again? She had to do what she'd come here to do and get back to the Beautyland.

She started down the corridor that ran the outer edge of the massive structure. Her flashlight barely disturbed the darkness, but the air stirred. A rustle above spoke of bats, and the sound of other footsteps faded in and out of hearing as if they might or might not be her imagination.

She stopped. Rubbed her head and ran her light over the walls, but was afraid to disturb the bats by training the light on the ceiling. Disappointing paintings of Buddha. Mandala. None of the small murals like the ones at Thatbyinnyu. She realized she'd been expecting them.

A rumble from the entrance stopped her. Her breathing rang loud in her ears.

Jeep engine. Idling.

Someone was here. Someone had come for her. How was she going to defend her presence out here in the night?

She looked for a place to hide as jeep doors slammed. She heard voices—Burmese. Soldiers, probably. The cavernous halls were like maws in front and behind her. If she kept her flashlight on, they'd find her.

She flicked the light off and the darkness came at her like a predator that would devour her whole. A small whimper escaped as she pressed against rough bricks. As she saw the flashlights run over the entrance nave and heard voices that flowed like bells under water.

Find safety. She opened herself to air movement, to rustles of sound. The voices came at her from a great distance and she was slipping, falling, down a great slide of time as she eased along the wall, and came even with a narrow door that gave onto a walled, side courtyard. Their voices told her the soldiers searched the corridors on the other side of the temple. If she were careful, she might sneak out the front entrance and make a run for home.

Every part of her strained, opened.

Something answered; old grief almost toppled her.

Run! Just run.

Just stay a little longer.

Kalla sought reality in the ragged brick. Footfall—came towards her. Move, dammit. Move.

But her body wouldn't respond.

And then, out of the darkness, something dragged her back as a hand smothered her screams.

Chapter 33 – Belling Shadows

Dhammayangyi.

General Ne Setkya paced the ground outside the courtyard walls of the huge temple, fighting back the sick feeling that had clenched his gut from the moment the soldier had woken him. The man had brought word that the researchers had returned from Popa.

And that someone had snuck out to Dhammayangyi Pahto and set it humming like a bell.

It was too much, on the heels of the message that had come for the woman.

Kalla Jervis's father was dead. Or else the message had another purpose. Like a goad to send her to the temple before she left. The powers in the world worked in strange ways.

He didn't need that. It was bad enough the fool nun had tried to take Kalla Jervis into Dhammayangyi. Age had obviously addled Daw Ma Ma Nang's brain.

When he'd returned to his headquarters in the middle of the night he'd found Colonel Aung had a troop of soldiers ready, and so he was here. Aung led the men in the search of the Pahto, leaving Ne Setkya to ponder what he was going to do if his men found the woman.

"I am going inside," he said to the driver who waited with him.

Inhaling the dust his footsteps raised, he stepped into the courtyard and stopped. He bowed his head in remembrance at all those who had come before him and felt the vibrations of the earth run up his legs and set his blood pounding.

Two of his men stood at the pahto entrance with Colonel Aung. They snapped to attention when they saw him.

"General. Sir," Aung said and snapped a salute. "The men search. There is no reason to trouble yourself with the mundane."

Ne Setkya waved Aung away and swallowed back anxiety. "I have not visited Dhammayangyi in a long time. Where are the men?"

"I have sent them around the right corridors to push the interloper towards us. We will have them, Sir."

The man's narrow eyes were lit from within. Avarice, Ne Setkya thought. He hopes for fortune in Pagan. At any cost. At least he did not seem to feel the change in Dhammayangyi—that only came with long familiarity and training.

"Then I will take the left corridor. You are aware, of course, that there are many exits from the temple. The builders made side courtyards from which a person might escape."

Aung's self-control demonstrated the care Ne Setkya must take.

"Thank you, General. I did not know. I had one man at the rear exit of the temple. I will increase the guard." He jerked his head at one of the soldiers and the man trotted off. Clearly Ne Setkya's soldiers were becoming Aung's men as well. The knot in Ne Setkya's belly tightened further.

He glanced back at the darkness of the pahto and inhaled a new scent—crisp and floral—felt the hum in the air like insect wings against his face. Felt the need of an old ox to fill the traces and lean into a solid weight.

"And I will take the left corridor, and between us we will trap this intruder."

He ignored the protest in Aung's gaze, the offer to accompany him, and stepped into bell-filled shadows that even he had not seen before.

§

Apples and roses took Simon's breath away.

So did the sharp elbow in his solar plexus as Kalla bit his palm and stomped down on his instep as he struggled to get them both quietly out of the corridor and into one of the side courtyards.

Merde! She was une sauvage—a wildcat.

"Be still. Someone comes."

Even in a whisper his voice echoed in the long corridors, seemed to become part of a vibration that was just beyond hearing, but that Taungbyon recognized. At least she quit fighting.

He eased his hands from her face, from that taut body that fit so neatly against his, and she whirled, faced him with a fierceness that only brought Taungbyon surging forward with the need to kiss her. Could he ever get enough of this woman to satiate the Nat? Himself?

Doubtful, but he/they would never find out.

He grabbed her hand and dragged her further into the tree-shadows of a courtyard surrounded by a collapsed wall, with her resisting every step of the way.

"I don't need your help," she hissed.

His answer was to crush her against the rough brick and inhale the heat of her anger and—fear. Something had truly frightened her.

Looked down at her and found those blue-black eyes still, waiting. Fear of further betrayals and want so clear it surprised him and sent the Nat coiling up in a cloud of black smoke that threatened his control.

Unfortunately, this was not the time to explain himself, nor to respond to such things, much as his and the Nat's desires were one.

He glanced over his shoulder. Soldier voices coming this way. But there was another scent on the air. Someone else came. Someone more cautious and more certain. Taungbyon told him that.

"If you are finished with your idiocy, we should leave."

Roughly he grabbed her wrist before she could respond, led her toward the gap in the wall where he had entered, following her scent and Taungbyon's certainty of her location.

It had been Taungbyon that had sent him speeding to the Beautyland from the travel agent's home with certain knowledge Kalla Jervis was in danger. He'd left Hue at the Beautyland and run across the dry fields following the Nat's unerring sense of direction.

The presence in the temple came closer and he had to get them free, but Kalla twisted in his grasp.

Never. Strong-willed to the end.

He yanked her against him, buried his face in her hair and felt her yield to him in a way that only filled the Nat with satisfaction. Quel dommage—a pity he could not take advantage.

"Do you wish to be arrested again, Princess?" he whispered into her ear.

She stiffened.

"Then follow me willingly. Someone comes and I sense he knows his business."

He turned, inhaled the night air. River water. Dust. The ancient scent of ox manure and the green scent of Lead trees. The faint scent of cactus and thorn, and from behind them the ammonia of bat guano. No scent of men.

He caught her slim waist, lifted her over the fall of brick, then leapt silently after her. Her eyes were huge, round with—what? Strangeness and confusion. Her hand went to her forehead and then her look hardened.

"I don't need your protection, Simon. I knew someone was here. I was leaving before you scared me within an inch of my life."

She started across the field, her footsteps raising dust, leaving a clear track across newly plowed furrows.

"Excusez-moi, Princess, but you leave a trail for men to follow."

Damnation, they did not have time for confrontation. The one in the temple was almost at the door. They could not afford this. In two long strides he was to her, grabbed her, threw her over his shoulder and knew he would pay a heavy price for his action. The only good thing was she did not scream. No, she belted his back and buttocks. Bit him as he loped the edge of the pahto ruins to a line of trees. There he set her down. Waited for the smack across the face, but the fury in her eyes was beyond that.

Flushed and beautiful, she turned, strode away, and left him to follow.

At least she kept to the shadows and seemed to naturally pick a path that led toward the Beautyland while still keeping to cover. At this rate they might make it home undiscovered.

In silence they covered the ground in twenty minutes, crossed the main road on the other side of the hotel and went around to the rear before entering the courtyard. Yes, his Kalla was smart. And sexy as hell, the way her butt filled out her jeans as she stepped up to her door.

"So tell me. What was so important that you would risk not being able to return home tomorrow?"

She stopped with her hand on the doorknob, as if it took all her effort to speak to him. Then she turned to him, a puzzled look on her face.

"I—I had to see Dhammayangyi before I left. The place has—intrigued me."

She looked both frail and fair as she stood there trying to explain. As if something was not right with her.

"That is not how Mei tells it. You had a fright there your first day, and would not enter, and yet now you creep there in the night."

She closed her eyes, but then they flashed open with a flicker of fear. "I don't know what's going on. I was so upset. I must have passed out or something and when I came around I was already at Dhammayangyi."

Her gaze dropped to the ground, her hands to her sides, in a gesture of defeat he did not like to see on her.

"It draws you, this pahto." He wanted to step up to her, slide his hands around her lower back and hear her sigh as she leaned into him.

"I don't know. All I know is things aren't working out the way I'd planned. Nothing is."

"But sometimes things are not meant to be as you planned. There is something better."

"Better?" her gaze flashed enmity at him. "Like you, I suppose? Is that what you're suggesting? Taking my puppet was better for you." She turned to her door again and he knew he had to stop her.

"Kalla, about that." He took a chance and grabbed her hand. "I know from our discussions how precious la petite Votaress is to you. I don't know how she came into my room, but I—I would not take her from you. Ever."

The darkness stirred far back in his head. Taungbyon knew something.

Tell me.

There was nothing. Perhaps it was only Simon's imagination.

But Kalla, still holding the doorknob, looked up at him searchingly. He hoped she saw truth and that he cared. He hoped she liked what she saw. Instead she looked away, hurt him as she pulled back slightly.

"You're asking a lot." Her voice was soft, tragically vulnerable, and the Nat hummed a soft response.

Min. Taungbyon's thought made him pause.

But Kalla looked back at him, making him ache with the haunted look that lingered in her gaze.

"She's very important to you."

"She's all I have. Now."

Simon frowned. She was so pale and clearly shaken by something. And hadn't a sister sent the telegram?

"Kalla, are you certain you are well?"

She jerked upright and pulled her hand away. "What's this all about, Reneault? Are you trying to butter me up, again? Because if you are, I'm not buying." Her rich mouth had gone hard and he wanted to kiss it to softness again. Or to grab her shoulders and shake her for suggesting such intent.

"Then I'll ask again, what took you out to the pahto? You could have been arrested, held. The General could have shut this whole research project down and you would have been responsible. Is that what you want?" He hadn't intended to be so harsh, but the question was out before he could stop it.

A flash of vulnerability cracked through her anger, but something wasn't right. Something about her smelled of—wilted jasmine and—dust? Then her gaze steadied.

"I've been arrested, abandoned, abducted, and told my father just died. I haven't slept well since I got here. How the hell would I know what took me to Dhammayangyi?"

But as she said it she half-turned toward the darkness that hid the huge structure. Her gaze said she hid something.

Taungbyon surged forward bringing with him the urgent need to regain her trust. Could he reach her—show her he cared after all he had done or was suspected of doing?

But before he could find the words, she drew herself up straight as a petite gendarme. All her boundaries had slammed into place—cool, collected, contained.

"I'm sorry. You don't need to see this and I don't need your help. I'm quite capable of dealing with things myself."

Breaking through to Kalla would not be easy. It would take time.

"I am glad the Votaress can go home with you."

She looked at him sharply. "Sure." Clearly she didn't believe.

Then a distant look formed in her eyes. "You know, at one point the thought crossed my mind about leaving her here. Part of Burma's legacy and all that. Like the general said."

She glanced at him, and he knew she'd told him just to prove she'd trust the general before Simon. Taungbyon actually growled his displeasure.

She turned stiffly back to the door, probably happy she'd injured him. "Well, good night. I suppose I'll see you in the morning when I leave for the airport."

"And there, Princess, is another problem." He caught the doorknob from her and held the door closed even though she'd unlocked it, just because he knew it would infuriate her. "Hue helped me find a travel agent. I was trying to get you on an early flight. There is a problem."

"Problem?" Her face was rigid with effort.

He released the door and chanced catching her shoulders, ran his hands up her arms and felt her tremble. From the darkness came the hollow cry of bells. How could he tell her the real problem was that he and an ancient warrior spirit did not want her to leave?

Chapter 34 – Pride and Prejudice

Mandalay: the name reeked of the British Raj and old layers of culture. A mythic city she had read of, home of dynasties, of temples and monasteries, of kings who had warred with Kalla's mother's people of Siam. She was there—in its midst!

And she couldn't describe a bit of it.

Well, maybe she could describe the concrete Central Telecommunications Office. Not exactly exotic. She stood in a stuffy glass booth in a grey room, an old-fashioned, black, telephone handset in her hand, waiting for the operator to connect the line so she had a dial tone.

"Air Mandalay has had to cancel a flight, and the one flight out of Pagan is fully booked by a European tour group. There are more flights out of Mandalay. I will drive you there in the morning." So Simon had told her last night.

He'd stood there with his thieving hands on her shoulders as if he expected her to suddenly believe him, after all he'd done. The trouble was, she *had* wanted those strong hands to cup her head, his mouth to take hers, and his body to make her forget her father's loss, lose herself in sensations of him.

Instead she'd held to her anger and grief, and told him in no uncertain terms she *didn't* want his help. She'd pulled loose and slammed into her room to pack and catch some sleep.

Like she'd been able to do that. She'd lain, shivering, in the bed with the Votaress in her arms, thinking about the disaster waiting at home for her to take charge. She knew it was disaster. With Sharon, it always was.

So, exhausted, she'd come out of her room determined to ask someone else to drive her to Mandalay. Unfortunately neither Khun or

Alex were prepared to have Simon at the hotel, so she'd been forced to sit, seething, beside the thieving bastard for the eight-hour trip to fabled Mandalay. Sitting stiff as a sphinx over all those potholes while she tried to plan everything that needed to be done at home had left her more exhausted and covered with a thick film of road dust.

They had barely made it into the city in time enough for her to phone home. Most of the telecommunications operators had already left at four o'clock, so only one had been available when Kalla burst into the building, and that man had required some serious convincing to make an international call.

Thank god for Simon's language skills. He leaned against the counter, now, and made small talk with the Telecommunications operator. She had to admit, even with all his faults he was a good looking man.

The buzz of the dial tone drilled in her ear and she punched in the numbers and listened to the ring at the far end of the earth.

It would be after midnight in Seattle. She prayed her sister would still be at her father's home. But knowing Sharon… god, her sister could be anywhere in Seattle—stoned out of her head, selling herself for drug money, partying hard with friends after selling off Dad's belongings. The meth-junkie sores on her sister's wasted arms and legs said there wasn't much Sharon wasn't capable of.

The thought of them still left Kalla cold with angry betrayal. Sharon was a screw-up and out of control, and yet Dad had always treasured her far more than Kalla.

Three rings. Four. Not home. Five. Typical.

Sharon with her spiky hair, a streak of red through the temple. She had vivid dragon tattoos on her upper arms and a rose and thorns on her left breast. Her fingers were stained betel-red from the cigarettes she smoked incessantly. Hell, the woman vibrated with her drug need even when she sat still.

"Hello?" A sleepy voice, and Kalla looked at the phone in surprise, fighting back a sudden resentment that Sharon actually was there.

"Sharon? You're home?"

"Kalla? Oh god, Kalla! Why haven't you called me?!"

There it was—the panic. She could see her sister sitting up, wild-eyed, still half-stoned from her latest hit of meth. Kalla stiffened with the need to just *be* there. Take over all the things that needed to be done. Protect what little there was of her Dad's estate, and stop all those ridiculous monthly contributions he made to psychic and spiritualist 'churches'.

Sharon was too vulnerable, too sensitive. So weak their father had always made allowances for her—and had expected Kalla to do the same. Sharon could never do things properly, even though she was the older sibling.

"It's alright, Sharon. I'm coming home. I didn't get your telegram til yesterday and all the phones were down. We had to drive through a godforsaken wilderness to find one. But I'm here now. I've made a list of all the things that need to be done. If you can't manage, I'm sure Aunt Micah can help until I get there to take over. I know this has to have been really hard on you, but hang in there—I'll be there soon."

There was silence at the end of the phone, then: "I'm managing okay, Kalla. I am. It was just so sudden. He seemed fine, you know? We had this wonderful talk the night he died. He told me all about how he and Mom met and fell in love and then about the way things were when we were a family."

Kalla stiffened, hating the way her gut twisted, the way she wanted to say 'Before I came along, you mean'. But she didn't say it. Sharon kept talking.

"I could almost remember how it was when he brought you home, you know? And it was so wonderful having you and so sad because Mom wasn't there. It was so hard on him—even talking about it was still hard on him. He cried. I wish you'd been there. It was like it was supposed to be—family, you know?"

A horde of old resentments flooded in. Yes, she knew. Yes, she should have been there—but their father had sent her away—again. Sent her on a mission she could never fulfill because she had never darn well been able to make her father happy, had she? Tears of frustration and hurt and anger fought her control.

It hadn't been fair. It wasn't fair. None of it. And now she'd never have the opportunity to tell him how he'd hurt her. Her fingers gripped the phone so hard she heard the plastic groan.

"He went to bed and he just didn't wake up, you know? The doctors say the cancer was pretty far gone. More than he ever told us, you know? It just spread to his brain and he just… stopped. He looked peaceful when I found him, Kalla. Not like all those years when he always looked so worried about money and us."

"He never worried about us." The bitter words slipped out. "You maybe. We *all* worried about you."

"Kalla?" Sharon's voice sounded injured even over the echoing distance.

"I'm sorry. I don't mean that." Kalla sniffed back her hurt and scrubbed at her cheeks. But she did mean it. Sharon had always been coddled. Dad and she had shared a circle of grief and an affection that Kalla was never allowed to enter. And look what Sharon had done with all that love.

"It's just—I've never been able to be there at the right time for Dad. All those years, and I swear he barely looked at me. I don't think he even knew I existed—or else he wished I didn't. It hurt him too much. We finally started to make amends and then I do something stupid like come here and he's gone. Now there's no chance to fix things."

Dammit, here came the tears she'd so carefully pushed away since she'd got the news. Even looking at Simon didn't allow her to hold onto anger and control. She brushed them off her cheeks and turned away from the glass door to the booth. She didn't want Simon to see her like this.

"What are you talking about, Kalla? Dad knew you existed. Heck, he was so proud of you—his brilliant daughter. Didn't you ever hear him talk about you? I did. All the friggin' way through school. Kalla won this award. Kalla got this grade. Kalla at the top of her class. Kalla's team winning at softball. Kalla in the State Martial Arts championships. Why can't you be more like Kalla? It drove me nuts."

Kalla knuckled her forehead because the headache was back. She glanced out the glass door. Simon was looking at her and she twisted away. His gaze was like a heat on her shoulders. Enough of this being weak and emotional.

"I'll bet he made sure all the psychics sent that message through to the other side, too." What her father might have said about her didn't matter. "Listen, Sharon, I've got this list of the things you need to do to deal with Dad's estate. We should go over them, so they'll be underway when I get home. Do you think you can do that?"

Again the silence on the phone. Was Sharon upset or was it the distance lag that caused their voices to echo on the line, so you had to talk while listening to your old words echo. Probably Sharon was falling apart. There was only the question of how badly Sharon would have fallen off the wagon by the time Kalla got home.

"Kalla, I think I'm managing pretty well, you know? When Dad died I dug through his papers and found his safety deposit box. His will named you and me as executors—go figure that. But I took the will to a lawyer and he's helped me figure out what needs to be done. I've been going through his things. Aunt Micah is helping."

Kalla looked at the phone. The quiet voice that reverberated through the line didn't sound like her sister—not when she spoke, and not in the echo. This voice—once the sleep was gone—it had a real clarity.

But Sharon had always been a great manipulator when she was after a fix. Kalla had lived through Sharon bringing home psychics to con her Dad out of money. Kalla'd been there through the thefts. Give Sharon the benefit of the doubt? From 5,000 miles away what choice did she have?

"It… sounds like you're doing pretty well."

The darn phone delay again.

"Thanks. That means a lot coming from you." A heavy sigh over the hum of the wires. "Kalla, I'm sorry, but I had to go ahead with the funeral. The mortuary was pushing, you know. I talked to Micah and she said we just had to get it done. It was this morning. Micah spoke. She said some great things. I got her to give me a copy of her eulogy so you can see. I'm sorry, Kalla. I wanted you to be there, you know? We should have been there together."

Damn the tears. Damn them. It wasn't fair. It just damn well wasn't fair. Nothing was, in this life. The bad things just kept on coming like never-ending echoes in a large, locked room. She squeezed the phone harder, held onto the small shelf at the back of the booth.

"Oh god, Sharon, what am I doing half way around the world when my Dad is dying and my sister needs me. I should be there. I'm the responsible one. I'm so sorry I'm not there—to take care of Dad. To take care of you. Oh god I'm sorry."

"Stop it!"

The venom in Sharon's words lashed across the miles and struck Kalla dumb. "Damn it, Kalla, stop apologizing for having a life. You're working. You're with Alex. Dad wanted you to go, you know? He said you needed to work things out—that you'd trapped yourself and you needed a chance to get out and find out who you are. He wanted you there—not here, you know?

"And if you treat me like an invalid one more time, I'm going to slam this phone in your ear. Understand? I don't need you here. Yeah, I've made some fucking horrible mistakes in my life, but—you know—I'm dealing with it. I get up every day and I'm tempted to use, but I deal with it. Having to take care of Dad, and now having to do everything about the estate is a test for me, but no more than just living is a test for all of us. I'm going to be tempted by drugs for the rest of my life—I know that. You've coped with everything in your life. You've done everything right. This is my turn to prove I can do the right thing too—you know? I'm not going to blow this chance, Kalla. And when I show myself I can do this, maybe I'll believe I can be more like you—strong and brilliant and perfect."

Perfect. What a lie.

Kalla squeezed her eyes shut. Sharon had never talked to her like this. Sharon had never been coherent enough to string two thoughts together. But this was a new Sharon. Someone who had found a strength she'd never had before. A strength Kalla felt a little helpless in front of.

How could the Sharon she knew so well be the one on the phone?

But it was, a small voice said in her head. It was and you should celebrate it with her—not distrust her and try to take over.

But she wasn't distrusting—she just knew Sharon's history. Her failures. Kalla squeezed her eyes shut. A light rap on the booth door turned her around. Simon tapped his watch and motioned to the operator. The telecommunications building was closing. She had to decide what to do.

"Kalla, you still there? How's it going over there? How's it going with Alex?"

"The site's fine. Alex's not. 'Nuff said."

The hum of the wire, then: "Dad wondered if it would work out; he hoped, but he wasn't sure even though Madam Renata had that vision. I'm sorry. Is there a place I can send stuff to you? I'm pulling together all the documents and I'll fax them to you. You can take a look and write your thoughts and then fax them back. Okay?"

Dad hadn't thought Alex and her would work out?

The realization made it hard to focus on what Sharon has requested. She glanced at Simon and he motioned to his watch again.

Choose, Kalla. What are you going to do? She'd never allowed anyone to take care of things for her. She'd never trusted anyone enough—especially Sharon. Take a chance, or go home and show her sister just what she thought. The air in the booth was too close. Sweat trickled down her back. She glanced at Simon, held up her finger for another minute.

Could she trust? Her stomach clenched as she looked at the little sign posted on the wall. It listed a fax number.

"Okay, Sharon. You can send the documents to this number and I'll pick them up tomorrow. I'll look them over and get them back to you. If everything's in order I'll think about going back to the site. If I do, I'll pretty much be incommunicado, though."

"I've got Micah, here, Kalla. And the lawyer."

Her sister's words were tight and Kalla knew her distrust had come through to Sharon loud and clear. Why was this so hard? "Sharon?"

"Yeah."

Simon tapped on the glass again. He made a motion to the operator and a 'T' with his hands. What should she say? Tell Sharon she trusted her? That it was great how well she was doing?

"Kalla, quit worrying. I don't need your mothering, you know? You just do what Dad said for you to do. Find yourself. You've worked so hard all your life; you've been so responsible that you've always seemed to miss out on living. This is your chance."

Kalla closed her eyes. This Sharon was someone she wanted to hold onto, cheer on. She opened her mouth to tell her.

And the phone went dead. It left Kalla with the same old feelings: hurt and anger.

And so many things left unsaid.

Chapter 35 - The Price

Ne Setkya stretched his neck from side to side to ease his tension. He barely noticed the pungent flavor of the pickled tea he chewed. Tried and failed to take comfort in the cool flow of air through the teak house, the call of the doves in the eaves.

"They have departed for Mandalay, but even now I worry. What happens there? I do not think we have seen the last of Kalla Jervis." His uniform sat stiff against his skin. It was not made for sitting cross-legged on the floor.

"And I told you, she will be back. Her place is here." Daw Ma Ma Nang sat across from him on the bamboo mat, serenity like a badge across her withered face. Once she had been a beauty, but years and harsh sun had taken all but the loveliness of her eyes.

And her heart.

"Her *place* is in America with her dead father."

"He is dead. It is life she must concern herself with. That is her gift." Her voice held the creak and groan of age.

"So you tell her old stories." He couldn't help letting his sarcasm slip and saw Ma Ma Nang's eyes glint with a moment of surprise at his unusual outburst.

"You do not like the fact she has a purpose here and that I teach her of it."

By all the levels of hell, the woman was calm - and perceptive. Her Buddhist practice had become a thing of beauty to see, where his bamahsan chin was worn thin these days.

"She is American. Who knows how she will react. That culture thinks only of money."

"You judge, Ne Setkya. You judge without knowing, and thus become like your Generals. Is that what you wish to leave for your people? A place that has forgotten itself, that sees everything as other?"

"You know I do not. But how can you—we—be certain of what she will do? She may be like those German thieves and take that which must remain behind."

Daw Ma Ma Nang sat silent, slowly chewing the green, pickled tea, and outside the breeze stirred the tree branches, rattled in the bougainvillea along the wall. It was peaceful here, but Ne Setkya still battled back nerves that had jangled since his visit to Dhammayangyi.

He had seen the woman there. And the man who had spirited her away. The fact they had been at Dhammayangyi, the fact the pahto had hummed like an old bell had stopped him cold. He should have called to arrest them. Should have stopped them.

Instead he had watched them go. And with their leaving the humming had stopped and he had felt like the earth shook the foundations of the ancient structure.

"There are signs, brother, and you know it. She is drawn to the temple. And there are reports of Taungbyon risen, are there not?"

Ne Setkya's gaze jerked up to her face. How did she know? But then Daw Ma Ma Nang always seemed to know everything.

"Yes, I hear the rumors. Three men beaten by a mighty warrior. Three men who admitted many thefts and an assault on foreign women. Kalla Jervis, perhaps?"

"You mean that he protects her?"

"Or takes revenge. Taungbyon is an angry spirit and his links to her are legend."

"The last thing I need is someone pretending to be a spirit raging across the countryside. I will not have order destroyed."

"But brother, are not the tales of Taungbyon that he returns in our country's hour of need? Was he not last seen leading troops against the Japanese?"

"We were a country in dire need then. The old tales surfaced to give us hope and strength to fight."

"And is the situation not as dire today? Would you deny the very thing we protect? I say Taungbyon returns because of the woman and of the age. Burma dies, and he will fight for her life—but he will not rage if the woman is here."

"So you think I should hope the woman returns. That she continues prying into our secrets."

Daw Ma Ma Nang leaned across the bamboo, caught his hand with warm fingers strong and rough from years of labor.

"Brother, who will take over when we are gone? It is a hard truth, but with each year the guardians of Pagan grow weaker. Look at us. I was already an adult when you were born to our mother, and yet there is grey in your hair and you yearn to return to the temple. I see it in your eyes." She shook her head. "We are old, and when we pass the only guards will be those placed there eight hundred years ago."

"They have stood this long."

"They fail. Walk the halls of Dhammayangyi with me and you will know it."

Ne Setkya pulled back, closed his eyes, remembered the ominous ringing in the mountainous temple. "I have. I do. Something in the temple responds to her, I think."

Daw Ma Ma Nang nodded. "I saw it when I met her. The covenant was always marred. She can make it whole, hold the place safe, and provide the power to undo so many ills. With her, our protection would not be needed. Would you deny Burma that chance?"

"She is the one, then?" The thought of it should fill him with joy, but all he could feel was the loss. It was ending. His purpose. His son's intended purpose.

"What one woman did, another must undo." His sister brought her palms together at her chest. "We must pray she returns."

He matched her gesture, feeling sick as he thought of the woman. Kalla Jervis who must return. Kalla Jervis who must pay the price to place the final seals.

Kalla Jervis. If she returned, he would ensure she did not leave Pagan again.

§

Kalla stumbled as she stepped out of the phone booth, and Simon caught her arm, felt the tremor in her hands as he steadied her. The phone call had taken its toll in tear-stains and new shadows under her eyes.

"How was it?"

Her gaze flickered up to him, seemed surprised at his gentle question, but her guards came up, shuttered her off, and she pulled her hand free, rubbed where he had touched her. This wasn't going well. He'd accomplished nothing on the trip—he hadn't known how to begin after she tried to have someone else drive her north.

"Fine. She's doing better than I'd thought." Preoccupation in her voice. "She thinks I should stay here. Says she's got things in hand back home."

A small burst of hope came from Taungbyon, echoing Simon's own, but Kalla only looked up at him with a healthy dose of skepticism in her expression. "Not the sister I remember, but I suppose I have to trust her. At least until I get the papers she's faxing."

"So we do not seek a plane ticket?"

She eased her neck, sighed. "Who knows? Knowing Sharon, probably. It's all up in the air." Shook her head. "I feel like Alice in Wonderland and nothing is what I expect. At least not Sharon."

Simon hid a victorious smile that would probably remind Kalla of the Cheshire Cat. He glanced at the telecommunications operator who was waiting to lock the building behind them. He herded Kalla toward the door, still lost in her ruminations.

"There will be electronic documents coming for her tomorrow. We will be back," he told the operator.

Then they were out into the car-exhaust-scented street and he glanced down at Kalla. So lovely even distracted, and suddenly he wanted her attention focused. Preferably on himself, because if she were staying it was more important than ever they sort things out between them.

Agreed.

Simon acknowledged the Nat.

"I have an old friend here. He runs a guest house. We can get rooms for the night and then perhaps I can show you ancient Mandalay. Does that sound well?"

An absent nod, that sent Taungbyon writhing in impatience. *Kiss her. Kiss her now.*

Simon shoved the urge back.

Wait. There is hope.

He would do his best to bring her back to them both.

§

The Silver Paya Guest House sat on a side street lined with small shop-stalls and shaded by broad-leaved teak and flame trees. Bicycle traffic, children, and old women smoking sausage-sized cheroots kept Simon busy steering through the narrow street.

Kalla left him to it, preoccupied by her phone conversation, until they pulled in beside a tidy, white-stucco building and Simon got out and began to unload.

"Thein Win will have rooms for us. We can shower and perhaps nap before we go out for the evening. I have a surprise planned."

The wicked rise of his brow caught her attention.

"I believe I have a say in that."

"And perhaps I will allow you that say in some things, but this will be my surprise."

"I think I've had enough of your surprises."

"Oui. I believe I recall you did not care for my sudden departure from the nun's home."

"Wasn't partial to the lead-me-into-the-woods-and-have-your-way-with-me, or the hands-over-the-mouth, yank-me-into-the-darkness thing either." She cocked her hip at him, glad she could keep control. She needed to keep focused on Sharon and Dad and the return home until tomorrow.

"You wound me." He struck a dramatic pose that almost made her laugh. "Aah, but I believe there was pleasure in our tour of Mount Popa." The raw darkness and desire of his eyes made her look away.

"And there's where you're wrong," she managed. "It was a momentary lapse in judgment. That's all. Nothing that's going to happen again." Her hand fell to her locked case that contained the puppet.

He only grinned and ushered her to the door, whispering. "You still have to live through another surprise. You cannot get my secret from me, no matter how you try."

"Great." She let her sarcasm show, hoping it would tame her awareness of the V of his shoulders, the strength of him, right behind her.

Thein Win was a thin man, dressed in traditional blue-plaid longyi and a white western business shirt carefully rolled to his elbows in Simon-fashion. He came out from behind his counter, face filled with pleasure.

"My old friend! You came back! Did I not say you would come back to Burma again? Have you brought magazines? Stories of Paris and the world?" He caught Simon's hand, pumped it more times than was necessary.

"Je regrette." Simon shook his head. "I brought issues of Paris Match, but the customs men found them in my luggage."

"No matter. You will tell me what the world thinks of this Myanmar we have become. Come. Sit. I have a room - " he eyed Kalla. "Two rooms for you. Please, who is this lovely lady?"

"Kalla Jervis. Thein Win, the manager of this most excellent guest house."

"Miss Kalla, very pleased to meet you." Thein Win stood very proper and formal, shook her hand, obviously proud he knew the custom.

"And I'm pleased to meet you and wish I could have made a better first impression." She looked ruefully down at her dust and sweat stained clothing.

"Travel in Myanmar is a dusty, hot business. All travelers say so." He busied himself over the register and their passports, nodded at two younger men who ran out to the jeep and hauled in their bags, then lugged them up three flights of stairs. Thein Win led them up the flights afterwards, talking all the way.

"Things have not been the same in Mandalay since the riots back in '95. People still anger over the rumor of the theft of Mahamuni Buddha's gold. And now…. " He shook his head. "You will see, friend Simon. The Chinese—they come and buy the businesses and it only makes our people poorer. There are people reduced to thieving from the tourists. Some places are no longer safe, though most people are still friendly."

"Does U Byin Nu still have his place?"

"Of course. What Chinese would know how to run his business?"

With a glance in Kalla's direction, Simon waved off further comment and she knew whoever U Byin Nu was, he had something to do with Simon's plans.

"Could you send him a message that I would like to bring a friend tonight?"

"Of course."

They were let into clean rooms at the top of the house. Fans circled, circled, circled above neat twin beds. An open window framed a silver spire as a flight of doves rose into the sky like spirits sent forth. Kalla inhaled the wonderful scent of growing things and life—so unlike Pagan.

"Lovely. Just lovely." She turned and smiled at Thein Win. "You must have given me your best room."

"For so lovely a friend of Simon's, how could I not?"

Kalla glanced at Simon. He was so obviously held in high regard it surprised her. Simon Renault was trouble—a thief and a womanizer—not someone that people regarded as a friend.

And yet he had tried to help her. Like trying to arrange a flight for her in the middle of the night. Like coming for her at the temple. Like volunteering to drive her all the way to Mandalay when his shadowed eyes said he had had very little sleep.

"Thank you." She said it to Thein Win, but somehow it was Simon who held her gaze, whose slight nod made her glad.

Chapter 36 - Old Wounds

The Eindawya Paya was small to Kalla, and filled with light and air after the huge, dark weight of the Pagan temples. White and silver, a single spire lifted shimmering tiers up to a slender pinnacle, forty feet up, against the fading blue sky of late afternoon. It seemed to lift her spirits with it. As did the dove wings.

The birds pecked seed spread around the paya's base, but had taken flight at her approach. The wind of their wings brought thoughts of the story of the swan maiden and her transformation. Was it really possible to change so much?

Kalla, drawn from her room, wandered the square, walled compound of the paya that was almost next door to the guesthouse.

Sharon said she had changed—heck, she'd even sounded like she had. But there had been other times she'd tried treatment. Other times when Dad had celebrated his elder daughter's salvation, only to have her slide off the cliff of addiction again. Each time it had sent him further into the clutches of the psychics for answers. It had left Kalla feeling his blame again, as if she'd pushed Sharon into using Meth in the first place. Or as if she were at fault for not knowing how to help her sister.

Sharon had done—could do—a lot of damage.

But she'd asked for this chance. For trust.

And trying to control everything, to make everything run smoothly, was exhausting business. It was why she'd come to Burma—to give up some of that control to someone else.

"Like that worked out."

In a corner of the white, marble-paved compound stood a small, wooden doll's house raised on a slim pedestal and fluttering with pink and yellow scarves tied to the ornately carved roof. Kalla paused inside a roofed walkway as a mother and two small children reverently placed a bouquet of flowers in front of the house and lit a stick of incense.

Then the children skittered away like small, wild things to chase the returning doves into the air. It would be wonderful to just fly away like that. To have wings.

She felt Simon's dark presence, smelled the incense-scent of his skin, before he spoke.

"What is the phrase—a penny for your thoughts?"

"That's a spirit house, isn't it?" She motioned to the small building.

"Yes. You see the small figures inside? That is - " He peered inside. "Taungbyon." His voice was surprised. "You see?" He stepped close enough she felt his damp hair on her cheek, his breath on her neck as he pointed out the two figures.

"They were brothers, Muslim sons of a great warrior and an ogress of Mount Popa. I spoke of them on the way to Popa. They did great feats of bravery for the King, but he killed them because they would not help build a Buddhist temple." He stepped up to the little shrine, picked a flower from the bouquet and handed it to her, but she hesitated to take something that had been given as offering.

"They loved greatly when they were alive. Beautiful women were always a weakness. They would want you to have this."

Simon's eyes were as dark as the space between the stars as he stepped up to her, eased the pale pink bloom behind her ear and her hair back from her face with a touch that sent a tremor through her. A sharp pain struck behind her eyes and she winced and jerked away.

"You shouldn't do that."

"Why? It looks lovely in your hair."

She touched the flower petals, soft as velvet, smelled the hint of sweetness it carried as she looked into the dark eyes of the man she knew was a liar and a thief.

A part of her wanted to encourage him, but the stronger part made her look away. The mother and children had circled the paya and were leaving the compound. She and Simon were alone.

"It's not your place to touch me, Simon. It was the crowning mistake of a trip made up of too many mistakes. I won't make another one." She stepped away from him, when she didn't want to. But she needed space to get her mind working again.

His study brought a heat to her cheeks she knew he couldn't miss. So darn cock-sure of himself. That was Simon Renault. He wouldn't even allow her to keep her distance. Instead he stepped close again, caught her shoulders and studied her face. She was forced to either look into his eyes or consider the dark hairs on his forearms, exposed by the neatly turned-back cuffs of his khaki shirt. There was hair like that on his chest, too.

She chose to look in his eyes.

"You did not sleep and now you are exhausted."

How did he know that? She'd showered and lain in her room for an hour until she abandoned trying to sleep and had gone out, telling Thein Win where she would be.

"I'll sleep better tonight, then, won't I?"

The way his gaze narrowed said he didn't believe her, but then he sighed and smiled that damned infuriating smile.

"Then we shall just have to tire you out enough to sleep."

She wasn't sure she like the sound of that, but he caught her hand before she could protest and led her out of the compound and into the busy streets of Mandalay.

They caught a rickshaw cab and he pointed out Zegyo Market and the gleaming temples that topped Mandalay Hill. He had the driver take them around the immense, crenellated walls of Mandalay Fort, telling her of how this had been the home of the last King of Burma before he was deposed by the British.

"See the spiral towers with their eight-tiered roofs? Those are signs of the King. The walls are three meters thick at the bottom. Once this area held the teak palaces of the king and queen, but the British took it over. The palaces burned during the Second World War."

"What a tragedy," she said as she scanned the length of the walls.

Simon shrugged. "It was as it should be in Burma. Each King built a new capital of teak, and when his reign finished, the palaces passed away. But it was a shame that all the rich murals and inlay were lost here. But then, the British Raj had already stolen most anything of worth."

"The way things were done then, I suppose."

"There are many ancient capitals near here—Sagaing, Amarapura. Perhaps you would like to see? There are only temples there now. It is the way of things. Natural."

"Not nowadays. Back home we build to last."

He nodded. "Here some would say that our American way is against the natural order of things. Only spirits last forever. And Buddha."

She shivered at his words and at how his gaze had grown intense in the gilding sunset. Her Dad would have liked this man. Dad would have liked this country and its preoccupation with spirits, too.

She rubbed her arms against the chill as the rickshaw wheels whined over the pavement and the driver brought them back to where they had begun. Simon spoke to him.

"So was that the surprise—the fort?" she asked, starting to climb out, because she really needed time alone to rid herself of her attraction to Simon and to focus on her father and what had to be done.

Simon stayed her with a hand on her arm, but her hard look at his fingers must have done its job. He released her.

"Not the surprise. We will go for dinner now—a Burmese dinner. And then will come the surprise." His smile seemed to weasel its way too close to her heart.

She used her hard gaze on his arm resting so easily across the seat and he removed it. Sighing, she eased back into the Simon-scented rickshaw and knew she should just tell him she was going to stay in her room.

"You are like the cat—too curious. It may get you into trouble, you know."

"I wasn't being curious. I was hoping it was over."

"Aah. I am sorry to hear that. But is not curiosity an aspect of the scientific mind?"

She nodded.

"Then be curious as we take our meal."

He paid the rickshaw driver to let them off at a large square filled with tables and people and noise. The vehicle whizzed off, and Simon caught her unwilling hand. "This is Mandalay's night market. Not so grand as those in Thailand or Hong Kong because Myanmar is a poor country, but it's where the people come to eat and socialize."

The square was lined with dusty-looking three-story hotels and shops that must have dated back to the colonial era, and small, low-roofed, teak homes with small, fenced yards that gave onto the street. Streetlights were virtually non-existent, so people had set up thin bamboo poles strung with miniature Christmas lights that Kalla found both strange and charming, given it was May.

"There are vegetable markets down closer to the canal, but here are the best restaurants in Mandalay." Simon pulled her through the steadily increasing crowd, toward a line of stalls and a scattering of trestle tables.

She would have fought free, but why? Hadn't Sharon shown her she should stop trying to control everything? Besides, this was probably her last night in Burma—she should enjoy it.

She forgave Simon enough to focus on the delicious scents of frying fish and curry and onion and ginger and garlic. Voices around her. Smiling faces and the laughter of children playing around their elder's legs.

"So what would the curious princess prefer?"

"You can stop calling me princess. It's not bugging me anymore."

Simon glanced over his shoulder, shrugged.

"Perhaps I think it suits you."

A little prickle of pique ran through her. "So you think I'm imperious and difficult?"

That grin of his that cut right through her.

"Difficult? Perhaps. But also lovely. And worth the trouble, as a princess should be." He pulled her closer to his side as slim Burmese in their longyi threaded past, and steam from bubbling vats of fat filled the evening air.

Kalla barely noticed, surprised as she was at his opinion of her. It embarrassed her that she'd questioned his use of 'princess'. She looked like she was fishing for compliments.

"Now this is interesting for the curious."

Simon broke her mortification and pointed out golden rounds of whole lake shrimp and small fish that had been formed into four-inch discs and deep fried. The air was filled with the scent of hot oil and sweet flesh.

"These are caught in small lakes nearby and are very good served with sweet and sour syrup." He raised his brows at her as she eyed the rounds.

"Whole shrimp and fish?" she said doubtfully.

"The entire thing." His grin said he laughed at her squeamishness because the French ate literally anything.

"They're good?"

"Shall we try one and see?"

Let the control go, Kalla. What's the worst that could happen? A little food poisoning isn't going to kill you. She nodded, and soon she was nibbling a crisp round of shrimp and trying not to notice the little black eyes that stared back at her.

But it was good. Very good in fact, with the sweet shrimp flesh and the thin shell cooked so it simply crunched in her mouth and was gone.

Simon led her to a table, told her to hold it for them, and disappeared into the crowd. She tried to watch him as she nibbled, but he seemed to meld with these people even though he topped most of them by almost a foot.

Such a strange man. Infuriating and dangerous and yet gentle. He seemed to straddle between the west and Burma and be parts of both and yet part of neither.

A thunk, and Simon set down two plates before them, then straddled the bench across from her. The noise of the market surrounded them, made it hard to hear.

"I thought you should try some of the best of Burmese food. This is magyi-ywe thok—a spicy salad made of tamarind leaves and lime juice and peanuts and chilies."

She took a fork he produced and tasted. Sweet spice and crunch and fire. Another bite and she smiled at him.

"This is good. It reminds me of Som Tam - green papaya salad in Thailand, but better."

"Same idea, but less spicy. Burmese food is the least spicy of Southeast Asian food."

He kept bringing her food, and she was caught up in the delight of new tastes on her palate, made more delightful because she just gave up discerning what it was that she ate and obediently tried what he brought her and laughed when she was surprised. Simon laughed, too, as the cool evening air settled off the river and the Christmas lights stained everything festive amber and blue.

The newness of flavors. The newness of letting go of her controls conspired against her anger and she had to admit that this Simon she was attracted to, regardless of what had happened before. The way he leaned in towards her, he was obviously attracted to her as well. She wanted to brush that wild forelock of hair from his eyes.

Finally, she caught his hand, stopped him from springing up to bring more food, and he froze, time stopped and the market noise disappeared as he looked down at her with those dark eyes, more brown than black now, and a softness around them she hadn't seen before.

"Yes, Princess?"

She couldn't seem to look away, nor release his hand.

"Maybe you should just stay put for a while. We haven't eaten all this." She waved her free hand at the litter of half-eaten dishes between them, feeling somehow guilty that she wanted to sit and talk to this man when she should be angry at him and focused on her father's death. That thought was a cold bath of water.

"It—it's a shame to be wasteful in a country that has so little."

Simon's gaze went to her hand still clutching his arm and she felt a slight tremor run through him—as if something quaked inside him. The weird thing was a part of her seemed to answer and she knew if she let herself she could really lose control.

It took effort to hold back, to release him.

Simon swallowed, checked his watch and smiled that taunting smile of his. No, it was more of a promise—a promising smile.

"Quel dommage." His voice rumbled in his chest. "It is time for your surprise."

Then his hands caught her shoulders and brought her to her feet. Strong hands ran down her arms, set fires flaring deep, but he only released her, turned, and led her through the crowd.

Chapter 37 - Yoke Thei

Taungbyon wanted her, and so did Simon. It was an ache to have her so near, to take her by the hand and lead her through the crowd, the wailing music, the voices and the scents that brought back so much of his childhood and a happier time. A time when he had been just-Simon and the world had been a whirlwind of travel following his anthropologist father from America to Paris to the country that would always be Burma.

Touching her also took him farther back—to the stormy life of just-Taungbyon.

Things had not changed much in Burma in all the years between those two lives. When Taungbyon overwhelmed Simon, he could catch glimpses of other lives, other times when the great Nat had possessed others. Simple lives, mostly. Village lives until the war.

At the edge of the square, village women sat with their backs to the shuttered stores, selling tomatoes and thannaka and dried shrimp, and gossiping with shoppers. He waved down a pedicab and climbed into the narrow space. It was built for Burmese—not his bulk—but having Kalla's softness squeezed in beside him was nothing to complain about. He left his arm draped across the back of the seat this time and felt her slowly relax, like a cat caressed into submission.

Caress now.

It is not the time.

The cab struggled up the slight slope from the night market to the fortress and turned to follow the old fortress wall the twenty or so blocks until the fortress ended and they were in an area of older buildings.

"Isn't the guest house back the other way?"

"It is."

She oriented quickly. A good thing.

The night was thick here, Mandalay experiencing another of its frequent brown-outs so the few street lights faded into darkness. The air smelled of curry and frangipani and neem blossoms.

"Where are you taking me?"

"I said it was a surprise." Ahead a lantern waved at them and the pedicab slowed, came to a stop in front of a large, teak house and adjoining building.

"Our stop, Princess." He leapt down and caught her hand, helped her down. It was an excuse to touch her, and the flash of her gaze said she knew it and accepted.

She *had* touched him of her own volition, even though he'd seen confusion in her gaze. He glanced at the lantern holder. Stouter that Simon remembered. More grey-haired.

"U Byin Nu?"

"Friend Simon? Is it you?" The man's fluid Burmese was overwhelmed by emotion as he caught Simon's hand, pumped it hello. "It has been too many years, old friend. Too many. I thought your mother held you prisoner in Paris and you would not come back to us."

Simon found a smile, even as the familiar old twinge of loss cut through him.

"I'm sorry for that. I missed Burma, but life…" He raised his hands in a what-can-you-do gesture and caught Kalla's hand as he switched to English. "This is my—friend. Kalla Jervis, meet U Byin Nu, a skilled craftsman and the keeper of my secret for this evening. Is all arranged?"

"For you old friend, it is."

Simon caught Kalla's strange look and leaned close. He inhaled her delicate apples and roses, overlaid with a hint of curry and wanted her.

"My father used to come here for his research. He worked at the Sorbonne before his death. It is why I lived most of my life in Paris—and why the Sorbonne administration put up with me."

A flash of sympathy and grief in her gaze and then U Byin Nu led them past the house and held the door of the larger building open.

Torchlight in the darkness, and faces crowded, staring, beyond.

§

Kalla took an involuntary step back, bumped into Simon's chest, and his hands found her shoulders, steadied.

"It is all right, Princess." His voice was soft, his breath warm in her ear. "It is yoke thei. I thought you should see a performance before you left Burma."

"Ohmygawd." She stepped inside, scanned the walls hung with small figures, and the musical instruments clustered before the torch-lit stage. She whirled to Simon.

"How did you know? I'd thought—hoped—maybe I would get a chance, but everything was so weird in Pagan I had no time to even ask if there was a troupe."

"There is only a poor performance by children in Pagan. The royal puppets only truly dance in Mandalay and Yangon, and I have heard of a troupe in Arakan. Unfortunately, it is only old men who hold the knowledge of the marionette construction, and old men die."

The comment made her cringe. She tried to hide it, but Simon stepped closer, shook his head in apology.

"Most only make tourist puppet," U Byin Nu offered. "They not skilled. Not so good. But once, puppets fly-fly apart and come back together on stage, so children screamed and Kings thought magic worked."

"Kalla owns a royal puppet."

U Byin Nu's eyes went round as he turned to her, and it made Kalla uncomfortable that she owned something that this man so obviously treasured.

"My mother came from Thailand. When she married my Dad, she brought the puppet with her. It was an heirloom passed down through her family. I don't know much about the puppet other than that."

"But you have only one?" U Byin Nu looked from Simon to her, concern on his face.

"Only one. The Votaress."

The little man shook his head as if he were about to say something, but then he turned from them. "I must get the performance started."

He scurried down the sloped stairs of the theatre as if he could not wait to get away. He disappeared behind the stage, all the while shaking his head.

"What was that all about?"

Simon did one of his Gallic shrugs that could have infuriated her before. Now she realized it was just him. His warm hand caught hers and he led her down between the raked rows of theatre seats to chairs next to the musicians.

"I warn you. It will be very loud when the music starts."

"You've seen the performances before, then."

"Many times. My father was consumed with the puppets. My mother as well. When he first came to Burma—as it was then—he met my mother and fell in love. He came back many times to see the performances, to speak with the old craftsmen. Most of them were dead by the time I was born, but I know a little. I have seen the performance here and have heard of a small troupe run by a retired Minister of Culture in Yangon."

In the torchlight his gaze seemed to deepen with memories, and suddenly she wanted to know more of this man, of his past. "Tell me."

Simon misunderstood. Or perhaps he purposely chose not to expose himself. "There are three types of performers in a yoke thei pwe. Puppeteers, Singers, and Musicians. The puppeteers dance the puppets and the musicians play, but it is the singers who make the performance whole. They tell the stories, and sing the parts. There are few singers of note left in Burma. The best is one of U Byin Nu's performers. Once, though, a top singer was revered almost like royalty. The royal yoke thei were given great patronage by the kings. They were the only performers allowed to dance on a stage higher than the King's head, and they could take license and criticize the royal family in performance in ways that would have gotten anyone else killed. They were valuable, these little performers."

In front of them, musicians had settled behind the strangest assortment of musical instruments Kalla had ever seen. There were drums in a circle, yes. And a clarinet-shaped instrument that whined up a scale, but there was also a musician sitting in the midst of a huge circle of brass gongs like a xylophone on steroids, and a massive, brightly painted, dragon-shaped structure that suspended a large drum from its belly.

A drum rolled and the flute wailed. The torchlight shone on the raised marionette stage with a background painting of fields and hills and trees. A puppeteer appeared on the scaffolding above the stage and a small figure swathed in red startled Kalla as it danced onto the stage carrying an offering bowl.

Votaress, Kalla recognized, but less ornate than hers. She shivered.

The small figure dipped and swayed, holding the offering bowl before her, offering it to the heavens, towards the painted hills and fields. Someone—an old man seated in the wings of the stage—began to sing.

A flicker of pain surged behind Kalla's eyes, and the music rose so loud she found herself pressed back in her seat, clutching the armrests. Then a warm hand enfolded hers and the pain became a building pulse. She knew Simon looked at her and could not control the expression on her face.

"What is that song?" Kalla leaned over to Simon, could barely make herself heard over the music, wild as anything at a nat festival.

"He sings the Votaress offering to the spirits, asking for strong crops and land and children."

She nodded, her gaze never leaving the stage. And then the Votaress was gone.

So many figures followed. Ogres and Kings. The Alchemist in scarlet with his staff and gold and red hat. Ministers and minions. Playful pages that somersaulted across the stage. Handmaids that suckled babes. Tigers and elephants and white horses and galon birds and naga. The Mintha and Minthamee—the Prince and Princess—who danced together more gracefully than many human couples, and all the while she felt Simon's gaze on her, felt the warmth of his hand on hers until she turned her hand, twined fingers with him.

It was like a sigh ran through them both, so when the music stopped and the performers took their bows, it was hard to straighten away from the way she had rested against him, hard to separate their hands so she could applaud.

Wildly. She stood up and continued clapping until finally U Byin Nu came to around the stage to join them.

"It was wonderful. Wonderful! It's hard to imagine that small wooden figures can transport you away like that." It was true. The entire performance had swept her up, taken her to some place simpler, where human story and the world were intertwined.

She caught U Byin Nu's hand. "You must thank the puppeteers for me. Please."

"The puppeteers come meet you, yes?"

"They will? Could they—would they show me how to work the strings?" She felt like a child at Christmas, knew she probably broke all kinds of decorum in her excited clasp of U Byin Nu's hand.

He called back to the stage and an old man and a younger woman came out from behind the curtains. The woman carried a Brahmin puppet, stood by patiently as U Byin Nu explained who she was.

The woman and the old man frowned, shook their heads, spoke.

"What's the matter?" Kalla glanced at Simon. He too, frowned in a way that brought a chill to Kalla's skin. "Simon?"

"They say they do not wish you to touch their puppets. The marionettes are their children. They do not want one who kidnaps a puppet to touch their charges."

"Kidnaps?" She looked up at Simon, a chill running down her back. Had he set them up to say this? Was this an attempt to get her to relinquish the puppet? "I haven't kidnapped anything. Did U Byin Nu tell them that?" The chill rushed away in a flood of anger.

Simon caught her hand, spoke in his fluid Burmese. The puppeteers replied sharply, hurried back behind the curtains leaving a contrite U Byin Nu behind.

"I most sorry, Miss Kalla. We are superstitious people. They do not wish others to handle their puppets. That is as it has always been." But that wasn't all of it. Kalla saw the way his gaze flickered away from hers, as if he hid something.

"Simon? What's going on?" She pulled loose, ignoring the comfort of his hand.

"U Byin Nu, the puppeteers were saying something about tree-brothers and ill luck. What's that about?"

The marionette owner avoided eye contact and sighed.

"It is old tradition. The twenty-eight traditional puppets are made from a single Yamani tree. That is a great tree. They say it holds great spirit that becomes part of whole troupe. They are joined. If part missing, the others wither and become nothing. Without Votaress, troupe cannot perform. Very sad thing." He shook his head. "You have such an orphan puppet. Not good. She should be returned to her troupe or destroyed as ill luck."

"I will not!" The thought of destroying her puppet shocked her. The little figure meant too much to even consider following such ridiculous beliefs. And yet. "I'm sorry, but she was an inheritance. She has been away from her troupe for a very long time. I'm sure it's no problem."

The little proprietor only bowed. "I am glad you like the show. Please tell others that they may come. Simon, friend, I must close the theatre now." And with that U Byin Nu eased them out of the theatre and the click of locks sounded behind them.

In the darkened city, Kalla inhaled the damp air of the river. The brown-out continued, but the pedicab waited for them and Simon handed her up to the seat, then settled himself beside her, warm, comfortable, even.

But part of her trembled inside. It was like the music still wailed in her ears and U Byin Nu's voice still chilled her. Made her aware of the headache that lurked quietly behind her eyes.

"You are very quiet." Simon's black gaze seemed to run over her face as a tangible thing.

"I was just thinking. My puppet must be very lonely, if what U Byin Nu says is true." And loneliness was something she could understand.

She hauled herself back from that maudlin thought.

"It was a wonderful surprise, Simon."

His knuckle smoothed a stray strand of hair from her cheek and she felt herself tremble at the touch and the desire in his eyes.

"And I am sorry the evening ended so. I had not intended to upset you. I wanted to—to make amends, I suppose."

"You—I guess you did." She forced a smile up at him.

"Kalla, I would not have taken the puppet. My mother always wished to finish her troupe, but at the same time I think she knew they were not a real troupe. Each of her puppets is beautiful, but they are different. Orphans. She mentioned to me once about the belief that they contained a part of the spirit of a single tree. I think she'd have been mortified if she realized she was holding those spirits prisoner."

Kalla couldn't meet his gaze. "Your mother believed, then—in spirits, I mean." She shivered, and was glad of Simon's heat.

"It is Burmese to believe."

"Aah. Well, then, my Dad would have made a good Burmese." She couldn't think about it—wouldn't think about it. She leaned out of the pedicab. "My god, it's a beautiful night. Look at the stars."

The pedicab whisked them past the fort walls and downhill before turning into the side street and depositing them at the Paya Guesthouse.

Inside, Thein Win greeted them. They spoke briefly and then went upstairs to their rooms. Simon gallantly bid her good night and turned to his room, and that was a problem.

"Simon." He glanced back at her, key in his hand, those black eyes something that could almost devour her.

"Thank you for the gift you've given me."

He straightened, shrugged. "It was nothing."

"No. It was something." How could she say this and not seem a fool? She looked down at the room key in her hand. "Simon, I believe you. I believe you didn't try to steal the Votaress, though I don't understand how she got into your room." She stayed his comment with her hand. "I really don't know how to do this other than to be blunt. I don't want the night to end just yet. Would you like to come in?"

'To talk,' she'd meant to end that sentence, but the words stuck in her throat. He stayed so still she was sure he was going to laugh at her, but then his gaze met hers. He knew what her request had cost her.

Only one stride of his long legs and then he was in front of her, predatory, intimidating, but his large hands gently cupped her face, the pad of his thumbs softly traced her lips. Then he lowered his mouth to hers. Kissed.

Gently at first, allowing her to be the guide, and she wanted him more. His touch left her breathless, weak, but his lips brought slow fire, flooding up from her core. Her hands slipped up, found the back of his head as her mouth answered, demanded.

And then she was pressed to the wall, lost, as Simon's lips found her cheeks, her eyes, her hair.

Chapter 38 - The Incense of Flesh

Simon pushed back the swirling Taungbyon presence. *No. This time it will be my way, not yours.*

Impatience beat at him, but he showed his strength by pushing himself back from the wall, looking down at Kalla with her bruised lips that demanded to be kissed, and her blue-black eyes. He could get drunk on her apple and rose scent.

"Are you sure you wish to do this, ma petite?" His voice rumbled deep in his chest with Taungbyon force.

Kalla answered with a palm stroke of his cheek. She handed him her key and looked away as if she could not believe she had done such a thing.

Submission. The Nat's satisfaction came through.

Not submission. It was a giving, a gift in response to the puppet show. Perhaps that was all it was. Paying him back in the only way she knew how?

He caught her hand, kissed her palm, and looked deep in her eyes. Not Kalla. Not *his* Kalla. She was far too complicated for that.

He unlocked the door and led her inside. Neat. Typical Kalla. Moonlight through the window exposed her things neatly folded in her suitcase. Her bed made, but showing signs she'd tried to rest there.

When he turned to her, in the darkness she had already released the top button of her blouse, exposing the exquisite delicacy of her collarbone, the curve where her neck became her shoulder. He could bury his face there, drown in her scent.

He ran his hands down her arms and smiled.

"I had hoped...."

"Shh." She unbuttoned his shirt, kissed his bared chest, ran her hands across his skin, down his sides until he shivered.

Taungbyon rose, rose, whirling at the sensation, lifting Simon on a cloud of pure arousal. *He would have this woman. Take her.*

No. This will be different.

He found she had stepped back, waited as his fingers went to her shirt, unbuttoned carefully and slipped it from her shoulders. Slim and pale as new poplar in a French mountain glade, her hair silk through his fingers.

"You steal my breath."

"No. This isn't some fairy tale. You just want a woman."

"Do I?" He knew why she demeaned what was to happen. Still wanting control. Wanting to not feel.

But her gaze traveled down his body, leaving jolts of fire in its path.

"I'd say the signs point to it." She leered up at him so the Nat roared. Simon held his breath.

"Peut-être. That might be so." He forced himself to move slowly, to run his palm over her bare shoulder, run his hands down her sides, then up to cup the underside of her covered breasts, feeling her tremble. Her body arched to meet his hands, her nipples engorged through the silk fabric of her bra.

He lowered his head to her mouth again, traced his lips down to her throat, and heard the hiss of her intaken breath as he lingered there, tasting. Yes, roses and strawberry. An underlying scent of apples as tart as Kalla's tongue.

His hands steadied her as he ran his mouth down to the upper curve of her breasts, as he mouthed the soft flesh through the cloth.

His fingers expertly dealt with the bra enclosure, eased the straps from her shoulder, freeing her to his lips, his tongue. Again the hiss of breath, a soft moan that made him smile at his work as his hands smoothed the skin of her back, her sides, cupped her breasts so he could better do his task.

He knew he worked well, when her arms came around him, when she pressed her body against him, wanting more. At that he lifted his face to hers, kissed her and felt the heat of her need, knew he would be the one to keep this slow, taking time to savor delights too long lost.

Taungbyon pulsed inside him, with him, but had settled to enjoy the savor of this encounter as the Nat had never done before.

Min.

The name echoed in Simon's head, as he eased Kalla's jeans down off her hips, as he discarded his own clothing to the floor and urged her back onto the bed.

He wanted to explore this willing creature. Know her and make her his, as he would give himself. How long had it been since he loved like this?

Years.

Generations.

Millennia.

He would make this last.

§

The wild music filled Kalla as she tasted him. Incense and musk and heated spice—clove, cinnamon and nutmeg. The burr of his five o'clock shadow. The feel of his lips. The hard length of him locked against her. She ran her body against his lean muscle and wanted.

His hands, lips, brought her small sobs of pleasure, brought her smaller hands to his body, felt him stiffen at her exploration. At her kisses.

Wild music, red curtain swept over her sight, and the sense she was two people—she locked in embrace, and another—watching—melting into the moment of passion. Set free.

She reached for him as their sweat mingled and she had not loved like this before. His body covered her as he cradled her hips, lifted her to him.

And found her.

She moved, frantic for more, and he answered. Filled her, moving slow as mountains, slow as eons, slow and building as an earthquake builds. Kalla shuddered as she looked into his eyes.

As the parts of her merged.

As he joined her and became one.

As they joined with the darkness of the world.

In the darkness he hung above her, intense gaze locked on hers. She couldn't look away. Was falling and lost, hopelessly lost, and she knew the only person who could help her was here. Now. Part of her.

She arched her body to meet him, desperately, desperately. He caught her legs, brought them forward and moved deeper. As if he would plow her soul. Find her. She held on for dear life. Never let you go.

"Never let you go," he whispered as he moved.

Moved faster as sweat found her eyes, her hair. Harder as she tasted, drank, thrust, was flooded, drowned in the sensations. Room lost. Darkness and moonlight. The pale light of Simon's eyes.

His power as he drove into her.

As she gasped for air. For him.

Cried for air.

Exploded in air and called out.

"Simon!"

As a warrior shout of triumph filled the air.

When the shudders stopped she lay with him, curled back to front in his arms as he stroked her, kissed her shoulder, her neck, cupped her breast with a care as if his hands sought to remember every feature of her. She lay, still slick with need of him, knew he wanted her, too, wanted the feel of him inside even more. It was quick work to apply another condom.

She shifted to accept him from behind, sighed at the smooth way they meshed.

"Aah." A soft whisper kissed into her ear. "And so you have gifted me right back, my Princess, my Minthamee, my Min."

Something in his voice evoked a memory she was not even sure she had, as he moved smoothly, slowly, as he held her to him.

"Who… who is Taungbyon?" It came out as a pleasured gasp and Simon pulled her to him, cupped her body as if he would not let her go.

"A great spirit, ma petite," he whispered in her ear. "Once he was a warrior and loved a woman, a Votaress actually. But she died."

She half turned her head at the sadness in his voice. Reached back to stroke his cheek.

"It was not the end of their love, for when the King killed Taungbyon he became a nat. Years later, when he possessed a young man, he fell in love with a woman who harbored the spirit of his lost love—his Min. But she, too, was taken from him—and he now seeks her through all time. Great love cannot be denied."

He began to move again. Slow, languorous strokes as his hands moved over her body, pleasuring, sparking lightning in her flesh, bringing them both to the brink again.

And beyond.

Gasping, they lay tangled together, he stroking her hair back from her face, softness in his gaze she had thought she only imagined before. He had called her his Min. Oh god, what was she doing? She was leaving tomorrow, probably.

"What is it? You stiffen as if you do not wish to be here." His voice came out of the darkness as his hands pulled her back against him, his heat scorching away her defenses. So strange. And so familiar.

"It's—nothing."

His arms tightened. "You cannot lie to me, petite. I know lies."

"Alright," she knew a tinge of exasperation colored her voice, knew she shouldn't say this, but what the hell. She'd already destroyed any professional distance she had with this man. At least there wouldn't be time to get more entangled.

"This is the first time in my life I haven't felt alone."

His arms curled her to him more tightly. "But you have a sister, a father."

"Sure. And they could barely stand to look at me. They won't admit it, but to this day all I do is remind them of my mother." There. She'd answered his question and not let it all out. It only hurt a little.

"You look like your mother?" His hand came up to explore her face, smooth her cheek.

"Maybe. Now. But that's not it." Kalla took strength from his arms, even as she wondered why she told him this. Probably because she *was* leaving. She wouldn't have to see his pity after she climbed on that plane tomorrow, because there was no way Sharon would have got things right.

"I killed my mother." Say it matter of factly, and it didn't hurt so much. Control was everything when it came to talking about this.

"Pardon? Kalla? You cannot say that and not explain, chérie. It is not possible." He leaned up on his elbow, turned her to him. "Explain, s'il-te-plait."

She couldn't meet his gaze, wondered why she'd said anything that could lead to this disclosure, but it was like something demanded it. Like Simon made her lose control in far too many ways. Like she needed to lance this boil in her soul.

"She died having me. It was a difficult birth. Then they couldn't stop the bleeding. She died. Dad and Sharon never forgave me. Dad loved her so much he spent his life savings trying to reach her on 'the other side'. Simple as that. You can't undo something like that."

"Oh, ma petite." He slipped down beside her, took her in his arms. Kissed her face, her hair. "But you tried, didn't you? You have tried all these years to undo it."

She didn't want his sympathy, his pity. She twisted to get free, but he wouldn't release her. "How would you know?" she spat.

"Puisque—because I understand old regret. I have spent many—years—trying to deal with loss and old actions, Kalla."

He said it so simply it took her breath away. No anger. No letting her push him away. No pity. Simply the warmth of his arms and his breath on her shoulder, the room distant, scented with their loving and the incense of flesh. The red haze colored the night. She thought of the puppets, her Votaress that she was taking away from Burma again. Leaving her lonely as well, if U Byin Nu and his puppeteers were to be believed. Another thing to feel guilty about and spend her years paying penance for. Perhaps she deserved to be alone herself.

Simon's breath had quieted, though his arms still confined her against his chest. Not confined. Perhaps cherished was a better word to describe how his hands smoothed her skin.

"Simon?"

No response, and she pulled away, began to sit up, but he pulled her back, nibbled her ear.

"I want you here." His voice was rough with sleepy passion and something more that made his voice almost echo in his chest.

It brought a shiver up from her depths, but she could not deny him. She lay in silence, listening to his breathing, to the strong, slow beat of his heart, and realized she liked his arms around her. Would like to stay like this. Always. The realization brought a small tremor of fear and a tightening of his arms as if he knew.

"Simon?"

"Hmm?" Sleepy. He nuzzled her neck, pressed himself against her so she could feel what she did to him, what he would do with her.

Her desire flamed on as she turned in his arms, used the ashes of her control to pause his hands for a moment and look up into those dangerous dark eyes. How did he do this to her? Make her give up her secrets and power? It was like something inside destroyed all her defenses.

Heat. His heat evoked hers. Left her burning with unrequited desire.

"I - I don't want to go back to the States tomorrow."

It came out as a confession, but his smile, the lingering kiss he gave her, made it fact as she opened to him once more in the moonlight.

Chapter 39 - Tragedy, Foreordained

The scent of sage and dust and sharp apples filled Simon's senses. He peered through the jeep's dusty windscreen, his fingers tap-tap-tapping the wheel in time to music the Nat hummed in his head.

Tap-tap.

Tap-tap.

On and on.

"Simon, stop the jeep!"

Tap-tap.

Tap-tap.

"Dammit, Simon, I think we've got a flat tire."

But it was the way she grabbed his arm that brought him out of his reverie. "What? What's the matter?" The jeep slewed under his hands, the thump-thump-thump as loud as the blood pounding in his head.

He slammed on the brakes and pulled to the side of the road.

"Merde!" He rubbed his head and eyed the woman next to him. He loved the fall of her hair, liquid as moonlight. The feel of her around him. Her small gasps and sighs as he loved her.

Right now her face was more concerned than anything else. Apple and rose and Kalla. *Mine.*

"How long?" he managed.

Not his. These are modern times. A man does not own a woman.

Mine.

There was no reasoning with the Nat. Especially not when their minds were of such accord. He was bound to Kalla, would protect her always. The need to do it was like the pulse of his life. Always.

Had failed her before.

"A couple of minutes, I guess. I heard the sound and thought you did too, but you just kept on driving and tapping the wheel like you had iPod buds in your ears or something."

"Or something." He managed a grin. "Internal music."

And more or less true.

"I think I may have picked up whatever has been giving you headaches."

Low laughter in his head. And something else. Something flashed into his head like an explosion going off. He groaned and went limp against the steering wheel.

"Simon? Simon, are you okay?"

He shook his head, hoping to dislodge whatever it was, but all that did was leave him feeling like the top of his head should—Mon Dieu, would it, please—come off, to release whatever was squirming inside.

"It has been building since last night. I woke with this—pressure." He pressed his knuckles into his eyes and swore he could feel his pulse in his hands. "Okay, let's take a look."

Blinking back the pain, he climbed out of the jeep to inspect the wheel. By the feel of it, it had to be the passenger front. It was. His prolonged driving had left the tire a shredded piece of rubber, the rim pitted and bent.

"Merde."

"Is it bad?" Kalla climbed out to join him.

He motioned at it. "Not good at all. Ruined—tire and rim both, probably."

And dammit, his legs were so wobbly he didn't even know if he had the strength to unload the spare from where it was stowed in the rear.

"What can I do?" She bent over to look more closely at the ruined wheel, and all that did was curve her jeans over that luscious ass of hers. Taungbyon stirred—not the usual roaring demand, but a smoky mist that seemed to drift and rise across Simon's vision.

"Yup, we did a number, all right," she said, and followed him to the rear of the jeep.

Around them the dry terrain south of Mandalay had given way to the rising terrain that surrounded Mount Popa. Kyaukpadaung was southwest after the mountain itself, and then they would turn north to Pagan.

Simon kept his gaze averted as they unloaded Kalla's gear from the jeep and hauled out the tire. She kept helping, almost getting in the way as she tried to lift her bag and boxes. As she climbed aboard to undo lug nuts, to help lift the wheel to him.

"Stop it. Just stop, Kalla. I can do this." Taungbyon's haze placed shrouds over his vision. It had never been like this before. He scrubbed at his face and then grabbed the spare, rolled it along to the ruined wheel and positioned the jack under the bumper, and levered the jeep up.

The wrench freed the first nut and he set it carefully down, only to have Kalla scoop it up.

"Dammit, Kalla, it was fine where it was." He looked up at her, silhouetted against the blue sky, the sun. The dark peak of Popa poked over her shoulder and he shuddered.

Shuddered again as his vision went dark, as Taungbyon rolled over him like a dense fog, and inside the fog was *another*.

Who? His thoughts seemed distant in his own head.

Not Taungbyon. An unfamiliar voice boomed out, and Simon was suddenly more afraid than he'd ever been before. He knew Taungbyon, had found some means to live with that spirit.

What the hell is going on?

"Yes. What's going on, Simon? You look—grey." By the sound of her voice she was crouched on the gravel beside him.

He opened his eyes and it was her—Kalla, concern etched on her lovely face. Precious Kalla, to whom he desperately needed to speak. Fog in his brain. Fog all around and something else was there and he was left useless as a bit of baggage tossed over someone's back.

"Kalla, it's me. It's Dad," he heard himself say.

§

Kalla slammed to her feet, staggered back the length of the jeep, shock stealing her breath away. Simon-who-had-just-called–himself-her-father stood to face her.

"What the hell are you talking about?"

Simon lurched toward her and she backed away, put the jeep between them. This wasn't any Simon she knew. This hulking being had a face like something out of *Night of the Living Dead*. There was no life in it. All his flesh had gone grey.

"We need t' talk, Girlie. We've needed t' talk for such a long time."

A small cry gurgled up through her lips, because that was her father's voice—at least his manner of speaking. Yet it couldn't be. She couldn't believe it was true. What *was* true was that Simon Renault was doing it to her again—Simon who she thought was her friend, who she thought cared for her.

"Stop it, Simon. Stop it this instant."

"Kalla, you left before we could put things to right. I'm sorry, Girlie. I realized it was hard for you all these years. I was too concerned for your mom, when really it was you I should have bin focused on. Can you forgive an old man?" Again he lurched toward her in the creepiest gait she'd ever seen on a living being. She kept the jeep between them, and her fear transformed to fury.

"Dammit, Simon. This isn't funny. Not at all. You know how I feel about this sort of thing." She stood her ground this time as the lurching thing came around the rear of the jeep towards her. Came up to her.

"I always loved you, Kalla." His hand came up in a too-familiar gesture, brushed the tip of her nose like the affectionate game between father and daughter and then twisted. "Got your nose, Girlie. What you gonna do about it?"

She stood locked to the ground. How could Simon know that was one game her dad had played with her and Sharon as children? She searched his gaze, but his eyes had gone blacker than she'd seen them before. His large hand was in front of her face, holding her mock 'nose', for her to try to get it back. As a child it had ended in tickling matches—mostly with Sharon, but occasionally with her as well.

Too many emotions welled up. Grief at her father's loss. Grief at this betrayal. The tears came full-formed into her eyed and her hand arched out, slammed into his face with such force he staggered back against the vehicle.

"You bastard! I've thought a lot of things about you, but I never thought you'd stoop so low."

Tears poured, unbidden, down her cheeks. Her nose ran. She knew her face was red and she didn't care, as she pounded her fists into his chest.

"Just get this dammed jeep going. If I hadn't told Alex I was coming back, I'd have you turn this thing right around and I'd be on the next flight out. You hear? You hear?"

Her fists connected again and again, and then suddenly he had her hands, had her arms down at her side, the weight of her caught against him.

"Kalla! Kalla! Kalla!"

He caught both of her hands behind her back, tried to gentle her with his free hand.

She bit him and he released her. She scrambled back.

"You bastard. How could you?"

"Kalla, I don't know what happened." He tried to touch her.

She jerked away. "Like hell you don't. The lies are written all over your face." They were, too. He knew something he wasn't telling.

"So tell me, Mr. Simon Renault. Is this what you do to all your women? Seduce them? Find their vulnerable spots and exploit them? So what was it for—the puppet? You were going to have my Dad tell me I should give you the Votaress? Is that it?"

She slammed her fist into his solar plexus and watched with satisfaction as he went to his knees.

"No Kalla," he gasped. "It's not like that. I would never." He shook his head like a dog shaking off a beating, and for a moment she regretted hitting him.

He staggered to his feet and caught his breath.

She crossed her arms. "What's it like, then?"

When he turned back his face was normal, yet he couldn't meet her eyes. Sweat glittered along his hairline as if just speaking to her took immense effort.

Well, it took *her* immense effort not to swing at that betraying face again.

"Kalla, I don't even know how to begin to talk about this." He started pacing across the road, as if only moving could he find the momentum to tell her what he wanted. "I don't know exactly what happened just then, but I'll take the look on your face as a sign it was bad. Really bad."

He waited until she nodded.

"You impersonated my dead father, is what you did. As if he sent a message from the grave." Dammit, the tears were still there. A new batch streamed down her face and she backhanded them away. "That's just about the most mean-spirited thing I think anyone could do to someone who just lost a parent."

"Especially when you're friends. Especially when you love someone." His black gaze was heavy on her.

"What? You expect me to forgive this just because you hint you might love me?" She snorted. "Not going to happen."

"Oh, Merde." He looked up at the sky, then back at her. "Fine. You want the whole truth, I'll tell you the whole truth." He kicked a pebble down the road, then turned back to her.

"I'm going to tell you something I've only ever told one person. You say you don't believe in spirits, but I'm here to tell you they're real." He paused, obviously waiting for her reaction, but she was too darn mad to give him even that much satisfaction. She just hugged herself tighter.

"When I visited Popa as a young man something happened. I was taken over like one of those Spirit Wives we saw. Only it wasn't a game or a matter of being too stoned to control myself. It was something huge and foreign suddenly moving into my head. It took over. It ruined my career and my life, until my mother helped me learn to meditate."

"You're trying to tell me my father moved into your head. Not going to buy it Simon. My Dad was alive and well then, remember?" She was so tempted to just go climb in the jeep and drive away, but Simon had would probably stop her before she got the damned engine turned over.

"It wasn't your Dad, Kalla. It was Taungbyon. Or one of them."

That stopped her, and a part of her she didn't recognize almost purred like a cat.

"One of the brothers you told me about? You're trying to tell me all that stuff on Popa is real?" And she didn't want to hear it because then it might mean that what she remembered of their time in the forest might be true, too. Something about a red woman dancing in her head. She shook herself. "No way, Jose. I'm not buying it."

He started towards her and she backed away.

"I don't care whether you buy it or not, but I'm telling you I have a nat in my head and that he-it-whatever invited something else in. Now I can't say whether it was your dad or not, but there was something there. Something that spoke to you."

He kept coming and she was at the edge of the road, her back to scrub brush and cacti and toddy palm when he caught her shoulders.

"I didn't make this up, Kalla. Truly I didn't."

But she shook her head, shook him off, and red seemed to bloom over her vision.

"No. All my life charlatans have taken advantage of my family with their tales of spirits, and I'm the one who paid. I'm not paying anymore."

He tried to catch her again, but she threw off his touch and marched to the jeep. Threw open the door and tossed the bolts at him so they skittered across the broken pavement. "Spare me your concern. Fix the damned wheel and take me to Pagan."

She'd been a fool to stay. A bigger fool to think something wonderful was growing between her and Simon.

§

Simon nursed the raging headache and the pain in his chest as he steered the jeep down into Pagan.

He'd lost her. They'd both lost her, and he didn't know how to fix it. All because Taungbyon had somehow allowed another to fill Simon's head.

Her father. He couldn't believe it had happened. Should never have happened. And now….

Sorrow choked him because history had a habit of repeating. He had lost her at least twice in the past.

At least Kalla was still alive. The thought brought a shiver up his spine, even as the hot Pagan wind blew through the jeep window. Late afternoon and they were home.

It was supposed to be a sweet homecoming because Kalla had reviewed the papers and sent a telegram home that congratulated Sharon profusely on a job well done. Her sister had apparently even remembered to cancel all their father's contributions to various psychic organizations.

And then this had happened.

Kalla hadn't said a word since he threw everything back in the jeep and climbed in beside her for the rest of the trip home.

He guided the jeep around the last curve on the road to the Beautyland Hotel. Only the straight stretch of pavement through the monuments separated them from their rooms.

His room or hers. Another night together. Always together.

Not going to happen, mon ami.

He shook his head and found Kalla looking at him, her face pale, her gaze frosty, her lips more vivid and—merde—so kissable he could stop the jeep right here.

This was madness. A good madness, but madness nonetheless. Last night Kalla had been like a wild thing, insatiable in her loving, had answered every lover's question with her body.

As if desperation rode her. A desperate need to prove she was alive in face of the death of her father? A need to deal with all her pent-up emotions?

It had been like a dam had broken in her. Or something had.

And today he had put the dam right back in place.

He glanced at her again as she peered out at the temples. Shwesandaw. Mingalazedi. Dhammayangyi. Her fever-bright gaze was drawn to the latter. Swatches of color highlighted her cheeks and the darkness under her eyes.

"You should have slept on the ride, chérie. You were awake all night."

"I'm not your 'chérie' and I'll thank you not to remind me of last night." She turned away, but the Nat made his hand touch her hair so she almost huddled against the far door.

Merde, he had not had need of a woman like this since the disaster at the Sorbonne. The difference was, this was a need for one specific woman. *To possess her.*

No, my friend, I fear it's too late for that.

The Nat swirled away, a sense of disgust and dissatisfaction coming from the creature like a strong whiff of smoke.

Kalla turned back as Dhammayangyi shadowed the plain on their right.

"It's waiting," she said quietly, almost to herself.

"What is waiting?" He glanced from her parted lips to the shadowed temple. Her breath was quick in her chest, her gaze, when she looked at him, huge and black and filled with confusion and layers of remembrance that brought a chill to the baking jeep cab. "Kalla?"

"We could make love in the darkness. Make the place live."

Her face and the strange words filled him with foreboding.

"Kalla?" He leaned over, caught her face in his hand and turned her face to him.

Her blue gaze suddenly burned into him and she jerked away. "I told you not to touch me."

"And I wouldn't—except you were spouting nonsense."

"Sure. Don't expect me to believe that anymore than I believe your story."

At least her attitude was Kalla, but the sweat on her brow, the heat of her flesh and the fever-light in her eyes suddenly concerned him. This was not just the passionate blush of a woman who had found her sensuality—and lost it. No—this was something else. Why *had* Kalla been at Dhammayangyi the other night?

Something was off. Even her way of speaking had been—different somehow. Formal and without the small lift of her chin that he now understood hid a massive insecurity.

He turned in at the Beautyland, paused while Hue ran out to lift the bar from the courtyard entrance, and then he was parked in the last drift of fading neem blossoms, out and around the jeep to Kalla.

She stepped out, the swing of her hair like a glistening river he would drink from again and again.

Hue looked at her oddly as she nodded hello, turned back to the road, and rubbed her head. Headache lines between her eyes.

"I think—I would like—to go back to the temple. See the murals."

Her hesitant voice said it took effort to find the words, as if they came from a long distance, and Simon caught her hand until she pulled it away with a snarl.

"Tomorrow perhaps would be better. You are tired, Kalla. Better to rest today."

But she was already shaking her head. "I'll do my research my way, thank you very much. It waits. She waits."

Now she was frightening him. Something was horribly wrong and the Nat rose in his head, slammed forward in a black gale that almost staggered him.

"Min." It slipped out before he could press the Nat back.

Taungbyon slammed forward again, again, as Kalla turned back to him, ancient hope in her eyes. "Min Gyi?"

"No!" He grabbed her. "You're Kalla. Understand? Kalla Jervis!" It was one thing for the Nat to recognize the incarnated spirit of his lover, but he would not see Kalla possessed by another. Not that. He knew the horror of where that could lead.

Kalla's blue eyes were swallowed by black as she hung in his arms, looked up to him and he suddenly wished she would strike him, do something to show the true Kalla was there.

Her palm stroked his face and sent a shiver down his spine.

"We are here, my love. For this lifetime."

Soft and echoing down through the years like a bell, tolling. Her body hummed in his arms with another power, another presence that brought the Nat raging—a whirlwind tearing at his thoughts, his body.

"Kalla," he named her, almost all he could manage. He saw her refusal, and then a battle in her eyes.

"Kalla." Merde, let her get free. At least let her be free of this hell.

"Kalla!"

The darkness wavered, dissolved in a gaze of blue, and Kalla—his Kalla—stared up at him with fury.

Then collapsed in his arms.

Chapter 40 – Returning

"The foreign woman has returned."

Colonel Aung stood at rigid attention before Ne Setkya's desk. So rigid, Aung was a model for the proper soldier, but his eyes said he waited like a snake for Ne Setkya's fatal mistake.

He must move cautiously. Not show his true interest in the Jervis woman.

"I thought she had left for Mandalay and was returning home?"

"So she said and so our informant thought. But she came back. Our spies in Mandalay say it may be because of the man. They have formed a relationship." The downturn of his lips showed he did not approve of the open sexuality of the foreigners who traveled Myanmar. It was a different way of being, against the moderation of Ne Setkya's Buddhist beliefs as well. But Buddhism also taught tolerance.

He looked back at Aung. 'Our spy', the man had said. So that source was compromised as well.

The walls of his office seemed a little closer at that news. They had steadily closed in on him since the foreigners arrived. Since Aung arrived. Removing his options. It was….

It was almost as if a great play were performed, now that all the actors were on-stage came a tragedy, the ending foreordained. The death of a dream, a legend.

And a woman.

The fact she had come back said it was so.

§

She teetered on the edge.

In the darkness, Kalla fought for balance on unsteady footing, looked down and saw she stood on a pillar of indeterminate height that disappeared into darkness.

A pillar of women.

Her feet stood on the shoulders of a woman—dark haired, dark eyed, and slight, but the shape of the square jaw, the tilt of the eyes—those Kalla recognized from old photos.

"Mother?"

The woman glanced up at her and smiled, pointed down at her feet, to the woman her mother stood on. Another resemblance to Kalla. Grandmother?

Who stood on another. And another. And another. Familiar faces peering up at Kalla while their pale hands pointed down, down, down into the darkness.

Something red there. Something flickering brightly.

Kalla fell, the wind rushing, roaring around her in voices, tearing the darkness, turning it red.

Or perhaps it was the red flooding up. The women below her dissolving into red, dissolving into one. Furious eyes. Thunderous voice. Dancing.

Long flow of hair and the red scarf trailing from her brow. Kalla looked in her eyes and knew Min. Knew her anger, her hope. Knew the moment was short, the lifetime was short. But the spirit lived longer.

As Min stepped up to her.

And inside.

Kalla woke with a sharp intake of breath, eyes flashing open, sweat stung. And she couldn't move.

Something held her and trapped her. She was locked away. Locked inside. Something horrendous and red was with her. *Someone* held her prisoner and fought the confines of her bed.

With her body.

She would scream if she could speak. Would beat at the—sheets— it was sheets tucked in around her that held her arms—if she could move. Control her body.

She couldn't control her body!

Fear slammed into her, made her reach for her controls, and the thing—smothering and crimson—swathed her. Made it hard to move, hard to think. Until:

"Kalla?"

Her name. Focus on her name. Hard to breathe. Hard to think.

Simon appeared above her, sat down at the side of the bed. Her bed. Her room at the Beautyland. How had she got here? She remembered Mandalay. Remembered going back to the guest house, making love—yes, love—opening fully to Simon. He stroked her face, her hair.

And he betrayed her.

Furious anger flooded in and she would have pulled away from his touch, but her body failed to respond.

"Kalla?" Concern in his voice.

Focus on control. Focus on telling him what you think. A simple word.

Her body stiffened with the effort as if the crimson fought her.

Wet her lips. "Bastard," she whispered and collapsed with someone else's shriek of fury in her head.

Kalla grabbed hold of the crimson and let it lift her free of where she was imprisoned. Her body. *Her* body!

But it was all she could do to reach forward through the screaming red haze, find her lips, form the words.

"Simon. Hate you." Almost inaudible, but it was there. She had done it, and the other presence wailed its anger, beat at her.

His hand didn't even pause in stroking her face, and he half-lifted her to sitting, pulled her into his chest. Her nose filled with the provocative scent of him and all she wanted to do was scream and send him away.

"Merde. Merde. How could this happen, chérie? My princess. Mon Dieu, I am so sorry. So sorry. I did not want this to happen. Never this." Kisses rained on her hair, her face. She could barely feel. Her skin numb to her control. Well, not numb. Distant. As if her body rested in the distance. Time and space.

"What's happening? I feel so strange." Sentences. Coherent. It took everything she had to make them happen.

This, Simon responded to, so he had to have heard her rejection but refused to acknowledge it.

He looked deep into her eyes and there was darkness there and anger and—fear. Fear most of all. For her. Kiss on her lips, tender and oh so full of despair, and she hated him regardless.

"You must not fight it, Kalla. It is the spirit of the one called Min. She wishes your body. To possess you." When he mentioned Min, anger flashed in his gaze. And old desire.

And that brought a choked laugh out of her. "Haven't you done enough with your lies?"

And now this latest attempt to make her believe in something that was impossible. There was no such thing as possession. Sure, ancient people told such stories—like Daw Ma Ma Nang's tales. Like Mei's comment about hungry ghosts. Some still believed. She understood the need to blame socially inappropriate behaviors on something supernatural. But she was a scientist.

Not possessed, just as Simon wasn't possessed. She managed a shake of her head, which was a good sign, but Simon had her face in his hands, turned her gaze and held it with his own.

"Kalla. Chérie. You must listen."

"Stop. Stop. Calling. Me. That." It came out no more than a whisper.

"You must listen, because I know these things," he rushed on. "Shwepyingyi Taungbyon has made my life hell, but I am alive because I knew that to fight him meant I would die. You cannot win a battle against a spirit. When I fought to reject him, a fever took me and weakened me. I almost died until my mother explained."

He was actually serious—or else he was the best damned actor she'd ever seen. Obviously the latter. She would have applauded if she could just get her hands free of the sheets. A part of her—the crimson part—welled up and brought laughter bubbling up her throat. She fought it, strangled on it, and felt the rage inside. Her body: she'd laugh when *she* decided.

But could Simon be telling the truth?

Her fight faltered at the possibility. Vermillion clouds plumed up to color her vision and her hand fought free of the bed, reached for Simon, stroked his face, felt the vibration of his life force as she looked in his eyes.

"We are both here, my love."

Not her words. Oh-my-god-no, they weren't her words. She should be clawing his face.

But to move was like swimming through mud.

Mine. This body is mine.

No more. There are things you must do.

Knowledge of Dhammayangyi lanced out of the crimson, stabbed into her head. Go there. Mend. The Votaress.

The force of the knowledge slammed Kalla back in her mind. She was small. So small in the face of the thing that took her. That inhabited.

Great need. Great rage and sorrow and so much left undone.

The confusing emotions left her weak and reeling and needing something to hold on to. Everything was distant—like she looked through the wrong end of a telescope. But Simon was there, seated on the edge of her bed, dark hair falling into his eyes.

Hold on to the sight of him. Hold to her anger. Hold to his touch.

But his caress was stolen by the other, so Kalla could not feel.

Simon, she cried, help me. But her lips did not move.

Mine. My life. My chance.

No! This is my life. My body, and you are dead! Kalla lunged forward through the suffocating haze. Rammed into it, opened to it, and grabbed for control.

See who possesses.

Flashes of light. Flashes of insight as Kalla forced herself back, swelled large.

She controlled this body. Hers.

Dark walls and death. Grief. A gift. Great gift stolen away.

A presence might be in her head, but she'd be damned if it was going to control her anymore than Simon was.

Remembrance. Guilt. And love. Through all time.

Kalla paused. She understood love. Had felt need so strong she could lose herself in another person.

No. This thing wanted her body for its own. She grabbed hold of the crimson and forced it down. Beat at it with the controls she had built through her life.

Crimson pressed back, back, coalescing into a flame. Desire. Burning bush, threatening forest fire.

Kalla tried to put the fire out. Failed. The presence was here to stay. She tried to erect barriers, but that failed as well. The thing—the spirit—would try again. Kalla grabbed hold of her body and—felt.

Simon's hands on her face. Cool cloths on her forehead. Bed under her. Heard her room door open. Voices. Mei-Alex-Khun. Concern.

She dared not move for fear the effort would incite the crimson thing again. And if it came back, would it incite the thing called Taungbyon? Would there be more episodes like Popa where she lost control? She would not take that chance.

The swirling fire rose in a blaze of flame. It seared her mind before she could react.

And she knew:

What she must do to protect him. What she must do to protect them all.

Escape and atone.

Chapter 41 - The Repeating Past

Merde, he was losing this battle for Kalla.

She burned under his hands, and the room stank of hot metal as if she were in Min Mahagiri's ancient forge. The King of Nats had been a blacksmith in the days before he died.

And she is his tool.

No. Simon swept back the Nat. He would not believe that. Kalla belonged to the spirits. She was a woman. His woman. Not some princess out of old legends or fairy stories. He caught her limp hand, twined his fingers with hers.

"Kalla you have to come back. Listen to me. Don't fight it. Don't fight. You will learn how to live with the new one inside you."

He placed a cool cloth on her head, but it warmed too quickly. She was burning up. Merde, with heat like this it could burn out her mind, and she did not understand—or refused to. All because of her father's actions and his.

A knock at the door and Alex pushed inside, Mei and Khun behind him.

"Simon. You're here. Hue said Kalla has taken ill again."

The accusation was clear in Alex's voice, as if Simon were somehow responsible.

Perhaps he was. It was surely the presence of Taungbyon that had opened her to the spirit, just as the Nat had opened him to her father. He sent a stab of anger the Nat's way.

No response.

"I—hope it is only the heat and the journey. Recall she had difficulty when she arrived."

Simon couldn't meet Alex's gaze because Alex would surely know there was something more. Something deadly. He felt Mei's and Khun's intent gazes, met Mei's eyes as she sat on the edge of Kalla's bed across from him.

"How long she be like this?" Khun's grumble brought Simon's gaze up.

"Since we returned." He checked his watch. "A few hours."

"That is not good." Mei took Simon's bowl of now-tepid water and went to replenish it. Returned and tried to take the cloth from him, but Simon motioned her away.

"She was with me when this happened. I'll care for her."

Mei's calm gaze met his, held, and saw too much, he was sure. She handed the bowl to him and stood.

"I will see about dinner. You will need food." Then she gently touched his shoulder.

He wasn't hungry, but if it would get Mei away from here, fine. He wanted to be alone with Kalla. Just get her well. Just get her back to him. Tutor her through these worst first stages.

Min. Taungbyon's voice. Gentle. The first time the Nat had spoken since the debacle with Kalla's father.

Your Min does this to her!

His anger sent the Nat reeling back in his mind. *Yes! Your Min will kill her, and then where will we both be?*

Taungbyon was a black curtain at the rear of his mind. Silent. It was the first time in many years Simon had felt such quiet.

He turned back to Kalla, and realized he still wasn't alone, even though Alex had disappeared. Probably gone to help Mei. Which left Khun still looking at him, gaze assessing.

"Things no good for her."

Simon sighed and looked down at Kalla, so pale except for bright fever patches on her cheeks and forehead. Her breath came in shallow gasps that seemed to take every bit of her effort.

Just breathe, Kalla. Just breathe.

"You worry for her." Khun slipped into Burmese.

Simon nodded as he renewed the cloth's cool water, dripped a few drops into her mouth before placing the cloth on her forehead. The scent of incense and jasmine came off her in waves and the cloth seemed instantly warm. If anything the fever was worse, and a spike of despair drove through him.

"Merde."

"This is not ordinary sickness."

Simon glanced over his shoulder. Khun stood, arms crossed and waiting. Simon nodded, turned back to his work.

"It's not disease. Or food poisoning. Or heat stroke, if that is your question."

Khun touched Simon's shoulder and he froze, then looked at the Burmese man. How long had it been since his father-uncle had touched him? How long had he mourned that friendship?

"Mei says you care for her very much." The comment was soft and brought Simon's gaze to Khun's.

"I do. Kalla—has grown in my mind."

"And your heart, it seems." Understanding in Khun's eyes. An old pain. "Once I hoped you would look at Mei that way. That our families would forever join."

Simon closed his eyes to try to shut away the memories. Once he had thought the same. And then had come Popa and everything had changed. Mei had happened.

"I'm so sorry, father-uncle. Je regrette… I never meant… I never wanted… there are no words to express my regret at what happened with Mei."

"She cried that night. She told me she loved you, almost gave in to you—but you ran away and left the country and did not come back. She thought she was ruined. Would not marry. My precious Mei thought she was unworthy of anyone but the blasted foreigners who use her. I hated you for that.."

The old anger in Khun's voice exhausted Simon. He deserved the other man's fury. Deserved to be hurt for all of the hurts he had caused over the years. But Mei's was the worst; the one closest to his heart. He bowed his head.

"I left because I could not stand the fact I hurt her—and might hurt her more. I knew I didn't love Mei—except as a sister—and yet I did that thing. Attacked her—almost raped her. I had no control. I had to leave—for her safety." He replenished the cloth again and Kalla murmured, tossed her head. The jasmine scent clutched at his gut. She was getting worse.

"I know."

The two words turned Simon back to his father-uncle. What he saw surprised him: not fury or anger. Only sadness in the smaller man's eyes. Compassion on his face as his gaze went to Kalla.

"I have seen this before, once in my life. It was a foreigner then, as well. Most cruel to one who does not understand. Living life as one being is difficult enough. Being two is a hardship." The older man's eyes looked deep into Simon's.

"You knew?" Simon tried to remember. Tried to recall anything that Khun had done or said so long ago.

"I suspected, but convinced myself I was wrong. Just as I suspect you love this woman. You were very ill when you returned from Popa, but I was afraid to speak for fear you would consider me a superstitious fool. I thought perhaps I was one. And so Mei was hurt and I must blame myself for not getting you the help you needed. Do not do as I did."

Khun went to the door, and then paused once more-. "Simon, I too, must apologize. I ruined the equipment out of revenge. I passed information to the General out of fear for Mei. I am sorry."

Simon nodded, understanding the emotions that could lead to such a thing. He forgave the betrayal. It was done now. Over. Perhaps it was time to heal.

If only Kalla could forgive as well.

"What is it the westerners say?" Khun asked. "Learn from past mistakes, or you will repeat them? We say such things in Burma, too."

"Khun?" Simon wanted to give his father-uncle a gift for his comfort, for the rekindling of old relationships. Khun paused. "I think Alex truly cares for Mei."

"So my daughter tells me."

And then he was gone, leaving Simon with a storm of feelings. Fear for Kalla. Grief for lost years. And love for the man who was almost his father. He turned back to Kalla.

"Do not do as I did."

§

The heat was too much. The sunset sent bright spears of light into Ne Setkya's eyes. He peered out at the river turned the color of blood, and blood was in his thoughts.

If only he could get cool. It was as if the whole plain held its breath. No air moved, even over the flowing river. But something came. Dread filled his bones. Perhaps he should just take soldiers and arrest the woman, then do what needed doing. But that would alert Aung, and Pagan's secrets would be revealed.

He could not chance that.

No, this required stealth; and if his sister would not help him, then he would work alone.

The decision released him from the window. He locked his papers in his desk, turned off the futile, ever-circling fan, and watched the shadows settle across the walls. He had occupied this office for fifteen years and it had never seemed so full of dark corners and pulsing heat as it did today.

Pagan had basked, then baked, then become more like a hell under the sun's assault. The world held its breath, and was caught between heartbeats until amends could be made. Covenants finally fulfilled.

If only it had not come in his time—but then, all men thought such things. He supposed his great forbearer, the Alchemist who had been the Alchemist's apprentice, felt the same in his time. He set his broad-brimmed hat on his head and flicked off the lights and went out to his jeep. A driver lounged there—not Ne Setkya's usual man—this one had formed allegiances with the Colonel.

"Home. The heat is terrible. You may have the night off."

The flicker of the man's eyes said that Colonel Aung would soon learn of this departure from Ne Setkya's usual routine. It could not be helped.

At home, he sent the man on his way but had the jeep remain, and stepped inside the walls that surrounded his home. He found his sister waiting. Daw Ma Ma Nang sat, unwelcome, in the shadows under his stilted house.

"What are you doing here?"

"The same as you. The woman has returned and Dhammayangyi waits."

Ne Setkya turned away from her. Another argument was not what he needed. It was too hot for arguments, yet the heat seemed to brew them like a yeasty beer. He had snapped at his men today and had seen Aung nearly snap back.

"Yes, Dhammayangyi waits. I felt it when I was there."

"She is the key." Daw Ma Ma Nang came out from the shadows and followed Ne Setkya, unbidden, into the coolness of his house. Usually it didn't rile him that she always acted like she still lived here even though the house passed to him from their parents. This time, with the heat….

"You think I don't know this? The temple purred like a cat, or an engine running smoothly. When she left it was gone, and there was only the emptiness and silence. I will fix this."

"Ne Setkya—brother—I beg you to rethink your strategy. I have meditated on this thing. The woman was sent to us. She has a purpose, but I do not think it is to be sacrificed."

Ne Setkya loomed above her.

"What, then? What are we to do? The seals crumble and break. The Generals send men to search for treasure. What is to protect the secret after you and I are gone, if we do not reseal the place? What do *you* suggest, sister?"

She fell back a pace—as much, he realized—from his sudden loss of composure, as his words. He swayed, rubbed his brow, under her dark, steady gaze.

"I'm sorry. There is much pressure these days. This heat makes it worse."

She still just looked at him, and he realized she was old. Very old. The child of the morning of their parent's marriage, as he was the child of the evening. He supposed that was why she always tried to follow lighter paths than he.

"It is our duty, sister. Our father placed the task on us. Beyond all else, we guard what waits. Now the chance to seal things comes. Pagan—perhaps even Burma—may bloom again. We must take this chance. To not do so is to court destruction as great as that the Generals bring to our country."

The shake of her head was almost imperceptible. Or perhaps it was only a tremor, but he knew she disagreed.

"You deal with things you do not understand. Do not assume you know the will of the nats." Her voice was quiet, almost a whisper.

"That is hope, not knowledge, speaking."

He turned from her and changed out of his uniform into his longyi. The air on his legs was a relief, but not enough to negate what must be done.

"I dream of the golden procession," she said. "That it is intact."

He stepped from behind the curtain, knotting his longyi. "And dreams are to be our solace now? Hopes and dreams? That is the only alternative you offer?"

"I spend more time at Dhammayangyi than you. I feel the place. It—they—want her...."

"I will give her to them."

"But..."

"Damn it woman, I will not have you question me like this. I am being pushed out of my job. If I am not in charge, there will be no one to stop the explorations and the digs. Who knows what will happen—what will be found? Do you want that?" He was almost shaking with his frustration.

"The Nats care for themselves."

It must be her age. Daw Ma Ma Nang spoke—thought—like a child. Repeating herself in her wish for resolution.

"Not now. Not in this age. You know it."

"Brother, they are more powerful than...."

"Stop! I will not speak of this again. I will go to Dhammayangyi. I will do this thing. If I must, I will drag the woman there myself."

He saw her stiffen—perhaps at his anger, perhaps with resolve, he could not say, but her eyes had gone black as night sky, her skin waxen.

"Take care of your soul, brother. Such action will not be necessary. The woman will go to Dhammayangyi this night. She knows what she must do."

Then she left him, the heated air and her words bringing a chill up his spine.

Chapter 42 - Electric Night

If she did nothing, it would destroy them all.

Kalla opened her eyes on darkness, and almost screamed as it pressed in. Darkness and death and hopelessness. It had come for her before. Smothering and heated.

Like her skin. Like the crimson cloud that tinged the darkness and made it hard to breathe.

Incense and jasmine.

Her senses full of them. She turned her head, saw a small brazier set up on her dresser, the Votaress puppet leaning against the wall.

Dresser? Wall?

She was in her room. The Beautyland.

Whirling red almost blinded her, but she needed to get up. Needed to go and do what had to be done.

The red fought her.

Stay still. Wait here. Be. Too long we have waited.

"This is my body," she hissed. Heard something and froze, as she became aware of someone else in the room. Crimson flooded around her, overtaking, overwhelming.

What the hell was the matter with her? It felt like another person was in her body, and the only way that could be true was if she were crazy—no matter what Simon said.

Move. Just move.

She fought through the red haze and swung her legs over the side of the bed. Covers fell back and the air chilled her skin. She shivered at the cold wood under her feet as her hair swung around her shoulders.

Naked except for bra and panties. Who had undressed her?

She knew. Sniffed and let the anger strengthen her. Incense and musk that betrayed her. Made the red lust. She turned.

Simon slumped in the room's lone chair, his long legs stretched in front of him, black hair across his handsome brow. A soft, exhausted, snore escaped his lips. Beyond him the room's door stood open, seeking a hoped-for breeze. Night noises of cicada and batwing hung on stagnant air.

Get past him. That was what she had to do. Protect them all because everything was coming apart. That was what she had learned inadvertently from the crimson. What it was terrified of.

Her open suitcase lay on the floor beside the bed. She dug into it, pulled out a t-shirt and a pair of jeans - no. The crimson longyi.

That was right. Proper for what she planned.

She pulled on the shirt and stood to wrap the loop of cloth around her. Smooth it, like skin. Sleek.

Her. The crimson beat at her, frantic.

Not this. Not this. Not this, again.

She swayed and pressed the crimson back. My body. My way. My task.

Fear stabbed into her and she clutched her head at the pain. Ancient fear and smothering. Hunger and death.

"No." It was no more than a whisper, but Simon stirred.

She had to get out of here. Away from him and get this done. She toed on her runners, grabbed the Votaress puppet and went to the door.

Simon sat in the way. Guarding her?

Will always guard, be there for you. Waiting. Want…. Her hand lifted to touch him, but she fought it back.

Not now! Not ever.

Now! Now! Now! Now or it will be never!

Oh god she wanted to touch him, kiss him goodbye. One last touch, but she dared not. Because he guarded. Because he betrayed.

In the distance she heard the plain hum under a rush of wind, saw a stab of dry lightning, and heard the low rumble of thunder. It seemed to echo inside her. Her hair lifted from her shoulders. A vanguard of clouds, white in the moonlight, filled the southern sky. Another stab of lightning, this time close by where Dhammayangyi stood and fallen bricks glowed in the night. Dhammayangyi became a blue beacon against storm and night-darkened skies. Storm coming.

She was coming.

Destiny.

She clutched the Votaress to her, hiked up the longyi, stepped over Simon's legs and out into the spirit-blue night. She started to run.

§

He woke to the Nat's wail and the knowledge he was too late. Simon lunged out of the chair, slammed it back into the wall. The bed lay empty. The air reeked of ozone and roses gone to dust.

Kalla was gone.

How?

You slept. Taungbyon raged forward, fury whipping the darkness to flame. *You sleep and will not hear.*

The rage shuddered against Simon, sent him half to his knees. He hadn't slept a full night since—when? Before Popa? Longer? Driving all night. And pleasuring himself with Kalla.

Pleasure for us both.

"Then it is both our faults, mon ami. Both our faults we scared her so badly." He swung to the door, wiped back the nat's darkness and stared out at the night.

Heat-lightning crackled madly at the edge of the plain, spitting thunder like an angry cat. There was only one place Kalla could be. The might of Dhammayangyi sat like a black presence on the plain, silhouetted in the bursts of blue-sparking energy. *There.*

He felt her like a pulse that answered to his heart.

Linked. Linked for always.

Simon shook his head. Linked they might be, but she was in danger. The whole plain reeked of it. Ozone and anger. Electricity that tingled every hair on his body.

He set off at a lope, vaulted the courtyard gate, scented the air. Bats wheeled like wild thoughts, like his imaginings of her danger. But merde, he knew. There were others who would not protect.

Who would not protect his Burma. Taungbyon railed against him, rose in his head, filled his body, and Simon felt:

Fear for Kalla.

Anger that history repeated.

The way evil crawled across the earth destroying all hope of life.

He increased his speed, pounding up the road, then cut across the fields. The sharp thorn of a cactus made him realize he was barefoot.

He didn't care.

Brick tore at his soles. Stone and more cactus impaled.

Didn't matter.

She was there. Already there, already in danger from those who waited.

"Non. S'il-vous-plait, pas ça. Please, not this." Not to lose her. Not to lose her now, when he had found her. He hadn't even known he had been looking.

Hot wind on his skin and sweat stuck his shirt to him as he came to Dhammayangyi from the side. She was—there. The main courtyard. Taungbyon joined him, rode him, seeking. Fear, his and the Nat's.

Not again. Not this. To have and to lose, the spirit warrior raged.

Not lost yet.

Following the collapsed walls of the courtyards that surrounded the massive temple, he made his way to the front in time to hear footfall and see through the darkness the flow of dark hair and the curve of a cheek.

Kalla.

He didn't speak, yet she faltered and clutched something tight to her chest as if she fought to hold something alive. Precious.

As she was to him. His hand fell on her shoulder and spun her around.

Heat of her body. Eyes huge and black stared back at him. Panic there, and resolve. She knew she had scared him and did not repent.

"Simon. You should not be here." Her face hardened.

Strange, how she spoke. Stiff. A little stilted in her inflection as if her tongue worked in unfamiliar ways. And her body was afire with a bonfire's heat.

"There's danger. We must leave."

The black of her gaze receded for a moment. She shook her head, and the moonlight gleamed burning-blue in her eyes.

"Not to me. You, perhaps. I am to be here." She turned away as if dismissing him, and that sent the Nat raging.

He tore her around. "You would leave me? Again? After what we have found?"

Simon fought back the Nat. He knew the Nat's pain, but this was not Min. This was Kalla. His Kalla. He caught her shoulders and shook her.

"Kalla. Come back. Speak to me."

She jerked free and glared at him, and it was Kalla. Kalla in control. Kalla with resolve, even as she shivered in the heat.

"I *am* speaking to you, Simon. I'm telling you to leave me alone. This—has to be done."

She turned and marched towards the temple's dark maw and Simon leapt after, suddenly afraid, suddenly realizing if she crossed into that darkness he might never see her again.

"Kalla! Ma chère! I cannot let you do this."

He caught her again, pulled her to his chest, and her body heat almost burned. But she fought him. Ripped her hands free to pummel him. Stomped down on his instep. He gasped, and the Nat raged forward. The double assault made him release her and she slipped towards the door.

He leapt for her again.

"Stay where you are." The voice stopped him mid-stride. He whirled as General Ne Setkya materialized out of shadows and moonlight.

The small man approached. He wore a simple villager's longyi and plain shirt, but a military pistol glinted in his right hand. Simon felt the Nat assessing whether there was a chance—any chance—of removing that threat.

Slim and none, Simon judged, but the Nat and he were prepared to try. For Kalla and Min.

"What do you want?" he snarled.

Ne Setkya glanced at him. "I could ask the same. She—I know what she wants—why she is here—but you are an enigma to me."

"I come for Kalla."

Ne Setkya shook his head. "A hopeless desire, I fear. For Kalla has duties here, don't you, my dear?"

Simon turned to her, but she stood, stricken. A blast of wind, the rumble of thunder said the storm was very near. Clouds overhead flickered and danced with power. The stones under his feet seemed to answer, pulsing with some unseen charge that lifted Kalla's hair into an unholy cloud around her shoulders.

"Tell him he's wrong. Tell him we're leaving now."

"I wouldn't go anywhere with you. It's too late for that. The bricks are crying. So is the earth." Her blue-black eyes were filled with such sorrow he thought his heart would crumble like the brick underfoot. She was not leaving.

"Kalla, no. Don't let the spirit do this to us."

She didn't look his way. "Go while you still can, Simon. It's not Min doing this."

"Damnation, Kalla." He grabbed her, ignored Ne Setkya's yell and pulled her into his chest again. "I'm not leaving you."

"Then you will go with her, Monsieur Renault." Ne Setkya glanced at the heaving clouds overhead and waved the pistol toward the yawning temple mouth.

"I have no time for arguing. The spirits wait and hunger."

Chapter 43 – Dhammayangyi—again

Dhammayangyi rang like a bell, and Kalla was what set it ringing. The sound-sense built through her bones, burst into her head, and she thought her skull would explode. The crimson woman shuddered inside her and went to her knees, hands outstretched.

Not this. Not this. She begged.

Kalla held her at bay—barely. Perhaps the effort was what set her shivering. *You should have picked a different person then, shouldn't you?*

She knew taunting whatever inhabited her head probably wasn't a good idea, but it seemed to help her hold onto her control. Of course, Simon's hold almost undid her efforts.

Betraying incense and musk. Betraying desire in her breast. She wanted the safety of his arms, wanted the warmth, because everything in this life was just so cold and hard, but Simon was not to be. He'd lied to her—played her like a fool—like less than a fool with his charlatan's game. It was time she finally made at least one thing right.

The darkness inside the temple flowed around her, came between her and the warmth of Simon's hands. Chill up her back. Her skin gooseflesh. The single, glaring eye of Ne Setkya's flashlight illuminated the empty halls where the chill breeze whispered. The General gave directions of where they should go—away from the outer corridor she had traveled before. Inward toward the heart of Dhammayangyi, as the structure's belling grew in her head.

And voices. Echoes. She strained and closed her eyes as she walked, felt the presence of others. Many had walked this way.

She had walked this way.

And she had and she hadn't. Cold. So cold. The crimson one was with her, now. Hands together clutching the Votaress. Both their tears came from her eyes.

Sorrow at endings and goodbyes. She must have sniffed, for Simon caught her chin, lifted her face to his.

"Kalla?" So soft it could break a heart.

"I'm fine." She pulled away, had to be strong because this was the most painful thing she had ever done. In front of her the long passage ended in tunnels to either side, filled in with heaps of fallen brick and debris. There was nowhere to go.

But there was.

Simon pulled her into his side protectively, when she did not need or want his protection. Still, he should not die to save her.

What is done, is done. Unending sorrow.

Kalla fought the feeling back, but it still chewed her gut. Sorrow was better than guilt. At least it was clean.

A sigh of regret and agreement from the Crimson.

"What now, Ne Setkya?" Simon faced the darkness like it was a demon, his eyes were pits that caught the flashlight's glow.

The General shifted his pistol at them. "Put your arms around Ms. Jervis and face the wall."

Simon did as he was told, an unwelcome warmth, Simon's breath on her cheek, his lips unbearably close. But Kalla watched Ne Setkya. The general used his left hand to trace a series of bricks up the wall, finally came to rest on a lone brick, and pressed.

Dhammayangyi's bell-tone changed. The temple seemed to shudder; spirit light—sparking blue—flushed through the walls, and the deep resonance she'd felt-heard in her bones began to climb the scales until it keened around her like a cold, lashing wind.

The crimson shrieked with it. Anger, guilt, and so much fear; Kalla could barely see. Ne Setkya flickered in and out. His flashlight bobbed across the walls as he fell back. His simple blue longyi seemed to fade away, replaced by red. A staff. A gold-crusted cap she recognized. Alchemist? He had been here the first time. She clenched her eyes shut against the madness of the scene, and Simon must have felt her shiver.

He clutched her more tightly. *He of the broad shoulders, leather clad and gilt in armor.*

She moaned and pushed him away. All too much. Her eyes betrayed. Her body betrayed just as much as he had, and the Crimson rose, fought to press the Votaress into Simon's arms.

A foretelling we will be together.

Darkness in Simon's eyes. She pulled her gaze away. Darkness Ne Setkya had exposed. Doorway she knew was there. Would have searched for.

The general stood back from it and motioned her towards the entrance. She would have gone, but for Simon's arms. *Taungbyon's arms.*

"I'm sorry, but your fate is there. Has always been there." The general's face said this was not easy for him. This was a decision that came from desperation and loss.

"And it is your fate as well." A new voice came out of the darkness.

Chapter 44 - Strength

The bang woke Mei with a start. She sat up in bed and listened, heard nothing else, but there was electricity in the air she had not felt before. It lifted her hair off her shoulders and made her cheeks tingle.

Something was not right.

She swung her legs out of bed, stood and went to the door.

Darkness and heat. A flash and a grumble in the distance, and a breeze that carried too much heat. At this time of year the monsoons should be bumping their way over Burma. But not here. It didn't look like the rains had been here for many years.

But something happened. A loud bang-bang almost made her leap out of her skin. She caught herself half-way to her bed and turned back to the door. Something was wrong and she needed to know what and do something about it.

Cautious of attack, she stepped out her room to peer down the length of the hotel. Kalla's room was open, the door caught in the strange wind and banging against the wall.

Not as it should be.

She stepped down the single stair and went to the room. Empty. When she'd gone to bed, Simon had been here, guarding the woman Mei was sure that he loved. Had they gone to his room?

That made no sense given Kalla's illness. No. She turned to look out on the plain, the hulking shapes of the temples caught in the flashes of heat lightening. Dhammayangyi. And she knew as surely as she'd known when she made her request of the nats, disaster came.

She half-ran to Alex's door, knocked softly, but he was there quickly, clad only in low-slung jeans and taking her in his arms.

"Mei. I wished you would come, and here you are." He lowered his lips to hers and she answered. Wanted to answer more in the sweet meeting of flesh, but now was not the time. No, there was disaster to be averted.

She pushed him away, saw the injured look on his face.

"I'm sorry. I want to." Would he understand? "Kalla and Simon are gone."

Alex ran his hands back through his hair, gone dark in the moonlight.

"So? They're adults. Let them go. This is about us." He reached for her again and Mei stepped back; she might have prayed for this man's love, but not at the cost of the others. Not even of Simon, who had hurt her so.

"Alex, you must listen. Something ill is afoot. I know it. I—I caused it."

A shake of his shaggy head and he caught her arm. "You keep trying to take responsibility for the actions of others. I love that in you, Mei, but not for this. Not for them."

"Listen to me!" She jerked out of his grasp, stamped a foot. "You don't understand. Not at all." She stepped down from the door, pointed out at the plain. "This is Burma, Alex. It is a place of spirits, and I did an evil thing. I wished for your love." She turned back to him. "I wanted you from the moment we met, but it could never be. So I asked the spirits for their help. For them to do so means someone must pay. Now Kalla and Simon do."

She saw Alex struggle with belief, saw him hesitate and look at her, saw the hesitation dissolve because it was her.

"What are you saying?"

"Something is after them. Something is going to happen. I think they've gone to Dhammayangyi. We have to stop them or it may bring disaster on us all." She caught his hand, began to pull him out of his room, though he was only half-dressed.

"All this because I love you? Does it scare you so much?"

That stopped her, turned her around.

"You love me?"

"Couldn't you tell? God, Mei, you're everything I could want in a woman. If you tell me there's disaster afoot, I'll believe you. Because I believe in you." He leaned down to kiss her, then released her, though the way his hands stroked her cheek, she knew he wanted much more.

He ran into his room, hauled on a shirt, shoes, and was back to her quickly holding a flashlight.

"Dhammayangyi, huh? I've had a hankering to go there." He fished in his pocket, produced a set of keys, and led her down to the jeep. In the vehicle they just might beat whatever was coming. She ran to lift the courtyard barrier, let it fall as she climbed in beside Alex.

They were off, careening down the road, skidding as they turned onto the long dirt road that led to the pahto.

It wasn't too late. Not yet, she could tell. But the lightning was close and the scent of ozone was heavy in the air. Alex skidded the vehicle to a stop and they both scrambled out into darkness. Nothing moved, but a strange hum filled the air and seemed to suck the breath from Mei's lungs.

"Do you feel it?" she managed.

Alex nodded, his gaze drinking in the structure as if it were a prize pet. "What is that?"

"Why don't you enter and see?" The thin-faced Colonel they had so learned to distrust stepped out of the darkness, speaking surprisingly good English. The machine pistol he held pointed at Alex, so Mei feared for both their lives.

Here was the danger she'd dreaded. Even in the shifting moonlight there were endings in the Colonel's eyes. Alex shoved Mei behind him, even as she wanted to protect him. She wanted to be strong. Wished she could be like Kalla.

"How touching and futile, Doctor. But I could use your archaeologist's eye. Thank you for your thoughtfulness in coming. You save me the trouble of sending for you."

He waved the weapon at the temple and Mei caught Alex's hand, took strength from him, and led the way into darkness.

Whispers and the soft hum were louder here. Something shifted beyond shadows. Shifted beyond the flashlights Alex and the Colonel ran across the walls. Overhead came a rustle and rush and batwings caught in her hair, talons on her skin. She could have screamed, but she would not show Alex she was weak. He sheltered her with his body and then the bats were gone.

But Colonel Aung was not.

"That way." The barrel of his weapon jabbed at them and Alex stumbled against her, steadied himself, and pushed her ahead of him toward a distant light.

Kalla and Simon and another. As she got closer she recognized General Ne Setkya, but did not understand what she saw—until a portion of the temple wall moved under the General's touch. Until Colonel Aung shoved her hard into the light.

Chapter 45 - Pictures of the Past

The new voice, the sudden appearance of Mei, stopped Kalla cold. She stood with Simon, still caught in the crimson haze, as Colonel Aung stepped out of the darkness, shoving Alex before him, an automatic pistol shoved into his side.

Then Alex spun, trying to overpower the Colonel, grappled with the smaller man. Simon pushed Kalla aside, leapt, but Aung's weapon bucked. Flashed, and Alex slammed back against the wall as Aung trained the weapon on Simon. Mei's screams filled the corridor. Shock filled Alex's face as he looked down at his gut. At the bright red bloom as he slid—far too slowly—down to the floor.

Mei lunged toward Alex, but Aung grabbed her by the neck, had his weapon at her head. Kalla couldn't move, fought against the crimson that made it hard to believe what had happened.

"One move and she dies, too."

Simon backed to Kalla and caught her hand. Warm. The only warmth in a too-cold world. Mei's sobs filled the tunnel.

"Alex," she begged. "Alex."

"Shut up. You are Burmese. He is foreign."

Aung pushed her into Kalla's arms, but turned the oily weapon's muzzle on them all as he glanced at Ne Setkya.

"The Old Man said if there were secrets in Pagan, you would be their guardian. It seems he was correct."

The elegant English sank through to Kalla, stunned her almost as much as Alex on the floor, as the humming in the temple. A slight groan indicated he still lived.

Go to him.

But Aung's English, his mention of the man who ran Myanmar like a puppet master, seemed to immobilize the general. Through the haze, she saw his throat work, until finally he found words.

"I should have known. You followed me—or had me followed."

Aung smiled like a snake tasting fear. The tunnel reeked of copper blood. *Should not.*

Kalla jerked at the inner voice.

Alex needed help. A doctor, but Aung clearly didn't care. Simon could do nothing. Shock seemed to have frozen him—them all. And something waited to be done.

Something distant and near. It took everything Kalla had to comfort the sobbing Mei and stay on her feet, still clutching the puppet between them.

"It was most unusual, you leaving work before the dusk, the hag's visit to your home. And all your concerns about the woman's return." Aung glanced Kalla's way, his gaze empty as the cold void

that waits through that door.

Again that voice. The pain stabbed her head and the crimson ran like Alex's blood.

"Kalla?" Mei's whisper. "You're shaking."

She couldn't respond. Knew Simon glanced at her in concern.

"I knew you would lead me to something." Aung looked back at the opening in the wall. "But this is more than I hoped."

It is death.

Had that come from her mouth?

Aung and the others looked at her. Aung pointed his weapon at Ne Setkya, his finger on his weapon's trigger.

"Let us make sure there are no more deaths than necessary. Your pistol on the floor, if you please."

"You think me fool enough to believe you will let us live?" Ne Setkya didn't look like he was going to relinquish his pistol. Then Aung sent a bullet into the wall near Ne Setkya's head. Sound exploded down the halls, echoes chasing after.

"Strange possibilities for strange times. The wall is open, so I think your usefulness comes to an end. Perhaps sooner rather than later. Now your weapon, if you wish for the chance to look upon what you have guarded."

It came out as a command that not even the general could deny. Slowly, the General placed his pistol on the floor and Aung seemed to relax, then motioned Kalla and the others to the passage.

"Shall we see what waits inside?"

No! The crimson rippled in Kalla's brain, *know what we will find.* Kalla staggered until Simon caught her arm. Mei faced Aung.

"We can't leave him here," Mei tried again to reach Alex, but Aung waved her back with his weapon. She moved to the door.

A deep part of Kalla screamed, and the stroke of fear knocked her knees loose. She crumbled, would have fallen if not for Simon's strong hands that caught her waist, lifted, steadied, warmed. She pulled away, not wanting his help. Needing to do this on her own, and Mei did the same. Setting the example. Reminding Kalla of who she was.

She would face this fear. Lock it away with the Crimson and her betraying heart, and do this thing that she knew needed doing. Shivering, she clutched the puppet and stepped across the threshold.

Everything went quiet. No bell tone. No throbbing, teeth-aching brick lament. Only the sound of her breathing, the heat of Simon's presence behind her, the flicker of the general's flashlight. And Mei's soft sobs.

Flashes of gold on the walls. Forests and leaves. A tiger peering out. Flowers and faces, stylized and brilliant as pictures in a fairy story. *Spirits.* The scent of dust and faded lotus filled her nose and sent the Crimson woman thrashing. It knocked Kalla against the wall and she moaned. Horrible double vision made her close her eyes and cold made it hard to move.

Spirits that lived.

A long procession. Many monks there. An alchemist. Spirit dancers singing and the gifts brought as offering to the great ones. She among them.

"Kalla. Let me help you." Simon caught her arms, and *it was another's hands that helped her when her legs gave out.* But it was the right thing she did. *Had done.*

Even leaving her daughter behind.

Here. She swung into the arms of the man who helped her, loved her, had to let her go. Take this. She grabbed from the pile of goods in the room. So many things, who would miss it? Give it to my daughter. A promise. I will return. To her. To you.

"Merde, Kalla! You have to stop this. You have to try." He shook her and she looked at him. Saw Simon/Taungbyon. Saw Mei's tearful face and darkness all around. She had tried before and had ended. It had not accomplished what was intended. Perhaps with a new life given...

"Move!" The Colonel's voice.

"He means it." The General's softer words as he urged them forward.

She kept going, half staggering with the weight of the temple, the weight of what she carried, and the visions that streamed through her head. *Torchlight fading. Darkness and sorrow and slow, slow death.*

The tunnel ended in a wall that flashed under Ne Setkya's light, but on her right there was more darkness. A door. Cold, she stepped through into sudden space, and hot wind blew around her. Lifted her hair. It felt like she was falling until Simon steadied her and anchored her in space.

"Is this what you were seeking, chérie?"

"I don't know." But she did. The pulse through the floor, through the Votaress, said this was her destiny. The general's light split the darkness, catching on golden figures, Nat houses, laquerware bowls painted with gold and spilling over with pearls and rubies.

"Mon Dieu."

"What is this place?" Mei asked, voice full of wonder.

Kalla pulled away from Simon's sheltering hands, inhaled the old scent of death and jasmine as she reached for a faded lotus blossom. At her touch it disintegrated. Grey dust coated her fingers like time.

"How long has this been here?" Simon's voice echoed in the darkness. Aung swore and shoved them farther into the room, but it didn't matter. Ne Setkya's flashlight sent wild light patterns over the walls. Didn't matter at all, because the Crimson cut through the strangeness, cut through Kalla's caution and brought feelings of...

home and resignation.

She was where she should be. Taking care of everything. Caught in a void. Walking with spirits. Wasn't that how Kalla Jervis lived her life, too? She strode forward into the darkness.

"General, please bring the light."

Behind her, Aung used his light. With his weapon still trained on Simon, he rummaged amid the gold and jewels, filled his pockets as his flash glittered on heaped offerings—bowls that once held fruit, now gone to dust. Nat houses crusted with gold. Figures the Crimson inside her named as Min Mahagiri, king of nats, Lady Three-Times Beautiful. Thirty six, she counted, each with his own gilt mansion.

General Ne Setkya and Mei came to her side, pushing past Simon who hovered protectively behind her. He could not save her from what had to be done. The Crimson returned.

She picked her way over the ancient, mural-covered floor. Against the wall lay a crumpled figure draped in red. Inside the Crimson stilled, sighed.

Kalla knew it was the Crimson. Min. Both she and the General went to their knees before the mummified figure.

"She has lain here a long time," Kalla murmured.

"She has."

"She gave herself."

"It was a great sacrifice for us all."

"It was not complete. She lives still."

She felt the General's gaze on her, met it, and saw sorrow.

"Old One." He bowed his head in acknowledgement. "I am sorry you must go through this again, but your sacrifice was not enough. The covenant must be completed or Burma—true Burma—dies."

The Crimson shuddered to life, struggled for dominance.

To run. To escape this second death.

Kalla pressed it back, fought it with all the controls she possessed. Locks and keys. Push away feeling, emotion. She was panting when she was done, and red haze still colored her vision and made it hard to think.

"I will not fight this duty." Kalla's voice came out thick, but true. "I give my life in payment for my mother's death." If Aung killed her, it would only increase the power of the covenant.

Her gaze slid from the body. The figure's position suggested she had died making obeisance to the wall.

Ne Setkya's flashlight followed her gaze. The murals, painted in a simple style reminiscent of the folk murals of Thatbyinnyu. Untouched by weather, they showed a bright procession across the wall. There were the temples of Pagan, huge and gleaming white under a younger sun. The plain between them was filled with teak palaces and teaming with people— filling the roads, streaming out of the city.

"It's the leaving," she said. "All of them go. They left of their own will—not due to disease or war." Awe filled her that these ancient people would do this, because she had no doubts the painting was true. Just as the other paintings had been. Offerings to the spirits, because here the spirits lived.

"The city was dying," the general said.

She glanced at Ne Setkya, saw the sadness there.

"They had forgotten to honor the nats and so the nats left the land. Without spirits, how can things grow, people thrive? They hoped this offering would bring them back, but something went wrong. And so Pagan—and Burma—has died a slow death ever since, though for a time it seemed the splendor of Pagan would bloom in Amarapura and Mandalay. Until the British came." The general bowed his head.

It was true, the Crimson knew it, had seen it over lifetimes. The sense of age left Kalla breathless as she followed the mural around the wall.

Pagan's people flooding out into the forest, the tiger, symbol of the wild countryside and nature, peering out at her from the side of the largest structure in the room.

A puppet stage.

It soared above her, its graceful awnings thick with gold, glittering with rubies. Bright curtains crumbled to dust as her movements stirred the air. Three dead trees stood on the stage, their trunks also crusted with gold.

"A royal stage," Mei whispered at Kalla's side.

Kalla nodded, moved forward to count what lay on the raised floorboards. Yoke thei—puppets. White faces still smiled. Ornate hands still gestured. Cloth-of-gold stiff with sequin and pearl.

There was ogre and horse. There the king and his ministers. Lovely Minthamee. Her prince. The others. All but one.

Kalla looked down at what she held, could almost swear the Votaress struggled toward the stage. Her clothing was different. Time had not been so kind on the outside world and the cloth had been replaced many times. Lovingly replacing the seed pearls on the bodice, the silken scarf, Kalla remembered the doing, though it was nothing she had ever done.

But the body of the Votaress was the same. The clever carving of the body with the illusion of life. The life-like face.

"I return that which was taken from you," Kalla murmured, knowing she did the correct thing as she placed the Votaress beside the other small figures.

An intake of breath, and cold wind against her skin.

Then the air shook as if a gong were struck, and reverberations sent her to her knees. Mei collapsed beside her, warm arms around Kalla.

"Kalla!" Simon leapt to her aid, helped her up, helped up Mei, when the vibrations would keep them from their feet. Kalla bowed her head. Had to show respect, but a shout came from the door.

A yell. They whirled as Aung fired, as lights lashed wildly around the room.

A flash of pink. Aung's angry expression.

Daw Ma Ma Nang, fury on her face.

Chapter 46 - Illusion of Life

Simon leapt as the temple trembled and rang like a bell. As Aung fired wildly. Someone screamed, and the flashlights went out.

Bullets whizzed too close to Simon's head and slammed into the wall, sending sharp shards of brick into his cheek .

Kalla. Stay with her. And Mei.

Deal with enemy, first.

He grabbed Aung, the Nat's spirit sight working in the dark. Slammed the Colonel back against the wall, grabbed his weapon hand as Taungbyon took over.

Darkness and rage. Death comes for YOU!

Aung's wrist snapped and he screamed. Screamed again as Simon/Taungbyon slammed a fist in his gut. Scream turned to strangled moan, barely heard above the reverberations in the room. Aung collapsed in Simon/Taungbyon's arms.

Unworthy man. He threw Aung across the room and his head cracked against stone. He slid down the wall to sprawl on the floor.

Finished. Taungbyon's satisfaction was clear.

Simon/Taungbyon whirled, satisfied and seeking. Kalla to protect. *His Min.* And Mei.

Too late. A flashlight flashed on to reveal that Ne Setkya had claimed Aung's gun. He faced Simon from across the room, Mei clenched to his chest.

"Forgive me, but do not try anything."

Simon ground his teeth, heard something in his jaw crack. Darkness and death. He had killed a man, and the continuing gong reverberations filled his head, his body, as the knowledge sank in. The air stank of ozone and incense as the world trembled around him.

What had he done?

But Taungbyon walked in his body. Taungbyon who would always rise to protect Burma and his love.

He advanced on the General as dust rained around him. *One chance. Just one.*

"Stay back if you want her to live." Ne Setkya tightened his hold on Mei as he edged around the room, his flashlight the lone beacon in the dust-filled room. She fought in his hold, fought like Kalla would fight. Simon took one step. Another. He could not let anything happen to Mei.

"Stop there." The General ordered. Simon still advanced.

"Simon, no!" Kalla stopped him from her place by the stage. "You can't take the chance."

"A wise assessment, Ms. Jervis." General Ne Setkya stopped beside the huddled pink form. "Ma Ma Nang?"

Nothing.

"Ms. Jervis, if you please?" He motioned at the fallen nun, but trained his weapon on Simon, knew the danger he posed. Around them bits of brick rained down.

There was no way Simon could reach Ne Setkya before he was hit. Taungbyon still wanted to try.

Death and rebirth. Taungbyon is eternal.

But I am not, mon ami.

Kalla obediently went to Daw Ma Ma Nang, gently turning the old woman over. Blood bloomed across the pink fabric that swathed her chest, but Daw Ma Ma Nang's eyes flashed open and she caught Kalla's hand. Spoke, but her words were lost in the painful tremors that filled the room. Then the nun went limp and Kalla checked her pulse, looked up at the General. His face hardened and Simon knew he had lost his chance.

"I am sorry for what I do, but my sister gave her life to save this place. Save it I will."

He leapt for the door, dragging Mei after, plunged into the corridor before Simon could react.

When he did, it was too late. Ne Setkya moved swiftly for an old man with a hostage, disappeared into darkness, and then there came the sound of stone grating shut. Simon/Taungbyon sprang after, slammed into brick. The door. The barrier closing.

He slammed again, but the wall would not be stopped.

"Simon!" Mei's cry filled him with fear. Her voice faded as the brick wall closed.

"No!" Taungbyon roared. Kalla would be trapped. Their lives would be ended. He caught the edge of the door and heaved. Still it moved. Simon slammed again, again, against the stonework. They would be locked in and he would have failed.

Failed Kalla.

Failed his love.

"Help Kalla," Mei cried. "You mus-"

And the door sealed shut. Again.

§

Darkness, and the gong-sound echoed and built as if demons pounded the drums of hell. It kept Kalla on her knees, huddled over the nun's body, inhaling the copper-scent of blood. It covered her hands, her clothes, as she smoothed her palm over the old woman's head.

Another sacrificed to this place. Another who would mummify here.

As she would. A gift that Burma might live. Perhaps Simon had won free.

But then strong hands lifted her away from the death and the chill of old stone. Warm arms around her. Warm breath on her face. Palm cupping her chin, her cheek. Lips on hers. She could barely feel as the numbness sank in, as the Crimson's screams filled her head.

"Chérie? Did he hurt you?" barely heard over the reverberations.

She shook her head, fought to get free and form words. "No. He didn't hurt me. He didn't want to do this, but he—had to—he thought. To make the sacrifice real. To give Burma a chance."

She looked up at Simon and found his dark gaze waiting, realized there was light to see. Turned and saw why.

Spirit light rose from the stage in a glitter of whirling blue sparks that coalesced above the puppets. Simon caught her in his arms and tried to pull her back as the whirling fireflies coalesced into a mass, and then exploded outward, fountained over, into, the small wooden figures…

that rose, stretched, yawned, and…

danced.

More graceful than the stage in Mandalay. More graceful than any strings could ever guide. More graceful than any ballet. Royal yoke thei, inhabited by the spirit of the Yamani tree.

And as if they knew her thoughts, the puppets swirled like eddying leaves across the stage and came together, their forms coalescing, joining wood-to-wood—branches of a tree growing, up to the roof of the room, up through the brick, sending roots deep, deep through stone and into the earth as the gong transformed to music, the heartbeat of the earth.

A tree. The great tree. Kalla knew the Tree of Life of so many folk tales and cultural traditions across the world.

The roaring sounded like a freight train approaching and shook the foundations of Dhammayangyi. Kalla feared it would come down. Simon dragged her towards the door as pieces of brick began to shower around them.

"I have to see," she shouted into the tumult, but her words were lost in the deafening maelstrom of sound.

She twisted in Simon's grasp, finally hit him and almost fell as he released her. She turned and ran for the stage.

She had to understand. It was almost at the tip of her tongue. The tree was key. The yoke thei were key.

A breath of wind and green growth blew off the stage. New grass. Young fern. Flowering jasmine. The small dead trees bloomed with new leaves. From somewhere over the roaring, her head filled with music and the wailing words of a singer as she stood transfixed. New leaves uncurled from the massive tree's white trunk.

Brick debris rained on her, bounced off of her shoulders.

"Kalla! We have to leave. The whole place is coming down," Simon shouted into her ear.

She waved him away. Knew she had to see, because the Crimson woman knew this was important, knew this was what should have happened so long ago.

The smooth bole of the new tree split wide and a small figure stepped free onto the stage's floorboards. Naked and perfectly formed, hair of moss, wood whorls visible through translucent skin, a three-foot tall woman danced onto the stage. She pointed delicate toes, arched her fingers more ornately than any Thai dancer, and came across the stage to peer down at Kalla.

She grinned, impish and yet filled with age's wisdom. Reached into the air and from nowhere pulled a pulsing ball of blue and white light.

Smiling, she pointed to a place on the gleaming ball. Kalla leaned closer and the singing voice stopped, the music stopped.

"*Pagan.*" A clear voice rang in Kalla's head.

The dancer's hand darted at the shimmering globe, spinning it as she spoke a list, a litany. Names, Kalla realized. She named names as she held the whirling blue ball out to Kalla.

Kalla hesitated. "I don't understand."

"You hold the key." Again that small voice that carried even over the roar that filled the room.

The falling dust made it hard to breathe. Kalla coughed, felt Simon hovering behind her.

"Key to what?" she managed.

"Many things. All doors. You have returned that which was stolen, and Daw Ma Ma Nang has taken your place. All is right, now. You are free."

The small woman held out the globe, and Kalla took it from her, inhaled the dancer's scent of sandalwood and green leaves.

"Be well, friend."

And then the voice was gone, the figure winked out, and in the fading light of the stage Kalla stood holding a small, round box. Laquerware, Kalla recognized.

And then the ceiling fell, concealing the tree and crushing the stage.

Chapter 47 - Sacrifice

Simon barely yanked Kalla back from the destruction. Sharp needles of stone and wood peppered Kalla with pain.

"We have to get out of here," he shouted above the roar. "The temple is coming down."

"No. Just here. Just the room. In protection."

"Peut-être, chérie, but it is not healthy to remain."

He grabbed her hand, and she followed still caught in the haze of crimson. Bricks pounded the gold statues. Stone smashed into the nat houses, and shattered the bowls of jewels until they were a menace on the floor.

Then they were in the tunnel, air cold on her skin; the roar diminished, but the tunnel walls quivered with the coming destruction. If the room collapsed it could take the tunnel with it. There was no way they would survive.

Simon crushed her against his warm chest and she realized she was cold, shaking with it. Shivers wracked her so she could barely stand as she clutched the tree nat's gift to her chest.

"Aah, ma pauvre petite. Stay here. I will get the door open."

"No," she whispered, but he released her and she heard the sound of his shoulder impacting the brick. Heard his effort, and she could no longer consider this man her betrayer.

"Simon. No. You'll hurt yourself."

"And I am your protector, non? I must get us free."

She found his arm in the crimson darkness. Stopped him.

"No." She ran her palm down his cheek. "I think—I think this door is my task. The spirit woman—she said something. Did you hear?"

 Karen L. Abrahamson

"What are you talking about?"

So the woman spoke to only her. Simon turned back to the wall, but Kalla stepped up to him.

"She said I was the key to all doors, and sure as heck this is one." She grinned though he couldn't see it, and the effort cost her. Keep things light even though the roar from the room, the vibration in the walls, the screams of the Crimson said there wasn't much time.

She turned to the wall, ran her hands over it, and the Crimson woman caught her like a cloud, thick and viscous.

No. She needed to think. She pressed the woman back, and a stab of pain pierced her skull and sent her falling against the wall. Frigid stone, and she was *freezing, falling, terrified and dying in the dark*. Couldn't think for the cold.

Simon had her in his arms.

"Kalla! Please, Kalla!"

She moaned, and tried to form words. Clutched her head against the pain, against the woman's screaming. "Her. Min."

"Kalla, my princess, you cannot fight her. You must live with her. It will kill you otherwise."

She couldn't think. Couldn't be. Possession was a lie. But there was something here, with her. Something screaming in her head. Crimson woman?

She had listened before, and used the knowledge.

The shaking rattled her teeth. The cold froze her bones. So cold, so cold in the dark. What use was there in buying into someone else's madness? She knew better. She always knew better.

She staggered up, went back to the brick, but just the touch of her hand sent the Crimson woman into madness, slamming into Kalla, wave after wave. She fell back against Simon, panting, and he caught her arms.

"Kalla, you must listen."

But how could she hear anything over the roar in the room and the Crimson's wail of frustration?

"Kalla."

She held onto her name.

"Kalla, if you are the key, there may be a chance. Spirits know things, Kalla. They have powers. And your spirit was here at the beginning of all this. She would know how the door works."

"She died here."

"And that was her sacrifice, chérie. She knew, and still gave herself."

The Crimson sent Kalla reeling into the back of her mind, but she would not let this wildness take her. Her heart stuttered, paused. Her blood hesitated in her veins, and the world slipped from her. Slipped, and she knew Simon was right. In this battle for her body, she could die.

Could he be right in other things? Had it been the truth that he told her? Had her father truly come?

The shivering made it hard to think about anything but the cold. *Listen.*

A word Kalla did not want to hear because always she was the one who decided, who knew the right thing to do. The shaking was worse and she knew her blood slowed. Heart slowed.

She collapsed against Simon's chest and knew it was only him that kept her upright and breathing. He lowered them to their knees.

"You must find a way to mingle." He shook her. "There can be no peace, no life, if you do not learn."

Give up control to this? He wanted her to live with this crazed madwoman shrieking in her head? How could she trust this thing? Or herself afterwards?

Like your choices have been so good.

She'd thought Sharon was crazy too, had thought Mei was weak, but look at the strength both women had found. Sharon was of hardier stock than Kalla had realized. So was Mei.

The same stock at the Crimson woman. As Kalla.

Maybe she was already mad. Buddhism said we each lived in our own delusions.

The shudders wouldn't stop. The noise roared in her ears, in her brain. Simon ran his hands up and down her arms—trying to keep her warm, she supposed. Pieces of ceiling brick pummeled his back, his head, his shoulders as he sheltered her. Blood dripped from his face.

She did this to him. Her delusions. If not for her, he would be free.

If she were going to find a way out, she would have to do it soon, but how do you take down all the walls of a lifetime?

Like temple comes down. I show.

The scent of jasmine slammed into her as the Crimson rose. She swayed in graceful dance.

Like this.

No! Kalla had managed all her life alone. She fought loose from Simon, struggled up as masonry showered down, as it suddenly struck her when Taungbyon's hands fell from her skin.

The door. She ran her hands over the rough surface. Brick. Mortar. Nothing more. Not even a seam. No breath of air. And the Crimson woman shrieked inside, her power taking Kalla's breath away.

Hands on bricks. Focus on hands on bricks, tearing them down, tearing at the lie of her control. Because it was a lie. She'd been fooling herself all these years. She'd built an illusion when the world was really out of control.

A way out. A way to hope. A way promised.

No! Not you.

Tears, blinding in the darkness. Blind fingers groped and tore at stone. Falling brick rained and the scent of dust and blood filled her nose. Hers. Bloody nails and fingertips.

Finally, exhausted, she slumped against the wall, and Simon's arms came around her protectively.

No hope except love.

"Help me," she whispered. "I can't let Simon die."

The Crimson stilled, and Kalla realized the rumbling had stopped in the tunnel, though brick still rained down.

"Help me."

The Crimson rose around her like the warmth of spring, like new love or lotus petals tight with new life—and opening.

All the power of new growth tore at her controls, all the walls shimmered.

Her back arched, her head snapped back, and Simon caught her once more as she fell down through the ages, down past the women, down past the pain to the Crimson and knew:

Strong arms around her.

Saying goodbye.

You don't have to do this, said Taungbyon.

Yes, I do.

She left him at the door. Stood and watched as bricks closed between them. Watched as her torch flickered out, as her candle withered and died. But would not let herself out, in payment for her people and a hoped-for future.

Chapter 48 - Sobbing and Rain

"Merde," Simon swore in the darkness, barely hearing himself over the thunder of bricks. He supported Kalla, Taungbyon using his power to hold back the dangerous hail.

But Kalla's body had gone rigid with internal struggle. Her breath came in short, uneven gasps and he felt her pulse hesitate and falter. She was losing the battle. The damnable woman would not listen. Must do things her way. He wanted to shake her. Do something to fix this for her.

But in this she truly had the control, and he hated his helplessness.

Her body radiated heat like forged iron. Radiated the ancient scent of jasmine and incense.

Min.

The other one pressed her presence, and that was what Kalla fought.

"You cannot leave me, Kalla. Must not leave."

As if in answer, she jerked in his arms. Once. Twice. Again. Choked for air as if she came up from deep water and fought her way from his arms.

"I will do this." Her voice held the distant sound of a bell.

And she did. Sudden blue light flared from Kalla's fingers, spread into the wall. Bricks hailed around her, seemed to glance away before they struck. The ceiling groaned, bent towards them. If they were to get free, the time was now.

There was only now.

And something answered.

Grinding sound, and the air shifted in the blue-tinged darkness. Fresh. Carrying the promise of the river, air shifted against his face. Darkness beyond Dhammayangyi's secret core.

He caught Kalla in his arms, leapt free of the tunnel, just as the ceiling gave a final screeching groan and collapsed in a roar.

Air and darkness in the temple's outer tunnels. No sign of Alex or the general or Mei. Simon ran. The whole place could be coming down for all he knew.

Safe. She is safe.

And how do you know that, mon ami? You are no seer.

Know. The Nat showed his disdain at Simon's doubt.

Down the connecting tunnel that led to the outer ways, past the white-faced Buddhas that gleamed in the night.

He stumbled out into a courtyard perfumed by new plowed earth, new rice and green leaves. Kalla struggled out of his arms, struggled to stand, did not release her hold on his hand, but clutched something else to her breast.

The soft sound of sobbing and the patter of building rain filled the space with music. Kalla led him to the shadows of a spindly tree. General Ne Setkya crouched beside Mei over Alex's body.

"He dies." The General's voice was choked with pain. "It should not be."

Kalla knelt beside them, her hair crackling out around her shoulders and moon-blue light in her gaze.

"You are free." Ne Setkya brushed at wet eyes, his voice full of— was it wonder?

"Non grâce à vous. No thanks to you," Simon muttered.

"Shh, love. He bears the pain of long duty and endings." Kalla's voice, and yet not. She was pale, gleaming, though no moonlight escaped the thick clouds, and two voices spoke with her mouth, two souls peered at him from her eyes.

"Min?" Taungbyon's question burst free of him.

"We are both here, beloved of now and before."

"And we are free." Taungbyon again, but with none of the wild madness Simon had known. Instead there was wonder and a stretching as if the whole world lay within his and the spirit's grasp.

Then Kalla set the lacquer box on Alex's chest, clasped his hand and Mei's.

"On such a night as this, all prayers will be heard. Pray, Mei, that Alex might live."

Her gaze turned to Ne Setkya.

"Your sister died well."

"I mourn the passing of many lifetimes' work, but mostly I am glad." He motioned at Dhammayangyi as the storm broke over the monument.

Blue lightning flashed from the temple to the sky. Blue lightning snaked through veins in the soil, flickered in the rain that deluged the dry earth. The air crackled with spirit power, spirit power coalesced around them, around Mei kneeling on newly sodden earth, Alex's hand clutched to her heart.

"My time is ended," Ne Setkya said.

"You are free to seek your rest," Kalla agreed.

She raised her face to the pouring rain, lifted up what she held—the small box, dazzling with the lash of spirit-blue fire.

"You have your sacrifice!" Kalla cried. "The nun, the Votaress and my long past. You do not need one more."

Silence, and then lightening spiked down, struck the box, and blue light poured down into Alex's chest. Alex spasmed, back arched, then slammed onto the earth. Ozone in the air. A moan on the wind, and Mei's cry of dismay as the heavens opened with monsoon rain.

Kalla stood. She turned seer's eyes on Simon as power returned to Pagan on the wings of the storm.

Alex opened his eyes.

§

"I still don't get it," Alex said over the research team's last cup of pathetic Sanka coffee. He sat at the Beautyland dining table flipping the laquerware box from hand to hand and making Kalla crazy with concern at each movement. His left arm wasn't that strong yet; who knew just how well the spirits had healed him.

Well, Min said, content.

That might be, but the box was precious, no matter what Alex said. The way the Crimson woman swelled at each small toss made her sure of it.

"What's not to get?" Simon asked, lounging in his chair. His arm was thrown possessively across Kalla's chair back, so she could feel the heat of his arm on her neck and mourn the day he wouldn't be there.

"You expect me to believe that the people of Pagan just up and left because they decided their city was dying?" Alex shifted uncomfortably. He still moved tenderly, his torso and left arm swathed in bandages from the Pagan military hospital.

"You've got to think from their point of view, Alex." She said. "I'm saying they got up and left because they realized *they* were killing the land that supported the city. Under the King's orders they had turned away from the nature spirits—the Nats who had been with them far longer than Buddhism. They neglected their offerings, and as a result the spirits left them and the land died. That's what the old Nun's stories and the other stories were trying to teach me. That's what the folk murals were saying, too. If you think about it, you can see it. These are people intrinsically part of their landscape."

"She is right, Alex." Simon joined in the discussion. "Nats dwell in each hill and rice field. There are great Nats like the Taungbyon brothers who are dedicated to the defense of Burma. They belong to Burma and Burma belongs to them. Even today it is like that."

Simon shifted behind her so his hand touched her hair, but Kalla cringed at his words. Taungbyon was the defender of Burma and always would be, while she had to leave. The expiration of her month-long Visa and the task given her by the Nats demanded it. Which meant Simon/Taungbyon would remain and their relationship would wither when it had barely bloomed.

She reached for Simon's hand.

"I still don't buy it and frankly I'm surprised at you, Kalla. I'd have thought you'd have looked deeper—found what was behind the superstition. You always have before." Alex flipped the box one more time and tossed it to Simon, nearly bringing a squeak out of Kalla. "Next you'll be telling me the rain is a gift from the nats."

She looked outside to where another afternoon rain soaked Pagan with life-giving moisture. The plain had bloomed with green since that fateful night. The birds seemed to sing brighter, the temples no longer loomed threateningly. "It is."

"For god's sake, Kalla. You can't believe that. It's all a load of bunk. No documentation of the room, and now you tell me it's lost forever. That box—hell, it's no more than a piece of tourist crap. I don't know how you could have chosen that as the one thing you brought out of the temple."

"You're sure?"

"As sure as I'm an archaeologist. I can generally tell when something is old even with all the fake antiques out there, but this thing.... The thing has a frigging map of the modern world on it. Like the ancient Burmese knew the world even existed."

His sarcasm turned to a wince of pain, but there was no way she was going to tell him all that she suspected—that this wasn't the end—that there were other places in the world that needed to be reawakened, just like Pagan.

Nope. Alex would require more than being shot to make a believer out of him.

"Alex, you really should rest a while. You are just out of the hospital." Mei's concern was palpable. She had spent every day at the hospital with him.

"I'm fine. No problemo. Aung's bullet just grazed me—one of your nat's miracles, I suppose?" He looked pointedly at the Nat Kadaw on the shelf, and patted Mei's hand. Kalla bit her tongue.

"Kalla says that belief in earth spirits existed in all cultures at one time, but our modern world has forgotten." Mei stood to refill Alex's cup with hot water from a kettle and poured another packet of Sanka into the cup. Alex used his good hand to pull her into his side.

"Thank you." A light kiss on Mei's hand demonstrated the bond that they had formed. Mei was the right kind of woman for Alex—smart, gentle and non-combative.

"So given your assessment, I shouldn't have any trouble getting the box out of the country?"

"Hell, no. Especially not with the papers your general-friend provided. He seems to have smoothed everything over—even Aung's disappearance."

"Good." She turned, satisfied, to Simon beside her, felt again the familiar shock of his intense gaze, the way the Crimson rose in readiness whenever there was contact between them.

And the grief that their relationship was almost over.

"So…," She said softly and stood. Simon stood with her as she walked to the door.

Arms around us. With us.

He gave her that smoldering smile as if he knew what she felt and that made her want to pull his head down to hers. Dammit, he knew the effect he had on her—and the trouble she had dealing with it in public.

"What are we going to do, Simon?"

"Do?"

A suggestive rise of his dark brows and he held out the box, her map. His scent of incense and musk left her fighting for control.

"Aah, Princess, perhaps you will lead me astray again? To secret, dangerous places?"

She gazed at the box she held. Small gold flecks caught fire in the fluorescent light and marked spots around the globe the puppet spirit had named—places that just might have their own spirits to evoke.

"I'd give anything for that. But I have to leave and… and Taungbyon is tied to Burma." She finally got out what she'd realized, looked up to find Simon's smile had turned soft.

"Taungbyon is many places, Princess. He dwells within many; he is the spirit of the people who fight for Burma, and so there are others who will rise to Burma's defense, just as the General did." He pulled her to him, one arm around her waist and nuzzled her neck, forgetful of Alex and Mei's presence. "I think Taungbyon is great enough to defend a world. As I will defend you through all adventures."

The promise of his words took her breath away. But the way he said it brought Min forth to warm Kalla's skin and heat the hidden places that knew Simon-Taungbyon so well.

Kalla-Min gripped the lacquer box more tightly as she hooked a finger in the front of his shirt, looked up at him and smiled.

"I don't think this is going to be easy, Simon," she said, trying to maintain some propriety with Alex and Mei so near.

Simon leaned in close to nuzzle her ear and whisper. "With the spirit upon us, Princess, how can it be hard?"

ABOUT THE AUTHOR

Karen L. McKee is a well-traveled writer who has explored Burma(Myanmar) and published nonfiction articles about the yoke thei. She is the author of literary, erotic, romantic and fantasy fiction. She lives on the west coast of Canada with two Bengal cats that aren't quite as well traveled as she is.

If you'd like to learn more about her, visit her at www.karenlabrahamson.com.

If you enjoyed this book, you might enjoy *Ashes and Light* by Karen L. McKee. Read on for an excerpt.

BOOKS BY THE AUTHOR

Written as Karen L. McKee
Ashes and Light
Shades of Moonlight
Judas Kiss
Second Spring
A Different Nightmusic
Shadow Play
Coming Down Christmas

Written as Karen L. Abrahamson

The Unlocking Series
Unlocking Her Heart
Unlocking Her History
Unlocking Her Grace
Unlocking Her Dreams
Unlocking Her Chances
Unlocking Her Doubts

The Sunshine Coast Mythical Beings
Surviving Safe Harbor
Dangerous Haven

KAREN L. ABRAHAMSON
Writing as Karen L. McKee
ASHES AND LIGHT
ROMANTIC SUSPENSE

Ashes and Light

Prologue

August 2001, Bamiyan, Central Afghanistan

The night ran thick with screams, just like so many other nights.

Michael Bellis willed himself motionless as he peered out into the half-lit carnage. Behind him, Yaqub quietly crouched in the collapsed mud house, working his healing wonders as he methodically triaged the injured.

Yaqub had the almost supernatural talent to ignore the madness, the sounds, the gunfire, and work calmly over his patients. Michael vibrated with the need to move, to protect the Hazzara villagers, even though he and Yaqub were woefully unprepared for the large force of Taliban soldiers that had taken the town.

Another rocket seared the night. It slammed into a stately, mud-daub tower and exploded in hellish flame no one could have survived. The concussion ran up his legs as mud brick and dust rained down.

One of the women shrieked—her voice ululating like the cries in the streets and the buildings around them.

"Silence!" he ordered.

Fire glared off the rugged cliffs and the yawning alcoves where the Taliban had destroyed the giant, awe-inspiring Buddha figures.

Panicked quiet filled the little group behind him. The women and children huddled together, masking the vocal woman's sobs with desperate hands.

To comfort them would be the right thing to do, but right now all his attention was on survival——theirs and his. They would live or die together depending on the women's obedience. At least that was part of Afghan culture——along with the pride and stubbornness that had kept Yaqub and the others fighting the Russians and now the Taliban.

He leaned back to his observations post, automatically inventoried the changes the explosion had caused to the ruined townscape. The knowledge would help their retreat from this shelter that would surely soon be discovered.

"We need to move," he whispered back.

Yaqub crawled forward just in time to see another woman dart towards their meager safety from across the ruined street. A sniper bullet spun her around and dropped her.

"The devil lives here, and his name is Hashemi," Yaqub muttered through his black beard. He was clothed, as Michael was, and as every other Afghani male, in the baggy trousers and long tunic and the black-and-white striped turban the Taliban required. "Praise Allah, Khadija is safe in London. These devils kill the women or they rape them and leave them for dead. We have to get them out."

He lifted his hairy chin at the cluster of bombed out structures across the street where more woman huddled hidden.

"Not easy." Michael muttered. In Afghanistan nothing came easy. In fact, all of Central Asia was a bomb waiting to explode into the flank of the West and the Taliban were looking to ignite it.

"When did Allah ever provide easy tasks?"

Michael grinned through his matching beard, then yanked Yaqub down as a jeep whined past bristling with Hashemi's armed men. The vehicle bumped over the woman's body, but didn't pause.

Michael held Yaqub's gaze.

"You know you're my brother in all but blood, and I would do anything for you, but to try to save the women trapped in those ruins is suicide. If we don't leave now, we won't be leaving at all."

"Then take them." Yaqub motioned to the frightened children and their mothers they'd managed to rescue. "I'll get the others."

"Like hell. You're too valuable."

"Then I'll just have to live, won't I?" Yaqub half-stood. "I'll see you in Kaabul, if not sooner."

Michael yanked him down.

"Damn you, Yaqub, I'm not kidding. A doctor's worth a damn-sight more than an agent. We came to bring messages. Not run a rescue mission." That was the trouble with Yaqub. He might be calm in the face of crisis, but he was no agent.

Except when he was providing medical care, he always ran head-long to do the right thing, leaving Michael feeling slow, stodgy and a trifle dishonorable when he proposed a more cautious approach. But caution had helped him live this long in a landscape where nothing lived out its natural lifespan.

Michael looked out at the flame-lit street, assessing each door, window, and slab of darkness in the ruins. Where the hell was that sniper?

"I swore a Hippocratic Oath to preserve life."

Michael glanced back at his friend and knew that look. Knew that tone of voice, too, and knew he was defeated.

Again.

Yaqub's expression was the same stubborn, passionate look Yaqub's father got when he'd decided on a mission. Or when he treated one of Hashemi's victims. The determined look meant nothing would dare to block his purpose. A typical Afghan expression when you discussed the fate of Afghanistan. There was nothing these people were *more* passionate about.

Getting in Yaqub's way when he was like this was like trying to stop one of Afghanistan's earthquakes. You only got crushed.

"Damn you, Yaqub…. What is it about all you Siddiqui?"

A palm tree's explosion illuminated the last mud tower of the city.

"*Khpel amal da lari mal,*" Yaqub said. What you do, will come back to you. His dark gaze was determined. Then he grinned, knowing he'd played the trump card between them. Michael owed Yaqub and his father so much.

There might be a way. There might. Yaqub with his beard and turban could probably pass for Taliban. He might have a chance to talk his and the women's way free even if he was spotted.

"Look, I'll go for the others," Michael said. "You take these women. There shouldn't be any problem once you get to the hills."

Yaqub caught his arm. "You sure?"

"*Inshallah*, I'll live to drink your father's tea and beat you at chess again. Now go."

Yaqub grinned and turned to the women, speaking in swift Pashto of the plan. He led the small group out the rear of the ruin and into darkness. Michael sent a prayer after them and stepped beyond the shattered wall, rifle ready.

He eased sideways through shadows.

Farther east the last tower in Bamiyan laid a shadow across the street. If he could cross there and find his way to the women, he might— just might—be able to lead them to safety.

Well-honed skills settled over him and the night reduced to him gliding silent as a shadow over fallen brick and mortar. He glided across the street and ducked into an empty doorway as one of the patrols passed.

Yaqub's need to help the women was understandable. The damned Taliban hunted Shi'ite female flesh. In their warped belief, they'd been "married" by the Imams in the *madrasas* of Pakistan. It gave them permission to rape any woman they found. Many of the victims in this honor-bound country took their own lives out of shame.

In Afghanistan the chasm that now separated the Sunni and Shi'ite branches of Islam was as bad as the schism between Islam and the West.

He slunk through another shadow and stopped. Ahead, the low walls held only half a roof and he ducked under to find five women cowering in fear.

"You must be very silent and very brave. Understand?" he whispered in Pashto.

The grandmother of the group—all of thirty-five by his estimate—nodded and clutched the hand of her daughter's daughter. The girl could be no more than eleven by the look of her, but she'd been found by the Taliban. The poor child whimpered into the woman's shoulder.

Michael had them clasp hands and led them out of the shelter down through the maze of ruins and across the street. He started to breathe. Miraculously, they were going to do it. They were going to get free.

But then came the scream. Sheer terror, it lifted into the night, going octaves higher than a human voice should, until Michael wanted to cover his ears. Gun fire. More shouting and screams. Screams to the heavens. Pleading.

And then there were Yaqub's shouts.

Chapter 1

May 2002, KAABUL, Afghanistan

The accident between the old man and the military convoy unfolded much like the many pleats of Khadija's blue *burka*. One thing leads to another, they say. In this case, the covering and incident only showed that Khadija no longer belonged.

First there were the boys kicking a soccer ball at the side of the rubble-strewn street. Even half-muffled by the *burka* their shouts raised a brief, painful memory of Yaqub playing with his friends when she was so much younger.

Then there was the man with no legs. The baker's son, Omar, who sat on a pram-wheeled cart beside the display of the huge rounds of flatbread. He harangued female customers with lewd comments so Khadija made a point of crossing the street when she passed by.

Then there were Khadija's shoes.

They were boots really—Marks and Spencer boots she had bought against the cold and rain while she was in medical school in London. They were the problem—just like everything she'd brought back with her and everything she'd become. If she'd never gone to London, would Yaqub still be alive?

The accident happened like this.

The shouts of the two boys filled the gritty Kaabul air and Khadija wished she was young again and running after Yaqub. Though at twenty-four she wasn't old, in her country she would never again be able to join the boys kicking the soccer ball as she had done on the side streets near Victoria Station. And now there was no Yaqub to play with, anyway.

She'd come home to this place that was a strange land. Like a nightmare really. Her city and yet not. No longer filled with gardens, no longer filled with picnicking families and laughter and well-dressed woman like her mother had been. No longer with Yaqub and his laughter.

Around her, shattered buildings lined the sewer-sided streets, and were inhabited by stick-thin men and blue-clad ghosts. That was all that was left of Kaabul. All that was left of the place her father had said the ancients called the Light City of the Angel King.

She raised her chin, wishing for the wind that lofted the kites above the rocky slopes of Kohi Asamayi—Asamayi Hill. Once Yaqub had sent his fierce red kite into the clear sky, but now the sky was masked with dust off the mountains and the smoke of cooking fires polluted the fading blue. Only the wind still blew—perhaps it could lift her away as well. The *burka* made her light—less than nothing.

That had been her mistake—looking away—because the bread-maker's son spotted her shiny boots, so different from the clack, clack, clacking plastic sandals on most women. When she'd raised her gaze, Omar rolled up to her and grabbed her shoe.

"Khadija Siddiqui, you must sit with me awhile," he said, shocking her.

It was *Haram*—religiously forbidden—for a woman to speak to a man not of her family. And he—Afghani decorum said he should not speak to, or touch, a proper Islamic woman. But that was the problem, wasn't it?

The street rumbled as yet another of the omnipresent foreign military convoys returned to its compound just south of Kohi Asamayi. She looked down at Omar's grinning face and broken yellow teeth. The foul scent of his unwashed body and diesel found its way through the *burka* and she wished she was home. She wished she was with Yaqub who always made her feel safe. She should be home, not out wandering the dying city, but marketing had demanded it. She closed her eyes against the fear.

"Come, sweet one. Let me see your face. You can go naked like you did in London, now that the *kofr*—the infidels—are here. You come to my room. I know of British ways." He worked his pelvis back and forth lewdly so his cart rattled. "I have money."

She jerked back in revulsion, and his cart rolled into the street. Its left wheel caught in a hole in the pavement, sent Omar sprawling, swearing, right into the path of an old, bearded man.

Who tripped and fell, directly in front of the military convoy's first huge, green-yellow troop carrier.

Grinding brakes and Khadija saw the too-bright eyes of the female soldier driving, but the carrier was too big, too heavy, and moving too fast, while the old man was far too slow.

Khadija dropped her marketing bag and leapt; in emergency rooms you learned to respond.

Grabbing the old man's arm, she tore him from the pavement, hauled them both out of the way in time to look up at the fair faces of the soldiers that reminded her too much of a pale-faced doctor in London, and even more of the graveyard her city had become.

She shivered and turned back to the old man. Brown-grey beard worn long like the Taliban had preferred. Pale turban over shaken, black eyes.

"*As-salaam 'alaykum.*" Peace be with you. "Are you all right?" she asked in her best medical voice, still steadying him.

His gaze changed from fear to disgust.

He spat. Right at the ornate grill that covered her eyes. Warm spittle sprayed her face.

"Worst of whores," he swore and jerked away. "Harlot! You do not speak to me!" His voice rose and Khadija realized the blue ghosts were whispering in the street.

Omar laughed as he hauled himself back on his cart.

"You see? I know what you are." He thrust his hips again and she grabbed her fallen market bag and fled.

Down the road towards the narrow streets of Kohi Asamayi. The skull cap of the *burka* was too tight. She couldn't breathe, couldn't breathe.

How could she ever think she could have saved Yaqub? She'd saved the old man and still she'd done wrong. Everything she did was wrong. All of her choices—going to medical school—allowing her father to send her to the west when the Taliban came to power. It was all one mistake after another.

Except coming home after Yaqub died. She had to help her father.

Catcalls and yells in the street behind her. She glanced behind and down the length of Darulaman Road to the ruins of the old king's palace and the fenced encampment of foreign soldiers who had come to "free" her country. Their flapping flags—red-white, red-white-blue—were an abomination given the state the country was in.

Closer, the stick men and blue ghosts called her the worst kind of whore, and the *burka* couldn't hide who she was.

Omar knew the abomination that was Mohammed Siddiqui's daughter.

Ashes and Light is available in print or as an e-book at all fine book sellers.

Romance and High Adventure from Karen L. Abrahamson

If you enjoyed this book, you might enjoy other
titles from
Karen L. Abrahamson in your local bookstore or
wherever e-books are sold.
www.karenlabrahamson.com